THE SHADOW CLUB

A JACK WIDOW THRILLER

SCOTT BLADE

Black Lion Media

copyrighted materials in violation of the author's rights. Purchase only authorized editions.

Published by Black Lion Media.

CHAPTER 1

E arl Jane Winston isn't afraid, but he should be.

Winston sits on a king-sized bed in a pricey suite at the Peninsula Hotel in New York City. His suite overlooks Fifth Avenue. Throughout the evening, he's gone out to the balcony and back in again. He'd smoke a cigar if he had one and if they allowed it, but he has none, and it's not permitted. It's a nonsmoking room, but that's not why he can't smoke in the room, or on the balcony. He can't, because *they* won't let him.

They are the three bubblegums babysitting him before his big day tomorrow. *Bubblegum* is slang for US Marshals. It's not a term of endearment. It's along the same lines as *pig* is for a cop. Not everyone uses it, or knows it. A lot of ex-cons just call any law enforcement officer *pig,* or sometimes *boss.* But *bubblegum* is more classic, and Winston likes the classics—the classics and the classy. That's why he negotiated such an expensive, swanky hotel into his witness deal.

The Peninsula Hotel in New York, like every other location they own, is top-notch, and comes with the price tag to prove it. The price for this suite is north of $15,000 a night. The federal government isn't happy to foot the bill. But they'll do it to get him to testify. His testimony is in the morning. He's got a tailored suit hanging in the bedroom closet, inside a dry cleaner bag. It's cleaned spotless, and pressed wrinkle-free. The government also paid for the suit and the tailoring. But not the cleaning and pressing. They're complementary; the hotel provides laundry service. The government caught a break on that one.

You can always trust the government to screw you over the first chance it gets, Winston thinks. He doesn't trust the bubblegums, the FBI, or that cheeky federal prosecutor lady who brokered his deal. Then again, he doesn't trust women at all. He doesn't like them, either. Not his thing.

The suite comprises a plush bedroom, a long hall with black marble floors and white walls, a lavish kitchen and dining room, a grand living room, and even an oak-paneled study. *What the hell am I going to do with a study?* he thinks.

It doesn't matter. He's not there to study. He's there to relax. All he's got to do is get through the night, get dressed in his new suit, and smile before a judge and jury. He's testifying about some Arab guy who's possibly involved in terrorism. Winston doesn't know for sure. He only knows a minor detail. But to the feds, it's some kind of big deal.

It's a lucky break for him. It's a lottery ticket. The feds offer him this deal, and he gets immunity on his own legal troubles.

He's really shocked by the whole thing. His legal woes are bad. He's facing life in prison, and that life wouldn't last long because child killers tend not to make it in general lockup. All that hinges on if the pigs could prove he did what they claim he did. Which, maybe they can prove it, and maybe they can't. He figures the answer probably leans more in the *they can't* column, because the feds gave him this get-out-of-jail-free card so easily.

A second element that affects their decision is that ever since 9/11, the feds have come down double hard on all terrorism investigations. The cheapskates in Congress rained hundred-dollar bills on them after that.

This new focus of the feds took the spotlight off regular criminals from sea to shining sea. Even pedophiles and child killers —like Winston—benefit from it. Of course, he doesn't view himself as any of those things. He thinks of himself more like a man who's minor-attracted. Although the term *minor-attracted person* won't become known in the public zeitgeist for several years, Winston first heard it from a priest in southern Alabama.

Winston was living there, and hanging out with that priest regularly. Winston worked for a church, cutting grass and taking care of other maintenance-man duties, in exchange for free room and board. One day, the priest made it known to Winston that he suspected they had something in common. They both enjoyed young men, even younger than what most would consider being of legal age.

Winston and the priest stayed up late, playing card games and drinking cheap vodka. They talked about everything under the sun.

At that point, Winston had never crossed the line. Not yet, but the priest made it sound like it's no big deal. He admitted to indulging himself with some of the altar boys in the past. "Not much they can do about it," the priest would say. "The legal age of consent is sixteen."

Winston would smile and nod along. But one time, the priest got especially drunk, and whispered to Winston, "In Mississippi, right next door, the legal age of consent for girls is sixteen, but for boys it's fourteen."

Winston, who was also drunk, exclaimed, "No it's not! Where did you hear that? How do you know that?" He also felt tempted to see for himself.

The priest said, "I read it online. In a chat room for guys like us."

Winston thought about it a long moment. The priest got up and walked away.

"Where're you going?" Winston called out. But the priest didn't answer. He returned a few minutes later with a cigar box. He opened it, and revealed photo evidence of his escapades with young altar boys.

It was the first time Winston had seen such a thing, other than in his own imagination. The feelings were overwhelming. Part shame, part excitement, part confusion, and all alcohol-enhanced. He flew into a blinding rage and beat the priest to death.

He regrets it now, because the priest was his only true friend, a man who understood him.

Winston buried the priest in a small cemetery on the church grounds. To this day, he's got no idea if they ever found the body. Winston took two things away from there that day. He took the knowledge of what he really was, because the priest, his dead friend, was right about him. And he took the pictures from the cigar box with him. It would've been a shame to throw them away, after all. Pictures like that would help him get by for years, until he couldn't hold back the urge any longer. And he did well for a long time. Until he saw that little black boy on the corner of Hudson and Chestnut, in Brooklyn. There was something about the ten-year-old. Something he couldn't get over, not even now.

Winston will never forget that kid. You never forget your first. That goes double for murder. He tricked the kid into his truck, and after he scratched that long-irritating itch, he killed the boy.

A year after he killed the kid was when his trouble began. This thing called DNA had gotten so much better since the nineties, and he got implicated. But the cops had problems with the case, and they probably wouldn't be able to convict him. *Sucks for them,* he thought.

Still, they might get him. So when the feds came to him, interested in the Arab guy he worked for part-time, he saw a window of opportunity. He escaped his troubles in one swoop. *It's better to be a living snitch on the outside, than a dead pedophile on the inside,* he thinks.

All this thinking about the dead kid riles him up with memories. Winston leans back against the oversized pillows, wearing an expensive hotel robe and nothing underneath. He clicks on the TV and finds a kids' channel. He stops on a popular show. It's not the purple dinosaur one; that's his favorite. But this one has plenty of boys on-screen. With one hand on the remote, and the other inside his robe, he watches.

Suddenly, there's a loud banging at his door. He yells, "WHAT!?" It's got to be the damn bubblegums. Getting interrupted by feds is so typical. Infuriated, he listens, but no one responds.

"WHAT!?" he shouts again. No answer. Winston rolls his eyes. He realizes they probably can't hear him answering their knocks. One of the great things about the Fifth Avenue suite is the thick walls. He could probably murder someone in here, and no one would hear a thing—not a scream, not even a chainsaw.

The bubblegums knock again, louder this time.

"I'm coming!" he shouts, then realizes again that they probably don't hear him.

Winston leaps out of bed, ties his robe up, and saunters down the long hallway to the door. The bubblegums knock again.

"I'm coming!" he repeats.

No response.

He makes it to the door, opens the spyhole, and glances out. There's a bubblegum standing off to the side, but Winston can only see part of him.

"What!?" he calls. He knows the bubblegum can hear him, because the spyhole is literally a hole in the door. No glass. It's an old-timey feature they didn't update yet. That's why the spyhole's got one of those round metal covers that has to be slid away first.

"Room service," the bubblegum says. His voice is low and monotonic, but like he's whispering as loudly as possible. It's like he's trying to hide something. Maybe it's an accent. *He's got an accent like an Israeli Jew*, Winston thinks. But that's not what gives Winston pause. He doesn't even bat an eye at it. It's the fact that it's room service, and that the man knocks. It's strange because the suite has a doorbell, and when room service brought his lunch, the bubblegums intercepted, and wheeled the cart in themselves, but not until after they rang the doorbell. They have a key, but they ring to warn him. They know what he is and don't want to catch him watching one of his kid's shows.

But what if the room service guy is a hired gun? What if he killed the bubblegums, and is posing as one of them, hired by the Arab to have me killed, before I can testify in court tomorrow?

Nonsense, Winston thinks. The bubblegum stands out of view of the spyhole, but Winston can see the top of his bald head. He's a white guy.

The Arab ain't got no high-level white guys working for him. He only hires white guys to do low-level work. Never in a million years would the Arab trust a non-Arab to take care of federal witness.

He breathes a sigh of relief, unlocks the door, and says, "You guys got terrible timing."

CHAPTER 2

B ut the bubblegum isn't a bubblegum at all.

He entered the Peninsula Hotel an hour earlier so he could recon the place. He wore a black overcoat, black suit, black leather driving gloves, and shined black shoes. A black tie with gold piping etched on it hung from around his collar. The man's hair was big, black, and curly. It was a wig, but only he knew that.

He's the only one who knows a lot of things. The man's height and weight are average. Underneath the clothes, he's cut like the statue of David. No one else knows. He's fit and strong, but keeps the bulk off in order to blend in.

The only thing about his appearance that's memorable, that might stick out, is a gold pin on his jacket's lapel. It's the scales of justice, two empty scales, but in balance. A symbol of the organization he does business with. It's only one of the organizations he does business with. But it's the most lucrative. He charges them a high price, and they pay it.

Of course, it's all just business to him. It's all about the money. However, he'd be lying if he denied the satisfaction he got from his work. That's one reason he wears the pin. Sure, he's done bad things. Working for this organization, this special club, he's done a lot of bad things, but to bad people. It gives him a sense of satisfaction. Why not embrace it?

The scales of justice man wandered the halls of the hotel for thirty minutes, then posted up in an armchair in a secluded area of the lobby, keeping two big objects out of sight on his lap, under his overcoat.

A copy of today's newspaper rested on a side table, like it'd been waiting for him.

The scales of justice man scanned the room before taking the newspaper to make sure no one was watching. No one gave him a second glance. He scooped up the newspaper and opened it casually, like a regular person. To anyone watching, he would appear to be just a guy browsing a newspaper. He took the time to read the front page, and then, slowly, he opened the newspaper to the obituaries. Taped over the death notifications was a rectangular keycard. It was white, and labeled *Hotel Use Only*.

Casually, the scales of justice man untaped the card and let it slide out of the newspaper. It landed on his lap. He glanced around the lobby, and still no one was watching him. He slid the card into his coat pocket. Then he sipped on his coffee and continued reading the newspaper, looking like he belonged there, like he was just a hotel guest hanging out in the lobby.

Long before he arrived, and long before Winston arrived, the scales of justice man did some research and found the right hotel employee: a disgruntled employee, one who likes money and who also has a rap sheet. The scales of justice man went through back channels to offer the disgruntled employee money for information.

A member of the staff texted him on a burner phone. Calmly, taking his time, he folded up the newspaper and set it on a side table, next to his armchair. He drank the rest of his coffee, and wiped the rim in case the FBI could use forensic DNA to identify him. Better safe than sorry.

The scales of justice man read the text message informing him that Winston was in his suite and had ordered room service. He smiles, returns the burner phone to his pocket, and stands up. He leaves the newspaper, and leaves the empty coffee mug with a five-dollar bill folded underneath it for the lobby waitress.

The scales of justice man walks to the elevators, takes out the keycard, and slips it into a slot at the bottom of the control panel. It unlocks the upper suite floors for him. He pushes the top floor button, and rides the elevator up.

At the top floor, the scales of justice man takes a quick look up and down the hallway. No one is watching. He knows the elevator chimed before it opened, so he waits, just to make sure the US Marshals didn't hear it and decide to investigate. No one comes.

He glances up at the elevator's ceiling. A small security camera stares back at him. The security camera is off, he hopes. That was also part of the disgruntled employee's job. The scales of justice man waits, and listens. The camera appears to be off. There's a light on it, and the light is dark. It's the moment of truth. If someone's watching, they'll raise the alarm if they see him do what he's about to do.

Time to find out if it's been money well spent or not.

The scales of justice man pulls a Remington Model 870 MCS shotgun out from under his overcoat. The weapon has a short barrel and a pistol grip, making it more concealable under his overcoat. A shotgun suppressor is screwed into the muzzle. A shotgun with a sound suppressor is rare. But this one is especially rare because it's specifically designed for bean bag rounds.

The gun hangs from a shoulder sling, so he won't drop it or have it ripped from his hands. The scales of justice man holds it out in the open, big and obvious, and waits. He looks at the camera. No alarm. No sign of anyone watching. He smiles. Then, he removes shells from out of a sidesaddle attached to the barrel. He loads the weapon, pumps the action, and drops it back out of sight, inside his coat. Dangling from the same sling is a thick, black metal crowbar. Which isn't illegal to carry in public in New York City, but it raises eyebrows, so he keeps it hidden with the shotgun, on the same strap.

The scales of justice man enters the floor, casually, and scans the long hall. He sees the three marshals. One roams the hall, down the opposite side. The other two face each other, standing in front of Winston's suite door. One of them leans on the wall. The other stands straight, his back turned to the scales of justice man. The standing marshal talks and laughs with the leaning one, like he's telling a long, funny story.

The scales of justice man breathes deep, closes his eyes, and slowly exhales. It's a calming technique he learned from a commanding officer in Sayeret Matkal, where he fought for nearly two decades. But that feels like a lifetime ago now. He's not returned to the holy land, Israel, in nearly a decade. He has no intention of ever going back.

The scales of justice man enters the hall, walking casually, like he belongs there. He glances at each hotel room number as he passes it, pretending to be looking for the right number. The marshal at the end of the hall is out of range, so the scales of justice man slows, and inspects a sign on the hotel wall, like he's having a hard time comprehending what it says.

The other two marshals continue talking, like he's not even there. The one marshal steps to the opposite end of the hall, then spins around and comes back. He sees the scales of justice man, takes the bait, and picks up the pace. He's the most diligent of the three officers. That's clear. The walking marshal is focused on the scales of justice man.

The scales of justice man continues the charade of reading the sign, until the walking marshal passes the other two marshals. He's extra vigilant. In a movement so fast a bystander wouldn't even notice it, the walking marshal opens his jacket, slips a hand over a gun in a holster, and thumbs the safety snap open so the gun can be drawn. He pulls his hand out of the jacket just as fast, and no one is the wiser. No one, that is, except for the scales of justice man.

The scales of justice man leaves the sign, and walks towards the marshals. The walking marshal puts a hand up, like he's signaling oncoming traffic to stop. His other hand slides to the flap of his jacket, where his gun is holstered. He asks, "Sir, are you lost?"

Even though the scales of justice man left Israel, and the Israel Defense Forces, nearly a decade ago, he retains the accent. It's his weak link, because it's an identifying trait. It's why normally he doesn't speak. He only talks if he has to. And when he does, he uses a deep whisper, which still displays his accent. But it's not the first thing listeners notice. They notice the whispers.

The scales of justice man steps towards the oncoming marshal, closing the gap between them, and getting in range of the other two marshals.

The walking marshal stops, opens his jacket to reveal both his holstered gun and his US Marshal shield, which hangs from his inside jacket pocket. He says, "Sir, we're federal agents. I need you to stay there. Don't come any closer."

The scales of justice man steps closer, and stops.

The walking marshal also stops, and asks, "What're you doing up here? You got a room here?"

The scales of justice man says, "Sorry, I'm lost. I think. I got on the elevator, and it brought me here."

The walking marshal lowers his jacket flap. The other two marshals take notice, like they just woke up from a hypnotic trance. The leaning one pushes off the wall, and approaches behind the walking marshal. The standing one turns, and follows suit. They step up behind the walking marshal, until they're definitely in range.

The walking marshal reopens his jacket flap, rests his hand near his gun, and asks, "Sir, how did you get up here? The elevator requires a keycard to get to this floor."

The scales of justice man smiles, and says, "It's nothing personal." Then, he erupts into a flurry of violence. The walking marshal is fast. He's proved that. But the scales of justice man is faster.

The scales of justice man levels the MCS fast—faster than the walking marshal could get to his gun. In fact, the scales of justice man is faster than all three marshals. He fires a bean bag shell into the walking marshal's gut. Bean bag rounds, though they can maim, disfigure, and, even kill, are normally nonlethal. The scales of justice man isn't here to kill marshals.

The bean bag round knocks the walking marshal off his feet. Just because the shells are nonlethal doesn't mean they're not powerful. He cracks his skull on the hard marble floor. He recoils in pain, and writhes on the floor. The pain is too intense for him to go for his gun.

The window of opportunity won't last long, because the first marshal's training will kick in. So the scales of justice man doesn't squander the chance. He pivots to the other incoming marshals. They both draw their weapons, or attempt to draw them. Before one of them clears the safety snap on his gun's holster, the scales of justice man pumps the action and fires. The shotgun sends another bean bag round bursting through the air. The bean bag slams into the next marshal's face. A couple of his teeth shatter. His nose nearly breaks. His head whips back, and his vision goes dark. The marshal plummets to the floor, and doesn't get back up. The round to the face knocks him out cold.

The last standing marshal's gun clears its holster, but he never gets a shot off. He doesn't get a shot off because federal agents are trained to aim, make sure they've got a legal target in their sights, and then shoot. The scales of justice man isn't worried about that. If he wasn't faster than the last standing marshal already, this little detail would still give him an extra split-second advantage. But he doesn't need it.

The scales of justice man shoots the last standing marshal in the forehead. The last standing marshal becomes the last marshal to fall. He flies back off his feet, slams into the wall, and slides down. His eyes stay open, which concerns the scales of justice man for a moment. He worries the guy is dead. But then, the last marshal's eyes roll back in his head, showing only the whites underneath. Dead people's eyes don't roll like that.

The first marshal reaches for his gun. He coughs in agony, struggling to pull the weapon out. The scales of justice man steps over him, steps on his hand, and shifts his weight over it. He aims the shotgun at the marshal's face. He whisper-asks, "This the room with Earl Jane Winston?" He points at a door, two doors down.

The marshal spits blood, and says, "You shot me with a bean bag round? I'm not scared of that."

The scales of justice man shoots him again, but in the inner thigh.

The marshal squeals in pain.

The scales of justice man pumps the action, and aims the gun further north of the marshal's inner thigh. He aims it at the place no man wants to get shot, lethal or not. Both have devastating outcomes.

"No! Please!" he yelps.

"Is he in there?"

"Yes!" the marshal says, and points at the correct room.

"Alone?"

"Yes!"

"Okay," the scales of justice man says, and punches the marshal with the combat shotgun's barrel. He hits him in the head, hard, and it knocks him clean out.

The scales of justice man scans the hotel doors, making sure no guests step out to check what the commotion is. Bean bag rounds are nonlethal, but they're not silent. A shotgun suppressor is fitted to his weapon, but, like regular sound suppressors, shotgun suppressors don't completely silence a weapon. Shotguns make a lot of noise—bean bag round or not, sound-suppressed or not.

It seems no one hears a thing, or doesn't question the noises they hear, because no one comes out into the hall.

Satisfied, the scales of justice man lets the shotgun dangle by his side, under his overcoat. He doesn't need it any longer. He walks to Winston's room, leaving the marshals where they lie. He eyeballs a fire door leading to a stairwell at the other end of the hall.

At Winston's hotel door, the scales of justice man removes his wig, stuffs it into a coat pocket. Long traces of black hair hang out, making it look like he scalped someone and shoved the scalp into his pocket.

The scales of justice man sidesteps the hotel door, mostly staying out of the spyhole's view. He bangs on the door. No answer. He hears a voice yell, "WHAT!?" The voice is faint, like the door and walls are super thick. And that's probably true. It explains why no one came out to check the shotgun sounds.

The voice shouts, "What!?" again.

The scales of justice man continues knocking. The voice says, "I'm coming!" He continues knocking hard on the door. The voice repeats, "I'm coming!" He bangs again, and again, until the spyhole cover squeaks open.

A voice says, "What?" It's Winston's voice. He's certain. He spent hours watching and listening to the guy's police interrogation videos from the dead black boy investigation.

Knowing Winston's expecting room service, the scales of justice man says, "Room service." He whispers in a low, monotone voice, trying to keep his accent masked, in case Winston recognizes that it's not one of the marshal's voices.

The door unlocks, and swings open. Winston says, "You guys got terrible timing."

There he is, standing in front of the scales of justice man, in the flesh—Earl Jane Winston. He's not the hardest target the scales of justice man ever had to get to, but he's up there. The scales of justice man had to expose himself to federal agents in a posh hotel in New York City. It's not like breaking into a military base, but it's not a walk in the park either.

Winston stands in the Fifth Avenue suite's doorway. He wears a bathrobe, and nothing under it. Cushy house slippers snuggle his feet. His chubby face is red. He pants, nearly breathless, like the scales of justice man interrupted him in the middle of doing cardio.

It's faint, but in the background, the scales of justice man hears a kids' show playing on a TV somewhere in the depths of the suite.

"Where's the food, man?" Winston says, eyeballing the man for the room service he ordered. The man stands there, holding nothing. He's supposed to be pushing a cart with a double cheeseburger and a double order of French fries, all of it under a heavy, silver cloche. But there is no cloche, no dishes, no tray, no cart, and definitely no food.

The man shoves his way into the room, and shuts and locks the door behind him. He turns back to Winston.

Winston says, "Hey man. What's going on?"

The scales of justice man asks in his normal speaking voice, accent and all, "You alone in here?"

"Yeah, man! Of course. You guys are watching the door. You'd know if someone came in. Wouldn't ya?"

The scales of justice man smiles, and pulls out the crowbar.

Winston stares at it, like he's seeing an old frenemy, someone he knows, intimately, but doesn't trust. He raises his hands, palms out in the universal surrender pose, and says, "Hey, man! What is this?"

The scales of justice man whacks him straight across the face with the crowbar, not hard enough to kill him, but the attack busts Winston's nose. Blood gushes out of three places—both nostrils, and a crack across the bridge.

Winston tumbles on his butt. His bathrobe nearly falling off. The cord that keeps it closed hangs on for dear life. He screams in agony, and paws at his nose, trying to stop the bleeding.

The scales of justice man inches closer to him. Winston scrambles away. He tries to shout, but the nosebleed chokes him, and he gurgles more blood. He scrambles to his feet, turns, and runs down the black marble hall, back to the bedroom.

The scales of justice man tracks behind him, staying close, but lingering. This is his favorite part. It's the sporting part. The victim tries to defend himself, just before he breaks completely.

A kids' show is playing on a TV. An audience of kids sings along with some animatronic characters. The music is loud, and annoying.

Winston dives onto the king-sized bed, and rolls across it. He flops onto the floor. But he does something the scales of justice man doesn't expect.

Winston pulls a snub-nosed .38 out of a nightstand. He thumbs the hammer back, aims, frantically, in the scales of justice man's direction. He shoots. Once. Twice.

The scales of justice man dodges the shots easily, because Winston fires haphazardly. The bullets slam into the wall. This isn't good because it speeds up the scales of justice man's timetable. Thick walls or not, someone's bound to have heard the .38's gunfire. He's got to stop Winston from shooting again. Luckily, Winston's two shots went into an interior wall. But the man shoots so wildly, what if he hits a shared wall? What if the bullet goes into the next suite over? No way will the guests miss that.

The scales of justice man quickly draws his own pistol. It's a Walther P99 with a sound suppressor on the end. He has a penchant for James Bond movies. Of course, his P99 isn't the Connery gun. It's the 2003 model, but close enough for him.

Winston half-squeezes the .38's trigger, but a 9mm bullet ruptures through his forehead, and rips out the back of his skull before he can finish squeezing the trigger. He rocks back over his bent legs, crashing into the corner of the room in a heap of dead limbs. He's dead before the bullet even leaves his head. Brains and blood smear across the wall.

A table lamp flickers. Blood is all over the lampshade.

The scales of justice man threads around the bed, and stares down at the dead man. Winston's eyes are wide open, staring up at the ceiling, lifeless.

The scales of justice man holsters his gun, stares at the .38, and asks, "Now how did you sneak that past the marshals?"

Winston doesn't respond.

The scales of justice man stows the crowbar, disappointed that he didn't get to use it more. It's not a requirement for him to kill Winston with it. He just likes the poetic justice of it all. Winston beats a child to death with a crowbar. Thus, he gets beaten to death with one. It's fitting, like a *what goes around comes around*, sort of thing—karma.

The scales of justice man shrugs. It doesn't matter. The job's done. He takes out a Motorola cellphone, selects the camera function, kneels, lifts Winston's head by a tuft of his hair, and snaps a picture of the dead man. He inspects the photo. The bullet hole is prominent, like a third eye, right in the center of Winston's forehead.

Satisfied, the scales of justice man drops Winston's head. It bangs against the wall. He steps back, making sure there isn't any blood tracking from his shoes. He leaves the room, putting his wig back on.

Several minutes later, the scales of justice man walks out of the hotel, and texts the photo to his contact's phone.

At a public trash can several blocks from the Peninsula Hotel, he removes his wig, tosses it into the trash. He breaks the Motorola phone apart, and stuffs it into the trash as well. The crowbar follows.

The scales of justice man pops his collar up to protect him from the chilly November air. He walks the street, merges into crowds of pedestrians, and becomes one of them.

CHAPTER 3

Juniper Brown walks home from church on a beautiful Sunday afternoon. Three of her neighbors escort her, right alongside her, matching her slow pace. Before the murder, they each walked to their own houses. But now, they walk her home first, making sure she gets inside safely.

That gruesome crime changed her life forever. Before, people told her she was a spry fifty-two-year-old. Now, people say she's aged twenty years overnight. Some even say thirty.

No one asks her how she's doing. No one speaks of the evil that killed her son, Miles. They all remember him, but they don't speak of him. He was just ten years old when a predator came along and plucked him out of the world, like he never existed. To the neighbors escorting her, Miles is a distant memory, but not to Juniper. For her, Miles's ghost is always standing there. It says nothing, but she sees it everywhere. She knows it's just her imagination, a guilty memory. It reminds her she wasn't watching him closely enough. It tortures her by reminding her of her secret. That unspeakable secret that she can never tell. The day Miles got abducted, she was with a married man from her church. He was the pastor, of all things, and married to a friend of hers.

The day Miles was taken, she had kicked him out of the house. "Go out and play. Momma needs adult time," she had told him. The guilt replays the events in her head, like a nightmarish home movie set on repeat. It's the part where she and the pastor were naked in her bed that sticks with her the most. She thinks that was the moment when Earl Jane Winston stopped on the curb in front of her house, and summoned her Miles over to his truck.

The police investigators said Winston lured Miles with the promise of a new Game Boy Advance, the latest successor to the Game Boy Color. And that sounded about right, because Miles had hounded her for the new Game Boy for two years. She finally caved and bought it for him. It was meant to be a Christmas present that year.

It's my sin that got you killed, my sweet boy, she says to the ghost, but it doesn't speak. It never does. It's there one moment. And gone the next. She knows it's a hallucination, a guilt-induced torment. But she still sees him.

The guilt makes her feel that she should be in jail alongside the man who kidnapped, raped, and killed her son. But neither of them are in jail. She still lives on the same street, and goes to the same church. She no longer sees the pastor, not outside of Sunday service.

The worst part—and she feels gut-punched by this detail—is that the pastor was the one who officiated at Mile's funeral. He asked to. And what was she supposed to do? She took Miles to that church every Sunday, for ten years. Miles was in diapers when he first met the pastor. But it never sat right with her; the pastor was the reason she hadn't been paying attention to Miles.

Whatever! It doesn't matter. Miles is gone. The ghost, real or not, induced by guilt or not, haunts her...until today. Today could be different. She feels it could be a day of balance, of justice. It's supposed to have happened by now. It should've happened last week. But she's losing faith. Then, she notices something about the front of her house, something unusual, and she walks fast, like her old self.

"Junie, let's slow down," one neighbor-escort says.

Another says, "What's gotten into you, Junie?"

But Juniper walks fast. They keep up behind her, as she gets within fifty yards to her house, then forty, then thirty. At twenty-five, she stops. And she knows she's about to get the news she's been waiting for.

Her neighbors catch up. She turns to them, hiding her smile. One asks, "Junie, what's gotten into you?"

Another says, "You drink a Red Bull or something, you old bird?"

She half-smiles at the jab, and says, "You know, girls, I think I'm okay today."

"Really?"

"Yeah," Juniper says, "I feel good today. I appreciate you walking me. But I think I wanna be alone for the rest of the day."

"Are you sure?"

"Aren't we playing bridge today?"

"Not today," Juniper says, and looks at the sky, "I'm going to spend the afternoon in my garden. It's a great day for it."

"It's November," one neighbor says, and tugs her coat in closer, like she's getting colder, which could be true. Brooklyn in November is cold.

"Plants still need love. Winter or not," Juniper says.

Her neighbors glance at each other, and shrug. They say their goodbyes, and part ways with her.

Juniper watches them all go. Once they're gone from sight, she turns back to her house. She walks slowly, glancing around the neighborhood, like there might be a trap. She stares at her mailbox. The flag is up, like she's sending out mail. But there's no mail on Sunday, and she put nothing out. She didn't put the flag up. She's certain it was down when she left for church a few hours ago.

At the mailbox, she glances around again, looking for anyone watching her. But there's nobody.

Juniper pulls her gloves off, cups her hands, and blows on them, warming them up. She opens the mailbox, and peers in.

Inside the mailbox, she sees a single white envelope. Carefully, she removes it from the mailbox, and glances around again. Still no one watching. She pulls the envelope close to her chest, like she's guarding its secrets.

She closes the mailbox, and darts into her yard. She walks up the steps to her house. Before she can fish her house keys out of her purse, the anticipation overtakes her. And she abandons her purse on the welcome mat.

Juniper plops down on her porch steps. She stares at the white envelope. There's no return address, and no postmark, of course, because the post office didn't deliver this letter.

It's the letter she's waited for. She knows because it's sealed, and the seal is *their* seal.

The letter is sealed with a special, and expensive, gold wax seal. The stamp on the seal is the scales of justice.

Juniper smiles with malicious glee. The gold wax seal is so elegant that she hates to break it, but she must know what's inside. She must see with her own eyes what they've sent her. She's got to put Miles's ghost to rest. She's got to forgive herself. She must know beyond a shadow of a doubt that justice has been done.

Her fingers rip the envelope open, breaking the seal, nearly breaking one of her nails, but she doesn't stop. She opens the envelope. Inside, there's a single sheet of archival photo paper, which is intended for high-quality photos.

She drags it out, slowly. The back of a photo is showing. The back of the photo is stamped with the same gold scales of justice. Slowly, Juniper turns the photo around.

The picture itself is grainy, and not high quality at all, despite being printed on this special paper. It's slightly distorted, like it was taken with a cellphone camera. But she doesn't care.

The photograph is all she cares about. She stares at it, and grins from ear to ear. She holds the grin for a long, long time.

Finally, her eyes fill with tears, and she bawls. She cries harder than when she found out her Miles was dead. She cries harder than the day she watched his coffin go into the dirt. She cries tears like storms rain.

The photo is of Earl Jane Winston, dead. Her son's killer is no more. She looks up at where Miles's ghost should be standing, but it isn't. No one is there.

CHAPTER 4

There're seven of them—*the* seven. They are distinguished members of their cities, of their professions, of the Club. Each wears a gold scales of justice pin. It's become the symbol of their club, of their vision.

They sit there, in one of their meetings, except they're not all in the same place. Only four of them are in the same room—the other three are not in the US. They're video-conferencing, using Skype to see and hear each other. Two of them drove in from New York City, not too far. One came from Hartford, Connecticut, and the leader, or *the founder*, as he prefers to think of himself, is from right there in Boston, Massachusetts. The three international ones are from Toronto, London, and Dublin.

The Seven are the original founders and members. There are actually dozens of members around the world, but they don't meet regularly, not like the Seven.

The other members span the globe, with most being American, inside the US. Not all of the people involved in the organization are considered members. Most are more like emissaries, or people of interest, or even potential members.

It's hard to approach someone about becoming a member, because once they're told about Club business, their lives are different. Their innocence is gone forever. Knowing the truth isn't something that everyone can handle. It takes a certain person, a certain view of justice.

Many people only have Club business once, and then they're never seen again. Some of them, a small number, join, and then decide it's not for them. And they leave, no questions asked. But they all know not to talk about it.

"Don't talk about us" is both the number one and number two rule of the group. The founder saw a movie that came out a couple of years before, called *Fight Club*. In it, actor Brad Pitt says, "You don't talk about Fight Club."

The founder's club already had these rules, but the founder circulates his club's rules the same way. Half jesting, he'll say, "Remember, members. You don't talk about *Fight Club*, and you don't talk about us."

Humorous, but they all understand the meaning. But what would really happen to them if they spoke about their club?

No one knows because no one's ever broken that rule. They have, in the sense that they spread the word. But the people they tell are victims, people who won't talk to the cops about it anyway.

One time, a new member asked, "What happens?"

The Seven stared at the new member in disbelief.

The new member glanced around the table at their faces, faces of people the world admires in their respective circles and professions. Everyone was silent.

The founder broke the silence, and said, "You don't want to know what'll happen to you if you talk."

The silence was deafening. It was brief, but notable. The founder chuckled, and smiled, and said, "I'm kidding. You'll just be hurting all the good we've accomplished, that's all. So keep our secret."

The rest chuckled along, and the new member joined in. But he felt a veiled threat underneath the laughter, a threat that he never wanted to see firsthand.

Meetings are monthly for the Seven, at night. Meetings involve Club business, and not much else. They're all friends. They chat in friendly tones, asking about each other's weeks and families, but when the clock strikes ten, they turn to Club business. They conduct the meetings like court sessions. There's a procedure. There's etiquette. And there're protocols in place, actions that are followed to the letter.

It's ten now. The founder gavels them in. The four locals sit around a round table with a Department of Justice seal engraved into the center. The room has oak paneling, thick wooden furniture, and high-backed leather chairs. The light is dim, like a law library after hours.

The founder says his normal spiel. Then he turns to a computer screen. Each member has a laptop, or PC, in view. The founder says, "Mr. Treasurer, how's our account?"

The one from Dublin says, "Money is good. Ms. Brown's donation was cleared, cleaned, and appropriated."

The founder says, "Okay, speaking of that, let's officially close the Brown case. All in favor?"

He hears six affirmatives.

The founder gavels, and says, "Good. Next order of business."

The Seven carry on with more Club business. The meeting lasts less than an hour. After the meeting concludes, they thank each other, patting each other on the back for another case closed. They go through their end-of-meeting rituals. The three across the world log off. And the four local founders stay, sipping on expensive brandy and smoking cigars. They talk about the upcoming annual event. It's not their event, not exclusively, but it's how they met. It's where they get their most interesting cases.

At the end of the night, nearly midnight, the two from New York City leave the building, and the ones from Hartford and Boston walk out behind them.

The founder glances up at the magnificent structure called John Joseph Moakley United States Courthouse, as he does after every meeting. The Boston courthouse is massive. The moonlight reflects off the glass windows and metal beams. He smiles, and walks away.

CHAPTER 5

It was a cold, breezy December night in 2003—twenty years ago. But Widow remembers it like it happened last year. Time flies by, but memories last a lifetime. Twenty years went by in the flutter of a hummingbird's wings.

Harper gives the orders, and Widow follows them.

Winter snow falls slowly and hypnotically around them, but Dr. Jaime Harper, or "Harp," as her friends call her, wants to sit in the courtyard in the back of English Mustache Coffee, a beloved neighborhood café about three blocks from the United States Naval Academy in Annapolis, Maryland. Snow or no snow, that's where she wants to sit and enjoy her night with him. And what Harp wants, Harp gets. At least, that's the trend Widow notices. He doesn't complain about it. He's a young man, but a sailor now—technically. The only *i* left to dot is the graduation ceremony. And the only *t* left to cross is his commissioning. The moment they hand him that diploma, Widow will simultaneously graduate from the Naval Academy and be commissioned as an ensign in the United States Navy.

Widow's twenty-two, but only by a little more than a month. His birthday was November 9th.

The snowfall calms and soothes, making the night's atmosphere one of peace and serenity. The sky is part starry and part moonlit, like something out of a poem describing a picturesque Maryland night. Christmas lights and wreaths are strung around the perimeter of the courtyard.

Cold or no cold, Harper gives the orders, and Widow follows them.

Harper doesn't outrank him, not officially. She's a civilian, and Widow's a non-commissioned sailor in the US Navy. Still, he's got a rank. She doesn't.

Harper is his instructor, from a semester that ended today, just a few hours ago. She teaches a course on Advanced Criminology and Criminal Investigation. It's her first year at Annapolis, and it's his last. Harper is one of the leading experts in her field. And she's top of the list in professors under the age of sixty, and a woman. Most of the other so-called expert investigation academics around Annapolis are old fossils. The youngest are in their sixties, some in their seventies, but the bulk are eighty and beyond. Teaching in a war college, like the USNA, provides a lot of perks. So, when instructors grab hold of tenure, they don't let go until their death. And they never retire.

Many of the aging instructors came out of the Baby Boom, the Silent Generation, or earlier. They got cushy jobs as college professors, and never left. Like many people in their golden years, they don't want to let go. They don't want to move on. And who could blame them? No one wants to let go of the only life they've ever known.

Such questions about life aren't on Widow's radar. Not then. He's too young. He thinks about the same things most boys think about—what most girls think about, too. Widow thinks about his own future, not his mortality.

Aging professors live their lives. They're worlds away from where Widow is in his life, in 2003. Some aging professors will probably die in their offices, at their desks. Some of them already have.

Harper tells Widow a story about the guy she replaced. He is...he *was* ninety-nine years old. One day, he didn't show up for his morning classes. The students sat in the lecture room, waiting, goofing off at first. But after he didn't show, they became worried because their professor, though old, isn't the kind of man to be late. He was infamous for being a stickler for punctuality. Still, he didn't show up for class. And he never would again. His assistant found the old man dead at his desk, which is now Harp's desk.

The guy was in the process of writing his lecture notes. He died before he finished the last sentence, on the last page—a life unfinished, just at the last page, last paragraph, last sentence.

The old guy's hand-scribbled notes are framed, and hanging in Harper's office. Widow sees the framed notes multiple times per week. He's been in her office many times more than any other students. There're only two others who might notice how often. One is her office neighbor, another elderly man who's got better things to do than keep up with Widow's comings and goings. The second is Harper's teaching assistant. Like Widow, he answers to her. Doubtful that he'll say anything to anyone.

Plenty of the academics in Harper's profession are from another time, another era, another way of thinking. They've got their ways, and she has hers. Hers are newer, fresher—some better, some worse. Her ways are updated. *I am the future* is how she put it to Widow.

Widow knows he's young and naïve, but he believes her ways are better. She's got him believing in her. He buys into her opinions. And why wouldn't he? She's the first woman to make him feel this way since he's become an adult. Hell, she's the first woman ever to make him feel the way he feels for her.

Widow believes the future is his. His generation is the best to come. But don't all young people think this? That they're the first to discover justice? That they're the first to discover equality? The first to know pain? To know love?

If only Widow knew then what he'll know twenty years down the line. It's a hard lesson. But it's a lesson that everyone learns the hard way. Widow is no different.

Being a woman at her level, Harper feels like all eyes are on her. Because Harp's a beautiful woman, Widow knows all eyes *are* on her. Whenever she walks into class, many of his classmates perk up. They give her more undivided attention than they do her male colleagues. Widow notices it, but says nothing. It doesn't bother him. His mother is a beautiful woman of authority. She's the sheriff of the small town he grew up in. So he's used to men ogling a beautiful woman he loves.

Widow wonders how his mother is? He's not spoken to her in nearly five years. It's personal, a family story about an argument over a lie she told him, over a secret she kept.

He means to call her. He's picked up the phone in his dorm twice. Hands trembling, he dials the number, but he always hangs up before the phone rings. Why? Maybe it's pride. It could be pain. It could be fear. Or it could be all three. He can't get himself to go through with it.

At first, he picked up the phone every month after he ran away from home. Then it was every few months, then six months. A year went by, and he dialed her number again. But he hung up again. This went on, and the years rolled by. Before he let his mind think too much about it, something usually distracted him, and life caught him up in its whirlwind.

Maybe he feared change?

It's not that different for the old men in Harper's field. Some fear the change that's inevitable. Others embrace it. But they all give it their attention.

Harper's become a minor celebrity in the criminal justice community. And not just on the Naval Academy campus. Right after she arrives, she's suddenly getting booked for crime shows on TV and being interviewed on national news outlets. She appears in an episode of *Dateline*. She's even been booked on a newer media called *podcasts*.

"Widow, you're doing it again," Harper says. Her arm wraps through his as they walk through the café's courtyard entrance together. She leans against him, the top of her head just above his shoulder.

Harper's not short. She's tall enough to have been eyed by a college basketball team back in the day. Even though those years are behind her, she can still compete physically. She still has the body for it—a height of five-eleven, hard muscles, and long legs.

Like many people, Widow thinks she can play basketball. Jokingly, he once told her that he doubted she had a good jump shot. She scoffed at him, and they took it to the court for a friendly game of horse. She won, naturally. She wins at every competitive thing they do together. Sometimes he lets her win. No reason to tell her.

Harper is a creature of habit. She's organized and smart. She's a planner, rarely leaving anything up to chance. She's in the gym every morning like clockwork, early too. Widow knew plenty of midshipmen who didn't get up as early as she did, or didn't put in the work like she did.

In fact, she's one of the most dedicated women he ever met. She boxes weekly. Her big secret for staying in shape isn't the gym. She lifts weights, but it's the boxing she loves.

Widow never sees her boxing. Not even a sparring match. Part of that is because Harper goes to an all-girls class, off campus, in Baltimore. The other part is she doesn't want him to see her. She thinks because he's young, big, and wears a Navy uniform, that he's some kind of expert brawler. She thinks she'll embarrass herself in front of him.

Widow responds with, "I've only fought a handful of times." Which is a lie. He's fought twelve fist fights by the time he's twenty-two. And he's won twelve fist fights. But Widow's fighting experience is mostly from when he was a kid, a teenager, and only a few times as a man. They were mostly schoolyard fights, not something *real*. He's not fought where there're stakes, not with his life on the line—not yet.

Though he's not seen Harper box, he knows he doesn't want to be on the receiving end of a right hook from her. She's tough. She reminds him of his mother in that way. The way she's built: tough, from the inside out. Harper doesn't take shit from anyone. His mom's like that. Of course, she's a sheriff.

Harper stops halfway through the café's courtyard, pulls her arm out of his, and says, "Widow! You're still doing it!"

Widow shakes away the daydreams, and asks, "What? Sorry, what am I doing?"

"You're off in la-la land. You've not said a word for like three blocks."

"I haven't?"

"Nope. You've not said anything since we left my house."

Widow asks, "Really?"

"Yep. We got in the taxi, even though I told you I could drive us here. You insisted on riding in a cab together. And then you didn't even say anything during the ride."

"I didn't?" he asks, reaches a hand into his pocket, and fidgets with an item inside. "Didn't I pay the cab driver?"

Harper stomps a foot down, turns, and stares up at him. She grins, pretends to be mad, and says, "I paid the cab driver. You don't have any money. You're a firstie, remember?"

Widow remembers. *Firstie* is Navy slang for first class midshipman. It's what they call a senior at the USNA. The Navy loves slang terms for various people, places, things, and even actions. The Navy, like the rest of the military, has its own language. Firstie, like a lot of other slang terms, can be insulting, but between them it's a term of endearment.

"I know," he says. "I hope that my lack of income doesn't deter you from wanting to be with me?"

She grabs him, pulls him close to her, gets up on her tiptoes, and says, "If I want a man for his money, I'll take a job in DC, find a mysterious senator who doesn't want his wife to find out about us. Then I'll milk him for all the bribe money I can get." She smiles, and kisses Widow.

Again, Widow fidgets with the object in his pocket, but he kisses her back. He hopes she doesn't feel the metal object, or notice him fiddling with it. She doesn't, and he breathes a sigh of relief.

Harper says, "You're not getting off the hook that easy. What were you thinking about so deeply that you zoned out?"

Widow smiles at her, and says, "My brain is exhausted from finals."

"Well, today was your last one. You're all done now. So, let's celebrate."

He nods, twists the object in his pocket, and says, "Yes, ma'am." He kisses her again.

Harper's hair is shoulder length and blond. During the day, it glistens in the sunlight, like the glass on a rifle scope. Her skin is fair. Her eyes twinkle blue. On top of all that, she's very stylish. She's the best-dressed woman that Widow knows of in Annapolis. Harper wears suits, skirts, expensive shoes, and a pair of designer eyeglasses that would've taken half Widow's monthly salary to pay for.

Widow knows because he looked it up. Trying to gauge Harper's taste, and her expectations. He's studied her closely for the last two weeks for a reason. The last thing he wants is for her to reject him. He got her something. And it's important. Harper doesn't realize it, but tonight is about more than just their first time out in public. It's about more than his passing his final exams. It's about more than his graduating the academy. It's about *them*.

At first, it was just a simple attraction. She's a beautiful older woman, and a woman with authority. He hadn't even known that was a feature that excites him about a woman. But it is.

Widow takes her class, and tries to focus on his studies. He tries desperately to ace her class, and keep it all student-teacher, as it's meant to be. But he's smitten with Harper. He keeps it to himself.

It was that first day of class, when Harper walked into the room. And Widow saw her for the first time. That was the moment he lost the battle before it began. He just didn't know it yet. Widow's infatuation is so bad. After that first class, he immediately leaves the building, crosses Ingram Field, and marches over to Nimitz Library and up to the second deck. He walks into the Registrar's office, like a man on a mission, and changes his class schedule for the semester. He takes more criminal justice classes. Unbeknownst to him, this will change his life forever.

In 2003, Widow's a young man, a young sailor. And like all young sailors, Widow does stupid, rash things to impress girls. Isn't that how it always goes?

One time, Widow read about this Olympic athlete and gold medalist. Competing, training, and living a lifestyle that enables someone to be good enough to win a gold medal is unfathomable to him. Their lives are grueling. It's years of sacrifice and hard work, and that's true of any Olympic sport. The gold medalist admits the whole reason he got into his sport is to impress girls. The gold medalist tells a story about his university team coach trying to get all the guys on his team to improve their performance, to raise their game to a higher level. The coach tries and tries to motivate them. But he has no luck inspiring them to perform better, to train harder. So, what the university coach does is: He moves their training facility across campus, near an all-girls yoga studio. He changes their practice times to the same as the girls' yoga hour.

Every time the girls leave yoga, the boys are training. The yoga girls can see the boys team through a set of large windows outside the gym's walkway. So, the yoga girls have to pass in front of these windows, and they see the boys practicing. The girls walk by, giggling and glancing. Their presence affects the boys, naturally. The boys, like most boys do, posture, and pretend their workouts and training are no big deal. In order to impress the yoga girls, the gymnast boys work twice as hard. It's all because the girls are watching. The coach's psychological trick works. His team wins a gold medal that year.

Widow likes Harper, more than likes her. He can't help but scope her out from across the classroom. It starts as an infatuation, then a crush, and then, one day, it's a student-teacher conversation that gets interesting, like two ships passing in the night. There's a connection. Then there's an accidental kiss. And beyond that, it escalates, as these things do. It's no one's fault.

Harper's the one who technically crosses the boundary. She's the one with something to lose. She's the one with authority. But the attraction between them is so strong, she can't help it either. They're only human.

Widow has liked girls before, but this is different. It's more like a calling, like raw attraction, like destiny. Widow *has* to know her.

In an everyday, normal kind of situation, a guy just asks around about her. He researches her, asking her acquaintances questions like: *Is she single? Think she'd be into me?*

Widow doesn't have that option. At Annapolis, it's forbidden for a professor to fraternize with a student in a romantic way. Which is understandable, and expected. So, he uses the internet to learn what he can about her. Mainly, he wants to know her relationship status. This is before the behemoth known as Facebook takes over the social media landscape. Widow has to use whatever public records he can find. Eventually, he learns she's single, or, at least, unmarried. And that's good enough for him.

Harper looks like the actress Michelle Pfeiffer looked at that age. So, the first time Widow stays after class to talk to Harper —under the guise of it being school-related, naturally—he starts with the line: *You know who you look like?*

She takes her glasses off, looks at him, and replies, "Michelle Pfeiffer."

Widow asks, "You've heard that before?"

"Yes. I have. This morning at a gas station. And then at lunch, from a barista. The cop who pulled me over on my way back to campus also mentioned it," Harper says, rolls her eyes, but she smiles at him. It's that smile that does him in. That smile pulls him in, like a tractor beam from an alien spaceship.

Widow says, "Oh. Well. That makes me feel pretty lame."

"Don't feel lame. It's not your fault. At least, you didn't ask me to do that Catwoman thing from the movie."

"What Catwoman thing?"

She smiles, and says, "Nice try. I'm not doing it."

Widow stays quiet.

Harper sighs, and says, "I'm not bad. I'm just drawn that way."

She says it with a little shoulder move, like she's doing an impression of something. But Widow doesn't get it. He's not with whatever she's doing. He asks, "Drawn?"

"Yeah. Like in that movie with the cartoon rabbit, and the redhead with the big boobs?"

Widow shrugs, and says, "Afraid I never saw it, ma'am."

Harper shrugs too, and says, "You've not seen *Batman*? And now, you don't know Jessica Rabbit. Have you ever seen a movie?"

"I saw *Gone with the Wind* once, ma'am. Sorry I don't get the references. We hardly ever watched movies in my house."

"Where're you from, Midshipman..." Harper asks, pauses, and glances at his ID badge. "Widow?"

"I'm from the South, ma'am."

"The South is a big place, Midshipman. What part of the South are you from?"

"Mississippi, ma'am."

"How old are you?"

"I'm twenty-one right now. My birthday is in November, ma'am."

"You don't have to call me *ma'am* every time you speak to me."

"It's protocol, ma'am."

Harper smiles, and says, "I'm not your momma, Widow."

"I know. I have to say it. It's regulation, ma'am."

"You don't have to say it so much."

Widow stays quiet.

Harper rolls her eyes, and says, "Never mind. So, what can I do for you?"

That's how their first interaction went. It didn't start out great for Widow because he had no plan of attack. He just winged it through the whole thing. Eventually, he got better at it. They talked more and more each day, and then they started seeing each other outside of class. Neither of them should've taken the risk. They both knew it. The problem was, neither of them could help it.

The day that conversation takes place, Widow is twenty-one, and Harper is thirty-one. They're ten years apart in age.

Although she doesn't confess to him her actual age, not for three more months, as they grow closer.

Widow already knows her actual age. He just never tells her. He learns it through more simple internet research and math. He uncovers the truth about his subject. Easy enough. He doesn't care about her age. The only person it's a big deal to is Harper. To Widow, at least back then, age is just a number. She's what's important to him.

Though some internet research tells him her age, and that she grew up in Maine, it doesn't reveal to him an important story. There's a secret that haunts Harper. It's something Widow will discover. And it's all too dark.

In November, Widow's twenty-second birthday comes and goes. He celebrates it with Harper, in secret. As a firstie, Widow sleeps in a private dorm room in Bancroft Hall. The Navy awards senior midshipmen with their own rooms to signify that they've progressed above their peers. They're recognized as a higher rank than plebes—freshmen—and other lowerclassmen.

Private room or not, Widow has neighbors—close-quarter neighbors, the nosy kind who see everyone who comes in and out of his room. Harper can't take the risk of being caught in Widow's room. It's doubtful they could explain a reason for that. Therefore, Harper and Widow celebrate his birthday at her house, where they spend quite a lot of time together.

Fast forward to today, a wintry day in December. It's another special day. It's not just the end of Widow's final exams, classes, and semester. It's not just that he finishes four years of school. And it's not only their first night out in public as a couple. There's another special thing about today. It all revolves around intentions and the future—their future, all that and the object Widow carries in his pocket. It's an item he spent more than a month's salary on. In 2003, a senior midshipman makes nine-hundred and eighty-five dollars per month.

On top of all that, Widow graduates in a week. His ceremony is later this month, not the traditional May date when most of his friends graduate. He doesn't care, because he made it. He's grateful to have so many wonderful things to celebrate.

Today, Widow's no longer Harper's student. Therefore, they're free to be out in the open with their relationship, or whatever it's technically called. Widow doesn't know for sure, because they never labeled it. They never had the relationship talk. They just enjoyed it. However, it feels like a relationship.

Now Widow's time in Annapolis is ending. He doesn't want to let go. Graduating, and moving on without Harper, doesn't feel right to him. There's something special between them. It's more than a fling. At least, he hopes it is.

Widow likes English Mustache Coffee House okay, but it's Harper's favorite place for coffee. She stops by a few times a week, stands in line, just to get her large caramel macchiato. And it's not an easy feat either. She has to deal with downtown traffic and fight for parking, which is on the street. After she gets her macchiato, she has to fight traffic to make it to work on time.

Other than English Mustache Coffee House being her favorite coffee shop, it's also the place that she "runs into" Widow off school grounds. It seems to be a happy accident to onlookers, but that's the point. Sometimes Widow will show up at the café the same time as Harper. They arrive separately, and act like it's a coincidence. "We're both here now. We might as well sit for a coffee," they say loud enough so listeners will hear them.

One time when they repeated this routine, no one from the Naval Academy was even there. That's the first time they got to sit together without worry of witnesses. As nice as that was, tonight is the special night.

The English Mustache Coffee House is set up in a Victorian brownstone. It's actually zoned for residential, not commercial, use, but because of an old city ordinance loophole, it's grandfathered in and authorized to operate as a commercial enterprise. A block away there're other businesses, so it's not far off the mark. The neighbors don't object to the café being there, because who doesn't love coffee? And the clientele is reasonably quiet.

The English Mustache Coffee House closes at around twenty-one hundred every evening. Most midshipmen are back in the dorms by then because of curfews, unless it's a weekend. No midshipman is going to spend his Saturday nights at a coffee shop anyway. Not when he can walk to O'Brien's Bar and Grill for happy hour drinks and oysters. The bar is a staple of Annapolis. It's one of the more popular hangouts.

Bars and popular hangouts aren't really Widow's thing. That's not where he wants to be. He *is* where he wants to be. Coffee's his drug of choice. Peace and quiet is his preference. Harper's his dream companion, and maybe more.

Widow sits down with her, and drinks his first coffee of the evening, but third of the day. It's a slow day. His nerves hassle him the whole day. The last thing he wants is to multiply it with too much caffeine, an unfortunate side effect of coffee. Large quantities of caffeine aren't good for anxiety and nerves. And Widow has more to be anxious and nervous about on this day than most others.

Widow's large coffee is black, imported, and Jamaican. Not his favorite bean, but a damn good one. Plus, it's a house special. He likes it. The bean never really matters to him anyway. As long as the coffee is black, hot, and caffeinated, he'll drink it. The flavor of that day's brew really packs a punch—a bonus for him.

Harper's trendier, with her large caramel macchiato. She likes to finish it, and then order Widow to get her a refill. She's not bossy or pushy about it, more like borderline.

She gives the orders, and Widow follows.

He's gotten so good at estimating her drinking time that he can time his coffee to coincide with when she finishes her macchiato. They sit out in the courtyard, talking for a while, until she finishes her first. And Widow goes to get another.

At the coffee counter, he chats with a barista. It's a girl his own age. She likes him, but he's so enamored with Harper that he has no clue about it. Even if he weren't so into Harper, he's so dense, he wouldn't know a woman was crushing on him if she hit him over the head with a rock and dragged him back to her cave.

Young Widow is far more tunnel-visioned than he will become.

The barista behind the counter is the only person in the world who knows about Widow's romance with Harper. Which is another reason she's kept her attraction to Widow to herself. In fact, she knows more about how Widow feels about Harper than Harper knows.

While making Widow's order, she asks, "Are you nervous?"

Widow snaps back to reality, like he's been daydreaming again. Which he has been. Involuntarily, he asks, "Why?"

She asks, "Isn't tonight the big night?"

Widow realizes he mentioned his plans to her before. It's been a week since he told her. He forgot, but who can blame him? He's got a lot going on.

"Yeah," he says.

"You nervous?"

"Yeah."

"Can I see it?" she asks.

Widow glances over his shoulder to make sure that Harper can't see him. She's outside, with her back to the café, and she's far away—too far away to see him. So he pulls out the object he's been fidgeting with all night. He takes it out, clasps it in his hands, leans into the counter, and opens his palms. She stops pouring for a moment, and stares at it.

Widow pinches a princess cut diamond engagement ring with a silver band between his thumb and index finger. No box. The tiny diamond sparkles under the coffee house's rail lights.

The barista stares at it, and stays quiet. Her mouth hangs open, but she covers it with one hand.

Widow's a dense man, but not completely. The one thing that causes him insecurity with Harper is money and status. She makes good money from her career, and has status. He doesn't.

The barista stares at the ring so long that Widow panics. His hand trembles holding the ring.

She looks at him, drops her hand from her mouth, and asks, "How much did you spend on it?"

"Why? It looks cheap?"

She sees his panic, grabs his hand, encouraging, and says, "No! Not at all! It looks expensive."

Widow breathes a sigh of relief, and asks, "Really?"

"Honey, I swear. She's going to love it!"

Widow nods. The barista continues making his coffee. She asks, "Have you thought about what you're going to say?"

The panic seeps back in when he realizes he's not thought it through. He says, "Not really."

She sees the panic, and says, "Just ask her to marry you. Keep it simple, you know?"

"I'm thinking that I'll just feel her out. Make it like it's not a big deal. If she seems open to a proposal, then great. If not, then I'll move towards more of a promise-ring-type of situation. What do you think?"

The barista pauses, like she's considering it, then she says, "Do you want to marry her?"

"I think so."

"You think so? Or you know? You need to be sure."

Widow pauses a beat. He's never proposed before. He's never had a serious relationship before. Not like this. He says, "All I know is how I feel about her."

"Do you see yourself having a future with her?"

"I do. I want one."

"Just tell her how you feel. Do it from the heart. It'll work out," the barista says, and hands him his order.

Widow takes the coffees—both in house mugs, no lids—and nods to her. He steps back out into the courtyard. The cold air hits him in the face as he traverses through the courtyard, passing a couple who is holding hands, sitting near the door to the coffeehouse. Widow passes empty tables, walking across the cobblestone slab. Snowflakes trickle through the air, landing on the cobblestones. White Christmas lights hang from a gigantic oak tree, which appears to be five or six times older than he is. The lights lace over and across long, twisting branches, thicker than Widow's arms at the thinnest parts.

Widow reaches Harper, and hands her the macchiato. She takes it, and sips it like she's dipping a toe in a hot bathtub to check the temperature. It's hot. She sets it on the table in front of her. Steam rises from the mug. She blows on it. And then she wraps her gloved hands around it, like she's using its heat for warmth on this cold, snowy night.

Widow circles around her, and sits across from her in an iron chair. He scoots it closer to her. The metal scrapes across the cobblestones. The sound echoes through the courtyard. He pauses, and glances at the other couple. They don't look back. They're too preoccupied with each other. There's something about the night. The snowflakes, the chill, and the quiet setting all create a romantic atmosphere. It's a night for lovers. Especially the other couple. They're holding hands, caressing, and kissing between sips from their own coffee orders.

Widow doubts anything short of air raid sirens would break their concentration. He continues sliding his chair closer to Harper until he's comfortable.

Harper watches and giggles. She giggles at him a lot. She catches him staring at her, and smiles. She turns away play-fully, watches the snow for a long moment, and waits for her macchiato to cool. She shivers. It's just a momentary, quick thing, but Widow notices. She's cold. Her breath escapes her lips in a soft, wispy cloud. It hangs in the air for a long moment.

Widow points to another table, and asks, "You want to move over there? There's a heating pole next to the table."

Harper says nothing.

"Harp? You wanna move tables?"

She glances back, and just smiles at him, giddy like a little girl, and answers, "No, I want to see the snowflakes."

"Okay. Want my jacket?"

"I got my coat on," she says, shivers, and pulls herself more into her coat. She wears this half-coat thing. It's like a bolero mixed with a quilted parka. Harper's more about style than comfort. It's one of her only flaws. If you can call it that.

"Yeah, but you're shivering."

"If I take your coat, what'll you wear?"

"I don't need it. I got my coffee."

Harper glances at his mug. It's already a third gone. She says, "That won't last long."

"It's okay. It'll stay warm in my belly."

"No, seriously. I'm fine," she says, and sips her drink.

Nervously, Widow says, "That's a fancy coffee you ordered."

Harper stares at him, narrows her eyes, and says, "It's the same thing I always get, and it's better than yours."

"What's wrong with mine?"

"I don't know how you drink it black like that. It's so bitter."

Widow stays quiet. He half listens, and half builds up the courage to make the move. Then he notices Harper. She goes quiet, and glances around, like she's canvasing the whole courtyard.

Widow asks, "What're you looking for?"

"Nothing."

"Are you still afraid someone will see us?"

"I don't want them judging me."

Widow says, "You don't need to worry anymore. Technically, I'm not your student."

"*Technically*, that's not true. Not until Friday, when the Commandant hands you a diploma."

"Class is over. Finals are over. You've got nothing to worry about."

"I don't want anyone to see us yet," Harper says, pauses, releases her macchiato, leans over, and grabs Widow's bicep. She squeezes it through his coat. She does this sometimes, when she wants to change the subject, or apologize, or make him shut up. He notices, but never protests. She says, "I'm sorry. I just don't want them to know I dated you when I wasn't supposed to. It's selfish. I do want to be seen with you." She kisses him, and he kisses her back.

After, they smile at each other, and Widow thinks this is the moment. It's perfect, like destiny. He doesn't see it getting any better. Nervously, he slow-reaches into his pocket to get the ring, while sliding out of his chair.

Harper slides back in her chair and stares at him, unsure of what's happening.

Widow freezes halfway down to his knee. The smile on his face fades. He digs through his pocket, frantic. His nervousness turns to fear.

Harper asks, "What's wrong?"

The ring is gone. Widow checks all his pockets—nothing. He remembers he was showing it to the barista. Maybe he left the ring back there by accident? Or maybe he dropped it?

He stops, stands up, and says, "I...uh. I need a refill. You want another?"

"You just got a refill," Harper says, and glances in his mug. Luckily, it's empty. She shakes her head, shocked. "I'm good on mine. I'm surprised you don't go to the washroom like thirty times a day, as much coffee as you ingest."

Widow nods, picks up his empty mug, smiles, and walks away. He hurries, threading back through the empty tables and chairs. The other couple stands up, stretches, and acts like they're on their way out. Because they're sitting near the entrance to the café, they force Widow to wait while they slowly gather their belongings.

Finally, they're out the door, and Widow scrambles into the café. He scans the floor for the ring. He combs over the rugs and hardwood floors. There's nothing, no sign of it. He glances at the counter. The barista is gone. He looks around. No one is in the café. The barista must be in the kitchen or the bathroom. Widow continues searching. He glances back at Harper. She's sipping her macchiato and staring at her Nokia phone. It's a newer one. Like many people of her generation, the new cellphones coming out seduce her. There's not much that can be done, not on these phones. But it's the possibilities of the future that grips them.

Great, Widow! he thinks, *You're ruining it!*

He searches and searches for the missing ring. He rifles over every square inch of floor that he remembers passing over. There's nothing. He tries the countertop, where he leaned earlier to show the barista the ring. He sets his empty mug down, abandoning it, and scans everywhere he can see. There's no sign of the ring, not anywhere.

Panic is taking hold of him. His heart races in his chest. Then he hears the barista's voice. She steps out of the bathroom. She sees him, and says, "Hey, you dropped something."

He stares at her. She pulls the ring out of her apron.

She says, "I found it on the rug. I tried to wave at you from the window, but you couldn't see me. I didn't want to go out there and raise her suspicions. I figured you'd come back in. And I was right." She hands him the ring, and smiles.

Widow takes it, relieved. He hugs her, and says, "Thanks! You're a lifesaver!"

"No problem!" she says, and glances at her watch. "You better go ask her, before we close up."

"Is that soon?"

"You still got thirty minutes, but I was watching you. The way you're going, it'll take all night," she says, and smiles.

Widow nods, and says, "I know. It's nerves, you know?"

"Want something stronger than coffee?"

"You got something like that? I thought you only served coffee?"

"Honey, we might be slow around here, but we're not boring. I got whiskey. Mostly, we use it to make Irish Coffee. You know?"

Widow nods, glances back out at Harper. She's still playing on her Nokia. He looks at the ring in his hand. His hand trembles. He says, "Yes. Let me get one."

"An Irish Coffee?"

"No. Black coffee, just give me the whiskey straight up."

The barista grabs a whiskey bottle from under the counter and pours Widow a big shot. She says, "This should calm your nerves." She slides the shot to him, and he stares at it. He's not much of a drinker, and not a fan of the hard stuff. Growing up the son of a sheriff in small-town Mississippi, he's seen plenty of lives crushed because of the hard stuff. Life in the rural south is boring for many people. And bored people drink and do drugs, a lot. Idle hands are the devil's playground, and all that.

Widow grabs the shot, closes his eyes, and slams it back. He nearly coughs after. It's powerful stuff. The smell alone nearly makes him gag.

When he opens his eyes, the barista puts a fresh mug of coffee in front of him. "Second time's a charm," she says, and smiles.

Widow nods, and puts the ring into his pocket. This time, he confirms it's secure there. Whether or not it actually does, or it's all in his head, Widow feels the whiskey loosen up his nerves. He takes the coffee and heads out to the courtyard.

The barista calls to him, "Good luck."

Widow doesn't stop. He's got the courage now. He's got the momentum. And he's got the grit. He's ready to ask Harper the question. Whatever answer she gives, he's ready for it.

Widow enters the courtyard and stares at their table. Harper's gone. Automatically, he scans the courtyard, but he doesn't see her. He spins around and checks the exit. He doesn't see her. *Did she leave him there? Did she walk out while he stood at the counter? Maybe she saw the ring? Maybe she overheard his conversation with the barista, and she dipped out before he could embarrass them both?*

"Harp?" he calls out. But there's no answer. He spins around again, glancing everywhere, at every table. There's no sign of her, and he sees no one at any of the other tables. No other patrons are there, nobody who can tell him if they saw her leave.

Widow's liquid courage drains from him, and he's left with fear. He steps out the exit, and looks right, looks left. He scans the street. There's no sign of her. He sees taillights in the distance, and asks himself, *Is that her? Did she get a cab and leave him there?*

The answer is no, he thinks. There's no way she caught a cab driving by on a Friday night, especially not after final exams are over. Most of the midshipmen will be out celebrating outside of Annapolis, or on the main drag where there are actual bars. Many of them will probably be in Baltimore, partying away the entire weekend. It's a waste of time for a taxi to cruise by here, looking for fares.

It's possible she called a taxi, but it's the same problem. No taxi is going to get there that fast, not on a Friday night. They're all going to be booked up, or far away.

Frantic, Widow heads back inside. He's about to ask the barista to check the women's bathroom, when he sees something. Right beneath their table, he sees Harper's Nokia phone. The big, boxy phone lay on the ground, a couple of feet from his chair, behind the table. It's like she flung it into the air, and it clattered across the cobblestones.

Widow approaches the table, and the phone, leaving the ring in his pocket. He stops two meters from the table. He sees that Harper's chair's knocked over. He scrambles to their table. Harper's macchiato is spilled on the ground. The hot liquid drips down a crevice in the cobblestones. The mug's shattered into four pieces.

Beyond the spilled coffee, he sees Harper lying on the ground. She's sprawled out on her side. There's blood pooling slowly under her head.

"Harp!?" Widow calls to her. He rushes over to her, kicking her knocked-over chair out of his way. He kneels and scoops up her head, inspects it. A wicked-looking gash cuts across her temple. It appears she hit her head when she fell to the ground.

Widow shakes her, shouts, "Harp!? Harp!?"

She's got a pulse, and she's breathing. But she's not responding. She's unconscious.

The barista hears Widow shouting, and runs outside into the courtyard. She rushes to them. She asks, "What happened?"

Widow ignores the question, and says, "Call 911! Get an ambulance here!"

The barista says nothing, nods, and runs back inside. She calls the paramedics.

Widow sits, holds Harper, and whispers her name to her, over and over, hoping she'll open her eyes.

CHAPTER 6

Widow rides in the ambulance alongside Harper, holding her hand. The paramedics ask questions. He answers, but never lets her hand go. He doesn't squeeze it, but holds it firmly so she knows he's there. She doesn't hold his back. Her hand is just limp, but not like a dead woman's hand. It's more like holding the hand of someone who's in a coma, like the light's switched on but no one's home.

Widow caresses her hair with his free hand. He moves away occasionally so the paramedic can do his job. The paramedic asks more questions, but Widow tunes him out, involuntarily. He laser-focuses on Harper, and nothing else.

At the hospital, the paramedics roll Harper into the emergency room. Widow stays by her side. Nurses ask him more questions. Doctors ask him more questions. Eventually they take her from him, and take her to ICU. She is hooked up to machines and to an IV drip. The doctors let Widow stay in the ICU room with her. It's smaller than his dorm room, but there's a chair next to her bed. He sits in it, twirling the engagement ring on his finger, hoping that Harper will wake up.

Widow steps out of her room only once. He goes to find a phone. The nurses let him make a call from their station. He calls his CO and explains what's happened, without naming Harper, of course. But he's got to check in, and let his commanding officer know that he's not coming back to the dorms tonight. His CO is understanding, and okays the reason, telling Widow he'll take care of it. It surprises Widow that the guy is so nice. It's probably because Widow's never given him any trouble.

Widow returns to Harper's ICU room, and falls asleep. He wakes the next day. His neck and shoulders are stiff from sleeping in the chair. He stretches and yawns, and inspects Harper. She's still out cold. He whispers to her, "Wake up, Harp. Please, wake up."

She doesn't move. She just breathes. Hospital machines hum in the background. He sees he fell asleep with her engagement ring above the top knuckle of his pinky finger. It's on tight. He struggles to get it off, and slips it back into his pocket.

Widow takes a walk. He leaves her tiny room, and asks a nurse where he can get some coffee. She points him toward a cafeteria. He thanks her, and heads through looping corridors and tight spaces until he finds it.

He grabs a tray of breakfast foods: eggs, bacon, and a biscuit. Then, he grabs two paper cups of coffee, black. He eats, and downs both coffees. Then he grabs two refills. He drinks one on the way back to Harper's ICU bed. He tosses the empty cup into a trash can on the way back.

When he gets to Harper's room, he sees that she's not in there alone. There's a doctor and a nurse in her room. They stand over her, blocking her from Widow's sight.

Then he hears her speak. She says, "I knew this would happen. I just thought I had more time."

Hearing her talk, Widow nearly bursts into the room, like a bull in a China shop. They hear him, and the doctor and nurse clear a path for him.

Harper and Widow make eye contact. She's awake, but dazed. He sets his coffee on a side table and hugs her, hulking over her in the ICU bed.

Harper wraps her arms around him, lovingly. She strokes his back. Widow whispers to her, about how he was worried.

She says, "It's okay. I'm okay. I'm here now."

After a long embrace, Widow lets go of her, and kisses her. Harper says, "Okay, Firstie. Careful, I'm not my normal self yet."

"Sorry," Widow says, and draws back from her. He tries not to crush her. "How do you feel?"

"I'm fine. Just weak."

Widow turns to the doctor and asks, "What happened to her? Is she okay?"

The doctor looks at Widow and pauses, like he's assessing Widow's relationship to Harper. He looks at Widow with condemnatory curiosity, like the obvious age gap is questionable. Harper is thirty-two years old. However, even though Widow's twenty-two, he looks young. He doesn't have a baby face, but he's a far cry from the rugged man he'll become.

Widow's six-four, and all-natural rock-hard muscle. He looks carved from stone. But there's a big difference between genetic gifts and life wisdom. Widow may be carved from stone, but the fires of life have not yet forged him. He looks young.

Plus, the doctor is older, in his sixties. And when you're over forty, all young people—whether they're twenty-two, or eighteen, or sixteen—start to look like baby-faces. Their ages can be hard to guess. But a thirty-two-year-old, man or woman, is more obviously an adult, with adult life experiences. And Harper's had plenty of life experiences. The doctor questions Widow's relationship with her, which he's supposed to do, to a degree, because he can't just share her medical information with anyone.

The doctor asks, "Are you her husband?"

Harper interrupts, "Boys, I'm right here. You can talk to me."

Widow turns to Harper, and says, "I'm sorry. I'm just…"

Harper takes his hand, and palms her other hand over the top of it. She says, "I know you're worried, and you want answers. And you'll get them. Okay?"

"Okay," Widow says.

Harper asks the doctor and nurse to leave them alone. And they leave, offering to come back if Harper needs anything.

"Come closer," Harper says.

Widow steps up, and sits on the bed next to her.

Harper grips his hand with both of hers, and says, "I need to tell you something. And I need to ask you to do me a huge favor."

"Of course. Anything."

"Just listen to me first. It's important. I'm going to lay a lot on you."

Widow nods.

Harper says, "I've been keeping something from you—a few things, actually."

Widow stays quiet.

Harper squeezes his hand with both of hers. She's weak. She's trying to hide it from him. But he knows it. He feels it. Her grip is weak. Her eyes seem heavy. Her voice sounds weak. She says, "You know you mean a lot to me. More than I let on, but I have secrets. I'm only thirty-two, and that might not seem that much of a difference to you. But I've lived a lot of life. Living a lot of life comes with secrets and regrets. And it comes with wisdom, but it also comes with a greater risk of death."

"I don't follow," Widow says.

Harper seems dopey, like the drugs they're giving her are having a toll on her facilities. She says, "I'm dying."

Widow doesn't realize it, but his eyes tear up. Softly, he whispers, "What?"

"I'm sorry, but it's true. I have something called *glioblastoma multiforme*."

"What's that?"

"It's cancer. There's a tumor on my brain."

Widow cries, but talks through it. He says, "We can fight it. We have to fight it."

Harper tears up, and gazes into his eyes. She says, "Oh, Widow."

"We can fight it, right?" he asks.

"I thought it would be fine. It was in remission. I thought I had longer. I hoped I did, but it's back."

"But we can fight it? There's gotta be a way. Surgery?"

"No. The tumor covers a vital part of my brain."

"Harp, what does that mean?" he whispers.

"It's inoperable, Widow. I'm sorry. I never meant to do this to you. To put you through this. I want you to know you mean the world to me. But it's over for me."

Widow asks, "How long?"

"They don't know. Three years ago, when I first learned about it, they told me I had six months."

"So, they could be wrong? Maybe you got years?"

"I don't think so."

"What about treatment? Radiation? Chemotherapy?"

Harper shakes her head, slowly. Her hair drapes across her pillow. She says, "No. I did all that last time. It's a nightmare, being deathly sick all day, just to die anyway. I'm not doing it again."

Widow pulls away from her. He stands up, and turns his back on her. There's a window with thin glass in it on the opposite wall. The window looks out onto a nurses' station and a shared walkway. He stares at a nurse talking on a phone. She's involved in a heated conversation with someone on the other end of the line.

"Widow?" Harper asks.

He sniffles, wipes tears from his eyes and face. He slow-turns back to her.

She sees the pain on his face, the sense of betrayal. She's not lied to him, but she's kept a vital secret. She never meant to hurt him, but she has, like Widow's mother did. And by the same means, a deep, dark secret, a lie. Harper's lie is a lie by omission. She let him fall in love with her, knowing there's no future for them. She knew her time was limited, and kept the secret anyway. She tries to sit up. She struggles to do it, and gets her head off the pillow. She puts her arms out, reaches for Widow, and says, "Baby, I'm so sorry I didn't tell you. I didn't think it would matter."

"You didn't think it would matter?" He says it emotionally, unintentionally heatedly.

"Widow, I know. I know. I shouldn't have hidden it from you."

Widow stays quiet, and stares at her.

"Say something," Harper begs, softly.

Widow half-opens his mouth to speak, holds it like that for a long beat, and closes it. He turns away from her, and walks out the room.

Harper can't hold herself up any longer. She drops back to her pillow, stares at the ceiling, and cries.

CHAPTER 7

Last week, the Seven gave him a new target, in Canada. This one took some planning, some extra effort, at no additional charge. The scales of justice man doesn't charge by the effort or by the planning. He raises the rate based on the risk. This one doesn't come with the kind of exposure that the kid killer in New York came with, but it isn't risk-free—far from it. The trick to that one was he had to get by the feds, kill the guy, and then get out clean. Plus, he didn't want to be caught later. So it also required *some* planning, but not like this one. This one is harder, but with less legal exposure. The risk here is death by resistance, which is higher than normal, because the target this time is Caleb Cobb, a biker guilty of raping several women and murdering one. The problem for the cops is they don't know about the rapes, because the victims never came forward. His rapes are all biker girls, and biker girls know better than to talk, especially to cops. Talking to cops is worse for them than running away. There's usually an alternative to going to the cops. Usually, if there's a crime committed in a motorcycle club—raping one of the girls, for example—the girl can plead her case to a figurehead within the club. Motorcycle clubs like to deal out their own justice.

But that's the crime that Jackie Tremblay considers, the sin against all sins in the biker world. Cobb rapes her, and after the third time, she goes to the head of the club. The guy assures her he'll take care of it. But he doesn't. So Cobb rapes her again, and again. And she's so doped up, and dependent on the club, that she can't leave. Where's she supposed to go? She's only eighteen, and a high school dropout. What's she supposed to do? Go out on her own? Is she supposed to get a job? It's not likely.

She could go home, but her father was angry with her for running with a gang. She thinks about going home. She misses her father. Her mother is a different story. She ran off years ago. Her father remarried. But she's not close with her stepmom. Her dad is all she has. And she's all he has. But they drifted apart. Her grades were poor. She was going to fail. She was high all the time. So, one day she hopped on the back of her boyfriend's bike, and they rode off into what, she thought, would be *the sunset*, like in the movies. Instead, they ended up broke, and riding with this motorcycle club in Toronto.

Her loser boyfriend tried to join the club, but joining an outlaw motorcycle club is hard, and taxing, and dangerous. And running away with him was a mistake. She knows it when Cobb, a member of the club, takes her, practically right in front of him.

She cried all night after. She asked her boyfriend why he stood by and did nothing when Cobb took her to his bunga-low, against her will. But he's got no answer.

Her boyfriend cried with her all night. He begged her to forgive him. He swore to her he'd kill the guy. He swore that in the morning, he'd go to Cobb and challenge him to a gun duel, and shoot him dead. Duels are sacred to this motorcycle club. They take them seriously. Any member can challenge any other member. Duels can be with or without weapons. They can be first to yield, or to the death. But they're always winner-takes-all.

Jackie stops crying that night. She doesn't forgive her boyfriend, but she hopes that he'll scare Cobb, or even kill him. Then her nightmares will be over.

In the morning, her boyfriend went to challenge Cobb.

The thing is, members can challenge other members, but her boyfriend is no member. He's a wannabe, like a peon intern for the gang. When he went out to challenge Cobb, the boy never came back.

Jackie thinks Cobb did something to him. Maybe he killed her boyfriend? But the rest of the club says he simply ran off— scared, like a coward. Witnesses claim they saw him go.

And her nightmares continue. She tells the head of the gang more than once, but her nightmares continue, until one day she decides she's going to go to the cops. Everyone knows it. It's being whispered around.

Jackie goes to the cops, but not the way she intends. She vanishes from the club, and a homeless man discovers her body under a bridge.

The crime was brutal too. Someone raped her and strangled her to death. The killer dumped her body under the bridge. Everyone knows Cobb did it. The motorcycle club knows. The cops know. They pick him up, but they can't charge him because every rider in the motorcycle gang comes forward and claims that he's never been out of their sight during the time of Jackie's death. They lie and say that Jackie ran off with her boyfriend when he left the club.

"You guys should be out looking for him," the motorcycle club figurehead says to them.

Toronto police drag in the rest of the riders too. And each one of them gives them the same line. They try to get the women to talk, but most of the women say nothing. They know better than to talk. The only ones who speak to the cops repeat the line about the boyfriend.

The cops find the boyfriend. Three weeks later, they find his body in a ditch. It appears he blew his own brains out. Which is believable. The kid left the club, and a week later his girlfriend was raped and murdered. He could've found out, felt guilt, and taken his own life.

But that's not what happened. The boyfriend found out, and heroically—or foolishly—returned to accuse Cobb of killing her. And it didn't go well for him.

The scales of justice man isn't here because of the boyfriend. He doesn't do *pro bono* work. He's not a charity. His services require compensation. And he doesn't come cheap. He's here because the Seven pay him. Where do they get the funds? He knows it's from victims of the target's crimes. He's not supposed to know exact details. It's for his and the Seven's protection. But he likes to do some homework himself, outside of their knowledge. That way, if anything ever goes wrong for him, he can point fingers at bigger fish. For Cobb, the Seven get their payment from Jackie's father.

Not only did the scales of justice man plan more for this one, but he also spent nearly four weeks trailing the guy, learning his habits. Habits are important. That's how he finds his targets' weak spots. If a target lives in suburbia somewhere, it's easy to walk up to his front door, ring the doorbell, and blow his brains out when he answers.

For Caleb Cobb, that kind of thing isn't possible. The scales of justice man couldn't go to the motorcycle club's front door, ring the doorbell, and ask for Cobb. That would've led to an all-out gunfight. Which the scales of justice man would probably lose. He's an expert in combat, especially firearms. But an all-out firefight with dozens of hardened motorcycle gang members isn't a winning hand. Especially when they're armed better than some third-world countries.

So, he follows Cobb, learns he rides with the gang nearly all the time. They must have a buddy system. There's never fewer than five guys together. The only exception is the Saturday morning rides. Every other Saturday morning, Cobb and two of his buddies take a long ride south of Toronto. They ride the long stretches of scenic roads through back-country. It's a shared bonding experience. This Saturday morning, the three riders would share more than they bargained for.

Cobb and the other two riders cruise for miles and miles. The early morning ride is serene, beautiful, peaceful. It's every-thing they hope for before they set out. They start in Toronto, ride through the local traffic, and then make it out to the country.

They weave and wind around looping roads, taking in breathtaking views of lakes, red fall leaves, and early-winter snowcapped mountain tops. They ride slow at times, and fast at others.

They know this route well. They ride it every other Saturday. Next Saturday, they'll head north, riding another route they like.

In a few minutes, they'll pass a looping bend, under a moun-tain, across a bridge. The bridge is over a river. It's a long drop. They like to race around this part, like an adolescent tradition. Bikers race around it from many motorcycle clubs. They've done it for years.

They see the thick trees, and know that's the spot to crank the accelerators. The other two riders take the lead, and Cobb follows. Everything's going normally, until, suddenly, the first rider's motorcycle explodes off its tires. He's flung off his bike and cracks his head on the blacktop. Luckily, he's wearing a half helmet, as they all are. But he hits the road so hard, the helmet barely keeps him alive. Blood sprays all across the road.

The second rider fares better. He clings to his motorcycle and tumbles over with it. Sparks fly across the road as the shredded tires melt away, and the metal parts of the bike skid across the road at high speeds.

Cobb is the last to go. He brakes, but it's too late. His tires explode like the others' tires, and his bike skids and rolls violently across the bridge's pavement.

The first biker skids into the guardrail. The second bike slams into him, crushing the bones in both his legs. The second rider flies off his bike and rolls to the guardrail, but is mostly okay. Cobb follows suit, but holds onto his ride. Hitting the brakes prevents him from slamming into the first biker.

Cobb gets the least damage. After his bike stops sliding across the road, he stands up and tears his helmet off, and checks himself for damage. He's got some scrapes, and bruises—but nothing serious. He runs over to the second rider, calls his name, and asks if he's okay.

The second rider waves him away, says, "Go help Conroe!"

Cobb says, "Okay! Okay!" He runs to the first rider, Conroe. But the man's not moving, and there's blood everywhere. Cobb sees Conroe's blood streaking across the road. He sees bloody teeth, skin, and shattered sunglasses on the pavement.

Two mangled motorcycles pin the one called Conroe to the guardrails. Cobb reaches him, turns the man's head, looks at his face. It's a heaping mess of burnt skin, mashed nose, and blood. The helmet saved his brain, but he looks doomed unless he gets an immediate medical evac to a hospital with some excellent surgeons.

The second rider shouts, "What the hell?"

It startles Cobb, who drops his co-rider's head. Conroe's helmet cracks on the road, and blood that was held inside comes gushing out, like a water leak on a boat at sea.

Cobb says, "Shit! Sorry, Connie." He turns back to see what the second rider is squawking about. He sees nothing. The second rider's gotten to his feet. He's dazed, bruised, has a sprung ankle and a couple of broken fingers, but he looks whole. He hops away from the bashed bikes, Conroe, and Cobb, back to the bend on the lonely road.

"Cobb, mate, check this out. What the hell is this?" the second rider says.

Cobb sprints back to him. They look down and stare in confusion at a long set of road spikes. They stretch across the road at the most dangerous part, the curve in the road.

The second rider says again, "What the hell?"

Cobb says, "Somebody laid that out like a trap."

The second driver's eyes widen. He grabs Cobb's shoulder, squeezes it, and says, "It's an ambush! Get your gun! It's probably those Devil Riders!"

Cobb turns, stares at his overturned bike. His gun is in the saddlebag. He runs back around the bend, to his bike and gun. The second rider finds his gun on the road. It came loose when he skidded across the road. He picks it up and inspects it. He calls to Cobb, who's halfway to his bike. He says, "Cobb!"

Cobb spins around to look, locks eyes with the second rider. The second rider says, "Hey, this is weird. The road spikes only cross our lane."

Suddenly, a big, white panel van comes flying around the bend, avoiding the road spikes by staying in the other lane, like the driver knows where they are. It slams into the second rider and crushes him beneath it. He's dragged several feet under the van. Blood smears across the pavement. The second rider's gun goes flying through the air and over the side of the guardrails. The second rider is dead.

Cobb stands there, flabbergasted and in shock. To his right, the heap of two motorcycles pinning Conroe catches fire. The flames are slow for a long second, until they hit a gas tank, then both bikes explode.

Cobb raises his hands, shielding himself from the flames.

The panel van stops on top of Cobb's crushed friend. The gears wind as the driver puts it in park. The driver's door opens, and an average-sized guy gets out. He wears all black —jeans, boots, t-shirt, and bomber jacket. But the most notable thing about him is a black ski mask. That and a suppressed pistol in his hand. He raises it, and points it at Cobb.

Cobb stands frozen. He stares at the man in black with horror and confusion.

The man in black steps closer. He gets ten feet away. That's when Cobb notices a gold pin on the collar of the bomber jacket. It's the scales of justice.

The scales of justice man says, "Caleb Cobb, walk towards the van."

Cobb stays still for a moment, and lies, "I'm not Cobb. Cobb's right there. You ran him over, mate."

The scales of justice man shoots Cobb in the thigh. Cobb grabs the leg and screams in pain.

The scales of justice man says, "Put your hands up!"

Cobb lets go of his leg, letting the bullet wound bleed. He raises his hands up.

"Go to the van, slowly. Or I'll put one in the other leg."

Cobb grimaces, and complies. He hops in pain to the passenger side door of the van.

The scales of justice man follows him. He says, "Not there. Go to the back."

Cobb reluctantly obeys, and hops to the back. He stands in front of the double doors, which have black windows. He asks, "Now what? You want me to open it?"

"You got it."

Cobb reaches for the handles, but the scales of justice man says, "Slow!"

Cobb slows his movement, and clicks open the doors. Inside, he stares at some kind of rig hanging from the ceiling. It looks like chains and leather. On the bed of the van, he sees a tripod and camera.

"What the hell is this, mate? I'm not into kinky shit, especially not with dudes," Cobb says. But before he can turn around to protest, the scales of justice man jabs a syringe into his neck. He presses the plunger, releasing a powerful sedative into Cobb's bloodstream.

Cobb paws at it, but the syringe is out of his neck. The job is done by then. He goes out cold, and falls over into the back of the van.

The scales of justice man holsters his gun, and lifts Cobb the rest of the way into the van. He hops in behind him, goes for a first aid kit hanging on the back wall. He wraps up Cobb's leg, covering the bullet wound with a bandage, stopping the bleeding. Then he cuffs the guy. He steps out of the van, checks the street. No one's coming. He runs around the van, pulls up the road spikes, and shoves them into the back of the van.

He closes the doors, removes his mask, and drives away to a pre-scouted location, a secluded location, the kind of place where screams won't be heard. And there will be a lot of screaming.

CHAPTER 8

Widow stares out a window in the hospital cafeteria, at a parking lot. A paper cup of old coffee sits in front of him, undisturbed. He stares for hours, from morning to late afternoon, to borderline evening. The sun sets to the west. He watches people come and go. Old families enter the parking lot, and leave in smaller numbers than they started with. Young families enter with small numbers, and leave with one new member. Life goes on right before his eyes.

Before he ended up in the cafeteria, he wandered the hospital halls and stopped at the maternity ward. He stood near a new father who stared at his newborn through a large window.

Widow chatted with the new father for a while. He thought about what it would've been like to have children with Harper. And now, he'll never know.

The image sticks with him while he stares out the cafeteria window. Suddenly, a voice interrupts him. A male voice asks, "Widow? Jack Widow?"

Widow looks up from his table, seeing his untouched coffee in his peripherals. He looks up to see a doctor standing over him. He's never seen this doctor before. The guy's middle-aged. He doesn't wear a white doctor's coat. There's no stethoscope looped around his neck. But Widow knows he's a doctor because not only does he have that doctor look about him, but a temporary hospital visitor badge dangles from his shirt pocket. It lists him as an oncologist.

He offers Widow a hand to shake, and says, "Philip Graze. I'm Jaime's doctor."

Widow takes his hand and shakes it.

"Can I sit with you a moment?"

Widow nods, drinks the cold coffee.

Graze sits across from him.

Widow says, "They call you in for her?"

"Indeed, the hospital always calls me if one of my patients ends up in here. I insist on it."

"That's very noble of you to come in on a Saturday for a patient."

"Cancer doesn't take Saturdays off, and neither do I. "

Widow nods, drinks more cold coffee, and asks, "How is she?"

"She's upset. She's been asking for you all day. She thinks you left her."

"I'm still here."

"Yes, well, Jack...er, Widow. You go by Widow, right? That's what she told me."

"Right, just Widow. Not even my mother calls me Jack."

"Okay, Widow, I've known Jaime for years. I can say without a doubt, she cares deeply for you. I'm sure she's sorry for not disclosing her condition to you."

"Yeah."

"Jaime's my patient, but also she's become my friend. She's fought through unbeatable odds, just to still be with us. I know she cares about you. I just think you should know that."

Widow stays quiet.

Graze rises from the table, and says, "Well, I'm not trying to cross any boundaries. It's just that I've seen a lot of cancer patients in my life. And a lot of them have strength and courage. But what they don't have is time. And Jaime's no different. I hate for her not to be able to spend what she has with you." Graze steps away, pauses, and says, "She's asking for you. I respect whatever you do. But if I were you, I'd want to know. That's all."

Graze starts to walk away, but Widow stops him. He says, "Doc."

Graze turns around and faces him.

"You're a good doctor," Widow says.

"Thanks."

"Let me ask you something."

"Sure."

"Is it really inoperable?"

"I'm afraid so," Graze says.

"How long's she got?"

"Not sure I should say any more, doctor-client privilege and all."

Widow says, "You already crossed that line, don't you think?"

Graze returns to the table, sits, and pulls the chair close to Widow. He leans toward him, and says, "I don't know how long."

"Years?"

"No."

"What about a year?"

"No. Probably not."

Widow swallows, stares into his coffee, and asks, "What about chemotherapy?"

"Doubtful. It could give her some time, but at what cost? She's done it all before. Some people get really sick from chemo and radiation. And I mean deathly sick. Jaime is one of those people. It's not worth it for her. To live on the verge of death for a few extra months, or live the time she's got, mostly as she lived normally. It's a quality-of-life issue. You understand?"

Widow nods, and says, "Thanks, Doc."

Graze nods, smiles, gets up, tucks in the chair, and says, "I won't tell her I saw you, in case you decide to leave. I can't blame you. She won't either. Watching someone you love suffer through this and die is about the hardest thing a man can go through. Trust me. I see it all the time."

Graze leaves Widow there to think.

CHAPTER 9

On a tree-lined street in Forest Hill, an affluent neighborhood in Toronto, a large house, a house that used to be elegant, sits quietly on a corner lot. The hedges grow wild and untrimmed. Fallen leaves cover overgrown grass. No one's tended the yard in months.

Inside the house, everything's quiet. Dishes pile on top each other in the kitchen sink. Old laundry overspills the lips of two hampers. House bills stack up on a countertop. Most are unpaid. Most are overdue. Some utilities are on the verge of being disconnected. It's too late for others, like the gas service. Thursday was the last day to pay it. And the house's owner didn't.

Last night, the house sat cold, nearly freezing the last remaining occupant, a man with an overgrown beard, matching the state of the yard. He lays in a sleeping bag on the floor of a bedroom that's not his. His bedroom is the primary bedroom, down the hall. But he doesn't want to sleep in there anymore. The last time he remembers sleeping comfortably in there was when his wife still lived in the house. A lot of time's passed since then.

His wife left him one day. She packed her bags and drove away in her car. She left without a goodbye, without an explanation. Their circumstances required no explanation. He knew why she left. He understood completely. She couldn't handle life with him anymore. She couldn't stand the sight of him anymore. And who could blame her?

So he sleeps on the floor, in his sleeping bag, in his daughter's old bedroom. She's not going to sleep in it anymore. She also left their family home. And she's never coming back. Not now.

He wonders what he did that was so wrong. Why did both his girls leave him behind? But of course, he knows why. Deep down, he understands their reasoning.

The man lies there all morning, only getting up to go to the toilet, and once to open the refrigerator door, looking for a quick bite to eat. But his refrigerator is empty, like it's been for a while now. He opens it anyway to check.

So far, his Sunday morning is just like his Saturday morning, and every other day this week. Nothing's happening. But today's different because a couple of hours into the afternoon, his doorbell rings.

It's been so long since he's had a visitor. His first feeling is one of excitement. Then, he thinks, it's probably that guy from the HOA, here to give him another citation for the upkeep of his house. They used to give him warnings, and because of his situation, they gave him extra leniency.

He thinks he should ignore the doorbell, but he gets up and runs down the stairs, excited to see a visitor. He scrambles down the stairs in his bathrobe.

The doorbell rings violently, like the visitor is pushing it multiple times, impatiently. It's loud in the house. He calls out, "I'm coming."

The doorbell rings again. "Okay! Okay!" the man says. He gets to the bottom stair, and leaps to the rug below. He hurries to the front door, which is a huge heavy thing. He unlocks the deadbolt and rips the door open. He stares out at an empty street. There's no one there. He steps outside, realizing it's the first time he's been outside in weeks. He steps past his front porch, and down the steps. He kicks through leaves and snow that cover his walkway, and stops at the end of his yard. There's nobody parked in his driveway. He looks up and down the street, and sees no one.

The man scratches his head and returns to his porch. Then he sees that he ran past something. There's a package on his doorstep. He picks it up and brings it inside.

Who's this from? he wonders. He inspects it. There's no post-mark, no stamps, no return address, and no sender address. The package is blank, all except one thing. There's a gold seal on it. The seal is the scales of justice.

Matthew Tremblay knows exactly what this is. A sober expression creeps across his face. *They really did it?* he thinks.

With excitement and anticipation, he takes the package inside his house and locks the door behind him. He rushes to his private study. Besides his daughter's bedroom, he's spent a lot of time in his study, because it's the place where he's got a fully stocked bar. At least, it used to be fully stocked. But ever since Jackie's murder, he's drunk a lot of the bar. The waste basket has long since overflowed with empty bottles.

It got so bad that he just started leaving empty bottles on the shelves. Frantically, he searches the bar for a bottle of liquor, but they all look empty. He's drunk the entire bar already. At least, it seems that way. But there's one last option.

Tremblay stops, sets the package on the bar, gets a stepladder, and climbs it to a top shelf of empty liquor bottles. He reaches way into the back of the top shelf, and pulls out a bottle that he has kept hidden from view. It's a very expensive scotch, the kind with a gold-encrusted bottle, and five hundred dollars per shot.

He gets it down, blows dust off the bottle, and sets it on the bar top. He stares at the package, and reaches for it, but his hands shake. He's too nervous to open the package because he's excited but also scared of the content. He knows what it is. He's the one who ordered it. He's the one who wanted it done, and wanted it filmed. Still, once he opens the package and sees the contents, then it becomes real.

Tremblay reaches over the bar, grabs a glass. He opens the bottle of old scotch, breaking its seal, and destroying its collector's value forever. He pours a large shot, and downs it fast. Then he reaches for the package, breaks the seal, and tears it open.

The package has no note, no letter. There's only one object inside, a digital camera. He takes the camera out, and stares at it. On it should be what he asked for, what he paid for.

Tremblay pours another stiff shot, and throws it back. Then, he screws the lid back on the bottle, takes the bottle, glass, and camera over to an armchair in front of a TV. He sets everything on a side table, except the camera. He hooks it up to the TV, after a lot of time figuring out wires and connections. He turns on both devices, and sees the camera's single video on the TV screen.

Tremblay dumps down into the leather armchair, pours himself another big shot, and sips it. He watches the video.

On the video, he sees a man in a black ski mask. The man blocks the camera for a moment, like he's adjusting it. Then, he steps out of frame to reveal beautiful, mountainous scenery, and the back doors to a white van. He steps back into frame, opens the doors up all the way, and reveals the man who haunts Tremblay's nightmares, his daughter's rapist, her killer.

Caleb Cobb hangs from the van's ceiling in a mess of chains and straps. He's bound and gagged. He's completely naked. He's wide awake and terrified. A gag muffles his screams and shouts.

The ski mask man takes the gag out. And Cobb begs and pleads for his life. Throughout the video, Cobb goes through the stages of grief, only with no one to grieve for.

Maybe he grieves for himself? Tremblay thinks during the video.

Tremblay watches the entire video from start to finish. It's forty-five minutes of unspeakable torture. The scales of justice man leaves no stone unturned, no piece of Cobb is left untouched by torment, unlike anything that Tremblay has ever seen before.

Tremblay started the video with a grin on his face, excited about retribution for his daughter. But by the end, he witnesses more than he bargained for. He witnesses the evils man is capable of.

His grin turns to sadness.

Cobb is finally dead, and the video ends.

Tremblay holds the near-empty scotch bottle in his hand. He stares blankly at the screen. The video dies, leaving behind static.

Tremblay chugs the rest of the scotch, and winces at his newfound pain. He thought seeing Cobb's death would heal him. He thought it would erase the nightmares of what his daughter went through. But now he realizes he was wrong. Now he feels she's left him all over again.

Tremblay struggles to stand, but slumps back into the armchair, drunk. He drops the bottle. It rolls off the rug, onto a hardwood floor, and vanishes into the shadows. He stares at the static a long minute. Emotions slam into each other inside his head, like subatomic particles in a super particle collider.

Suddenly, Tremblay reaches the final stage of his emotions, and buries his face in his hands. He sobs harder than he ever has in his life. After a long time of crying, he says, "What have I done?"

Several minutes later, Tremblay finds himself in his garage, where he keeps his camping equipment. He and Jackie used to camp together when she was a little girl. Looking back, it's still the best time of his life. This is where he kept the sleeping bag when Jackie was still at home.

Drunkenly, Tremblay digs through the mess of tents, tools, and other camping gear until he finds a coil of rope. He takes the rope and stumbles through the house. He takes a long time to make the climb up his stairs. He stops in Jackie's bedroom. Other than the sleeping bag on the floor, every speck of dust is the same as the last day she slept in her bed. It's still unmade. The sheets and blankets are still ruffled from the way she left them, the day she ran away from home.

Tremblay stares at a photo of her as a little girl. She's holding up her first catch, a walleye they caught together at the river. She holds the fish up, with his help, and the two of them smile for the camera.

Jackie's missing several teeth in the picture. But her smile is the last memory he wants to have. Not what he just witnessed. He never wants to think about what he saw the ski mask man do to Cobb. He never wants to think about how he is the reason.

What would she think? he wonders. Tears roll down his face.

He stumbles away from her room and finds the pull-down stairs to the attic. He climbs them with the coiled rope in hand. Carefully, he walks the beams across the attic, barely avoiding mis-stepping and crashing through the house's second floor ceiling.

He searches for the right spot. He takes a long time. His vision blurs in the attic's darkness. Then he blunders his way to the right location. He tosses the rope over a roof beam, a structural one. He ties a hangman's noose, tightly, slips his neck into it, and pauses. He says, "I'll see you soon, baby girl."

Tremblay jumps up high into the air, hoping to crash through the floor on his way down, turning his own lights out, ending his suffering, and freeing himself from his guilt at the horrible thing he's done.

CHAPTER 10

The scales of justice man waits in the van, down the street from Tremblay's house. It's been a couple of hours since he dropped the package off. After he killed Cobb, he buried the body out in the wilderness and cleaned the van. Now it's time to clean up the last piece of evidence.

He steps out of the van, closes the door, and walks the street, checking it for witnesses and security cameras that might be a factor for him. He sees Tremblay's neighbors going about their own business. Some wave at him, but none let their eyes linger on him.

The scales of justice man goes up to Tremblay's front door. He rechecks that no one is watching him, and slips his ski mask back on. He rings the doorbell and steps back away from the door. It's not uncommon for clients to want video. But even the Seven understand the need to recover it after a client views it. They can't allow the videos to stay out there in the wild. As good as he is at concealing himself, and protecting the Club, it's still video evidence of a crime. Though he can't be connected to it right now, who knows how technology will advance ten or twenty years from now?

No one answers the door. The scales of justice man rings the doorbell again. Nothing. This time he knocks, violently. But Tremblay doesn't answer.

The scales of justice man glances around. No one is watching him. He looks through the windows and sees no one inside the house. He takes out his tools and picks the lock. He's inside the house within seconds. He closes the door behind him, and pockets his lockpicking tools.

The scales of justice man stands in the foyer, and calls out. He says, "Mr. Tremblay?" He waits, but there's no answer. He calls the name several more times. No answer. He takes out his gun, holds it at his side, and calls out, "Matthew?"

No answer.

The scales of justice man walks the house, and hears static from a TV. He enters a large study, and finds a TV playing the static. Then he finds the digital camera, hooked to the TV. He disconnects it and pockets it.

He should leave, but curiosity grips him, and he searches the house until he finds Matthew Tremblay.

In the daughter's bedroom, Tremblay's head, torso, and legs dangle from the ceiling. He's dead. Broken ceiling tiles and dust cover the girl's bed. Tremblay hung himself in the attic and crashed through his daughter's bedroom ceiling.

The scales of justice man feels no emotion about it. He leaves the house, like he's never been there, and vanishes into the day.

CHAPTER 11

Widow stands in Harper's ICU room's doorway. Dr. Graze is with her, talking to her. She sees Widow, and gestures Graze to step aside. She stares at Widow, and says, "You came back?"

Widow smiles, and asks, "Still wanna come to my graduation ceremony?"

Harper smiles, throws her arms up, like she's waiting for a hug. Widow goes to her. Graze sidesteps out of their way. Widow and Harper hug. She squeezes him tightly, and whispers, "I'm sorry I kept this from you."

"It's okay, Harp," he whispers back.

They embrace a long, long time. It's so long, Graze considers leaving the room. But he doesn't.

Widow pulls away from her, and brushes her hair out of her face. She stares into his eyes. Sorrowfully, and choked up, he says, "I hope I didn't ruin it?"

Tearfully, Harper says, "Of course not! It's my fault. I shouldn't have hidden such a thing from you. I lied to you, and I'm sorry."

"Nah, you didn't lie."

"I kept an important secret from you. It affects you too. You're my boyfriend. It's lying by omission."

"Boyfriend?" Widow asks. His hand inches to his pocket, with the engagement ring in it.

Harper smiles at him, and says, "If you want to be. I want you to be."

"I thought I already was that?"

"I meant officially. I don't mind the world to know," she says, pauses, and corrects herself. "I mean I want the world to know."

Graze interrupts them, and says, "Jaime, I need to say a couple more things, and then I can get out of your hair."

Widow stops going for the ring. *This isn't the right time or place*, he thinks. There's too much happening to Harper right now. Both of them turn to Graze.

Graze explains to them that Harper needs to rest before they release her, and he explains more possible symptoms, including forgetfulness, seizures, slurred speech. Before he leaves, he also tells her she could black out again, and that she may not wake up from it.

They thank him, and Graze leaves the room. Widow's relieved he didn't propose to Harper at that moment. She's got enough on her mind.

Harper says, "I'm so glad you came back."

"I wasn't going to leave you." He sits on the edge of her bed and holds her hand.

Harper slides a bit towards him because of his weight on the bed. She says, "I hope I can make it to your ceremony. I'll just die if I miss it."

"Me too. You're the only person who'll be there for me."

Harper pauses a beat, and asks, "Have you thought about calling your mom?"

Only every year, since I left home, Widow thinks. But he says, "It's been a long time."

"I know. And I'm not saying you're right, or she's right. I'm just looking out for you."

Widow nods, and changes the subject. He asks, "How long did you say you've been sick?"

"Well, I wasn't sick. Not for a long time. It's been couple of years. I thought it was in remission. I guess, I kinda thought it went away. Or I hoped it had."

"Do you hurt?"

"My back hurts from falling at the coffee shop. I guess. I don't remember. You went inside for something. Next thing I remember, I'm here."

"Anything I can get for you?"

"You being here is all I want right now," Harper says, and squeezes his forearm. She stares at him for a while. They sit in silence, until her face brightens, like she just remembered an appointment she forgot. She says, "Widow!"

"Yeah?"

"I do need something."

"Sure, anything."

"No, I need something huge. I forgot. I was going to tell you earlier. I need a big, big favor."

Widow brushes her hair and cheek, gently. He says, "Tell me, I'll do it."

"Did I ever tell you about my sister?"

Widow stares at her, and says, "You only told me you're from Maine. You don't talk about your family. I figure it's like my situation. I have my mom, but that's it. And I don't even have her anymore, not really."

"Yeah. So, my situation's a little different. My father and brothers are...what're the right words?"

"Difficult?"

"They're simple folk."

"What do you mean, like they're Amish?"

"Let's just say they're judgmental. They don't like the way the world is, and they prefer to keep to themselves. It's one reason I worked so hard to leave. I'm from a place with small minds, and I wanted more."

Widow relates to this, but stays quiet.

Harper shivers, and pulls her blankets up higher. She says, "My sister was murdered."

"I'm sorry. I had no idea. I can't imagine what that's like," Widow says, sincerely, not knowing that he *will* know someday.

"It's why I went into criminology."

Widow stays quiet.

"It's been a long time. Someone murdered her, back in eighty-four. It's a cold case now. She's been gone for more than nineteen years. I was only twelve. I remember her, and think of her often. She left home with her boyfriend. They went to college together. This was against Daddy's wishes, of course. But she did it. She got a full scholarship. She went off to college, and I never saw her again, not alive and in person, anyway. They showed her college pictures in newspapers and on the news. Her story got national attention." Harper pauses, stares at him, but looks through him into a faraway past, at a deep wound that never closes.

Choked up, Widow asks, "What happened to her?"

"Her boyfriend murdered her. He raped her, strangled her, and ditched her body in a stairwell. It happened at college. No one found her body for days."

"That's horrible!"

"That's not even the worst part. Her boyfriend got away with it."

"How?"

"Lack of evidence. I've been over the case files many times. Collected everything I can get my hands on. I even stay in touch with the detective who worked her case. I think it haunts him like it does me. There's just not enough evidence to convict her boyfriend, a man named Peter Stamos."

"Nineteen years is a long time. What happened to him?"

"That's the favor I need from you," Harper says, and turns to Widow. "The police questioned him, arrested him, and held him on suspicion of murder. But eventually the prosecutors dropped the case, because they didn't have enough to convict him. I was so angry. I still am. It's the reason I left home. My father acted like she never existed. And I couldn't stand it."

Widow nods, and says, "He sounds like a type of man I'm familiar with. I bet he hurts, but is too proud to show it. Or too afraid."

Harper's face turns red from anger, thinking about these painful memories. Widow strokes her hands softly. She calms, smiles at him, and says, "Sorry. Where was I?"

"You're explaining what you need from me. You said Peter Stamos killed your sister, and the prosecutors dropped the case."

"Right, they dropped it, and the charges went with it. The police asked Peter not to leave town without telling them. In the eyes of the law, Peter's seen as innocent until proven guilty, so cops can't make him do something. He's got rights just like the rest of us."

"He left?"

"Yeah, and he must've changed his name because we can't find him."

"We?"

"Snyder and I. Oh yeah, Howie Snyder is the detective who worked my sister's case. He's as obsessed with it as I am, even though he's an FBI agent now. It's his...what do you call it? Jennifer case. You know what that is?"

"I never heard it before."

Harper says, "It's a cold case. It's that one case that every detective gets. It goes unsolved. It haunts them. The one they can't forget. Snyder wants to bring Peter to justice for what he did. Remember how I told you I'm going out of town this week, but I'll be back for your ceremony?"

"Yes."

"I told you I had a conference to go to?"

Widow nods along, he remembers.

"That's sort of true. I was going to a conference, but not the normal kind. I'm supposed to meet with Snyder," Harper says, and struggles to scoot herself up. She sits up, adjusts her pillows, and falls back against them.

Widow stares at her, confused about what she means by *sort of true*.

Harper says, "Have you ever heard of The Vidocq Society?"

Widow stares at her, blankly, and asks, "The what?"

"The Vidocq Society."

"What's that?"

"The Vidocq Society is a secretive organization. They meet once a year in Philadelphia. The members are world-renowned criminologists, detectives, forensic experts, profilers, former law enforcement officers, and the like. There's even judges. They come from all over the world. It's by invitation only."

Widow puzzles at the name, and asks, "Wasn't Vidocq like some kind of European detective, like Hercules Parrot?"

Harper giggles uncontrollably for a long minute. She laughs so hard, she nearly goes into a choking and coughing fit. Finally, she relaxes, and says, "*Hercule Poirot* is the name of Agatha Christie's Belgium detective. A parrot is a talking bird."

"Yeah, that's what I meant, the guy with the mustache."

"The Frenchman, Eugène François Vidocq, was a nineteenth century criminal-turned-detective. He's often considered one of the first private investigators. And he was very good.

"The Vidocq Society assists law enforcement agencies from all over the world in solving cold cases. They've got a penchant for unsolved homicides. The members volunteer their time and expertise to help investigate and provide insights into difficult, unsolved crimes."

Widow nods, and says, "That's sounds mysterious, and kind of great."

"Exactly! They've solved numerous cold cases all over the world."

"And you think they can help with your sister's murder?"

"Yes! I do!"

"But I thought you said that this Stamos guy is guilty? So what's left to solve?"

Harper glares at him, like he's not been listening. She says, "Ideally, they'll find a missing puzzle piece. Maybe they'll find the smoking gun we need to prove that Peter killed my sister."

"I see. So, you're not looking for them to find him, just to see if they come up with evidence the cops have missed?"

"Yes. That would be great. If anyone can, it's them."

Widow nods, thinking about mentioning that he's not bad at murder cases himself. His mother trained him for years on how to look at evidence. He'd even solved some cases with her, where she credited him with the victories. But he doesn't mention it. It seems pretentious to tell his world-famous crim- inologist girlfriend that he's got the training to solve her sister's murder, even though she, and a hardened detective- turned-FBI-agent, couldn't solve it themselves. So he stays quiet about it.

Widow says, "So, what do you need from me?"

"I was supposed to attend their yearly meeting to present Mia's murder case. But I can't go now...not in my condition. And I can't afford to miss this opportunity," Harper pauses, a tear streams down her face. She says, "We gotta face reality. I may not live long. I want to see Mia's killer brought to justice before I go."

Widow freezes. The thought of Harper dying so young gut-punches him. He empathizes with her. Her position is hard. What would it be like to die before getting justice for your sister's killer?

Widow asks, "What do you want me to do?"

Harper swallows, and says, "I need you to go in my place. The meeting's Tuesday night. Snyder's going to be there, but I need to be there. And I can't. So, I need someone I can count on. And you're the only person. I would just let Snyder handle it, but I also need you to bring something there for me."

"But this week is Commissioning Week. It's jam-packed with stuff I'm supposed to take part in. I'd definitely miss it for you, if it's possible. You know that, but it's mandatory. I can't just leave."

"What does it take for you to get a few days off? It's important."

"Well, I have to go up my chain of command. I have to put in a formal request with my CO."

"Will he give it to you?"

"I don't know. He's given me a break, letting me stay overnight here. I guess I could go to the platoon commander. Not really supposed to go over my CO's head though," Widow says, trying to think of how he could get the time off. What's he supposed to do? He can't tell his CO that his secret instructor girlfriend needs him to take a few days off during a critical week in his career.

Harper says, "Don't worry about that. I'll make some calls tomorrow. I think I can help."

"How?"

"I'll call Harrington."

Widow looks blank for a moment, until the name registers. He asks, "You know the Superintendent?"

"Sure. I work for him, technically."

"Yeah, so do I, *technically*. But he doesn't get involved in small matters like me."

"You're no small matter. But also, this is important to me. I can get him to approve your leave. You only need Tuesday. Philly's only two hours away. You can be there and back the next morning," Harper bats her eyes at him, smiles, and says, "If I can get out of here by Wednesday, I can still go with you to the Commissioning Ball. You know that black dress I got in my closet?"

Widow nods, half-smiles.

Harper says, "I'll wear it. And I'll go with you."

"In front of everyone?"

She nods.

"You better be cleared to get out by then," Widow jokes, and kisses her.

"I will be. I feel better already. And look, if they let me out Tuesday, then I'll go. And you can stay."

Widow shrugs, and says, "I'll call my CO and put in the request. Maybe he'll approve it under the circumstances. You are in the ICU. I got to call him soon, anyway."

"Why?"

"I gotta tell him I'm not coming back to the dorms tonight, either."

"You're not going home tonight?"

"No. I'll be here, with you."

Harper smiles at that.

Widow leaves the room to use the phone at the nurses' station. On his way out, he twists the engagement ring in his pocket.

CHAPTER 12

Saturday night comes and goes. Widow's CO approves his leave, with the caveat that Widow's got to be back on campus and in his dress whites Monday morning, and ready for the day's ceremonial events. His CO's never been this nice to him before. It's like suddenly, they're chums. Widow knows he needs more time away from the school than just *till Monday*, but he didn't feel like pushing his luck. So, he takes the leave from his CO with grace and thanks him, like Brutus lying to Julius Caesar's face—*Et tu, Brute?*

Traditionally, the USNA holds graduation and Commissioning Week in late May every year, as they will the next year, and every year after that. But some midshipmen excel in their courses and graduate early, in December. Widow falls into this category. A lot of the activities that are jammed into the regular May schedule don't apply. One such example is the Herndon Monument Climb, which is quite a sight to see. Widow did it his first year. It's where the plebe class slogs together to climb a greased-up Herndon Monument. The cat's out of the bag on how to climb it. The plebe class stacks and climbs up on each other to reach the top, replacing a "dixie cup" hat at the top with an officer's hat. This marks the end of their plebe year and symbolizes their transition to the next class year. The Herndon Monument Climb, an iconic marker in a sailor's life, is a longstanding tradition at the USNA. It dates back to the 1940s.

The week before the graduation ceremony, a lot of midshipmen will skip various events, without consequences. It's all meant to be an unofficial week of leave, which would work out great for Widow; he could stand in for Harper on Tuesday night. The problem is his CO. He might not be willing to overlook Widow missing every event.

Widow spends Saturday night sleeping in the chair again. Sunday morning, before Harper wakes up, he takes a cab back to her apartment. She told him what to get the night before. He grabs her a set of clothes, personal items, and a locking document bag, which Harper says holds Mia's case files and other evidence that Harper's collected. It's resting on her home desk, next to her plane ticket and invitation to The Vidocq Society.

Widow takes it all, double-checking before he leaves that he's got everything she asked for. The document bag's key is already on Harper's key ring. The bag is heavier than Widow anticipated, but he carries it without a problem.

Instead of taking a taxi, Widow drives Harper's Mercedes-Benz SL 55 AMG, brand new and fully loaded, black, with leather everything. Harper likes expensive things. He can't blame her. It's her money. And she's earned it. Plus, she has a terminal illness. So why not live the good life?

Thinking about her cancer shines new light on who Harper is. It explains so many things. She's a woman who likes money and elegance, and she lives in the now. Widow supposes it's because she's only got the now. He guesses everyone only has the now, but Harper's fate is all but sealed. She's gotta live every day like it's her last, because one day, soon, it will be her last.

Widow detours, and stops at Bancroft Hall, avoids seeing his CO, and enters his dorm room. He shaves, showers, brushes his teeth, changes his clothes, and contemplates taking his dress whites with him. But then he's got to avoid getting them wrinkled or smudged.

Widow returns to the hospital to find Harper awake. She greets him, and they kiss. He gives her the items he's brought. She's pleased to see he got all her stuff. He asks, "Doctors say anything new?"

"Ugh, bad news. They want to run a million tests on me. So, I won't be out of here by Tuesday. They say that I might not be out by Friday."

Widow shrugs, and says, "So what? We'll miss The Commissioning Ball. Big deal."

"Don't you want to go?"

"Not without you."

"Widow, it's your life. You only get this stuff once."

"I don't care about that. I'd rather spend time with you. Besides, you know the big Commissioning shindigs were back in May. There'll probably be a dozen people at this one. It's too cold, anyway. People will find any excuse to skip it."

Harper smiles, and says, "Well, I'm going to your graduation ceremony Friday night. The doctors will have to shoot me to stop me."

Widow and Harper spend the rest of Sunday together. The only time he leaves her side is to get coffee from the cafeteria, which ends up being several times. The last time, he takes four coffees with him back to her room, holding two in each hand. Harper pretends to want coffee too, but Widow ends up drinking most of hers.

By Sunday night, the hospital transfers Harper out of ICU and into a shared room with an elderly woman recovering from her second endarterectomy.

Harper falls asleep early, being doped up and exhausted from the entire ordeal. Widow stays with her overnight, again. This time he sleeps in a different chair, but ends up with the same stiff results.

Monday morning, Harper wakes up at dawn, with Widow. She reminds him where he's got to be on Tuesday, gives him Snyder's phone number, and tells Widow to call the FBI agent when he checks into his hotel in Philadelphia. She goes over everything he needs to do when he gets there. He's supposed to let Snyder do the talking about the case. He's there to represent her, the family, and Mia. She tells him it helps the Vidocq members to feel pressure from the victim's families.

"They're more likely to give it their best shot if there's a face representing the victims," she says.

Widow reassures her he's got it all locked down in his head. He reminds her to call Harrington's office, and fast-track his leave. Widow doubts it'll happen, but he doesn't share that with her. If anyone can convince Harrington to give a midshipman he's never heard of a few days leave, it's Harper.

Widow starts to leave, when Harper says, "Oh, and you better dress nice for The Vidocq Society. You're representing me."

"What should I wear?"

She shoots him a sideways look, and says, "A suit and tie."

"I don't have a suit and tie."

"Bring your dress uniform."

Widow asks, "Which one?"

"Either, but I like the blue."

Widow agrees, kisses her goodbye, and tells her not to worry. If he gets the leave approved, then he'll see her on Wednesday. Maybe he'll have good news. Perhaps the so-called expert investigators at The Vidocq Society will help solve her case. It seems like a long shot to Widow, but he sees the desperation in Harper's eyes. Harper wants to catch her sister's killer.

Widow's got his reservations about the whole thing, but he keeps his doubts to himself.

Widow returns to his dorm, showers, and dresses for the day. Luckily, he's not required to be at his first event until eight hundred hours, which is a breakfast event for the early graduating class, in the banquet room at the Naval Academy Club. Even though Harper wants Widow to stand in for her at this Vidocq Society's event, right then, he couldn't stop thinking about breakfast.

Widow's been to ceremonial events with food before. There's nothing like a fancy breakfast. This one's held in Widow's honor. Well, not *his* honor, but his class's.

At breakfast, Widow sits with his company and eats eggs, bacon, and toast with jam. It's all good, like a feast for statesmen. The early graduating class looks small, or perhaps many of them took the week off. Many COs don't require their guys to be present the whole of Commissioning Week like Widow's does.

Towards the end of the hour, a group of men enters the banquet hall, and everyone stands up, at attention, like one man is the president. Widow can't see who they are, but like his brethren, he stands at attention. One man, a short gray-haired man, commands everyone to sit, and they do.

The man is Rear Admiral Fred Harrington, the USNA's superintendent. A small entourage of high-ranking officers follows him.

Harrington tells everyone to be seated and continue eating their breakfasts. He gives a rousing speech; the same one he gives every year. At the end of it, he goes around the room to the various tables, shakes hands, and has his picture taken with Widow's classmates. At one point he stops at Widow's table. Widow's CO greets him, standing at attention, even though Harrington says *At ease.*

Harrington says, "I understand you have a sailor named Widow?"

The CO glances at Widow, who sees it, and stands up again, setting down a fork with egg dripping off the prongs. Widow stays at attention.

Harrington sidesteps around the front of the table, over to Widow, and says, "Son, I hear you're needed for a special mission?"

Widow says, "Sir?" Figuring he couldn't be talking about Harper's request. *Did she actually get his attention that quickly?*

"I heard you put in a leave request, so you can stand in at an important event for someone special to you?"

"Sir, yes I did."

Harrington nods, glances at Widow's CO, and says, "I take it they approved your leave?"

Widow looks at his CO, who slow-nods, like he planned to approve it all along. The CO answers, "Yes, of course it is, sir."

Harrington says, "Good." And he puts a hand out for Widow to shake.

Widow takes it and shakes it. Harrington's hand looks like a bear cub's inside Widow's grizzly paw.

Harrington says, "Congratulations on graduating. Now, go out there and represent Harper in her family's time of need. And remember, you're representing the Navy too. Carry yourself appropriately."

"I will, sir," Widow says, and stops shaking the man's hand.

Harrington says, "I expect you to be back as soon as it's over. And don't miss your graduation."

"Yes, sir."

"Good. Gentlemen, we have an understanding," Harrington says, and makes eye contact with Widow's CO, as if to psychically tell the man to back off this week. The CO nods like the message is received.

Widow finishes breakfast with his classmates, and his company. After, his CO dismisses him, and Widow returns to his dorm and changes into street clothes, wearing the bomber jacket Harper bought for his birthday. She had said, "A sailor needs a proper, warm, bomber jacket. Isn't it a rite of passage for you guys?"

"You're thinking of jet pilots."

"I saw it in that eighties movie about pilots."

Widow responds, "I'm not a pilot."

"So you don't like it?"

Widow quickly course-corrects, and says, "I love it. It's just too expensive. You shouldn't have."

"Widow, you're important to me. I want you to have it. I saw it, and couldn't wait to give it to you."

Now, that bomber jacket is Widow's favorite possession. And he'll need it. It's going to be cold in Philadelphia, he figures. The Navy's uniform code covers attendance at private civilian events, such as The Vidocq Society's annual meeting. Normally, it requires Widow to wear civilian clothes that are appropriate to the venue. A suit and tie would be the right attire. But Widow doesn't own a suit and tie, and time is a factor. He's not sure he could find a civilian suit that would fit him, not in time for the event. Much less likely is finding a tailor that'll be able to accommodate him in twenty-four hours. Besides, Harrington says to represent Harper, her family, and the US Navy, which is code for dress his best. Widow figures his dress blues fit the occasion, just as Harper had suggested. So, he packs them, still takes his dress whites, and an extra set of street clothes, with shoes, into a rucksack —navy blue, of course.

Widow walks to the door, stops, and glances into the bathroom. He stares at the toothbrush, and realizes he'll need a toothbrush if he stays in Philadelphia overnight. So, he jams the toothbrush into a pouch in his rucksack. Then he leaves the dorm, and drives Harper's car back to the hospital.

She's awake, lying in her new hospital room. She's excited to see him again, even if it is only a few hours later. He tells her the good news, that he got a couple of days off. She says she told him so.

Harper had bought a hotel room and plane tickets for her to go to The Vidocq Society event to represent her sister. The plane tickets are nontransferable. But the hotel suite is a different story. So, Harper gets on the phone, fixing it so Widow can stay in her room.

Philadelphia is only a two-hour drive from them. Widow thought she might loan him her car to drive there, but she'll need her car when she gets out. Which could be before Widow gets back. So, she offers to buy Widow plane tickets instead. But he thinks that's too much of a waste of money. Tickets bought the day before a flight are price-gouged, marked up too high.

Harper asks, "How're you going to get there?"

"I'll ride the bus."

Harper frowns at first, probably picturing being stuffed into a bus in a third-world country, which isn't reality. Widow smiles, and assures her it'll be fine. He spends the rest of the day with her.

Harper calls Snyder, and tells him to expect Widow instead of her. They eat more hospital food, and drink more hospital coffee. Widow's fast asleep by twenty-one hundred hours, in the chair. Harper watches him sleep for a while, thinking she's lucky to have him.

Tuesday morning goes the same as Monday. There's coffee, breakfast, and more conversation. Harper talked little about her sister, or her sister's murder. She refers Widow to Snyder on that, like she doesn't want to think about it.

Harper reserves Widow a bus ticket at the closest depot, all by phone. It's an automated system: *press 1 for English, say the name of the passenger*, etc.

By noon, Widow's gone. The bus ride is fairly short. He gets on, sits, and stares out the window for two hours, until he sees the City of Brotherly Love in the window. On the way in, Widow sees the Philadelphia skyline, historic neighborhoods, the Walt Whitman Bridge, and other landmarks. On the way to his hotel, something that entices him is the I-95 and I-76 interchange, a massive transport hub. He stares at it, leers at it, nearly the way he leers at coffee. It calls to him, like a siren hiding in the rocks at sea. But will it lure him to his death? Only time will tell.

Staring at it, he's struck with the idea of possibilities. *Where could I go? What adventures wait out there for me? Who will I meet?*

Widow lets himself daydream about it. He imagines a life of leisure, travel, and adventure. He imagines a life of freedom.

Widow's bus arrives at the bus depot on Filbert Street. The bus pulls into the terminal bay, and unloads. Widow gets out with the rest of the riders and grabs his rucksack from the undercarriage.

Widow makes his way to the hotel Harper booked for him. She never gave him the hotel's name, only the street address.

Widow loops through the Ten Avenue of the Arts, going around Logan Circle once, where he sees Alexander Stirling Calder's Swann Memorial Fountain. That's when he realizes Harper booked him a suite at The Ritz-Carlton, not far from The Franklin Institute, a famous science museum.

Widow checks into his hotel, and gawks at his suite for a while, like it's his first foray into upper middle class. He can't help but think about his own personal flight path. At this moment, he feels pretty good about his future. He's accomplished everything he set out to. He's passed his classes, final exams, and, in a week, he'll be a commissioned officer in the US Navy—not too shabby. Officer pay ranges, but it's all upside from here on out.

Sure, he'll have hard times, and tough decisions, but if he plays by the rules, he can have it all. He'll be able to afford a suite like this, one day. He'll probably be wearing two silver bars on his collar by then. Still, it's in his future.

Widow snaps out of it, realizing he's staring out one of the suite's windows at Philadelphia. It's midafternoon, which is too early to go to the event. The invitation says eight pm. So, Widow unpacks, hangs his dress blues and whites, pockets his ring—because he doesn't trust leaving it—and goes out to explore the city.

CHAPTER 13

All's quiet on Locust Street when a taxi pulls up to the Warwick Hotel in Rittenhouse Square and stops at the front door. A middle-aged man steps out. He's dressed in a clean, but worn, black suit and tie. The city night is windy, and it's an icy wind. It slaps his face as he steps out of the taxi. It surprises him, how cold it feels. He's originally from Maine, which makes him impervious to cold weather, or so he thinks. Unfortunately, he's been in Miami for too long. The nice beach weather has eroded his cold-weather armor.

The taxi driver calls out to him from the passenger window, reminding him to pay for the ride. He apologizes for nearly forgetting, and pays the taxi driver in cash. The taxi drives off a split second later, leaving the stranger in the cold, on the lonely street.

The man looks up and down the street. He sees virtually no signs of life, not out on the sidewalks, anyway. There's a restaurant with some life inside it, but it's mostly waitstaff. He glances at the address on the Warwick Hotel's awning. It's not his destination, but close. He glances next door, and that's wrong too. He looks across the street, and sees the right building. There're cars parked on the street in front of it. He looks up to the building's top, inspecting the windows on the way up. The lights are all dark. It looks like the building is asleep.

Is this the place? he wonders. He's forty-five minutes early. But he figures there should still be people there. It's such an exclusive club to get into, he figures that people would arrive early and not late. He's heard rumors of this club for decades. He's heard rumors of these people for decades, too.

The most elite people in his field, in the world, come here when they can't do the job alone. These aren't the kind of people to be crossed. Don't be late for people like these. Their time is valuable, more than boardroom executives, more than Wall Street bankers. Some might say their time is even more valuable than heads of state.

These elite people have murder on their minds.

The man in the clean, but worn, suit crosses the street, and goes up the steps to the door at the right address. He stares into the window on the door, and sees a dimly lit foyer and the bottom of a staircase. It descends out of shadows like the stairs from a dark attic, holding dark secrets.

He steps back, and glances over a plate on the outside wall. The plate lists the occupants of the building as several law firms, all under one umbrella. Still, the name of the club he's searching for is absent.

The man in the clean, but worn, suit reaches into the pocket of his overcoat, feeling his gun on a hip holster, and takes out his invitation. He checks the date, time, and location. They're all correct. Other than being early, he's right on the mark.

Cold air wisps out of his mouth as he exhales. He glances up and down the street again. There're parked, silent cars, and not much else.

Suddenly, he sees someone coming. From South 15th Street, a man turns the corner, and walks towards him. The man is tall, very tall. He's got broad shoulders, and short dark hair cut to military standards. He carries something like a briefcase. The guy's young too, maybe early twenties. There's something terrifying about him, like a dark angel walking among the shadows.

The man in the clean, but worn, suit involuntarily reaches for his gun. He doesn't draw it, or put a hand on it. He just inches his hand into a position where he can get to it in case he needs to. Something about this stranger makes him uneasy. It's not his FBI training or his law enforcement background that gives him this feeling. It's more instinctual. It's primal, like something in his brain passed down over the generations, from when men worried about natural predators like bears and wolves.

Even all of that isn't what sticks out the most about this stranger. What really sticks out is that the guy's dressed in a military uniform, like he's going to some kind of formal ceremony.

The man in the clean, but worn, suit comes down the steps and edges to the street. He watches the military stranger. The guy walks right towards him.

The man in the clean, but worn, suit doesn't know much about the military, only what he's seen on TV. But from what he's seen, this military guy's dress uniform looks right. It's navy blue. He knows that color is for the Navy. So, the guy must be a sailor.

The sailor in the blue dress uniform glances at the man in the clean, but worn, suit and passes him, but walks up the same set of steps to the same quiet building. He stares through the same door window, then at the plate on the building wall. He puzzles over it.

The man in the clean, but worn, suit says, "Are you here for the thing?"

The sailor turns to him, descends the steps, and stops five feet from him. He says, "That depends. What thing's that?"

The man in the clean, but worn, suit reads the sailor's name tag out loud. He says, "Widow."

"That's my name."

The man in the clean, but worn, suit withdraws his gun hand, reaches it out to Widow, and smiles at him. He says, "I was told you'd be here. I'm Howie Snyder. Jaime told me to expect you instead of her."

Widow stares at him suspiciously, and asks, "Can I see your badge?"

Snyder's smile recedes a fraction. He says, "You're chary? I like that."

"I'm just optimistically cautious."

Snyder takes an FBI badge and ID out, flips the billfold open, and shows it to Widow. He says, "I think you mean cautiously optimistic."

"If only it were that simple," Widow says, and checks out the badge. It's him—Howie Snyder, FBI agent—the cop who worked Harper's sister's murder case nineteen years before.

Snyder looks at Widow, confused by his statement. He re-pockets his badge, ID, and wallet. He took it out right-handed, out of his left side inner coat pocket. His gun never shows. Widow notes Snyder is right-handed, so his gun must be on his right hip.

Widow sees Snyder's puzzlement, and says, "Forget it. It's a stupid joke."

"Jaime never said you were funny."

"She thinks I'm goofy."

"She didn't mention that you were so young either."

Widow stays quiet.

Snyder asks, "How old are you?"

"Twenty-two."

Snyder nods, with a judgmental look on his face.

Widow says, "Why? You don't approve?"

"I didn't say that. It's just that Jaime's a lot of woman. She's a good woman. Just a lot of woman."

Widow glares.

Snyder changes the subject, and says, "Of course, she's still a kid to me too."

"You met her working her sister's case?"

Snyder says, "I did. Her and her folks."

"What're they like?"

"Her mother ran off one day."

Widow interrupts, "Was that because of the sister's murder?"

"No. She ran out on the whole family before that. I had to find her and inform her that someone killed her daughter."

"How'd that go?"

"She cried about it, but she never called her ex-husband, or her other children. She'd remarried and moved on."

"Well, it's cold out here. Should we go in?" Widow says, looks back at the cold, dark building, and pauses, "How do we get in?"

"That's a good question. I got here just before you did. I don't see anyone here."

"The building looks all wrong. It's empty."

"And The Vidocq Society isn't on the wall plaque."

Widow says, "It's the right night. Is this possibly the wrong address?"

"It's right. My contact told me to come here. And it's on the invitation," Snyder says, and looks at his wristwatch. "We're a little early, but people should be here."

Just then, the driver's door of a parked black sedan opens, and a gray-haired man steps out. He shuts his door and walks over to them. The car's running quietly. Snyder notices the exhaust pooling out of the tailpipe, and curses himself for not seeing it earlier, like he's gotten rusty in his many years.

The sedan driver shivers, and makes a big show of it, like he's not used to the cold at all. The sedan driver is well-dressed. He wears a pin on his lapel. It's gold, circular, with a crest on it. It's too dark for Widow to make it out without squinting and staring hard at it, so he doesn't bother trying.

The sedan driver says, "Gentlemen, do you have invitations?"

Snyder says, "Who're you?"

"I'm the doorman. I make sure the right guests get through the right doors."

That's ominous, Widow thinks.

Snyder takes out his FBI badge again, quick, and flashes it to the doorman. He says, "I'm FBI, so you need to direct me to the right door."

The doorman says, "Respectfully, I need an invitation. That badge is only one of many inside our club."

Snyder gets annoyed, and starts to protest. Widow knows this game. He's never been a part of it, but he saw it with his mother whenever she dealt with outside law enforcement. When there were cases that tracked over into their jurisdiction, Widow witnessed a lot of pissing contests, especially with men. If she went to their door for help, they usually made her jump through hoops to get information that they could've just shared with her.

Widow stomps out this charade before it drags on. He takes out his invitation, and shows it to the doorman. The doorman takes it, smiles, and looks it over. He says, "Dr. Jaime Harper? That's not you."

"No, I'm here representing the family. Harper's in the hospital," Widow says.

The doorman stares up at him, and then back down Widow's uniform. Before he can object, Snyder flashes his own invitation, and says, "He's telling the truth. Harper's confirmed it with me."

The doorman reads Snyder's invitation, and holds onto it for way too long, like he's inspecting it for flaws. Then, he says, "Okay. Agent Snyder. What's Harper's representative's name?"

"My name's Widow."

"It's right there on his name tag," Snyder remarks, and stows his invitation.

The doorman stares at Widow's name tag, and says, "Oh, yes. I see. I can't say we've ever had a man in uniform inside the chambers before."

"All right, now you've confirmed our invitations, can you let us into the building?" Snyder asks.

The doorman says, "This isn't where you're going. This is the mailing address. One of these law firms handles our mail. And for tax purposes, this is our headquarters. They hold the conference somewhere else, usually in Philadelphia, and every year it's a different venue."

Snyder, annoyed, asks, "So where are we supposed to meet, old man?"

"Tonight's meeting is at the Union League of Philadelphia. I'd take you, but I have to wait here for other attendees. But you can walk there. Just head that way, turn left on South Broad, and it's up a block on the left," the doorman says, and points.

"Thanks a lot," Snyder sneers to him. He turns to Widow, and says, "Guess we're walking."

"I'm pretty sure I passed what he's talking about on my way here."

"Good, then you know the way," Snyder says. Widow nods, and leads them back the way he came.

Forty-seven minutes later, they stand in front of The Union League of Philadelphia, a sprawling, gothic building, somewhere between a castle and a European museum. Right smack in the city's center, this is where, throughout American history, big players have made big moves. The monolithic structure is all massive columns and stone carvings, a throwback to a time when powerful and prestigious men seemed to be carved from marble.

Inside, it's a haven for Philadelphia's old money, the movers and shakers, the men who pull the strings from the shadows. American secrets are carved here, many older than the cobblestone streets outside. Enormous portraits of long-dead generals line the walls. They gaze down and watch rich and powerful men strike deals, form alliances, and plot deeds.

The Union League is where the American elite play their high-stakes games, where every conversation is a dance of hidden agendas, and trust is as scarce as a straight flush in a poker game. It's a place where power brokers meet, where a raised eyebrow can mean more than a handshake, and where the line between friend and enemy has as many twists and turns as the mazelike corridors.

Widow gazes at the lit-up League building. People line up outside in front of massive double stone steps. They're dressed in professional attire, like this is one of his Navy graduation ceremonies, only the audience here is all civilians.

The building is old, and oozes American history. Armed police keep pedestrians moving along the sidewalks and out of a roped-off area.

Snyder says, "Huh. Well, this is fancy."

They move through the crowds and police and the roped-off area by showing their invitations to another doorman. He's similar to the one back at Locust Street. They could be brothers. The doorman is instructing the police.

Widow asks, "You suppose he's a cop, too?"

"Could be. The Vidocq Society comprises cops, prosecutors, judges, and investigators from all around the world."

"I know, Harper told me that part."

"It's a special event, and it's only held once a year, but I didn't know it would be so swanky. Did she mention that to you?"

Widow shakes his head.

The two men show their invitations once more at the top of the gigantic steps, and enter the building. They pass old-timey smoking and sitting rooms, and an old café, where Widow's nose immediately smells coffee. It's something special too. The aroma is something worthy of the American Revolution. House staff work their various stations, guiding Vidocq Society invitation holders through a Founders room, with paintings of founding fathers—some presidents, and some not.

People mingle and dillydally. The invitation holders range from young to old, from American to Asian, and from black to white, but it's mostly white. Service staff go around carrying trays of champagne flutes, some full and some discarded.

Snyder says, "Damn fine year I picked to quit drinking."

Widow nods, and smiles. Not that he doesn't find it funny, it's just that he's feeling the pressure to keep the night about business. He's here to represent Harper, her sister, and the US Navy. His uniform is a constant reminder that he's in plain view of everyone as a sailor.

Several invitation holders and members thank Widow for his service, and he responds politely, per Navy protocol.

A large grandfather clock strikes the hour, and a man in a suit speaks with a deep radio voice over the crowd noise. He says, "Okay everyone. It's time to get started."

The house staff turns into ushers, and guides invitation holders up more stairs. On the second floor, more ushers wave the crowd into an enormous ballroom with high ceilings and crown molding. Crystal chandeliers hang overhead. The hardwood flooring is set in herringbone parquet patterns. Dozens of large round tables are set out with fine linen coverings and place settings—no dishes, only glasses. They're not serving food. But there's a bar, apparently.

There're more paintings of dead presidents and famous generals. This place is called Lincoln Hall, or Lincoln Ballroom, depending on which house staff member Widow asks.

The radio voice guy gets up on a stage at the front of the room. He stands behind a podium. Widow has never seen the seal on the front of the podium before. It's The Vidocq Society's seal. The seal is all gold, and at the center of the seal is a fleur-de-lis, circled by words, in English and in Latin: *Truth Begets Truth - Veritas Veritatum.*

The radio voice guy tests the microphone. There's feedback for a moment. He signals to a house staff member, who adjusts it for him.

The radio voice guy says, "Good evening. Please, everyone take your seats. You'll find your name is on your placemat."

Widow and Snyder search the room, threading through people, until Snyder makes it to a table in the front corner. His name is there, and Widow's is not. But Harper's is. So Widow sits in her chair. If people don't look at his name tag, they'll assume his name is Harper. Or not. Either way, it makes no difference.

The radio voice guy says, "Welcome, all, to The Vidocq Society, where truth begets truth. We shine light on the darkness. I'm Commissioner Mautner, and I'm honored to introduce you to a world like no other.

"Here, we're united by our relentless pursuit of justice, delving into the mysteries of cold cases. Just as our namesake, Eugène François Vidocq, pioneered the art of detection, we carry forward his legacy.

"Thank you for joining us on this journey of forensic investigation. It takes unwavering dedication and brilliant observation to do what we do. But together, we illuminate the shadows, and bring light to the dark.

"Let's get started and dole out some justice."

Lincoln Hall erupts with applause. Commissioner Mautner explains how the night will go. The people sitting at the tables with and around Widow are all investigators who've come to present their cases before the members, hoping to solve them and provide justice for the families.

The night goes on. Widow sits through two hours' worth of grizzled detectives, PowerPoint presentations, and tragic, but engaging, murder mysteries. Investigators present each case with care. They use images of evidence, witness testimony, DNA reports, forensic data, and of the murder victims, themselves.

One case projects images of three dead children, and one missing. Those are nightmares that Widow will never forget. There's a case about a sniper who shot five people from a water tower and got away with it. But one of The Vidocq Society members, a world-renowned forensic expert, offers a theory about weapons, and climbing the ladder up the tower. That sounds like something interesting. Maybe it'll lead to an arrest. Maybe not.

Widow orders a coffee from a waiter. The coffee tastes peculiar, and it takes him a while to realize the issue. It's an Irish coffee. There's whiskey in it. It reminds him of the night at English Mustache Coffee, when the barista offered him one, and his failed attempt to propose marriage to Harper.

One of Widow's life rules is he doesn't turn down coffee. His second life rule is he doesn't throw away coffee, unless it's decaf. So, he nurses the Irish coffee for the first hour, until the case with the murdered children comes up, and its images. That's the tipping point for him. And he finishes the Irish coffee, and orders a second one.

For his third coffee, Widow switches to regular, no whiskey.

Widow returns with it to his table, and finds Snyder sitting there sweating and nervous. Widow asks, "What's wrong?"

"We're up next."

"We?" Widow asks, wondering if Snyder expects him to go up and participate in their presentation.

Before Snyder can respond, Widow's question is asked and answered right then, because Commissioner Mautner stands up at the podium, and says, "Okay. We've saved the last presentation for our longest unsolved case. This one is baffling. It dates back to the 1980s. Please welcome FBI Special Agent Howie Snyder, and..." Commissioner Mautner pauses, and says, "Sorry, son, I don't know what rank to call you. Please welcome Widow, a sailor in the Navy, who's representing Dr. Jaime Harper. I'm sure many of you are aware of Jaime from her work in forensic investigation, and teaching at the prestigious Naval Academy. Sadly, like some of us, Harper also has a murder story that hits close to home. Please welcome Snyder and Widow."

Commissioner Mautner steps aside from the podium. The audience applauds. Widow and Snyder stand, and climb the stage. They shake hands and exchange pleasantries with Mautner. Widow suddenly wishes he had drunk another Irish coffee. He's not good at standing in front of crowds of people, not yet.

Snyder takes the podium, which is good, because Widow is totally unprepared. Harper asked him to guard the locked document bag. She never gave him permission to open it, so he didn't. He knows very few details about her sister's murder, far too little to give a presentation on it to the world's most elite investigators.

Widow remembers Harper gave him the locked document bag to give to Snyder for his presentation. He glances back at their table, where he left it. It's sitting underneath his chair. He scrambles offstage, back to the table, and scoops up the locked document bag. He unlocks it with Harper's key, so if Snyder asks for something out of it, it'll be easier to access. After he unlocks it, he holds it closed with his fingers.

Widow thinks this is a good idea, but he's underestimated the Irish coffees. He scrambles back to the stage, and stumbles and half-trips on the steps behind Snyder. The document bag comes open. Important case documents slide out, along with a green leather cash bag with a zipper, but the zipper isn't zipped all the way. Widow peeks inside and sees bearer bonds. There's a thick stack of them, thousands of dollars' worth. It might be tens of thousands of dollars' worth, or more.

Harp must've forgotten it was inside the locked bag, Widow thinks.

Snyder glances back, and asks, "You okay?" The crowd chuckles.

Widow says, "Oh yeah. I'm good. Sorry. Please continue."

Snyder smiles, returns his attention to Lincoln Hall, and introduces himself, "I'm FBI Special Agent Howie Snyder, and nineteen years ago I was a detective in a college town in Maine."

Widow gets back up. He zips the cash bag closed, fumbles it and the documents back into the document bag with care, trying not to ruin the order of Harper's collection of investigation details. He's not sure what Snyder might need.

Widow gets straightened out and stands at attention onstage, behind Snyder. He holds the document bag with care this time, and listens.

Snyder clicks on a laptop. On screen is the PowerPoint presentation that he's prepared. He shows slides about Mia Harper's unsolved cold case, starting with a picture of Mia Harper herself. Only the image isn't just a picture of Mia Harper. It's the image of her newspaper obituary.

Snyder says, "This was nineteen years ago. On December 7th, 1984, Mia Harper was twenty years old. She escaped her small-town life in rural Maine to get to college. And as you can see, this is the age she'll always be. She was robbed of another birthday and another Christmas."

Snyder flips to the next slide. It's a picture of an old New England college shrouded in coastal fog and perched at the edge of Maine's Atlantic shoreline. The sea is literally feet from the edge of several eastern buildings.

The college campus's architecture is a fusion of eerie gothic spires and ivy-covered walls. The dark blend whispers secrets of forgotten American centuries. The campus grounds are nestled beneath towering pine trees. Old wrought-iron gates close the campus off to outsiders.

Snyder says, "Atlantic Shores College. Look at it. It's picturesque, right?" The crowd nods. Widow stands like a sailor at post.

Snyder continues, "It's in Bar Harbor, Maine, about an hour from Bangor, but about three and a half hours from a town called Bridgton, Maine. Bridgton is another picturesque place. It's the quintessential New England small town. That's where Mia Harper grew up." Snyder glances back at Widow, and says, "That's where Jaime Harper grew up. But the last time Jaime saw Mia, she was only ten years old."

Twelve, Widow corrects in his mind.

"The story goes like this: Mia Harper left home the first chance she could. She and Jaime grew up in a difficult, broken home. Their father was a hardworking man, but by all accounts, a tyrant. He drank heavily, abused their mother. And last time I spoke with him, his sons—their brothers— were going down the same road. It was only the two sisters who got out," Snyder says, and looks around the room, from face to face.

"Mia was Jaime's hero. The first in the family to escape, and go to college. She was doing well for herself. She had a full scholarship, good grades, and a serious boyfriend. Her professors said she wanted to be a veterinarian. All sounds like a bright future, right?"

The crowd is silent.

Snyder switches the slide to images of Mia dead, with close-ups. The audience doesn't gasp, but Widow does. It's under his breath, so only Snyder notices.

Snyder says, "On a snowy Friday night, at the end of the semester in December 1984, on a wintry, gothic college campus, Mia Harper was studying for her final exams. Most of the students had already finished their exams and left for the rest of the year. So the campus was pretty empty that night.

"Mia and her boyfriend, were in the school library, a massive building with floors of books," Snyder says, and shifts from one foot to the other. "This is her boyfriend, Peter Stamos."

Snyder clicks the slide to a picture of a man, younger than Widow is now. He's got that 1980s hair, like he used to be in a hair band, but he was conformed by *the man*, and now he's bettering himself in school.

"Peter was—is —my number one suspect. Anyway, Mia and Peter were in the library. Because of the time of year, the library stayed open twenty-four hours for students during finals week. Peter was there till midnight. This is according to

Peter. He said that he started getting sleepy, and told Mia that he was going to return to his dorm. But Mia, worried about her biggest exam on Monday, wanted to stay and study.

"Peter claimed he left Mia alone in the library. We know he was in the library with Mia after eleven pm because a couple of students who left the library between eleven and eleven-twenty saw the two of them in the stacks. Plus, the library staff clocked out at eleven, and they also saw Peter and Mia.

"Peter claimed he went back to his dorms around midnight. Only Peter's roommates had all left for the year. In fact, his entire hall had left for the holidays. No one saw him enter the dorm that night. No one can corroborate his whereabouts after the students and the library staff left the stacks that night.

"Peter said he showered and went straight to sleep. Then he said that he never saw Mia again after that. Not alive, anyway.

"No one saw Mia alive again, in fact. On Monday, three days later, a pair of students found her," Snyder says, and flips to an image of Mia, dead, in a stairwell, "like this."

Mia's dead body is shoved beneath the fire stairs. Her jeans are thrown into a corner. Her sweater and shirt are ripped off her, tossed in another corner. She's nude, face down on the cold concrete. Her knees are bent, and tucked up underneath her, like her buttocks were up in the air when she died.

"Her assailant attacked her in the library, dragged her into the stairwell, raped her, and..." Snyder says, and flips to another slide. This one is Mia on an autopsy table. Her body is nude. Bruises cover her face and neck. There's a black and blue ring of bruising around her neck. "...strangled her to death."

Widow's seen dead bodies before. He's seen murder victims before, in real life, because his mother investigated homicides back in his hometown. But never has the dead body been the sister of a woman he intends to marry. It takes away the numbness that comes with being a total stranger.

Snyder says, "You're probably saying to yourselves: *Why's it so hard to arrest and convict Peter for the crime? Tell us about the evidence.* Well, here's the problem. We know someone murdered Mia between midnight on Friday and six in the morning Monday. We know because one of campus police officers checked the library around midnight, making his normal rounds.

"The officer saw Mia's books and backpack at a study table, but no Mia. He says he checked the bathrooms, as is standard protocol, and he saw no one. He said they don't walk the entire building because the professors have offices up there.

"After finding the library empty, the officer continued his rounds. This is where it gets unfortunate for us. On Saturday morning, the janitor came in to clean. He said he found Mia's chair knocked over and her books open. He said he cleaned up the area, picked up all her belongings, and put them in the lost and found box, which is procedure. He said he found snowy footprints and scuff marks on the tiled sections of floor, and he cleaned it all up—mopped and everything. When we came to the crime scene in the stairwell, it was all cleaned spotless."

A few members of The Vidocq Society *hmm'd,* like things just got interesting.

Snyder says, "The way the body was pushed under the stairs, it was hidden from plain view. The janitor claimed he never saw it there. He said he found scrape marks in the stairwell, along with knocked-over boxes. He straightened and cleaned it all up, as was his job. He said he thought a student got in there and intentionally messed everything up. Some of them are teenagers, after all.

"Because the janitor cleaned up our crime scene, all we had to go on was his witness testimony. Everything he described to me back then sounds like signs of a struggle," Snyder says, and steps away from the podium, forcing Widow to step back further upstage, and reenacts the violent scene, like he's doing an improv class. "The way we reconstructed the crime scene was, Mia's assailant came up behind her while she was at the study table, and wrapped an object around her neck. We don't know what he used, but we suspect it was a wire from a lamp. We found a lamp in the library, not too far from the attack. Someone had ripped the cord out of the lamp and the wall. We never found the cord.

"We think Mia's attacker slammed her face into the table, hard, which dazed her. Then he threw the cord around her neck. Strangling her, he dragged her away from the study table, knocking over her chair. He took her into the stairwell, where he raped and killed her," Snyder says, and returns to the podium, hidden laptop, and the horrible slideshow.

"We interrogated two campus police officers. Both worked that night. One patrolled, and one stayed at base, in case there was a 911 call on campus. The one who checked the library never saw Mia or Peter. And neither did the one at base. Our witness list included Peter, the two police officers, and the janitor."

Commissioner Mautner shouts, "What about the two cops?"

Snyder makes a show of glancing around the room, like he's trying to locate the source of the question. He stops on Commissioner Mautner, and says, "We cleared them."

Snyder flips the slide to the next frame. It's four images, lined in two columns. Each image is of a different man's face. One is a college-issued ID photo of Peter Stamos, Mia's boyfriend. The other three are college-issued employee badge photos of the janitor, Anton Idris; and the two campus cops, Joel Bernabe and Bret Nabors.

Snyder says, "Idris is a little slow. We looked at him hard. We looked at all of them hard. He cleaned up after the killer, making forensics impossible. And remember, DNA wasn't a thing yet. We ruled him out because the medical examiner timed the rape and murder at some time in the wee hours of Saturday morning, before Idris gets to campus. And Idris had an alibi. It checked out. As for Bernabe and Nabors, both men had clean records, and pretty long careers as cops. Bernabe is the one who checked the library that night. There's no evidence that suggests he murdered and raped the girl. And Nabors was a Marine before he became a cop. His service record was good. And he was inside the base all night."

Another Vidocq Society member, from Commissioner Mautner's table, asks, "Is there any physical evidence that wasn't ruined?"

Snyder says, "Just Mia's body."

"If the janitor tainted most of the physical evidence, and there're no witnesses, how can you be sure it was Peter?" Another member blurts out.

"We looked at Peter the most. Their friends say he was abusive, jealous, and that Mia planned to dump him during Christmas break. And," Snyder steps away from the podium, and paces, like he's at home in this setting. "Even though Mia ran away from her ultra-strict, ultra-religious father, she was a devout Catholic. It's likely she was a virgin, saving herself for marriage. We corroborated this with her church and friends, who also told us that Peter was constantly pushing her to go further with him. Tired of waiting, of her constantly rejecting him, and discovering that she planned to dump him, we think Peter flew into a rage, and attacked and raped her."

Commissioner Mautner nods, and says, "Stamos had motive."

Snyder nods.

Then Commissioner Mautner says, "Murder cases have gone to trial on less. So what's the real problem here?"

"Even though DNA wasn't a part of police work then, we kept all of Mia's belongings. At least, what we found. One item we kept was her underwear. There was semen on it," Snyder says.

Another member asks, "Have you DNA-tested it?"

"Of course, but we didn't extract it properly because we didn't know this stuff back then, so the results were inconclusive. And because of how the underwear was stored, the semen is all but useless now," Snyder says.

"So, what about Stamos? Where's he now?" Commissioner Mautner asks again.

"Peter Stamos vanished six months after Mia was murdered. He dropped out of college and disappeared, like he never existed. To this day, I can't find him. I should've charged him back then. I know he did it. He had evil eyes. There was no remorse there. I knew he was guilty, but couldn't prove it. And he ran," Snyder says, choking up. "For nineteen years, Mia Harper's murder has haunted me. I'd do anything to bring Stamos to justice. Anything. Thank you."

The crowd cheers for Snyder's presentation, and his commitment to justice. Snyder tears up. Widow feels more pain for Harper than he ever did before. He didn't know a lot of this stuff about her. *This is why you're so tough, Harp,* he thinks.

CHAPTER 14

The Vidocq Society's meeting lasts till eleven-thirty at night. It ends with Commissioner Mautner thanking the presenters for coming all this way and sharing their cases. The crowds stand and mingle again. The house staff does a round of last call on beverages, and picks up trash.

Snyder explains to Widow that the investigators who have theories or ideas will come up to them afterward, and either share their ideas or exchange information. Then he says, "If we're lucky, one group will take an interest in Mia's case."

"Group?" Widow asks, checking that Harper's document bag is locked. He doesn't want to spill its contents again, especially with those bearer bonds inside the cash bag.

The two men edge away from their table and back to a grand hallway, near the top of a marble staircase. Reluctantly, Widow turns down another coffee from a waiter. Which he wouldn't have done if the waiter had the coffee right there, on a tray.

"Yeah," Snyder says, "The Vidocq Society is made up of world-famous investigators. Some of them are close friends in real life. They form cliques, like most humans, and if they're interested in Mia's case, they'll offer us help. If we can get six or seven investigators from around the world to help us, we might come up with either evidence that'll convict Stamos, or a bright idea about how to find him."

Most of the crowd exits the hall and leaves the League building.

Widow and Snyder don't have to wait long. A couple of minutes later, Commissioner Mautner approaches them and offers a hand to Snyder to shake, which he does. Commissioner Mautner says, "Great presentation, Howie. It was very intriguing. So much bad luck in this one."

"Thanks, Your Honor. I appreciate it."

Commissioner Mautner turns to Widow, thanks him for his service, and says, "You represent Jaime?"

"Yes," Widow says, and nods.

"So, why isn't she here herself?"

Snyder says, "She's in the hospital."

"Oh, heavens! Is she okay?" Commissioner Mautner asks.

Widow says, "She's okay. But she couldn't make it. They're observing her for a few days."

Commissioner Mautner says, "I see. So she sent you, like an emissary from the royal courts of history?"

Widow stays quiet.

"What's your relationship? Are you one of her students?" Commissioner Mautner asks.

Snyder says, "Jaime really wanted to be here, Your Honor. She's hoping to find some answers."

Commissioner Mautner says, "That's why I came by. I'd like to invite you to discuss the case with my group. We're meeting in the cigar room right now. It'll be a private affair. Mia's case is the only one we're taking this year."

Snyder smiles, and says, "Thank you!"

"Right down the stairs, and before the entrance. We'll see you a moment," Commissioner Mautner says, and turns to walk away. He stops and looks back, says, "Bring Mr. Widow."

Snyder nods, but looks surprised. Commissioner Mautner walks down the hall. Snyder says, "I guess you're joining us."

"Why do you keep calling him *Your Honor*?"

"He's a federal judge," Snyder says.

Widow nods, impressed.

Snyder leads Widow down the marble stairs. Most of the members and guests trickle out and exit to the city streets.

In the cigar room, Mautner and six other men, all wearing scales of justice pins, greet Widow and Snyder as they walk in. The well-dressed men sit around in leather armchairs, looking distinguished: smoking cigars, sipping brandy, and carrying themselves with a certain pride. Widow feels like he's walked into a room full of statesmen, like he took a wrong turn.

The men introduce themselves to Widow and Snyder. Hands shake. Pleasantries are exchanged. They thank Widow for his service.

Widow and Snyder take a seat on a pair of armchairs near a roaring fireplace. Commissioner Mautner comes in, and closes the double doors that lead into the room. He takes a seat across from Widow, and asks Snyder to recount the entire case to the group. Only this time, he asks if there're case files to go along with the story. Snyder nods to Widow for Harper's locked document bag. This time, Widow doesn't hand him the bag. He opens it with the key and takes out the files that Harper's collected, then passes them to Snyder.

Snyder hesitates, like he's confused why Widow just doesn't hand him the bag. He leans to Widow, and says, "I need the rest of it."

Widow glances into the document bag, sees there's nothing left in it but the cash bag. He shakes his head, and whispers to Snyder, "That's it. That's everything."

Snyder stares at the files, and back at Widow. He whispers, "There's not anything else? I thought there was more."

Widow realizes why he thinks that, and whispers, "Oh, because the bag's heavy. It's a mistake."

"A mistake?" Snyder whispers, his face turns slight red, like he's getting agitated.

"Yeah. I'm sorry. That's all the files. Are you expecting more?"

Snyder stares at Widow, coldly.

"Sorry, man. That's all that's in there," Widow whispers, glances around the room, and whispers even lower, "There's a cash bag in here with a bunch of bearer bonds in it. I think Harper must've stored it in this bag, and forgotten about it when she put her sister's case files in it. She's under a lot of pressure right now. It's understandable."

Snyder stares at Widow, and then slow-nods, like he's finally understanding. He whispers, "Jaime put her money in the wrong bag. And then sent you here with it by mistake."

"Yeah. I'll just be sure to keep it close to me," Widow whispers.

Commissioner Mautner asks, "Everything okay, gentlemen?"

"Yes. Just a little confusion. Everything's good," Snyder says, and goes into the entire case presentation once again, using Harper's files instead of the slideshow. He passes around the files, and the seven men study them.

Widow studies the files as well, and something leaps out at him. At the end of Snyder's presentation, Widow raises his hand, like he wants to ask something.

"You're not in class, Widow. If you got a question, just ask it," Snyder says.

"Sorry, I literally was just a student last week. Anyway, I'm looking over this sheet," Widow says, and flips one sheet around for them to see. "It's a police list of Mia's items. It lists her belongings. The ones that were recovered from the crime scene and collected as evidence."

The seven distinguished men nod. Snyder gives Widow a puzzled look.

Widow asks, "Is this the full list of Mia's belongings?"

Snyder says, "Yep. That's what it is."

"It's exhaustive?"

"Of course."

"And there's no chance it's abbreviated?"

"Abbreviated?" Snyder asks.

"Yeah, like shortened? Did the police leave stuff off, to save space?"

"The police you're referring to were me and my guys. And no. We didn't abbreviate it," Snyder says, and turns back to the seven men, like he's done answering Widow's questions. After all, Widow's not the one who can help him.

Widow raises his hand again.

Impatiently, Snyder asks, "What is it?"

"So, it's a very thorough list?" Widow asks, and hands the list to Mautner. Mautner takes it, looks it over, and two of the others lean over to look along with him.

Widow recites the items listed, in order. Mautner and the others follow along. Widow says, "It lists Mia's backpack, textbooks, notebooks, bookmarker, pens, pencils, purse, ID, cash, coat, scarf, reading glasses, nail polish, various other makeups, the number of tissues in her purse, jewelry, jeans, sweater, t-shirt with the college logo, friendship bracelets, bra and panties, the lint in her pockets, and two hair barrettes."

Everyone but Mautner stares at Widow and stays quiet. Mautner reads the list again. Once he finishes, he looks up and says, "Incredible. That's what it says, and in the same order."

Snyder asks, "So, what's your point?"

Widow says, "December 7th, 1984."

"Yeah, and?" Snyder asks.

Widow says, "Mia was murdered on campus in December. In Maine."

All eight men stare at him, waiting, like he's about to give them a punchline to a long joke. Widow says, "Night temperatures in that part of the United States, in December, would've ranged from twenty-five to thirty-five degrees Fahrenheit."

Widow looks at each of them, into their eyes, waiting for one of them to see it. He doesn't want to be the only one. Collectively, the eight other men in the room have a combined two hundred and forty years of real-world investigative experience. And who's he? Widow's just a twenty-two-year-old runaway turned sailor. He hasn't even graduated Annapolis yet, not officially. He doesn't want to appear some kind of know-it-all, punk kid. So, he waits. But in a room with investigators and a federal judge, there's no answer. No response. No one else sees it.

Finally, Mautner asks, "Son, what's missing?"

Widow breathes, and says, "On a freezing cold winter's night in Maine, a ninety-eight-pound, twenty-year-old girl born there would know to wear all her clothes."

Edgily, Snyder asks, "What is it?"

"Where's her shoes?" Widow asks.

The room is silent.

Mautner studies the list again. He says, "They're not here."

Thunderstruck, Snyder takes the list from Mautner and stares at it, reading it over intensely.

One man says, "Maybe your police forgot to list them?"

"They didn't forget!" Snyder barks.

Another asks, "Did they miss them at the crime scene?"

A third one says, "The janitor accidentally cleaned up the crime scene. Maybe he picked them up?"

Mautner says, "Yes. That's plausible. Perhaps the janitor saw the shoes, and mistook them for lost items because they came off somewhere along the way of Mia being dragged to the fire stairs."

Snyder speaks in a low voice, like he's embarrassed and broken, because he, and his cops, missed Mia's shoes. He says, "That's not it. If the janitor found them, he'd have put them in lost and found, with the other stuff."

Widow says, "There's another thing."

Mautner puffs on his cigar, and says, "Her socks."

Widow nods.

The seven men smoke and drink and whisper among themselves. This new development intrigues them. And Widow impresses them.

Finally, Snyder says, "It's strange. I admit. But it's just an oversight. Her shoes and socks are in the evidence locker in a long-term evidence storage building in Bar Harbor."

Widow asks, "Are you sure?"

Snyder pauses a beat, glances at the floor, like the answer is sewn into the fibers of the rug. He says, "Yes! Of course they are. I would've noticed if they were missing. It changes nothing. I still want to find Peter Stamos. He's gotta be brought in."

Mautner slow-nods, and puffs his cigar, like he's considering some offer that Widow doesn't know about. Ultimately, he takes a last puff and says, "Okay, gentlemen. It's time for us to talk."

The other six Vidocq members nod. Mautner stands, and the others follow suit, like he gives them their cues. Mautner says, "Mr. Widow, it's been a genuine pleasure to meet you. But we have club business to discuss, briefly. Would you mind waiting outside?"

Widow and Snyder both stand.

Mautner says, "Howie, you stay."

Snyder nods, and says to Widow, "I'll be just a few minutes."

Widow says, "No problem. I'll wait outside for you." He ignores the loose files, because the group might still need to look at them for whatever they can't discuss in front of him. He scoops the document bag up, tucking Harper's cash bag deep into it, closes and locks the document bag, readying it to go out with him.

Snyder puts a hand on the bag's handle, grins, and says, "Leave it. I'll make sure all Harper's files are back in it. Then I'll bring it out after."

"No can do. I gotta watch over it. Harper will freak out if I let something happen to her money."

Snyder pauses a long beat, glances at Mautner, who stares back at him, like they're sending psychic messages. Then, Snyder smiles at Widow and releases his grip on the locked document bag's handle. He steps back and over to Mautner.

Widow takes the bag and nods to Snyder. He departs the cigar room, leaving the eight men to talk among themselves.

CHAPTER 15

Widow waits by the exit to South Broad Street. He stares up at the Wells Fargo building and the famous Philadelphia skyline beyond. He can feel the cold outside, even from behind the door, inside the League house's nice warm temperature.

Snyder walks out of the cigar room meeting, and the seven men follow. They laugh and say their goodbyes. They must've offered their help on the case, because Snyder is thanking Judge Mautner profusely. And he's smiling, more than Widow's seen him smile all night.

Snyder parts from the group and walks over to Widow. He hands Widow Harper's files, and says, "Okay, let's go." He leads Widow out onto the sidewalk. The cold air hits them both. Snyder closes his coat up and blows into his hands.

Widow stuffs the files back into the document bag, locks it, and says, "You should get some gloves."

Snyder glances at Widow's gloves, and says, "You military people are always prepared."

"It's part of the dress uniform. The Navy likes to take all the thinking out of mundane things for us."

"They like their servicemen not thinking?"

"Not really. They just don't want us distracted by the cold when we need to concentrate on the mission."

Snyder nods, smiles, and says, "I'm sorry. I'm not trying to act like a jerk or a has-been agent."

"I'm sorry if I commandeered your meeting with those guys. I know you're just trying to solve this case for Harper."

"I'm just trying to get justice for Mia," Snyder says, and sighs.

Widow shrugs, and asks, "So, what did they say? What was that at the end?"

"Sorry about kicking you out. These guys are really into ceremony, and you're uninitiated into their little club. So am I, but I've been in law enforcement for thirty years."

"You didn't really answer my question. What did they say after I left? If you don't mind my asking."

Snyder says nothing.

Widow smiles, and asks, "What? Are you sworn to secrecy, or something?"

"This town's full of secrets."

"Okay. You don't have to tell me."

Snyder looks at his watch, and says, "Hey, what's the oldest bar you've ever been to?"

"Not sure. I'm not much of a drinker."

Snyder looks Widow up and down, and says, "A sailor in his early twenties, who doesn't drink? Now I've seen it all. Next you'll say you have no tattoos."

Widow shrugs, and says, "I don't have any tattoos. Maybe someday. And I didn't say I don't drink. I just have other priorities."

"Didn't you just graduate from college?"

"Technically, yes."

"Come on. Let me buy you a celebratory drink. Right down the street is the world famous McGillin's Olde Ale House. It's been around since the 1860s."

"I thought you don't drink?"

"I don't, but I can live vicariously through you."

Widow looks at the locked document bag, thinks about Harper's cash bag inside, filled with her misplaced bearer bonds, and says, "I don't know. I got this."

"Oh, come on. When's the next time you'll be in Philly? Plus, it sounded like your weekend after you passed your exams wasn't what I'd call a celebration."

Widow thinks for a moment, glances at the locked document bag in his hand, and says, "I'm at the Ritz. I think it's just over there. Let me stop in, drop this off, and I can change my clothes." He pauses, and points north, in the Ritz's direction.

Snyder takes him by the arm, points to the east, and says, "Forget all that. McGillin's is right there. We'll be in and out."

"I don't know. I gotta watch Harper's money."

"Listen, you don't want to leave it unguarded in your hotel room. Thieves love to stake those places out. They wait for the guests to leave their rooms, and they pick the locks. Trust me. I'm FBI. It happens all the time. At least, if you take it with us, you can watch it."

Widow stays quiet, thinking it over.

Snyder says, "McGillin's beer taps have run for like a hundred and forty years straight. Try some."

No response from Widow.

Snyder says, "I saw you like coffee."

Widow's eyes perk up but stay guarded, like he faces a real moral dilemma.

Snyder says, "McGillin's has a stout beer on tap, made from coffee beans. It's incredible."

Widow grins, and says, "Okay. One beer."

"Yeah! Now you're talking!"

The two men walk the couple of blocks to McGillin's, and have more than one drink. Widow drinks the coffee-bean stout, and Snyder drinks a nonalcoholic beer. The night goes on. They talk about both the living and the dead: the Harper sisters.

Snyder keeps looking at his watch, like he's expecting a hot date. Widow thinks maybe he wants to leave, and offers to go, but Snyder says, "One more round, and then we'll go."

After two and a half pints of the coffee-bean stout, Widow starts to worry about Snyder's suggestion of thieves in hotels. He's glad he has Harper's engagement ring in his pocket. All his other possessions are replaceable, but he doesn't want to if he doesn't have to. So, he insists it's time to leave.

Right on cue, the bartender mentions they close in fifteen minutes, and asks if they want a last call round. Snyder rejects it, and pays their tab. Widow finishes his last pint, and they get up to leave. Widow's halfway out the door, when Snyder calls to him.

"Widow?"

Widow spins around to see Snyder standing back by the bar, holding up Harper's locked document bag. He says, "Don't forget this."

Widow smacks his forehead, goes back, takes Harper's bag, and says, "Thanks. I can't believe I almost left it."

"You okay? You only had a few beers."

"I'm not a lightweight; just I had a couple of Irish coffees at the Vidocq meeting too."

Snyder glances at his watch again, and says, "Want to grab a bite somewhere?"

"Nah. I'll be okay. I just want to get in my room, and sleep. I can always raid the minibar for snacks," Widow says, and they leave together.

Out on Drury Street, the night air is freezing cold, and the street is empty, all except a large, dark green Range Rover, parked at the corner. The engine idles. Exhaust pools at the tailpipes. There's a sticker on the rear window. It's a skull with green cloverleaf eyes.

When Widow and Snyder get within five yards of it, all the doors open, and the dome light comes on.

Widow stops. Snyder freezes in front of him. He turns around, grabs Widow by the biceps, and tries to push him back, only Widow doesn't budge. He stands and stares. Snyder pushes harder, but it's like trying to jerk an oak tree up out of the ground with a warehouse forklift.

Five tall, but gangly guys rush out of the Range Rover. They wear thousand-dollar track suits under thick coats. Face tattoos and silver teeth grills stare back at Widow.

Snyder says, "Come on."

Widow follows Snyder. They don't run, but they walk fast and turn down an alley, then another, and stop.

Snyder says, "Here. Go in here." He points at another turn. They duck into a small dead-end alley.

Widow asks, "Who are they? What's going on?"

"Did you see the skull decal?"

"I did."

"Those are the Fenian Boys."

"Who?"

"It's a local Irish street gang. Fenian is a word associated with Irish nationalism."

"What're Irish nationalists doing here?" Widow asks.

"They're not nationalists. They might not even be Irish. They might just like the word."

"They looked right at me. Were they waiting for us?"

Snyder walks back to the lip of the alley, and looks around the edge of a building. He says, "Not us, but maybe a couple of drunk suckers to rob."

"They're driving a hundred-thousand-dollar Range Rover. What're they expecting to get from a couple of guys who came out of a dive bar?"

"It could be a gang initiation. You know, like rob a couple of strangers, and you're in the gang."

Widow shrugs, and says, "You got a gun on you. And a phone. Get your gun out and call 911."

Snyder freezes, like he doesn't hear Widow.

Widow says, "Howie?"

Just then, Snyder throws his hands up in a surrendering gesture, and backs away from the edge of the building.

The five Fenian Boys come face-to-face with Widow and Snyder. Three of them point guns at Snyder and then at Widow.

Having guns pointed at him isn't something Widow is used to—not yet. However, he handles it pretty well. He stays calm, stands feet planted on the ground, strong like an oak tree, raises his hands slowly, and stares into the eyes of the five Fenian Boys.

All five are lanky, scrawny guys, but they have that street gang look in their eyes. The kind of men who don't fear death, but walk around with it. They've seen things, done things—terrible, terrible things.

One of them, a guy with short, bleached hair, takes the lead, and the others follow suit. In a Philadelphia accent, he says, "Okay, fellas, do as you're told, and you don't have to get tuned up, understand?"

Snyder says, "Take it easy. We're complying. Just tell us what you want."

Widow stays quiet.

"Fast to cooperate? We like that, fellas. We like it a lot," Bleached Hair says, and looks from Snyder to Widow. He stares at Widow, says, "And look at you. Hey boys, we got a sailor here."

The Fenian Boys laugh. One says, "He's a giant sailor, too. "

"Yeah, he looks like he's been eating his spinach," another says. "You know like, what's that old cartoon?"

Bleached Hair gets up in Widow's face, stares at him, and says, "Popeye the Sailor Man. Isn't that right, fella?"

Widow stays quiet, looks down at the bleached-hair guy.

Bleached Hair gives Widow the stare-down for a long moment, a primal challenge seen all over the world, every day, from gorilla troops to schoolyards.

Snyder says, "Don't resist, Widow. He's just trying to antagonize you."

Bleached Hair asks, "Widow? What's a Widow?"

"It's my name. It's written on my name tag," Widow says, and just can't help himself. "It's on the right side of my Navy dress blues. It's placed roughly a quarter inch above the right pocket, centered from left to right. Its placement aligns with the US Navy's general uniform regulations. Name tags are positioned on the right side to distinguish them from ribbons and medals worn on the left.

Bleached Hair cocks his head, and asks, "Are you being smart, guy?"

Widow says, "Smart? Smart would've been for you to find something else to do with your time. It would've been smart to find a new hobby, boys."

"Oh yeah? That right?" Bleached Hair says, and glances at two of his guys. The two he glances at step up to Widow and shove guns into his chest, like they're synced to Bleached Hair's commands.

Widow glances at both of them in the eyes, and he sees the truth. They won't hesitate. They won't blink. These are two guys who probably have killed, but definitely would kill, and on command.

Snyder says, "That's enough. He doesn't know what he's talking about. He's been drinking. Forgive him. We didn't expect any trouble."

"Is that right, Mr. Widow? You're a little drunk? A little tipsy? I should look the other way because you're not in your right mind?" Bleached Hair says, and stares at Widow, along with his two armed guys. Like the gorilla troop, or kids on the schoolyard, it's important that they don't back down.

Since Widow doesn't want to die, he smiles, and slurs, "Right, fellas…I'm so…drunk. That's how…I'm not drivin'." He busts out in fake laughter.

Bleached Hair stares for a second, and then, he, too, laughs uncontrollably. Soon the other Fenian Boys join in.

After a long bout of laughing, they stop and continue their business. Bleached Hair gets up in Widow's face again, and stares at him like he's contemplating whether or not to believe Widow's lie. Widow doesn't think he's buying it. Widow's not much of a liar, not yet.

Still, Widow doesn't budge. Finally, Bleached Hair steps back, and says, "Okay, enough fun, you boys hand over your cash, jewelry, and valuables. We don't need your wallets, just the cash."

Widow has three major problems. One, he doesn't carry a wallet, but he has a bank card, military ID, and some cash. Two, he's still carrying Harper's locked document bag, with her bearer bonds inside the cash bag. And three, he has Harper's engagement ring is in his pocket.

The last two things, Widow doesn't want to part with. He couldn't care less about his own cash.

Snyder and Widow slowly reach into their pockets. Snyder's wallet is in a rear pants pocket, and he is able to avoid revealing his badge and gun when he reaches for it.

Snyder pulls out his wallet, opens it in front of the Fenian Boys, and hands over a wad of cash. One of the unarmed Fenian Boys takes it and brushes through it. He nods to Bleached Hair, and says, "Nice."

They turn to Widow. Widow does the same, takes out his cash, and hands it over. His cash is in the same pocket as Harper's engagement ring. So when he pulls the cash out, the ring comes out in his hand too. He closes his palm around it, to hide it. But the Fenian Boy says, "Hey! What's that?"

Widow stays quiet, keeps his fist closed around the ring.

"What is it?" Bleached Hair asks.

"It's nothing," Widow says.

The unarmed Fenian Boy paws at Widow's closed fist, and says, "Hand it over!"

Reactively, instinctively, Widow headbutts the guy full on in the face. The guy's nose *cracks,* and he falls back into one of the other guys. They tumble over onto their butts. Widow freezes, unsure what to do. But he's not the only one to freeze.

The two armed Boys left standing freeze, waiting for instructions from Bleached Hair, but he hesitates as well. There's a quick moment of opportunity. That happens. If Widow blinks, he'll miss it. But he doesn't.

Bleached Hair glances at Snyder, like he's waiting to react based on what Snyder does. But Snyder does nothing.

Widow seizes the opportunity, and swings Harper's heavy locked document bag at the nearest armed Fenian Boy. The bag slams across the guy's face. It impacts hard. The locked document bag is full of case files and that stack of bearer bonds inside the cash bag. It's essentially all paper, but paper can be heavy. In large amounts, it's like concrete. And this is a large amount of paper.

The impact knocks the guy back, and spins him around. He nearly drops his gun. The other Fenian Boys, including Bleached Hair, stare at their unfortunate friends for a second too long. Which gives Widow time to act. And he does.

Widow smacks the gun in the other Fenian Boy's hand. The gun muzzle arcs down, startling the Fenian Boy, who pulls the trigger. The gun fires. The gunshot booms and echoes off the brick walls and the surrounding buildings. The bullet ricochets off a cobblestone and into a dumpster, piercing the metal and getting lost in the trash.

Widow scrambles to the right, jerks the guy by the gun hand, and spins him around to face the others, like they're dance partners trying to kill each other.

From behind the Fenian Boy, Widow rips the gun from his grip, and points the muzzle at the Fenian Boy's head. With adrenaline pumping, and his inexperience hindering his judgment, Widow says, "That's it! It's over! Drop your guns, and return our cash."

Bleached Hair stares at Widow. The other Fenian Boys recover, and aim their guns at him. The one with the busted nose draws a gun. They all aim at Widow.

Snyder keeps his hands up, like he's unsure what to do. Widow had hoped Snyder would've drawn his service weapon. He could've shot them. It's a justified use of force. But he didn't. He's either too old and slow, or dumbstruck by Widow's reaction. Either way, he misses his opportunity to act.

Bleached Hair reaches around and draws his own gun. He smirks at Widow, like he's saying: *Good job, but what now, fella?*

Bleached Hair doesn't point his gun at Widow, like his boys do. Instead, he aims it right at Snyder's face, and says, "I'm counting to three, and pulling this trigger. And nothing's going to stop me except you giving that gun back to my boy and letting him go."

Widow stays where he is. His Fenian Boy human shield quakes nervously. The other Fenian Boys look at Widow in disdain. They want his blood. Widow can feel it.

Dammit, Snyder, he thinks. If Snyder had acted when he had the chance, they might get out of this.

"One," Bleached Hair says.

Widow calculates his moves, but he's not the man he will become, not for a long time. He could shoot a few of them. They would all return fire, killing their partner, for sure. But looking at their faces, Widow isn't sure that matters to any of them. If he shoots a couple of them, it will end badly for him, end badly for Snyder. He'll never see Harper again.

"Two," Bleached Hair says, and pushes the muzzle into Snyder's cheek.

Snyder says, "Shit! Widow, please?"

He sees no moves. Anything he does short of surrender will end with him and Snyder both dead. The Fenian Boys would shoot the two of them dead in this alley, and steal Harper's money and her ring anyway.

Before Bleached Hair says *three*, Widow lets go of his human shield and reverses the gun, offering it back to him. The guy steps away from Widow, surprised and dumbfounded. He stares at the gun for a long second, like it's a trick. He rips it away from Widow and steps back, putting a large distance between them.

The human shield points his gun at Widow, and says, "I should kill you, fella!"

Bleached Hair lowers his gun, stuffs it back in his waistband, and says, "Good boy."

Snyder sighs in relief.

Bleached Hair barks orders at the others. To the human shield, he says, "Holster your gun. Go get the truck ready to roll." He glances around at the others, and says, "Come on, fellas, someone will have heard the gunshot. Let's get it and get going."

Two of the guys keep their guns trained on Widow out of fear, and don't deviate. The busted nose guy picks up the cash he dropped, and rips the locked document bag out of Widow's hand. Widow resists at first, making the guy jerk it with all his strength. Even then, he only gets the bag from Widow because Widow allows it.

Bleached Hair takes Snyder's wristwatch and saunters over to Widow, stares him in the eyes, again, still like a gorilla in a troop. He grabs Widow's clenched fist with both hands, and pries Widow's fist open. He takes the engagement ring and says, "Count yourself lucky, fella."

He takes the ring, turns, and runs back to the Range Rover around the corner. The other Fenian Boys follow. The last two keep their guns pointed at Widow, and back away until they're at the alley.

At the alley, they turn and run back to join the others.

Snyder lowers his hands, and sighs again. He breathes heavily, nearly hyperventilating.

Widow walks to the alley's opening, and steps out. His eyes follow the Fenian Boys back to their Range Rover on Drury Street. He memorizes the plate number and watches them until they're gone from sight.

Slowly, Snyder joins him on the street. He's breathing normally now. He puts his hand on Widow's shoulder, and says, "I'm sorry. I didn't want them to discover my badge and gun."

Widow shakes the hand off his shoulder, and says, "You should've backed me up."

"We would've died."

"You don't know that. We could've stood a chance."

Snyder shakes his head, and says, "You don't understand. I know who these guys are. We did the right thing. Plus, I can't reveal I'm FBI. Not here. I'm under a prime directive. I'm on a task force, and I'm not supposed to be active here in Philadelphia. If I'd shown my cards, they could've done a lot of damage to a case here. It's best this way."

Widow stays quiet.

Snyder says, "Sorry about Harper's bag."

"Her money's in there. And…" Widow says, but trails off.

"What?"

"They took the engagement ring I bought her."

"Oh?" Snyder says, and pauses. "Well, hey, I'll make some calls tomorrow. Philadelphia's finest can recover it for you. It might take a little time, but they recover stuff like this all the time."

"You're not a very good liar, Howie," Widow says, and walks away.

"Where you going?"

Widow says, "Back to my hotel."

"Okay, call me tomorrow."

Widow stays quiet, and walks away, back to the Ritz-Carlton.

CHAPTER 16

In the morning, a man sips coffee with cream and sugar at his kitchen counter in Atlanta, Georgia. He's only got three payments left on his house in Peachtree Hills, a prominent neighborhood for the wealthy. The only bad thing that ever happens here is the weather, like today. Outside, it's windy and rainy—a cold rain. That's why he's happy to be him. He's happy to be one of the bosses at his firm.

Sean Casey's built a good life for himself. Ten years ago, he joined the architecture firm of Baldwin, Kelly, and Pierce. Now, it's Baldwin, Pierce, and Casey, because Elton Kelly—named "Elton" because his parents loved the singer—is dead. He died from a heart attack, while he was with his mistress in a seedy motel near Adair Park.

Kelly's death left a giant hole in the company, and the remaining partners decided to give Casey a junior partner role. They even put his name in place of Kelly's. They didn't pay him as much, of course. But eventually, he got there.

Casey enjoys being a partner. He no longer works those long hours for little pay. Now he has subordinates who do that grind, just as he did.

And it's not just for the pay. For him, it's really the chance to see his family more. Today's a good example, because his wife has to go to work early, and she takes the kids to school on her way. She does this a couple times a week, so Casey can sleep in.

But sometimes, he surprises them. Today is one of those days. He gets up an hour early, even though he doesn't have to be in the office today until eleven. He sneaks out of the house and drives down the street to their favorite donut place. He picks up a box of the glazed for his wife and chocolate for his kids. Everyone gets a big box of their favorite, except for his teenager. She doesn't eat donuts, because she's *watching her figure,* or so she says. She won't say it's because of peer pressure, but it is.

Still, her favorite donuts are paczki, which are filled donuts, Polish style. He gets them anyway. She doesn't eat them, until one day, when he figures he'll get a small order of them in a small box, big enough to only hold two or three donuts. He stops announcing the paczki to his family. He simply puts them by his daughter's keys. She always leaves them beside the family's key tray. Sometimes the box of paczki is gone. And sometimes it's not.

Today, the kids are all excited to see him up early, drinking coffee and reading his paper, because they know that means their donuts have arrived. His wife kisses him as passionately as the day they married. His kids are happy, especially because he bribes them with the donuts.

Even his teenager thanks him for the paczki, which shocks him. But a trick he's learned over the years is that when his teenager is excited about something he's done for her, the best thing to do is play it off like it's no big deal. If he makes a big deal about it, then she'll go right back in her shell.

Shortly after breakfast and coffee, his wife is downstairs, dressed and ready for work. She's wrangling the kids, wants them to get downstairs, fully dressed, and ready to go to school in five minutes—which turns into ten, and fifteen for the teenager.

After a while, the whole Casey clan is downstairs and ready to go, all while Sean Casey is still drinking his second coffee.

His wife kisses him again before leaving. She's running so behind, she forgot she kissed him the first time. So, she planted one more on him for good measure.

She waits in the kitchen, near the door to the garage, for the kids to line up so they can go. The last straggler is the teenager. She finally comes downstairs, wearing a midriff top that might get her sent home from school. Her mother warns her she better not get another call from the school.

The daughter says she'll keep her jacket on. "It's an ensemble piece," she adds.

The mother rolls her eyes, and shuffles the teenager out the door, then the boys. She says goodbye to Casey before she leaves. He returns the sentiment, unsure that she heard him over the morning chaos.

The door to the garage shuts, and he's left alone, at the kitchen counter. He hears the garage door open. His wife's car starts, backs out, and drives away. The garage door closes.

Casey gets up, pours another coffee, switches off the machine, and dumps the rest. He won't have another cup till he gets to the office.

Casey sits down with his last morning coffee, grabs a leftover glazed donut and starts to eat it, but the doorbell rings. He gets up, sets the donut back into the box, and goes to the front door.

Somebody forgot something, he thinks. He smiles, unlocks and opens the front door, expecting to see his wife's car parked in front of their house, and one of his kids at the door. It's a quick *run in to get whatever one of them left behind* kind of situation.

But Casey doesn't see his wife's car idling at the curb. He doesn't see one of his kids at the door. Instead, he has a visitor he doesn't recognize, a stranger.

Standing in the rain, outside Casey's door, is a man of average height and weight, wearing a dark suit under a rain slicker. His hood is up over his head. Rain pounds the slicker. It pounds the concrete on the walkway behind him.

Casey's wife's car taillights are down the street at four-way stop, near a duck pond. He glances over the stranger's shoulder, and sees them, his family, his clan.

Casey stares at the stranger, and says, "Hello. Can I help you?"

The man in the rain slicker is unremarkable, or at least unmemorable, to onlookers. If police asked Casey to describe the man, or pick him out of a lineup, it'd be hard. The only thing he would remember is the pin on the guy's suit coat lapel. It's a familiar, gold pin. It's the scales of justice.

The scales of justice man asks, "Sean Casey?"

"Yeah," Casey says, "That's me." A look of confusion overtakes his expressions. "Do I know you?"

The scales of justice man pauses, reaches a hand into his slicker, and stops. He grabs something, an object, but Casey can't make it out. There's too much rain, and too much shadow under the man's slicker.

The scales of justice man asks, "Are you Sean Casey, or Peter Stamos?"

Casey's eyes grow wide. He hesitates, and says, "I don't know any Peter Stamos. You got the wrong house, buddy. I want you to leave. Don't come back here." Casey closes the door, fast, but it stops abruptly, halfway open.

The scales of justice man stopped the door from closing with his left hand. But that's not the part that's got Casey's attention. It's what's in the man's right hand.

The scales of justice man draws a gun with a sound suppressor screwed into the barrel. He points it at Casey, draws his elbow back, and punches Casey in the solar plexus with the business end of the gun's barrel. It's one quick, unexpected blow. Casey stumbles back into his foyer, nearly falling on his butt.

The scales of justice man follows him into the house. Water drips off the scales of justice man's slicker and all over the tile floors. But Casey doesn't pay attention to any of that. He just gasps for air. The scales of justice man's strike knocked the breath out of him.

Casey breathes heavily and looks at the intruder, who is shoving a gun in his face. Casey stares at the little hole at the end of the gun's suppressor.

The scales of justice man doesn't wait any longer. He shoots Casey between the eyes. And the man born Peter Stamos falls back dead, landing on the floor of the house titled to his fake name, Sean Casey.

The scales of justice man glances back at the open front door, to see if there're any witnesses passing by. And there are none. He steps to the front door, checks outside to be thorough. He sees Mrs. Casey's taillights fade away in the rain.

The scales of justice man closes the door, holsters his gun, and steps to Stamos's body. He takes out a digital camera and snaps a photo of his target.

Minutes later, the scales of justice man is back on the street, hood pulled up over his head. He eats the last bite of a stolen glazed donut, brushes the crumbs off his gloved hands, and stuffs them in his pockets. He walks away, just another stranger walking in the Atlanta rain.

CHAPTER 17

At seven hundred hours, Widow calls Harper's phone from his hotel room. It's a gamble, because she might be awake, or she might not. He doesn't want to wake her up. But Widow can't wait any longer to talk to her. He nearly called her at six hundred hours, but talked himself out of it. Just because he didn't sleep well doesn't mean that she should suffer too. It's going to be bad enough that he's got to tell her that her money got stolen.

The phone rings, and Harper picks up, groggy, like he woke her out of a deep sleep. She isn't quite awake, but answers the phone anyway. She says. "Hello?"

"Hey, it's me. Did I wake you?"

"Ah, yes. What time is it?" she asks, but glances at her phone. "It's early. Is everything alright?"

"Yeah. I just wanted to hear your voice."

Harper yawns, and says, "Widow, what's wrong? Did something bad happen at The Vidocq Society? You know I can tell."

Widow assures her the conference went well. He told her about their meeting with Judge Mautner and the other six members of his elite faction of The Vidocq Society. And he told her about their interest in mulling over her sister's murder case, and seeing if they can help find Peter Stamos, or any evidence missed by the police.

"They seemed eager to help," Widow says.

"That sounds wonderful. It's really great news," she says, but sensing there's more, she adds, "So, what aren't you telling me?"

Widow pauses a beat, then he says, "Last night Snyder took me to a pub here. It's a famous place. I went, and we had a good time. But when we left, there were these local thugs. They jumped us."

"What? Are you okay?"

"I'm fine. Just got my pride knocked down a few pegs. But they took your document bag, with all of your Mia files."

"Firstie, that's okay. It's just stuff. It served its purpose. Snyder got The Vidocq Society to take my sister's case."

"There's more," Widow says, nearly asking if she's sitting down, because the news that her savings is gone will shock her. But he knows she's already lying in bed.

I dropped the bag at the conference, and your cash bag spilled out,"

Harper goes quiet.

Widow says, "It was full of bearer bonds. I know you're iffy about banks. You must've forgotten you left it in your document bag with Mia's files."

Harper stays quiet.

Widow asks, "Harp?"

"Yeah," she says, clears her throat. "Yes. I forgot about it. Shit, Widow, that's part of my savings."

"I'm so sorry. I tried to keep it from them, but they had guns and there were five of them."

"Wait! You said nothing about guns. They had guns?"

"Oh yeah. They shoved them in our faces."

"Widow, I don't care about the money. Just that you're okay!"

"I'm fine. I honestly think Snyder's more shaken up about it than I am. He's the FBI agent who let a bunch of low-rate thugs get the jump on us."

"As long as you're fine. That's all that matters to me. Why don't you get your ass back here? I miss seeing you."

"I'll head back later today. I gotta do something first."

"What do you have to do?" she asks.

"I gotta take care of something is all."

"Widow? You're not planning to get yourself in trouble, are you?"

"I'm getting that bag back for you."

"What? No! Let it go!" she says.

Widow stays quiet.

Harper senses his uneasiness. Like a woman scorned, Widow's need to correct injustice can't be still. It can't be suppressed. It can't be silenced. She's known this about him since the day he first walked into her classroom. She knew it about him, even if he has yet to see it in himself. It's something she loves about him. She used to feel that way herself.

She used to be idealistic, and innocent, and determined to do good. Her sister's murder drove her to criminology and the forensic sciences. Her sister's death is the light to the wick of life that's driven her this far.

Harper knows she's lucky to have found a calling at all. Many people live and die without knowing their calling, their purpose in life. But Harper's known her calling since the day police detective Howie Snyder came to her dad's house in rural Maine and told the family that someone raped and murdered her big sister, leaving her body to rot in a stairwell.

Unfortunately for Harper, her sister's murder wasn't the only gut punch life held in store for her. A few years ago, life hit her again, this time with a tumor in her brain. She nearly died trying to fight it. The battle to kill the cancer was killing her too. So she was thrilled to find out that it went into remission. *It's a tiny miracle*, she thought. Shortly after the tumor went into remission, she got this great job offer to teach at the United States Naval Academy in Annapolis, Maryland. She was excited for the opportunity at a real life. Maybe she would be able to catch her sister's killer someday.

Then she met Widow, a student, a younger man. It's forbidden to date a student, so she resisted the attraction, the urge. But like the calling to catch her sister's killer, she couldn't hold out for long.

Being with Widow, even though it's in secret, gives her new ideas, new purpose. And she wishes she could have a future with him, that she could live a life with him. Is it possible? Can she forget the skeletons of her past? Can she ignore that calling from the grave?

She tries. And for a while things are good, better than she thinks possible. But now, her tumor's back. This time, life gut-punches her so hard that she can no longer ignore her sister's ghost. She can't ignore what haunts her. She knows her time is limited.

If it weren't for Widow, she could've missed her chance to get her sister's killer. Because Widow's there for her, she feels hope that The Vidocq Society will come through for her. It may not be too late.

Widow repeats, "I can get it back for you."

Harper smiles. Widow's so good. His goodness shines around him, unlike the darkness that shrouds her life. Shaking off the thoughts of her dark past, she jokes, "How? What're you, Hercules Parrot?"

Widow laughs, and says, "You know I thought he was called that for a minute?"

"You know I've graded your tests?"

"Yeah?"

"So I know you're dumb, but not that dumb."

Widow smiles, but stays quiet.

Harper sits up in bed, and brushes her fingers through her thick, blond hair, frowns, and asks, "Do you think I'm pretty?"

"Of course. You're beautiful! Why?"

"I don't know," she pauses, and asks, "What if I lose my hair?"

"Why would you lose..." Widow says, stops, and realizes what chemotherapy does to a person's hair. He asks, "Are you thinking about doing chemo again?"

"I don't know. I'm just thinking maybe it could give me a chance," Harper pauses, and whispers, "And more time with you." She cries.

Widow can't see her, but he hears her sniffles. He says, "You know, I think bald chicks are hot."

"You do?"

"Oh, yeah."

"Like who? Which bald chicks?"

Widow pauses a long, beat, trying to think of examples. Finally, he says, "Like that singer."

"Which singer?"

"The Irish one, from when I was a kid."

"Are you talking about Sinéad O'Connor?"

"Yes! I loved her in GI Jane!"

Harper gasps, and says, "That's Demi Moore, not Sinéad O'Connor!"

"Yeah! I like her in that movie! Very hot!"

Harper palms her face, and giggles. Of course, Widow can't see her, but he knows her. At least, he thinks so. He pictures her smiling, forgetting about her stolen money, forgetting about her cancer—for one precious second.

Harper asks, "What's your favorite part about me?"

Widow thinks, and says, "You're smart."

"You know I mean my body parts. Which is your favorite?"

"Body parts?"

"Yes. And don't cop out on me. Give it to me straight! I'm a big girl, I can take it."

Widow's automatic response is to say her brain, which would be the truth. Harper's very smart. She's accomplished a lot in her life. It's admirable. But he doesn't say that. He pauses. *Can he say brain?* It might make her think about her tumor, which probably already haunts her 24/7 already.

"Earth to Widow. You're off in la-la land again. I'll repeat my question. What's my sexiest body part?" Harper says, and lists the contenders, like she's giving him multiple choice. "Do you like my legs, or my eyes, or my stomach, or my back, or," she pauses, and sighs, like the next items on the list are cliché. She says, "Do you just like my boobs?"

"Hmmm," Widow says, and acts like he's thinking hard on the question.

"What? Is it my butt?" she asks, excited, like that's the answer she hopes to hear. Which she does. She works hard doing squats to get the glutes she's always wanted.

Widow stays quiet.

"Oh, no! You're not one of those guys who likes feet, are you?" she jokes.

"Feet?" Widow asks, and freezes.

"Yeah, feet. Some people are into feet. You know?"

"Feet?"

"Yeah, what're you doing, an impression of Hercules Parrot? Feet are a strange fetish, I know. But who am I to judge?"

Widow says, "A foot fetish."

"Widow?"

"Yeah? Hey, I gotta call you back," Widow says, and hangs up on Harper. Scratching his chin whiskers, he realizes he needs to shave before wearing his uniform again. *A guy with a foot fetish*, he thinks. Then he dials another number on the hotel phone. It rings, and rings. The phone's owner doesn't pick up. He gets the voicemail.

Widow waits for the beep, and says, "Howie, I'm in my hotel room. I got a crazy thought. Man, it sounds really crazy. I know why the shoes are missing. The killer took them. Okay, call me back. If I'm not here, then I'll call you back."

CHAPTER 18

After eating room service bacon, eggs, and toast, Widow drinks coffee, sits in an armchair, and stares out the window at Philadelphia City Hall. The masonry building looks magnificent from his view. He glances at the clockface, then all the way up to a statue of William Penn, a city founder. The statue sits atop the 548-foot-high tower.

Widow stares at the statue and the skyline, and thinks about Mia Harper and that horrifying crime scene. He knows how Snyder must feel, because Mia's haunting him now. He can't imagine nineteen years of that crime replaying in his head, over and over. William Penn founded a city, and they put a statue up for him. No one will erect a statue for Mia Harper.

Howie Snyder is aging. Most of his life's behind him now. Jaime Harper's dying from brain cancer. After them, who'll remember Mia? If her killer is never caught, how will she ever get justice?

Widow pictures the suspect list in his mind: Peter Stamos, Bret Nabors, Joel Bernabe, and Anton Idris. He pieces together the chain of events in his imagination.

Snyder and Harper are convinced the killer is Peter Stamos. Judge Mautner and his core group of six others seem to agree. Snyder suspected him back then, and suspects him still. It could be Peter. According to the investigation, he was the last person to see her alive.

College police officer Joel Bernabe claimed he entered the library to check it out around midnight. He saw no one and continued his rounds. Peter said he left around midnight. Factoring in that witnesses are often off on exact times and dates of events. Bernabe may have gotten there after midnight, and Peter could've left before midnight. This was in 1984. They didn't have smartphones. They could both be completely off on their times. Even conservatively, there could be a window of opportunity there for a totally different party to be in the library, watch Peter leave, see Mia in there all alone, and take advantage of the situation.

If Bernabe went into the library, called out to anyone inside to leave, and no one responded, would he check the stairwells? Probably not. Widow doesn't know how big the library building is, but colleges often have libraries with several floors. There could be a lot of hiding places.

Widow searches his mind for the medical examiner's reports. He sees the time of death is in the early Saturday morning hours. It could be possible that someone not even on the suspect list grabbed Mia and dragged her out of the library and into the fire stairwell. They could've done it right after Stamos left, and before Bernabe checked the library. It's possible. Maybe the killer strangled Mia while Bernabe was in the library, checking the bathrooms?

Widow's mind wonders to Mia's feet. He doesn't recall seeing them in the images that Snyder showed in the presentation at The Vidocq Society, but Widow's seen Harper's feet, many times. He thinks about her feet. If the killer is a foot fetishist, then Widow needs to think like one. The problem is, he's not one. All he can do is think about what might be considered an attractive foot.

Harper's got good feet. They're clean, shapely, and manicured. *Is that what a foot fetishist would look for?* It's hard to say.

Widow glances at a clock on the nightstand. It's eight in the morning. Time to get going. He already showered and dressed before breakfast. He's wearing his street clothes: bomber jacket, sweater, undershirt, underwear, jeans, shoes and socks. He picks up his military ID and bankcard, and stares at the bankcard for a moment, grateful the Fenian Boys didn't take it.

Widow pockets his ID, bankcard, and hotel room keycard, and leaves the Ritz-Carlton. He retraces his steps from the night before, and returns to the alley where the Fenian Boys mugged him and Snyder. He looks around.

The streets, the alley, it's all the perfect chokepoint to trap someone. A tourist would fall right into it because the surrounding streets have lots of foot traffic, making them feel safe. The Fenian Boys picked the perfect spot to rob a couple of tourists like him and Snyder.

The Fenian Boys had set up at the corner in a gang vehicle with the cloverleaf-eyed skull decal plain as day—their calling card, and symbol—part of their intimidation tactics. Gangs and mob families are as much about branding as any other organization. Even terror groups use branding, and symbols, as a part of their arsenal of fear.

Widow revisits the pub, which doesn't open till eleven-hundred on Wednesdays. But through a window he gets the attention of a bartender who is attending to his opening duties. He asks the bartender about the Fenian Boys. The bartender is reluctant, at first, to say anything. He does a side-to-side look around, up and down the street, like he's making sure the wrong ears aren't listening.

Widow remembers seeing in a movie that bartenders like to get paid for information. So he's glad he stopped by an ATM outside the Ritz-Carlton before retracing his steps. He flashes a wad of cash at the bartender, says, "I just got five hundred dollars from an ATM, the most I could take out of the machine."

The bartender smiles at the cash, and steps out of the pub. He leads Widow out to the street, and they talk.

The bartender's first piece of advice is to go to the police. Widow thanks him, but indicates they both know that'll lead to nothing. And the Fenian Boys took something valuable from him. The bartender says, "I'm afraid your money is gone. I'm sorry, but they've already passed it up the chain, probably. The Fenian Boys usually work at the orders of the higher-ups. At least the street gangs do. So, if they took something valuable, they've already sent it up the ladder. It's gone."

"The item in question is of a personal nature," Widow says, referring to Harper's engagement ring, but also the cash bag.

The bartender glances at the cash money in Widow's palm. What he sees is a stack of money, with a hundred showing on top. What he doesn't see is under the hundred is a folded stack of fives. The whole amount Widow's offering him appears to be the full five hundred, but it's a hundred and fifty bucks. Still more than the information is worth, Widow believes. He's not sure how much to offer the guy. He's never bought information from anyone before.

But the bartender works at a famous pub in Philadelphia. He didn't get to this position by being stupid. Cautiously, and before he answers, the bartender reaches for the cash. Widow clamps a hand down on top of the bartender's, as he touches the showing hundred-dollar bill.

Widow says, "Not so fast! Tell me more!"

The bartender stares at Widow and asks, "How old are you?"

Widow squeezes the guy's hand down into his, crushing it like a hostile handshake. He speaks in a raging voice, so the guy gets the message. He says, "I'm not paying you for questions. Just tell me more."

The bartender shivers, partially from the pain in his hand, and partially out of fear. He says, "The Fenian Boys are into all sorts of petty crimes. But the bulk of their business involves cars."

"Cars? Like stolen cars?"

"Yeah, like for chop shops. They own several of them all over the city."

"What about the cops?"

"The cops know about it, but hardly ever interfere. Every once in a while, they'll raid one for show."

"For show?" Widow asks.

"Sure, you know, for the theater of it. It looks good for the public to see the police raiding another Fenian Boys chop shop on TV. It makes the mayor look good. But it's all just the cost of doing business. The cops mostly allow the Fenian Boys to operate. It's a type of economy here. Every city has something like this. You know?"

"Where can I find a chop shop?"

"Hey, man. I don't know that kind of thing. I just know what I've seen and heard. That kind of information's not worth the money to know. If the Fenian Boys got wind of someone ratting out their chop shop locations, they'd cut their throat and dump them in the Delaware River."

Widow squeezes a little harder. A look of pain streams across the bartender's face. Widow asks, "Who would know that information?"

The bartender flicks his eyes left and then right, like he's hoping someone will come along and save him from the young musclebound maniac who's crushing his hand, but there's no one there. Finally, he says, "The taxi drivers!"

Widow eases up on his hand, and asks, "Taxi drivers?"

"Yeah, man. Ask a taxi driver. Some of them make money on the side from the Fenian Boys."

"How so?"

"The drivers are like bird dogs for the Fenian Boys."

"Bird dogs?"

The bartender looks at Widow, like Widow's some young kid who has a lot to learn. The bartender says, "Yeah, it's for a kickback. The taxi drivers all know this. They drive around all day with customers, and they keep their eyes peeled. If they see a certain car, then they text a phone number."

"A certain car?"

"Yeah, there's a list. It's online. The Fenian Boys update it every week with cars they're seeking. They strip, refurbish, and sell them on the black market to private collectors, I guess. I don't know exactly what they do with them after they steal them," the bartender says, "But the taxi drivers all do it. If they find the really high-priority stuff, they can earn a lot of extra money."

Widow releases the bartender's hand, and the money. The bartender grabs the money, rips his hand away, spins around, and walks back to the pub. He stops halfway, turns back, and says, "Hey! These are fives!"

Widow's already walking away. He says, "No, it's a hundred and fives."

The bartender says nothing to that. He just stomps away angrily and goes back to the pub and his opening duties.

CHAPTER 19

Widow spends the next couple of hours riding in taxis, asking drivers about the Fenian Boys, and getting a lot of silence. No one, it seems, wants to talk about them. Next, he tries asking them directly for the website where the Fenian Boys list their most desired cars. Still, no one is talking. He tries offering money for information, but it doesn't work. One friendly driver, who swears he doesn't partake in the scheme, informs Widow the reason no one will take his money isn't because they're loyal to the Fenian Boys or anything like that. They won't take his money because the Fenian Boys pay for the information about car locations, but they also pay for silence.

So, Widow tries a new tactic. He rides in more cabs, around the city center, hoping to spot one of those skull decals, or a car that might be of interest. He figures that if he's lucky enough to spot some kind of rare, expensive car, maybe he can keep getting rides around it, and see if a taxi driver texts the Fenian Boys' phone number to report the car.

Widow gets luckier than he expects, because the very next taxi he takes stops at a busy intersection, and he sees a black

Aston Martin parked in a department store lot, far away from the other cars, like the owner didn't want anyone to park near it. He doesn't recognize the car, but he knows the name. It's the James Bond car, only not the original model. This car's great-great-granddad is the Bond car.

But he's not the only one who takes note of it. The taxi driver does too. He sends a text while they wait at the light. Widow watches. The texting itself isn't indicative of him contacting the Fenian Boys on its own. But when the driver snaps a photo of the car, immediately texts it to the same number, and then gets fast responses, Widow knows it's them.

There's the driver's initial text, then a response, another text, and response. And so it goes, until the driver sets his phone down and smiles at Widow in the rearview mirror.

Widow smiles back, and asks, "You happy about something?"

The driver says, "Yes, my friend. It's a good day. I just get a bonus."

"I see."

The light turns green, and the driver moves forward. Widow points to another section of the department store's parking lot, and says, "Drop me off right there."

The taxi driver nods and pulls over. Widow gets out, pays the fare, and goes back to the Aston Martin and waits.

* * *

THE SCALES of justice man speaks with the Founder before he gets on the plane in Atlanta. The Founder asks him about the target. The scales of justice man informs him it went, like they all have, flawlessly.

The Founder seems apprehensive, like something's weighing on his mind. But when the scales of justice man presses him, he denies it. So, the scales of justice man doesn't push the questioning.

The Founder asks where he's headed to next. And the scales of justice man tells him. They get off the phone.

A couple of hours later, the scales of justice man picks his car up from long-term parking at the Baltimore/Washington International Thurgood Marshall Airport. Of course, his plane tickets, credit cards, IDs, and cars are all under various fake names.

The scales of justice man checks the gun he's left in the car's glovebox. It's still there, undisturbed. He ejects the magazine and racks the slide, making sure it's still loaded and chambered. Then he slides the gun between the driver's seat and the console, so it's tucked away out of sight from any police officers that might pull him over for a traffic stop, but easily accessible should he need to draw and fire it quickly.

The scales of justice man leaves the airport and drives to his next destination, Annapolis, the same city that Harper's in.

CHAPTER 20

W idow figures he won't have to wait long.

The Navy does a lot of recovery efforts as a part of their operating duties. If a piece of US spy hardware such as an advanced spy drone crashes in enemy waters, it's often necessary to deploy a Naval team to recover it, and fast. Widow imagines stealing expensive, rare cars is no different. When a high-value target car is identified, having a team ready to go is essential. The faster they deploy, the faster they secure the car.

Widow waits on a sidewalk that wraps around the department store. Behind him there's a café, with patrons sitting outside on a patio. Even though it's cold out, they're staying warm by outdoor heaters. Widow's not so lucky. He shouldn't have to wait long for action on the Aston Martin, but he still freezes, standing out in the cold, hoping the car's owner doesn't leave before the Fenian Boys crew shows up.

And they don't disappoint. He gets even luckier than he expects, because the crew drives into the parking lot in the same Range Rover he saw the night before. At least, the Range Rover looks the same. It could be a different one, with the same colors and with the skull with the cloverleaf eyes decal on the back window.

Widow counts only two guys in the SUV. He gets a good look at both of them through the windshield, which is the only window that's not tinted too dark to see through. He doesn't recognize either guy. They're a different crew than the ones who held him and Snyder up the night before. The guys from the night before are the night crew, and this is the morning crew, he figures.

They drive up and circle the lot for a while, scoping things out, like they're making sure the car is there, and that the coast is clear to take it. *They're pretty cautious for a gang of their brain power*, Widow thinks.

Finally, the Range Rover pulls up behind the vehicle and the passenger door opens. The passenger hops out. He doesn't glance around. No scanning the parking lot for danger or witnesses. They don't care about witnesses. Not even the driver is paying attention to anything but his partner.

The partner is at the Aston Martin's driver's side window. He's got some kind of electronic box in his hand. He taps away at various buttons on it, and stares at a screen, as the device is looking for the right signal to bypass the car's alarm, unlocking the door.

Widow seizes the opportunity, hops off the curb, and walks straight to them and the Aston Martin. The driver doesn't look at him. Widow assumes since these guys throw their weight around the city with little to no repercussions, they think they're invincible. The problem with criminals like that is, regarding their own personal security, they relax too much. They don't think in a million years a stranger would come along and start something with them.

Widow figures their lax security means they don't lock their doors. It turns out they don't. Widow walks right up to the driver, who's staring in the other direction, watching his partner. Widow grabs the door handle and wrenches the door open, fast. The driver, stunned, whips around and stares in shock and horror as Widow punches him straight across the face. The driver's nose cracks and his teeth rattle. Widow grabs the guy, rips him out of the driver's seat. It happens so fast, the driver's got no time to even touch his nose to check if it's broken.

Widow jerks him out onto his feet. He spins him around like a human shield and headlocks the guy, tight. Widow squeezes his biceps around the guy's throat. The driver kicks and bucks, trying to get Widow off him, but Widow's too strong for him. The driver doesn't even get Widow to move an inch.

The driver slaps at Widow's forearms like he's tapping out. But he's trying to break Widow's grip. Only his strikes get weaker and weaker. And Widow's arms don't budge. It's as if Widow's arms are forged from stone. Within seconds, the driver goes limp. He's out cold.

Widow drops him to the concrete, and turns his attention to the partner. He looks through the Range Rover's front cabin and out the passenger window at the other Fenian Boy. The partner's so busy trying to get the Aston Martin's door open that he's not even noticed what's happened to his friend.

Widow threads around the hood of the Range Rover and heads to the partner. Customers at the café are taking notice. Some rise to their feet, watching the violence unfolding. Others take their phones out and frantically dial 911.

Widow presses on, ignoring them. He comes up behind the partner, only he doesn't sneak up on the guy. The partner, having trouble getting the device to crack the car's alarm signal, glances back to the Range Rover and says, "Hey Frankie, I can't get the thing to work."

But the one called Frankie isn't there. Instead, he sees a hulking young guy standing directly behind him. The partner stares at Widow, for a long second.

Widow stops an arm's length away, explodes from the hips, and jabs the guy straight in the solar plexus. The impact is intense. The partner drops the box and goes flying back into the Aston Martin's door and window. The guy hits the car so hard; the alarm starts blaring. The noise is loud in the parking lot.

Widow glances around. Now more department store holiday shoppers are dropping whatever they were doing, and turning their attention to Widow and the Fenian Boy.

The Fenian Boy is stunned, but he reacts faster than Widow anticipates, and pulls a nine-millimeter from seemingly out of nowhere. He coughs and winces, like Widow's jab knocked the wind out of him. But he scrambles to his feet, planting his free hand on the alarm-screaming car to help himself up. The other hand has the gun, and it's pointed in Widow's direction.

Widow doesn't flinch. He had thought that if one of them pulled a gun on him, he would. But he doesn't. His adrenaline pumps, and pushes him to react to the weapon. Widow waits till the guy is half-situated back on his feet. Once the guy stands, he still wobbles, because the strike to the solar plexus not only knocked the wind out of him, but disoriented him as well.

The guy can't aim straight, but he does what many inexperienced gang members do. He blind-fires the gun in Widow's direction. But Widow's ready for it. He steps right, clamps a huge hand down on the guy's weapon, and, simultaneously, jerks the gun up, so it points to the sky, and strikes the guy across the face with a right hook hard enough to send the guy to a dentist for emergency surgery.

Two things happen, fast. One, jerking the guy's gun up like that forces him to bump his finger around in the trigger housing, and he shoots the gun, twice, into the sky. The gunshots boom over the car alarm. And the bystanders no longer remain as witnesses. Most of them hear the shots and, confused about what's happening, scramble away in a mad dash to escape, like the two shots signal to them there's an active shooter in the area, and they better run for cover. Two, the Fenian Boy's two top incisors break off and fly out of his mouth, leaving behind a bloody mess.

Widow jerks the gun out of the guy's hand, and gut-punches him once again for good measure. He points the gun at the guy, but there's no need. The guy drops to his knees, folds over, and throws up a mess of blood and whatever he ate for breakfast.

Widow scans the parking lot and the café's patio. All the witnesses have run off. No one watches them. Still, Widow's sure several people called the cops. They'll be there, eventually. And he doesn't plan on sticking around to greet them.

Widow gives the guy a couple of seconds to puke up the rest, and catch his breath. Then he bunches up the guy's jacket, hauls him to his feet, and shoves the gun in his face, under his chin. He searches the guy with his free hand for any other weapons. He finds a folding blade in one pocket, and no other weapons. He pockets the knife. Then he points the gun straight up, like he's going to shoot the guy up through his throat, towards his brainpan, and says, "That's enough. You'll live. Get moving."

Widow pulls the gun back, and shoves the guy back to the Range Rover. The Fenian Boy coughs and wheezes, confused about what's happening. He assumes Widow wants him to get back in, so he goes for the passenger door. Widow stops him, and hauls him around the rear, back to the driver's side door, where he sees Frankie on the ground, unconscious.

"Oh, no! Frankie? You killed him!" the Fenian Boy says, spitting out more blood. He sounds ridiculous, because he can't pronounce his words correctly. It turns out he needs those broken incisors to pronounce several letters.

Widow says, "He's not dead. He'll live too. If you cooperate!"

"Yes! Take whatever you want, man! Just don't kill him!"

Widow says, "Good," and shoves the guy into the driver's seat. He cracks a hammer fist once on the guy's head, just to keep him dazed for a moment. The guy can do nothing but paw at his face.

Widow steps back, slams the driver's door shut, grabs the driver's leg, and drags him back, and over into one parking stall, next to a car. He doesn't want to leave the guy lying in the road. Not that he cares, but he's not trying to get the guy run over. He dumps the driver there, returns to the Range Rover, wrenches open the driver's side rear door, and hops in the backseat. He shuts the door and shoves the gun behind the Fenian Boy's ear. He says, "What's your closest chop shop to the city center?"

The Fenian Boy hesitates, like he's thinking of giving Widow a line of shit. Widow notices, so he grabs the headrest, slides forward, and says, "Stop stalling! Where is it?"

The Fenian Boy looks at Widow in the rearview, his hands up in the surrender position. He says, "What're you, like twenty years old? I don't think you're going to shoot me."

Widow smiles, withdraws the gun, moves it around the seat, and jams it into the guy's crotch, hard. The guy winces again, discovering a new fear. Widow says, "You want to find out?"

The Fenian Boy shakes his head violently, and says, "Okay! Okay! It's in North Philly! I can take you there!"

In the distance, police sirens blare. Even far away, Widow and the Fenian Boy hear them over the Aston Martin's car alarm. Widow says, "You better get driving then."

He sits back, buckles his seatbelt with his free hand, and says, "Buckle your seatbelt, and keep your hands high on the wheel. If I don't see them at all times, I'll shoot you through the seat. Got it?"

The Fenian Boy nods, and says, "I got it!"

"Okay, take me there. And drive safely. We don't want to get pulled over."

The Fenian Boy doesn't wait any longer. He drives out of the parking lot, abandoning his partner, and takes Widow where he wants to go.

CHAPTER 21

I n North Philadelphia, the Fenian Boy drives Widow past the Broad Street Line, over train tracks, and through large swaths of industrial areas. It's cold out, but there's still a lot of vagrant activity on the street. Homeless people push rickety shopping carts. Young men, Widow's own age, walk in groups, looking like they're up to no good.

The Fenian Boy turns the Range Rover into Kensington, and drives near the river until they get onto the garage's street. Widow shoves the gun into the Fenian Boy's ear, and asks, "How much farther?"

"The garage's just right up there, over the hill," the Fenian Boy says.

"Good, pull over into that empty parking lot, right there," Widow says, and points at an abandoned parking lot, full of loose bricks and broken concrete and nothing else. They drive into the lot. "Put it in park."

The Fenian Boy parks the SUV in the middle of the lot. Widow says, "Step out, and keep your hands up."

The Fenian Boy does as he's told. He tries nothing, but he thinks about it. Widow can see the thought process on his face. But Widow reminds him who gives the orders by pointing the business end of the gun at him.

Widow steps out with him, forces the guy to the cargo door at the back of the vehicle, and makes him open it. Widow hopes to find something to restrain the guy with. He can't just let him go—not this close to the chop shop, where he can try to warn his gang buddies.

Widow's a skilled fighter. He's skilled with guns and other weapons. And he's got a lot of street smarts. But he's only twenty-two. What he's missing is wisdom and experience. Which he'll have someday, but not today.

The Fenian Boy takes advantage of being closer to the Range Rover's cargo space than Widow is. As soon as the door opens, he scrambles for a weapon. And, of course, the Fenian Boys keep extra firepower in their cargo space. Why wouldn't they?

Despite being beaten and tired, the Fenian Boy remains quick. He grabs the closest gun he can get his hands on, a shotgun. He spins around, pumps it, and fires in Widow's direction, the muzzle inches from Widow's center mass.

A shotgun shell from this close should gut-shoot Widow. He should fly back, reeling in pain. At that range and angle, his life should be cut down to a timer with only twenty minutes left on it. He should be lying on the concrete, bleeding out, and dying in horrible agony. But he's not.

Although the Fenian Boy's plan mostly went off without a hitch, there's one flaw in it that he should've known, but didn't. The Fenian Boys, like other long-lasting organizations, divide themselves into departments. Each department specializes in a specific task. And each must perform their tasks properly in order to keep the whole machine running right. If one spoke on the wheel malfunctions, everyone suffers.

This Fenian Boy is in the car theft department. However, if he had been in the armory department, then he'd have known that it's dangerous to drive around with their heavy duty weapons loaded. Also, shotguns and assault rifles are expensive. They require a lot of upkeep.

The Fenian Boys hardly ever use their long guns. Their handguns are their daily-use weapons. That's different. Their handguns get shot often enough. But not their long guns. Leaving their shotguns and assault rifles fully loaded and lying around in the back of their vehicles can cause the springs in the magazines to warp and break, which causes them to malfunction. Therefore, the gang's armory department stores the guns unloaded. The gang typically loads them before they plan to go on a raid or a mission that requires that kind of firepower. But they don't just drive around with them fully loaded.

The right way to go about it is to only load a shotgun's magazine part of the way, leaving slack in the spring, so the gun is at least partly loaded in case it's needed for use. The situation the Fenian Boy finds himself in is the perfect example. But even the boys in the armory department don't think of everything.

The Fenian Boy squeezes the trigger, and the shotgun shoots out nothing but air. Still, it surprises Widow. He flinches. It's only a split second, but it happens. It surprises him as much as it does the Fenian Boy.

The second mistake the Fenian Boy makes is that he tries again. He pumps and fires, but the shotgun is empty.

Widow only flinches once, then he pistol-whips the guy full on in the face, shattering more teeth, blackening the guy's left eye, and knocking him out cold. The Fenian Boy crashes backwards into the Range Rover and folds over, toppling onto the concrete.

Widow hit the guy out of anger. It's a reflex. He looks down at the guy, thinking he killed him. It doesn't look like he's breathing. Widow checks the guy's pulse. It's there. It's slow —not faint, but slow—like the guy is in a deep sleep.

Widow tucks the handgun into the waistband of his pants and looks around for witnesses, like he did at the department store parking lot. Only here, there are plenty of pedestrians, and plenty of them saw the whole thing go down. Unlike the department store's patrons, these folks couldn't care less. They see violence daily on this side of town. They're used to the Fenian Boys. It's not even a factor. Widow figures even if one of them called the cops, Philadelphia PD probably wouldn't even show up for forty-five minutes, or an hour, or hell, they might not even show up for ninety-plus minutes.

That's life in the big city, Widow thinks.

Widow shrugs, and leaves the Fenian Boy where he lies. He checks the cargo space, and finds boxes of ammunition. One of them is the box of shotgun shells that the Fenian Boy needed. He picks up the shotgun and loads it properly. It'll come in handy for him.

He sees the Fenian Boy has more guns back there, but Widow won't need them. At least, he hopes he won't. There's some other stuff of interest: bulletproof vests, road flares, ski masks, a roll of duct tape, and much more. He takes off his bomber jacket and puts one of the bulletproof vests on. He covers it with the bomber jacket. It's not a bad idea to have a bulletproof vest on when going into the lion's den. Especially when that lion's den is a Philadelphia crime gang. He also takes a ski mask and puts it on. He's already wearing knit gloves. It's probably a good idea to keep his anonymity in case they try to track him down. Which they probably will. Gangs hate to let attacks go unpunished, and he's planning an all-out assault on them. Still, he's not too worried about them tracking him down. He's leaving the Ritz-Carlton today. And what're they going to do? Track him to Annapolis, and attack him there? Let them try an assault on a 158-year-old school guarded by the United States Naval Academy Police.

Wearing a bulletproof vest and ski mask, and armed with the two guns, Widow racks the Range Rover's driver's seat all the way back and climbs in. He shuts the door and drives out of the lot, down the street to the Fenian Boys' chop shop.

CHAPTER 22

The Fenian Boys' chop shop in Kensington takes up half an abandoned warehouse. Besides a strip mall housing a convenience store, a pawnshop, and scam businesses like same-day paycheck establishments, deserted warehouses occupy most of the street. Most of their signs have faded into the past. The last time this street saw better days was back in the eighties.

Parked in their lot are mostly regular vehicles, not stolen, just old beat-up cars and trucks. They're parked there to make the garage look legit. The name on the garage's sign doesn't read: *The Fenian Boys Chop Shop*. It just reads: *Joe's Autobody*. There's a rusted chain-link fence around the lot, with two gates. One's an entrance, the other is the exit. Both are usually closed to keep people from driving in, thinking it's a legit garage. But they're open today. They leave them open whenever they're expecting deliveries. They've not had someone come in and mistake them for a real auto shop in a long while. The locals know what the garage really is. And tourists usually don't make it this far from the safety of the city center.

The bleached-hair Fenian Boy sits inside a heated office in the garage, with the door closed to keep the cold air out and the heat in. Five other Fenian Boys are in the garage. Only two of them were with him last night when they robbed the old FBI guy and the sailor. The two who were with him last night are sitting near the garage entrance at a table, playing poker, and freezing their nuts off because the bleached-hair Fenian Boy insists they keep the garage door open while waiting for the day crew to bring in the stolen Aston Martin. The bleached-hair Fenian Boy says it's one they've not had before. He knows just the collector for it, too.

One of the two from the night crew is the one who got his nose busted by the sailor, named Widow. He spent the morning at their off-the-books doctor getting it set. Now he's sporting a shiny nose splint.

Two of them work under the hoods of two stolen cars, and one works on a stolen motorcycle that's worth more than the bleached-hair Fenian Boy makes in a month, which is a hell of a lot.

The bleached-hair Fenian Boy makes good money, more than all five of the underlings in the garage. Which makes him wonder about the guys higher up the chain. *How much do they make?*

Of course, these types of questions stay in his own mind. He doesn't share them. His job is to keep this garage in order. He oversees the daily operations of his territory, and only his territory. The only time he deviates is when one of the higher-ups gives his guys a special mission, like last night's excursion to the city center.

The two Fenian Boys playing poker put down their hands. The one with the nose splint jumps with excitement because he just won a day's wage from the other one, with a straight flush. "What an amazing hand!" he says. "This'll make up for that shit last night." He touches his nose splint, and winces at the pain stealing his enjoyment from beating his associate. The other one gets up and slams the cards down. He says, "You cheated!"

And the two start arguing, heatedly. No one pays them any attention, because the guy with the busted nose is known for cheating. The other Fenian Boys think it's more the other one's fault for risking his money by playing the guy with the busted nose, so they continue working on their assigned vehicles. The bleached-hair one ignores them until they get too loud. Then he yawns, and curses them. He jumps up from his desk and stares down at them through the window.

The five Fenian Boys down in the garage all wear warm coats, gloves, and hats, keeping themselves as warm as possible with the cold air blowing in through the open garage doors.

The busted-nose Fenian Boy and the other poker player argue louder. It sounds seconds away from going to blows. But it goes worse than Bleached Hair thinks because the Fenian Boy dumb enough to play Busted Nose pulls his gun out.

Bleached Hair sighs and steps out of the office, without his coat, which pisses him off even more. Yelling at the two arguing Fenian Boys, he curses and hurls slurs, the kind that're unsuitable for television broadcast in any country. He comes down the stairs, cursing them the whole way. But he slows at the bottom because he sees something out the garage bay exit. He says, "What the hell're they doin'?"

The two arguing Fenian Boys stop and turn to look. The mechanics stop what they're doing to look. One of them says, "Is that Frankie?"

Across the street from the exit gate, the Range Rover comes to a stop, turned toward the garage, nose aimed through the exit gate, and the driver hops out, leaving the driver's door open.

He leans back in, like he's doing something in the footwell. The SUV's engine roars, like someone's stomping the gas all the way down. The driver does something else, and then hops back quick from the vehicle. The Range Rover roars to life and speeds up fast towards the garage. The driver's door slams shut from the speed. The Range Rover bumps through the open exit gate, nearly hitting the fence rails. It veers a little to the right, but it slams through the open garage bay and runs over the stolen, worth-more-than-Bleached-Hair's-monthly-salary motorcycle, destroying it, and nearly running down the Fenian Boy working on it. He dodges at the last minute.

The Range Rover doesn't stop at the motorcycle. It slams through the garage until it crashes into one of the other two stolen cars. Dust kicks up everywhere. The car slides violently, slamming one of the Fenian Boys into a heavy worktable, pinning him. One of his legs snaps the wrong way, and he screams in agony. It's mostly expletives.

In utter shock and panic, Bleached Hair runs down the remaining stairs and onto the garage floor. His jaw drops open, and his eyes open wide.

Bleached Hair shouts expletives. The two uninjured mechanics try to help the one who is pinned by the work-table. They try to move the table at first, but it won't budge because the Range Rover is jamming the car against it.

The motorcycle mechanic figures it out first, and wades through a colossal mess of overturned tools and diagnostic equipment. He gets to the Range Rover's driver-side door and wrenches it open. He peers in and stares, dumbfounded.

Bleached Hair barks at him, shouting, "Michael, Frankie better have had a stroke in there!"

The one called Michael says nothing. He just stares into the Range Rover's front cabin.

"What the hell is it? Is Frankie hurt?" Bleached Hair asks, a look of genuine concern on his face, but not because he cares about Frankie or any of the rest of them. Their lives are meaningless in the bigger structure of the Fenian Boys' organization. But Frankie is the best one at boosting cars. Today, Bleached Hair sent him out with a newer guy to train to do the same. And something's gone wrong, obviously. Bleached Hair's immediate thoughts are to blame the new guy.

But what Michael's about to find inside the Range Rover will tell a completely different story. Michael dips into the Range Rover and grabs something, which causes the accelerator to stop completely. The SUV's engine stops revving, and just idles. The tires quit smoking.

Michael comes back out with a brick covered in ripped duct tape, and says, "This was taped to the gas pedal."

Right then, the Fenian Boy with the splint on his busted nose sees something out of the corner of his eye, inside the doorway of the open garage bay. He glances out and sees a tall, masked man aiming a shotgun at him. The Fenian Boy poker player turns around and sees him, too.

Widow steps straight to the busted-nose Fenian Boy, recalling that he's one of the ones who took Harper's locked document bag from him, and strikes the guy full on in the face with a quick butt-strike of the shotgun. The guy's splint busts and his nose cracks again. It's too fast and too unexpected for the poker player Fenian Boy to stop him. The second after Widow cracks the busted-nose Fenian Boy in the face, he pumps the action, and points the gun in the poker player's face.

The busted-nose Fenian Boy topples over in pure agony and rolls on the ground, pawing at his new and old injuries. His nose is now broken in too many places to guess.

Widow ignores the busted-nose Fenian Boy. He's out of commission.

Widow sidesteps, herding the poker player to the left. Now the guy's between Widow and the others.

The other Fenian Boys slowly raise their hands in surrender because they don't want to get shot. But not Bleached Hair. Bleached Hair keeps his hands by his sides, and says, "Do you got any idea who we are?"

The motorcycle mechanic is Widow's biggest concern, because he's positioned in such a way that he could duck down the other side of the SUV, draw a gun, and shoot at Widow. If he has a gun, which he may not. It's hard to imagine these guys carrying a gun while sweating in uncomfortable positions, working on vehicles.

Still, Widow ignores Bleached Hair, aims the shotgun at the motorcycle mechanic, and yells to him. He shouts, "You! With the brick! Drop the brick, and walk this way!"

The motorcycle mechanic does as Widow orders, dropping the brick and joining the others. Bleached Hair continues to curse and protest. The others stay quiet, and stare at the masked giant with the shotgun.

The motorcycle mechanic stops short of the bleached-hair guy.

Widow aims at Bleached Hair, and barks, "Shut up!" Bleached Hair shuts up. Widow says, "Get your hands up! I want to see everyone's hands in the air! If I don't, I'll kneecap you!" The Fenian Boys who didn't have their hands raised, raise them.

Except right then, the poker player, being the closest to Widow, makes a move. Unlike the mechanics, he is armed. He draws a pistol out quickly, driving it towards Widow. He's not bothering to aim, just quick-draw fire. But before he can pull the trigger, Widow reacts. The reaction comes from a place Widow's not yet that familiar with. The primal mind, somewhere at the core of his brain, sparks, and he reacts.

Widow shifts from the waist, aims at the poker player, and fires. A shotgun shell ignites, blasts out the barrel. The shotgun kicks. But Widow's ready for round two before round one's bell even dings. He pumps so fast he nearly beats the first shot.

The first shell sends clusters of buckshot through the air. The spread tears through the poker player's knees and thighs. He tumbles forward from the impact, dropping his pistol. It clatters across the concrete, passing under Widow's legs.

Bleached Hair is the next one to prove he's down to a skeleton crew of brain cells. He goes for a gun tucked into his waistband. He's farther away than the poker player. Being that time and distance are relative, he's got more distance to make a move. But as for time, it's a different story altogether. With gunplay, speed is also a factor. And Widow's got the speed. But the distance inhibits the shotgun somewhat, because a shotgun is more of a close-quarters weapon.

However, shotguns shoot a whole range of ammunition. And Widow's loaded this shotgun with buckshot, which has a significant spread, meaning more pellets and more range. Even though Bleached Hair is farther away, the spread gets him.

Widow shoots the gun in the same direction. He pumps and fires. The speed is just as fast as before. The spread catches Bleached Hair in the legs. Some of it clips his upper kneecaps, but most gets him in the upper thighs. It nearly hits his groin.

Bleached Hair drops the gun, and, like the poker player, he doubles forward, landing hard on his face. His nose doesn't break, but he lands on his jaw, rocking him to the core.

Widow points the shotgun at the last two, reiterating that they need to keep their hands in the air, or he'll kneecap them both. And they do. The motorcycle mechanic and the last car mechanic stay where they are, keeping their hands up. The mechanic with his legs pinned claws at the table, hoping to free himself. Widow doesn't worry about him.

Widow aims at the motorcycle mechanic, because Widow figures he's the most trustworthy, or at least the one with the best survival instincts. Widow figures that because the guy had the chance to turn the tide in their favor when he stood on the other side of the Range Rover, but he didn't make a move. He follows orders, like a sheep, like a guy who doesn't think too much. And Widow needs one of them, preferably one who won't think too much.

Widow says, "You. What do they call you? Michael?"

Michael nods.

"Okay, Michael. I'm going to give you one chance. You deviate from any of my instructions, and I'll kneecap you next. Got it?"

Michael swallows hard. It's audible, even over the wide open space and the agonized cries of the four wounded Fenian Boys. He says, "Whatever you say, I'll do!"

Bleached Hair struggles to get himself up on his knees, but the pain is too much, and he buckles, falling back on his face. He doesn't attempt it again. Instead, he rolls over on his side, and barks at Michael, saying, "Don't you dare help this man!"

Widow steps forward, stops, and kicks Bleached Hair's dropped gun clear across the floor. Bleached Hair watches it.

The gun slides out of sight, and out of reach, under the Range Rover.

Widow steps to Bleached Hair, stops, and hovers over him. He slowly lowers the shotgun, one-handed, and aims it into Bleached Hair's face. Bleached Hair stares up at the shotgun's muzzle, then eyeballs Widow over the gun.

Widow stares down at him, slow and menacing, and says, "BANG!"

Bleached Hair flinches, shuts his eyes, expecting it to be real. He opens his fear-filled eyes, and stares back up at Widow, who says, "Speak again, and I'll kill you."

Bleached Hair nods, obediently and cowardly. Widow looks up at Michael, who's still holding his hands up in the air. Widow asks, "Any of you got any more guns on you?"

He looks at the two able-bodied mechanics. Both deny being armed. Widow says, "Okay, Michael, where do you guys keep your spoils of war?"

Michael stares at Widow blankly, and asks, "Our what?"

"Where do you keep items you steal from people? When you guys mug them? Do you keep them upstairs in that office?"

Michael stutters out of fear. He says, "Ye…es…sir."

Widow says, "Okay. Got any guns up there?"

"Yes."

"Like what?"

"Well, he keeps that gun," Michael says, and points toward the handgun Widow kicked away. "And there's rifles up there, but they're usually locked up."

"Are they locked up now?" Widow asks.

"I don't know."

"Who would know? This guy?" Widow asks, looking down at Bleached Hair.

"Yes," Michael says.

"Okay, are the rifles locked up?" Widow asks Bleached Hair.

Too afraid to speak, Bleached Hair just nods.

"You're sure?" Widow asks.

Bleached Hair slowly reaches into his sweater's collar, and pulls out a key on a chain, and shows it to Widow.

Widow says, "That's the key?"

Bleached Hair nods.

"Okay. Michael, go up to the office, and look for an engagement ring and a locked document bag. Bring it down for me."

Michael nods, lowers his hands, and slow-walks past Widow to the stairs. He climbs them.

Widow says, "Michael?"

Michael turns around and looks down at Widow.

"Be quick, and don't nothing stupid. Stay visible in the windows. So I can see you. Got it?"

"I got it," Michael says, and goes up the stairs. He enters the office, leaving the door open too.

It doesn't take him long before he comes out with Harper's bag. He holds it up and asks, "Is this it?"

Widow glances at it, and says, "That's the one. What about the engagement ring?"

"Yeah, it's here. Are you sure it's an engagement ring? It's... cheap," Michael says.

"That's it," Widow says, frowning.

Bleached Hair speaks, involuntarily. He says, "The money's gone. There's no money here. If that's what you want."

Michael stays at the top of the stairs, holding up the engagement ring, which Widow could barely see, and the bag. Widow stares down the barrel of the shotgun at Bleached Hair. He asks, "The bonds that were in that bag, where are they?"

Bleached Hair stares at Widow's ice-blue eyes, like he's putting it together. And then recognition falls over his face, and he smiles, and chuckles. He says, "You're the sailor."

Widow stomps a heavy boot down on Bleached Hair's shot-up knees. Bleached Hair yelps and cries in pain. He bucks and struggles, trying to get away, but he can't. Widow asks, "Where's the money?"

Half wincing in pain, Bleached Hair says, "Money is picked up every day by our gang's courier. He collects it. After that, I don't know what he does with it. But that's not what happened to your bonds."

Widow stares at him, confused, and asks, "So, what happened to the bonds?"

Bleached Hair stays quiet, defiantly. Widow scans the shotgun down the guy's torso, passing his waist, and stops over his groin. Bleached Hair's eyes widen in a greater fear than he's ever felt before. But he doesn't give an answer.

Michael slowly descends the stairs. He says, "Your bonds are gone. This guy picked them up."

"Shut up, Mikey!" Bleached Hair barks.

Widow stomps down hard on Bleached Hair's knees again. This time, it's so hard, Bleached Hair nearly blacks out from the pain. Widow looks to Michael, and asks, "What guy?"

"It was this guy we never seen before. He was...," Michael says, and pauses, like he's scared to say the words. "He was terrifying."

"What do you mean exactly?" Widow asks.

Michael descends the last step, and slowly walks to Widow. He says, "I mean I've seen a lot of scary dudes, working with these guys, but I never saw someone like this. He wore an expensive suit. He's an older white guy. But he had an aura about him."

"An aura?"

"Yeah, like a ghost. When he walked, he made no noise. He was more like a specter, than a man. It sounds crazy, I know, man, but it's true."

"This ghost man. What else do you remember about him?"

"He drove a black Mercedes. His suit was expensive. He was clean, like a rich guy, but I can't really say much more, because he just kind of looked like a lot of well-off guys. It was just his aura that gave him away as something else. I'm telling you; he gave me the creeps."

Widow glances around at the other Fenian Boys, and asks, "Can any of you tell me more than you just saw a scary dude?"

No one spoke. Their silence gives Widow chills. Widow says, "There's got to be more."

Finally, Bleached Hair says, "He told you what you wanted to know. The guy's like he said. He came by, picked up the bonds, and left."

"He just got the bonds?" Widow asks.

"Yeah. Just the bonds. I was told to expect him. He walks in, takes the bonds, and doesn't say a word," Bleached Hair says.

He didn't want the other cash? Widow thinks, and he asks, "Who told you to expect him?"

"My bosses, man. They called me yesterday, told me where you'd be, and what to get."

Widow freezes, stunned. He realizes what Bleached Hair is saying. He and Snyder were targeted on purpose. Widow asks, "They told you to mug us? Specifically, us?"

"Yeah, man! They told me to rob you and that FBI agent. Then I was to give the bonds to that scary dude."

FBI agent? He knows Snyder is an FBI agent, Widow thinks.

"Who wanted us targeted?"

"I don't know."

"Was it the FBI agent I was with? Did he know about this?"

Bleached Hair pauses, like he's looking for the answer. He says, "I don't know. I just know that the order came from the top."

"What does that mean?"

Michael steps to Widow, hands him the engagement ring first. Widow pockets it. Then Michael hands him Harper's bag, but Widow doesn't take it, not yet. Michael says, "It's someone important. Someone powerful, is my guess."

"Someone powerful?"

"Yeah, that's the only time our bosses come to us with specific requests like that."

Widow stares at Bleached Hair, and asks, "Who was it that ordered the robbery?"

"All we know is it's someone powerful."

"What? Like the mayor or something?"

Michael says, "Could be. It's someone from high society. Powerful men are no better than us. They get us to do their dirty work from time to time, but they ain't better."

Widow takes Harper's document bag, feels it's lighter without the bonds inside. He checks it, one-handed. Harper's collection of Mia's murder files is still there. He zips it closed, and tucks it under his arm. He orders the other mechanic to join him and Michael. Then he steps back, putting distance between them. He says, "Turn around, close your eyes, and count to a thousand. If I see you turn around, I'll shoot you."

The men do as they're told, knowing Widow will be gone when they open their eyes, but they follow his instructions anyway.

Widow backs away, past the Fenian Boys writhing around on the ground in pain. He leaves them there and vanishes around a street corner. He dumps the guns and the folding blade, the bulletproof vest, and the ski mask in a dumpster behind a Sunoco. He calls the cops from a payphone, tells them about hearing gunshots at the chop shop.

Widow hails another taxi and returns to the city center.

CHAPTER 23

B ack in his hotel suite, Widow calls Harper to tell her he's on his way home, but without recovering her bearer bonds. A nurse tells him she's fine, but is down the hall getting exercise. Widow thanks her, and doesn't leave a message.

Widow stepped over the line when tracking down Harper's case files and recovering them. He knows it would displease her that he risked his life to get them, taking on part of a criminal gang and all. He realizes it was a stupid and dangerous thing to do. But for the first time in his life, Widow feels something he's not felt before, at least not on this scale.

Widow's always stood up for victims. He's always stood up to bullies. He's always stood up for what's right. But this is different. It's more than that feeling, much more. He feels drawn to it, called by it, like it's destiny.

In Annapolis, the Navy teaches midshipmen about honor and integrity. They teach duty. All of that fits Widow's character, but Widow also feels a calling to right wrongs.

Widow plans to return to Harper today. He starts to pack Harper's document bag up with the rest of his belongings into his rucksack, but he stops and takes out the files again. He looks through them. He scans the images of the faces of each person of interest. There's Stamos, Bernabe, Idris, and Nabors.

Peter Stamos is out there somewhere. Snyder said he changed his name and ran, six months after the police investigated him. But does that make him guilty? Snyder and Harper both think so. Mautner seems to agree. Why else would Stamos run, and change his name?

Widow puts Stamos aside, and looks at the others. There're two college police officers: Bernabe and Nabors. Then there's the janitor who cleaned up the crime scene, supposedly without realizing what it was. The year was 1984, making a lot of modern technology and investigation tactics unavailable, because they didn't exist yet. Security cameras existed, but they were big, bulky, and expensive. Tons of colleges and universities have them now, but few utilized them back then. Everything that's in the files, all the police work, is all there is.

Could one of these others, besides Stamos, be the killer? Could one of them be a foot fetishist?

Widow goes back and stares at Stamos's picture. He was just a kid in the photo, only a few years younger than Widow is in 2003. Did he kill his girlfriend? Sure, it's possible. And Snyder seems convinced that's the answer.

Widow studies the faded photo, and looks at Stamos's eyes. Slowly, Widow closes his own eyes, and imagines the scene.

Mia Harper is twenty years old. Her blond hair's cut and styled in a 1980s way. A bright smile beams from her face as she studies with her boyfriend in the college library that cold, dark night.

Stamos finishes whatever he's doing, and gets anxious. He's ready to go back to his dorm, ready for bed. They've both had a long, exhausting week. Widow can relate. His final exam week just passed. It was also long and exhausting.

The library staff tells them, the last students, that they're leaving for the night. Peter and Mia thank them. And the last workers in the library are gone, leaving Mia and Peter alone.

Another hour passes, and Stamos grows more tired. He rushes Mia to finish up so he can turn in for the night. But she's not having it. She's got a lot more studying to do. It's important to her. Perhaps it's the most important thing in the world to her. When Harper talked about her sister, she described her leaving their Maine hometown as escaping. *Mia escaped our hometown with her boyfriend*, she had said.

In front of The Vidocq Society, Snyder told the story similarly. He said Mia *escaped her small-town life in rural Maine to get to college.*

Both Harper and Snyder describe Mia as desperately escaping her small town life. Harper said she left with her boyfriend, Peter Stamos. So, was she so desperate that she escaped with a killer? Or did she trust Peter Stamos? Did Stamos conceal what he really was?

Widow's not so sure.

In Snyder's scenario, everyone leaves the library that night, except for Mia and Peter. Peter gets up, insisting they leave, but Mia doesn't want to leave. They get into a heated argument, and Peter clubs her over the head, or punches her. Then he rips a cord from a nearby lamp, wraps it around Mia's neck, and drags her to the stairwell, where he rapes and strangles her to death. And what? Then he steals her shoes and socks?

If Stamos was the killer, and he kept the shoes and socks because he had a foot fetish, then why rape and kill her? Mia was his girlfriend. They *escaped* their small town together. She probably was sexually active with Stamos, as most college-aged boyfriends and girlfriends are. So, why rape her? It makes little sense.

Alternatively, they could've argued, things got heated, and Stamos killed her in a blind rage. But that doesn't account for the rape, or stealing her footwear. Unless he was desperately trying to cover up a crime of passion. Perhaps, after he strangled her, he thought he could throw the police off by staging a rape-and-foot-fetish-murderer-type scenario. But that's not possible either. If the killer sexually assaulted Mia post-mortem, the cops would've known.

Widow shakes off the dreadful images of such thoughts.

A third scenario is Stamos told the truth. He left around midnight, as he claimed, leaving Mia all alone in the library, or so he thought. How well did the library staff really check out all the stacks before they left that night? How easy would it have been that they missed someone? How hard would it have been for someone to hide, wait for the library to clear out, and see Mia there all by herself?

A modified version of this scenario is a serial killer with a foot fetish. Perhaps someone she knew saw an opportunity, and took it. What if Bernabe watched Stamos leave, then entered the library, attacked Mia, raped and killed her, stole her shoes and socks? What if Nabors did it? Or Idris, the janitor? He could've been there. Janitors have keys to things. He could've known there would be students in the library that late. There was a good chance the last one left could've been a young girl. Perhaps he saw Mia, and seized the opportunity?

Stamos makes little sense to Widow. To Widow, the most plausible scenario is a someone with a foot fetish murdered

Mia. That explains the missing shoes. But Widow needs to confirm it. He can think of only one way to do that, but there's a problem. After the mugging last night, and the conclusions he's drawn from what the Fenian Boys said, Widow doesn't trust Snyder, but he needs Snyder's help to follow his hunch.

It's not his place to solve a nineteen-year-old murder. And Harper's not asking him to. She only asked him to present her case to The Vidocq Society, which he did. She's expecting him back in Annapolis.

Widow files away the murder investigation records, and returns them neatly to the document bag. He closes it and packs it into his rucksack. He stands, and checks the hotel room one last time before he leaves to make sure he's not forgotten anything. He hasn't.

Widow walks to the door, stops, and stands there at the door to his hotel suite. He grabs the knob, and freezes. Something's wrong. He can't make himself turn the knob.

He's got to return to Annapolis. It's literally his orders. His company expects him back today. His CO expects him back. He's been ordered back. But how can return without pursuing his theory? He owes it to Harper. He owes it to Mia. He owes it to the oath he took. Part of that oath is: *I will obey the orders of the President of the United States and the orders of the officers appointed over me.* Which clearly requires him to return to school and check in with his CO. There's no question.

However, the first part of the oath is: *I will support and defend the Constitution of the United States against all enemies, foreign and domestic; that I will bear true faith and allegiance to the same.* Support and defend the Constitution of the United States. True faith and allegiance. Isn't it his duty to follow this lead for Mia? Mia had the right to life and liberty, and it was stolen from her. She's a citizen, like anyone else. Isn't it his duty to protect and defend her as well?

No, he must return today, as ordered. No question. He's already told Snyder about the shoes. He's mentioned it to Mautner's club of elite sleuths. Let them take it from there. So Widow opens the door, steps into the doorway, but stays there. He can't cross the threshold. He licks his lips. They're a bit chapped from the cold. His shoulders slump, his gaze drops to the hallway carpet, and he sighs.

Widow struggles a long, long moment, looks back over his shoulder into the hotel suite, at the phone. He whispers to himself. He says, "Shit!"

Widow steps back into the room and closes the door. He picks up the phone and dials Snyder's number from memory.

Snyder picks up the phone, and says, "Yes?"

"Howie, it's Widow. Did you get my voicemail?"

"How come you can call me, a Special Agent with the FBI, and your elder, by my first name, but I got to call you Widow?"

"Somebody's grumpy."

"Sorry, I didn't sleep so well. We got mugged last night, remember? It's embarrassing for an FBI agent. You know? It kept me up half the night. I feel bad about it. I should've pulled my gun, saved Harper's money."

Widow avoids telling Snyder about what he did to recover the files, bag, and engagement ring, he just says, "Don't worry about it. If you'd pulled your gun, we'd probably be dead. It was stupid of me to make the move that I made. I'm surprised they didn't kill us." Widow listens carefully, to see if Snyder indicates he knows more than he's saying.

But Snyder glosses over it. He says, "That's good to know. Thanks for being understanding. So, what can I do for you?"

"Did you get my voicemail?"

"I did. You got a theory?"

"I do."

"I'm all ears."

"You got any fetishes?"

Silence over the phone. Then, Snyder asks, "What're you talking about?"

"Many people have fetishes. You know? Like sexual turn-ons, or kinks?"

"I know what a fetish is, Widow."

"Ever heard of a foot fetish?"

Snyder goes quiet for a moment, and then he answers, "You think Stamos raped and killed Mia, and took her shoes, because why? He's got a foot fetish?"

Before Widow can answer, Snyder says, "Hold on," he pauses. Widow hears him mumbling to himself, like he's saying it out loud, and listening to it. The idea clicks for him. Snyder says, "You think someone saw Mia alone, dragged her to the stairwell, raped and killed her, because of her feet? And they took her shoes and socks as a sick, twisted reminder?"

Widow stays quiet. He's letting the theory turn the wheels in Snyder's mind. Snyder may be deceitful in some unknown way, but he's still trying to catch Mia's killer. And he's an FBI agent.

After a long silence, Snyder says, "If some sicko with a foot fetish raped and killed Mia, and took her shoes and socks, that sounds like a keepsake? A souvenir?"

"Or a trophy."

"A trophy? I never heard of a boyfriend taking a trophy."

"Serial killers take trophies."

Snyder goes silent again, and then he says, "A serial killer? I don't know, that's a stretch. But it doesn't mean Peter wasn't the killer. In fact, your theory could explain why he vanished, and changed his name. Mia could've been his first victim. There could be others."

Widow didn't indulge in Snyder's Peter theory. Widow says, "Let's not jump to any conclusions. It's just a theory that explains her missing shoes and socks. That's why we need to look at the evidence in person. So, where is it now?"

"It's in evidence storage."

"Where's that exactly? The Bar Harbor police station?"

Snyder chuckles, and says, "Oh no! The Bar Harbor Police Station is a small, rickety building, no bigger than a double-wide mobile home. They wouldn't have the space to keep a nineteen-year-old box of evidence. All that stuff's probably still in a storage building on Highway 3."

"Is that in Bar Harbor?"

"It's just outside of it."

Widow asks, "Do you have the rest of the day off?"

"I'm off the whole week, in case Mautner and his guys come up with something."

"Can you take me up there? We can look at the evidence."

Snyder pauses again. Widow hears the self-talk mumbling, like he's working out if he should take Widow or not. Finally, he says, "Yeah. Let me make some calls first. Are you still at the Ritz?"

"I am."

"Okay, meet me out front in thirty minutes," Snyder says, and clicks off the phone.

CHAPTER 24

Widow stands out in the cold, with his rucksack slung over one shoulder, and waits on the curb out front of his hotel. Just by coincidence, or because McGillin's pub is only a couple of blocks over, he sees the bartender who gave him the information about the Fenian Boys and their use of taxis to scout for rare cars.

The bartender walks by on the other side of the street. He's dressed in street clothes, like he's off work. Maybe he's on a break. He looks like he's heading somewhere important. After Widow catches the bartender staring in his direction, they make eye contact, briefly. The bartender breaks it and moves on.

The thought crosses Widow's mind about the bartender being a little agitated at how Widow tricked him with the five-dollar bills, and that he might be tempted to inform the Fenian Boys about spotting Widow.

A minute later, Snyder picks Widow up in his car, a white 2003 Chevrolet Impala. Widow figures it's a rental, since Snyder mentioned he's normally stationed in Miami. He must've flown here and rented a car.

Snyder stops at the curb and pops the trunk, but doesn't get out. He buzzes the window down and says, "Put your bag in the trunk."

Widow nods, puts his rucksack in the trunk, closes it, and gets in. Hot air from the car's heater warms his face, and he welcomes it. Before they drive away, Snyder says, "It's a long drive. You sure you want to do this?"

Widow pauses, glances out the windshield to the street. He says, "I don't have a choice."

"Didn't you mention something about having to return today?"

"Yeah, I'm supposed to."

"Won't you get into trouble for that? Isn't it like deserting your post? Or something?"

"Not the same. I'm already on approved leave. Abandoning my post would be if I vanished from an assigned post, or left the base, telling no one and never returning. Here, I'm just going to be a day late."

"But won't you get in trouble for that?"

"Probably, unless Harper can do her magic again. She pulled strings to get me off for last night. I hope she can do it again. I think she can."

Snyder says, "I might pull some strings. If her influence doesn't work out. Being an FBI agent has its perks."

"You would do that?"

"Sure, I want to make up for wimping out on you last night."

Widow inadvertently glances at the side mirror, thinks about the trunk, where his rucksack holding Harper's recovered document bag is stashed, and thinks about his one-man mission earlier to retrieve it. He says, "No need to apologize. It'll work out."

Snyder jokes, "Hell, I could always arrest you on suspicion of a crime. Then say I made a mistake. That'll buy you a day or two."

"It wouldn't be the first time I've been falsely arrested, and it probably won't be the last," Widow says, and smiles, not realizing how much truth is in that joke. If he knew the future, he'd find humor in that old saying: *Be careful what you wish for*.

"You've been arrested before?"

Widow stays quiet, and is saved by the bell. At least, he's saved by the car horn. A car behind them honks its horn. Widow glances in the side mirror again. The car is a Philadelphia police cruiser, and the horn is more like a quick siren blip. The cop speaks, over a speaker mounted on the grille, and says, "Move along."

Snyder salutes the cop in the rearview and drives away. He takes Widow back through the city, only heads north on I-95. It's slow-going at first. The lunchtime traffic is brutal, but not as bad as the five o'clock traffic.

At various points while sitting in traffic, Snyder receives and responds to several text messages. He doesn't tell Widow what they're about.

After twenty minutes of fighting through the traffic, they get north of the city. Widow watches North Philadelphia through the windows as they pass by. He checks the on-ramps, a little nervous, like he's waiting for the Fenian Boys to regroup, get a posse, and hunt him down. He pictures a Mad Max road chase scenario. But nothing happens.

Once they hit the open road, Snyder puts the car in cruise control, and speaks again. He says, "Okay, it's roughly nine more hours till we get there. So, you told me about your foot fetish theory. You got anything else?"

"Not yet. Just what I told you."

"Okay, well, before I picked you up, I made a phone call to my office. I got a support worker back in Miami working on tracking down all the players we know. She's been texting me. We know she's not going to find Stamos. At least, no one has been able to all these years. But she found two of the other persons of interest," Snyder says, and takes the car out of cruise control. He moves to the left lane and passes a cluster of slow vehicles, then returns to the right lane. He resumes cruise control.

He says, "We got lucky. Two of them are still in Bar Harbor. And they're still at the college. So, we can talk with them.

"Bernabe rose through the ranks and is now the head of college police department. Which makes sense. He seemed smart, but not too smart.

"Anton Idris is a whole different story. He's still the janitor, which doesn't surprise me. He wasn't the ambitious type. My impression of the man was that his book has a few pages missing from it. If you catch my meaning?"

Widow asks, "You mean he's mentally challenged or something?"

"No. Not exactly. He can read and write and do arithmetic. He's just no brainiac. Idris has got to be pushing his retirement age by now."

Widow nods, and asks, "What about Nabors? He was there that night too."

"Right, so Nabors is out there somewhere. He quit the college's force a little while after Mia was murdered. The last thing he said to me was he couldn't live with the guilt of knowing he was probably just a few buildings away from her while she was being murdered. And he didn't save her. He struck me as a hero type. And now, my girl's having a hard time finding him too."

"So, Stamos isn't the only one who's vanished?"

"It was nineteen years ago. I didn't say he's vanished. I just said she can't find him yet. Stamos is completely different. I know he changed his name. I searched for him many times over the years to follow up. His trail went cold years ago. No one knows where he is."

"What about his parents? Harper told me about Mia's bad relationship with hers, but what about Peter Stamos?"

"Well, he had a mother. His father died a long time ago. But his mother might've known where he went."

"But?"

"She also died, about two years after Peter killed Mia."

"Allegedly killed Mia. We don't know he really killed her, remember?"

Snyder stares blankly at the road, and says, "Right, that's what I meant."

Widow doesn't believe him. He sounds like it'll take a lot more than a new theory to change his mind about Stamos. Or maybe he doesn't want to be wrong about Stamos? It's like he's already signed the guy's death warrant or something. And to prove Stamos innocent now would jeopardize his own innocence.

Suddenly, a thought occurs to Widow. It's a new idea. Excitedly, he asks, "You know what?"

"What?"

"I bet I can find Nabors."

"How?"

"Nabors was a Marine, right?"

"Right."

"Give me your phone," Widow says.

Snyder glances at him, and asks, "What's wrong with yours?"

"I don't carry a phone."

"Why not?"

Widow shrugs, and says, "I guess I don't like to be so accessible."

Snyder says nothing to that, and hands his phone over. Widow takes it and dials Annapolis's main phone line. He gets the operator, and asks for the number to Marine Corps Criminal Investigation Division, or CID. Snyder listens. Widow gets the number, and memorizes it. He clicks off the phone and dials the number to CID. He waits, and gets another operator. He gives her his military ID number, explains the situation, and then pauses, like he's hit a brick wall with the operator. He says, "Hold on one second." And he covers the phone, looks at Snyder, and says, "Give me your badge number?"

"What for?"

"They're not going to cooperate with me. I'm just a midshipman in the US Navy. But an FBI agent will get this done fast."

Snyder nods, holds the wheel with one hand, and reaches into his jacket pocket. He takes out his badge wallet and hands it to Widow. Widow takes it, flips it open, and reads the number to the operator. He pauses a long beat, waiting while she checks it out. He closes the wallet and hands it back to Snyder, who pockets it.

Widow listens. He nods a few times, explains the situation again, and finally, thanks the operator and clicks off the phone. He puts the phone in a cup holder, near Snyder.

Snyder asks, "So, what'd they say?"

"She said she would pass along the information request, and someone would call us back."

CHAPTER 25

Widow and Snyder drive the interstate. They start at I-95, will switch to several other routes, and then they'll be on I-95 once again when they're closer to Bar Harbor. But they're not there yet, far from it.

Northbound from Philadelphia, the road stretches out like a gray ribbon tossed casually across a rolling landscape. Interstate 95, a critical vein that provides lifeblood for commerce and travel, cuts through the heart of the East Coast.

Philadelphia's roads expand into New Jersey, where the land patchworks into a quilt of fields and towns, peppered by the random clusters of oak and maple trees that stand guard like the Navy Police at Gate 1 in Annapolis.

Widow sees signs for New York City. It's only eighty-nine miles from where they started, but traffic's heavy around both Philadelphia and New York City, making it two hours to get past New York. Pretty good time, relatively speaking.

As they drive the scenery changes, the Northeast's lush wintry countryside replaces New York City's concrete sprawl.

The trees appear to grow denser and taller. They loom over the roads like long-dead, petrified monsters. Icy wind blasts the outside of the vehicle, keeping the heater working overtime. The sky opens up, becoming massive, making the horizon seem like a blue bubble that rolls into eternity.

They drive with jazz music playing on the radio. It's Snyder's choice. Widow enjoys jazz as much as he does blues: He tolerates it, but doesn't love it.

Jazz is good, but not his preferred music. It's not great long-car-trip music. Jazz is a little too sleepy for long car rides, which are already sleepy by nature. Especially when they pass New York City, because then they're on rural, scenic routes.

Winter trees line the sides of the interstate, and the jazz music plays on. The blue sky vanishes, and gray skies overtake them and the roads ahead. There're hints of rain on the horizon as they drive further north. Snow blankets distant hills and the farm building rooftops.

Widow dozes off, not just from the monotonous scenery or the jazz music, but also because he's had a long night and morning already, without this long drive tacked onto the day. Last night he presented Mia's murder, met Judge Mautner, and got mugged. Today he tracked down the Fenian Boys, recovered his ring and Harper's bag, and now he's neck deep in a nineteen-year-old murder case, where he might just be on the trail of a serial killer.

It feels like Widow's only out for a few minutes when Snyder's phone rings, loudly, killing the ambient quiet created by the jazz music. Widow's eyes pop open like shutters thrown back in a storm. He comes to and finds himself curled in his seat, which crams his feet and legs into the footwell. Being nearly stuck, he struggles to pull himself out.

Snyder answers the phone, says, "Hello?"

The caller speaks, but Widow can't hear it.

"This is Agent Snyder," Snyder says, pauses, and listens, and then he says, "He's here. Hold on." Snyder passes the phone to Widow.

Widow takes it, puts it to his ear, and says, a little groggy from being awakened from a deep sleep, "Hello?"

The voice on the line is a woman. Her voice is smooth, but commanding. It's like Snyder's sleepy jazz music slams into Widow's preferred rock and roll, and merges into one strong, silky-smooth sound. She says, "Midshipman Widow, I'm Special Agent Cameron with the NCIS."

"Yes, ma'am. This is Widow."

"Midshipman, you called about a former Marine named Bret Nabors. Is that right?"

"Yes, ma'am. But I called CID, not NCIS."

Cameron says nothing to that. She says, "Midshipman, help me understand what's going on."

Widow pauses and glances at Snyder, whose eyes are on the road but who's listening intently. Widow gives Cameron the entire story, starting with Harper, Annapolis, The Vidocq Society, how he got hooked up with Snyder, and Mia's murder, omitting his theory of a killer with a foot fetish. He's not ready to disclose that yet. And he left out the Fenian Boys, and the botched proposal.

At the end of his description of events, Cameron says, "Wow! That's quite an ordeal you've gotten yourself into, Midshipman."

"Yes, ma'am," Widow says, pauses, and asks, "Ma'am, why're you calling me back instead of the CID?"

"Thank you for explaining it. So, here's the thing: first off, I'd never communicate about official investigations with unauthorized persons, especially a twenty-two-year-old midshipman who should be partaking in Commissioning Week right now, instead of out there playing detective," Cameron says.

She looked me up, Widow thinks.

Cameron says, "However, the FBI's vouching for you, and I've heard of Jaime Harper. In fact, I saw her at a conference once, on something about forensic sciences. It was required for agents who work homicides. Strangely, I never heard about her sister's unsolved murder. Which I guess makes sense. Why would she go around talking about it? It was nearly twenty years ago. That said, I'm going to answer your question. It could be a coincidence. But, and I'm sure Agent Snyder will back me up here, in homicide, there're no coincidences."

Widow glances at Snyder. He says nothing, just drives and listens.

Cameron says, "The reason they sent this to me is that I've got this old murder case on my docket. I inherited it from a guy who inherited it from another guy. It's from 1981. And it sounds awfully similar to how you're describing Jaime's sister's murder."

Widow speaks loud, so Snyder can hear him. He asks, "You've got a cold case homicide from 1981 that sounds like Mia Harper's murder?"

Snyder's eyes widen, and his jaw drops. He turns and looks at Widow.

Widow nods to Cameron's response. She says, "I do."

"So if you didn't know about Mia, then why did the CID send this to you? Why're you calling me back?"

"Because Bret Nabors was stationed at the post where my murder occurred all those years ago."

Widow goes quiet. He stares through the windshield at the gray skies ahead. Dark thunderclouds rumble on the skyline, like a far-off enemy army marching towards them.

For the first time, Cameron doesn't call Widow by his student rank. She asks, "Widow? You there?"

"Yeah, I'm here."

"Let me read you the highlights of my case. The victim was PFC Elena Torres. She was raped and strangled at Marine Corps Air Station Tustin, in Tustin, California, back in 1981. She was only nineteen years old. Of course, I was only four years old back then. But I've seen photos. And Widow, believe me, you don't want to see them. It's one of the most brutal murders I've ever come across. The original agents described it as a *nightmare murder.* Over five thousand man-hours went into the investigation alone. But it went nowhere. After years and years, the Corps didn't want to think about it anymore, and it got handed down from the first agent to me," Cameron says.

"Anything weird about her remains?"

"Like what?"

"Anything missing?"

Widow hears noises, like rustling papers, like Cameron's actually got the physical files in front of her. She asks, "Like a body part? Nope. She was all there."

"What about her personal belongings?"

Cameron pauses a beat, and asks, "Like her clothing?"

"Yes."

Cameron pauses, a long, long beat. Widow hears more papers rustling, like she's double and triple checking. Finally, Cameron says, "We never found her shoes."

"The thing is, Nabors is a person of interest in our case, and Mia's shoes and socks were never found."

"So you think the killer took them? Why?"

"I have a theory. I know it sounds stupid," Widow says.

Snyder glances over. He's been listening to a one-sided conversation, but he understands the context of everything Widow's said. Loudly, so Cameron can hear him, he says, "It's not stupid, Agent Cameron. The more and more time passes, the more I think Widow's got something."

Cameron says, "Tell me your theory, Widow."

Widow says, "I think our killer has a foot fetish."

Silence, and then Cameron says, "You think he kills them, and takes their shoes like a trophy?"

"And their socks too."

Cameron says, "Widow, I think we might have the same killer. And Bret Nabors is the common denominator between Elena Torres and Mia Harper. Where're you now?"

"We're on the road. We're headed to Bar Harbor. We're going to check the evidence in storage to confirm Mia's shoes and socks are indeed missing, and it's not just an oversight."

Impressed, Cameron says, "That's thorough police work."

"Thank you. We also need you to find Nabors. Can you help us?"

"I can do that."

"We're also going to interview the other cop, and the janitor. They're both still employed at the college where Mia was murdered. We'll see what more they can tell us. Now we know to ask them about Nabors. Maybe the years have shaken some information loose," Widow says.

"Okay, I'll find Nabors. Don't worry about that. The Marines keep up with their own."

Widow asks, "Could you do me another favor?"

"Sure. What?"

"Would you look into Mia's boyfriend? Peter Stamos. He's the original suspect. Even if it turns out to be Nabors, we want to find him. He's probably changed his name. Snyder and the FBI can't locate him."

"Sure. I can do that."

"Okay, thanks, Agent Cameron. Call us back at this number. Or we'll call you if we find out more," Widow says, and clicks off the phone. He puts Snyder's phone back in the cup holder.

Widow reviews his conversation with Snyder as they drive, aligning them, putting them on the same page. Snyder's demeanor changes, and Widow notices. The change starts when Widow talks about Cameron and him discussing Peter Stamos. Widow asks Snyder about Stamos, but he gets uncomfortable and changes the subject. Widow reckons it's out of a feeling of guilt for possibly blaming the wrong man for all these years.

For nineteen years, Snyder's believed that Stamos killed Mia. It's haunted him right along with Mia's ghost. It makes sense. Widow imagines how hard it would be for him to live with, knowing that he let a woman's killer get away for nearly two decades. Widow can't blame Snyder for thinking it was

Stamos. How many murder cases does it turn out the killer is the boyfriend or spouse? The answer is most of them.

Idris coming along and cleaning up after the rape and murder muddled the crime scene. In a lot of ways, it completely destroyed it. Sure, they found fingerprints in the library, and on the fire stairs doors. But they found too many. They found hundreds, because lots of students and faculty were in the library on a daily basis. And sure, they found Stamos's fingerprints on Mia's personal stuff, but he was her boyfriend. He probably touched everything she owned. Even if they found her shoes, with Stamos's fingerprints all over them, it wouldn't be enough evidence because he probably had touched her shoes before. It could all be explained.

Snyder might be acting uneasy because he's slowly realizing that he's been chasing the wrong man all these years. Plus, the actual killer, if it is Nabors, has been under his nose all this time. That's double the guilt for Snyder.

Widow cuts Snyder some slack. It would be difficult carrying around hate and certainty for one suspect for nineteen years, only to discover that you were wrong.

They drive on, crossing into Connecticut, where the snowy hills rise and fall, like the cadence of one of Snyder's melancholy jazz songs. They follow the curves of the freeway through the state, skirting around cities and towns, tunneling their way through quiet forests.

At one point, Widow calls Harper and talks with her. She sounds okay, but is questioning why he won't be back today. He explains some of the situation to her, telling her they have a lead, and it may not be Stamos who murdered her sister after all.

Harper reacts unexpectedly to this news. Widow thought she'd be excited that they got a lead, and that he's the one who came up with the theory. Instead, she's quiet about it, like she's upset by it. Widow figures his same logic about why Snyder feels guilty over blaming Stamos all these years probably applies to Harper as well. She's also blamed Stamos for nineteen years. And now she's hearing it may have been this guy, Nabors.

To bring her back to feeling happy, Widow credits her feet for his theory. And she laughs about it. He asks if she can pull some more strings with Harrington, and get him leave till Friday. She says she'll do her best. Then she says she's not feeling well again. So they hang up.

Widow and Snyder stop for gas twice. Each time, Widow gets a large coffee. And each stop, he visits the men's room before refilling his coffee. They press on further into the heart of New England. They reach Massachusetts. Widow admires the scenery. It commands his attention with its storied blend of rich American history and snowy landscapes. The Berkshires loom in the distance. It's a series of gently rolling hills, rising and falling like waves on the ocean.

At hour four, Snyder asks Widow to take over driving because his feet are starting to really hurt him due to his arthritis. Widow informs Snyder he doesn't have a license, but he can drive. Snyder pauses, then rejects the offer, like he's worried how it'd look if Widow got a ticket for not having a license, and with an FBI agent in the car. So Snyder decides to stop for the night.

By the time they'd arrive in Bar Harbor, it'd be late anyway. They wouldn't be able to get into the evidence storage building until Thursday. Widow realizes Snyder's right, but he feels anxious about it, because not only is he overstaying his leave, but he's also risking missing his own graduation ceremony.

They stop in Worcester, Massachusetts. Snyder rents two hotel rooms for them at the Blackstone Inn, next to a river of the same name. He tells Widow not to worry. The Bureau will reimburse him. Widow ends up with a river-view room, only because they were out of all the others. And when Snyder showed his badge, the innkeeper hopped to attention, like Widow did when he saw Harrington at breakfast back in Annapolis.

"Best rooms in the house, for our best guests," said the innkeeper.

Snyder tells Widow it's only because they were out of cheaper rooms. He says, "It happens all the time."

They get to their separate rooms and turn in for the night.

Before he even unholsters his gun, or takes off his shoes to let his feet rest, Snyder calls Mautner's direct number. Frantically, he waits, hoping it's not too late. There's no answer. He gets Mautner's voicemail. He freezes, nervously, and then he hangs up. He texts Mautner: *NEED TO TALK! ASAP!*

Snyder waits ten minutes, then twenty, then thirty. Finally, he removes his gun and shoes. He sits on the bed, rubbing his feet, and waits.

Forty-five minutes later, there's still no response. Snyder can't wait any longer. So he calls again. He gets the voicemail again. Panic-stricken, he gets the outgoing message, and the beep, and he hesitates, then he says, "Can you put a pause on our arrangement? We might be wrong...God, I think we're wrong. Allan, please call me back!"

Snyder pauses, takes a deep breath, and says, "I'll be back in Bar Harbor tomorrow. I think Widow's right. We're going to check out the evidence, but I'm positive the shoes and socks are gone. I think we're wrong about Peter. So, call me back. I need to be certain, before we go forward. Okay?"

The voicemail timer runs out. Mautner's phone hangs up on Snyder. He sets his phone down and returns to massaging his feet. He focuses on breathing exercises that his doctor tells him will help with his stress.

CHAPTER 26

Beacon Hill, a historic neighborhood and a stronghold of Boston's old money, hovers over the city like its name suggests, as a beacon. Its gloomy cobblestone streets narrow into shadows, winding tightly between rows of elegant, centuries-old brick townhouses. Gaslit lamps flicker at night, casting dancing shadows over polished brass door knockers and window boxes flooded with the remains of autumn flowers.

Beacon Hill emanates a dark sense of exclusivity like a members-only club, the kind of thing that's inherited, not earned or bought—a legacy whispered through generations of elite Bostonians, through long bloodlines going back to the Founding Fathers. The old houses, red-brick and stately, stand shoulder to shoulder; their facades, while a welcoming testament to Boston's Federal-style architecture by day, are cold and uninviting on winter nights. Even the cheerful Christmas lights barely mask their dark coldness.

The snowy streets, while dark and quiet, drone like the dark hum of a tuning fork with the silent power of their citizens: politicians, literati, and judges—the kind of people who wield quiet influence and near-absolute power. The wintry air heightens the dark unspoken truths. Even now, centuries after the American Revolutionary War, residents of Beacon Hill meet in smoky rooms, behind heavy doors, to decide things. And their decisions shape the city, and the nation.

And yet, Beacon Hill doesn't flaunt its status. It doesn't need to. The power players know who wields the power. Beacon Hill doesn't ostentatiously display wealth. There's no need for it.

Judge Mautner's house is tucked away inside Beacon Hill. Christmas carolers move about the neighborhood outside his doors. He hears them spreading holiday cheer.

The Seven's founder sits in his big house alone. His wife's been dead for years, from a heart attack. His children are all grown up. He's got grandkids who're having babies now. They'll all visit him on Christmas Day. He knows it. They come every year. Of course, his grandkids want their presents, and his kids want their inheritances. So, they visit each year, and call often enough. Some call him more than others. What's ironic is that the one son who rarely calls him, the one who dislikes him, is the one he respects the most. Of course, he doesn't tell that to the rest of them.

Mautner sits in a timeworn Chesterfield armchair in front of a roaring fire, puffing on a cigar, and sipping his favorite brandy out of a hundred-dollar crystal snifter. He finishes presiding over a celebratory virtual meeting with the other six members of the Seven. They've been patting themselves on the back for another successful assassination of a criminal lowlife who thought he got away with rape and murder— Peter Stamos.

Mautner congratulates them once more, wishes a happy holiday season to them all, and reminds them they won't meet again until 2004, after the holidays. The other six echo the same sentiments, and one by one they click off their screens. Mautner clicks off his laptop, closes it, and sets it on a coffee table. He's pleased with the Seven, pleased with the year of assassinations they've had. He's pleased with the number of vermin they've gotten rid of. He feels euphoric, thinking about all the justice that's been done, around the country and around the world. He thinks about all the victims he's helped. He feels righteous, and justified, for overseeing the elimination of so many murderers.

His Wednesday night is going pretty well until his cellphone rings—not his personal line, but the burner phone that's designated for club business only. Mautner also has another, completely different, phone designated just for communication with the scales of justice man.

The number on the phone screen is for one of his last clients. And hearing from clients after the job is done is frowned upon. They're told not to call again. There's to be no communication once they complete a contract. Many of them want to call and express their gratitude for ending their respective nightmares. Mautner informs them this is unnecessary, and dangerous. Once their business concludes, they're forbidden by the Seven to communicate again. All interaction should stop. It's like they never met. It's best this way to maintain the integrity of each case.

Therefore, when his phone rings, and he recognizes the number as Special Agent Snyder's, Mautner pauses a beat. Snyder understands the rules. He knows after the job is done, there's no more communication. Normally, Mautner would scold him for such a grievous breach of protocol. However, Snyder's an FBI agent. Mautner watches the phone buzz on an end table between his armchair and a ten-thousand-dollar leather sofa. He reaches for it, but hesitates. He's not sure what to do.

Mautner lets it go to voicemail. The phone goes silent. He puts out his cigar and sips his brandy. The phone buzzes again. It's one simple blip, indicating there's a text message.

At first, Mautner ignores it. Maybe it's a mistake. Or maybe Snyder doesn't know the job's done. It's possible. Sometimes, the scales of justice man doesn't present the evidence to the client for days or even weeks. This could be one of those times. Still, the job's done. No reason to hear what Snyder has to say.

Mautner sips again from the crystal snifter. He glances at the phone. Curious, he sets down the snifter and picks up the phone. He stares at the screen. There's a text message from Snyder. It reads: *NEED TO TALK! ASAP!*

Getting frustrated, Mautner pauses, and asks himself if he should call Snyder back, but he decides not to. He grabs his brandy, and sips. And he's left in peace, or so he thinks, because after forty-five minutes and a second crystal snifter of brandy, the phone rings again. And, again, it's Snyder. Mautner ignores it. It goes to voicemail, and blips again, again indicating a voice message.

Mautner listens to the message. Snyder talks, running through the voicemail's timer. He says, "Can you put a pause on our arrangement? We might be wrong…God, I think we're wrong. Allan, please call me back!"

Snyder goes silent for a beat, then his voice returns, saying, "I'll be back in Bar Harbor tomorrow. I think Widow's right. We're going to check out the evidence, but I'm positive the shoes and socks are gone. I think we're wrong about Peter. So, call me back. I need to be certain, before we go forward. Okay?"

At first, the message horrifies Mautner, but not because he may have ordered the murder of an innocent man. Judges sentence innocent men all the time. It comes with the job. Judges aren't perfect humans. They get it wrong from time to time, and he's no different, no better than any other man on the bench. It's the cost of doing business. How many men has he sentenced to death? Technically, Massachusetts abolished the death penalty back in 1984—ironically, the same year Mia Harper met her death. The last time Massachusetts executed a prisoner was 1947.

Just because Mautner technically never sentenced a man to death doesn't mean he's never handed down a death sentence. A life sentence is ultimately just a prolonged death sentence, after all. How many of those has he wrongly given out? It's probably dozens. So why should he care if Peter Stamos was guilty or not?

It's too late now, anyway. The scales of justice man has already executed the sentence. Killing an innocent man isn't Mautner's concern. His concern, the thing that's frustrating him, is Snyder's phone call. He sounds like a man who's losing resolve, like he's cracking under the guilt. Surely, Snyder's arrested innocent men before. He's the one who convinced the Seven that Stamos killed that girl. He's the one who came to them, and presented their court with the evidence. Stamos's death, innocent or not, is on Snyder.

The issue that gnaws at him is the way Snyder sounds. He sounds like he has a guilty conscience. And a man with a guilty conscience tends to talk. Snyder sounds like a loose end.

Mautner sips more brandy, letting ideas simmer in his mind until the call to action is clear. He chugs the last of the snifter's brandy and picks up the phone. He dials a number, and waits.

CHAPTER 27

The scales of justice man sits in his car outside of Harper's apartment, like he's waiting for something. His phone rings. He sees it's Mautner, and he answers it. He says, "Yes?"

Mautner says, "There's a problem." He explains that Stamos might've been innocent. Killing him might've been a mistake.

"That's not my department. I retire who you tell me to retire," the scales of justice man says. He knows Mautner's a little upset by the prospect that an innocent man was killed, but he also knows Mautner isn't that upset by the prospect. And, Mautner will get over it. They'll move on with business as usual. Out of sight really is out of mind. Still, Mautner likes to pretend it matters to him. So the scales of justice man listens, lets the Judge vent about it.

"We're only here for justice, not blind murder," Mautner says, like he's supposed to say. He feigns outrage.

"That's your thing, your rules. I'm just the tip of the sword. I go where you point me."

Mautner breathes heavily, and says, "Yes, you're right. The most important thing now is damage control."

"What do you want me to do?"

"Snyder's involved this sailor, Widow. He's a kid, but still he struck me as an idealist."

"Idealists usually cause problems."

Mautner says, "I agree. If they involve anyone else, or discover the whole truth...all we've done together, all the good we've done, will be exposed and perverted to be something else. And all the good we could do would be prevented. It'll all come down like a house of cards."

All the good we've done? If that's how you see it, the scales of justice man thinks, but he says, "So, what do you want me to do about it?"

Mautner says, "You need to correct the situation."

"How?"

"See if you can find out who the right target is, and take him out. If you're not sure which one is the right target, then take them all out. All three of the remaining suspects. That'll right the wrong, but also," Mautner says, and pauses. "Tie up the loose ends. All the loose ends."

"I need to get paid for this. I don't work for free."

"Fine. I'll do it out of my own pocket. Take care of it. I booked you a flight to Bar Harbor. It leaves out of Baltimore in two hours."

The scales of justice man smiles, and says, "Consider it done."

CHAPTER 28

Wednesday night, before he goes to sleep but after he eats a room service cheeseburger and fries, alone in his hotel room, Widow calls the number he memorized from Snyder's cellphone. It rings twice, then a voice answers.

NCIS Agent Rachel Cameron says, "Hello?"

"Agent Cameron? This is Widow. I assumed you'd be awake, because I'm on the east coast, and here it's only twenty hundred hours. I have no idea where you are, but if you're in the US, then I should be okay. Was I right?"

"I'm at Naval Weapons Station Charleston, in South Carolina. We're in the same time zone. What's this number you're calling me from? Is this your phone?"

"No ma'am. This is a hotel phone in Worcester."

"So, you boys are halfway to Bar Harbor?"

"Yes, ma'am. We've stopped for the night."

"I see. So what can I do for you?"

Widow says, "May I speak bluntly, ma'am?"

"Yes, Midshipman, and quit calling me ma'am. I know it's protocol, but it makes me feel old. So knock it off."

"Okay. I'll stop if you just call me Widow, then. Deal?"

"Deal. So, what's going on, Widow?"

"I'm alone in my room. Snyder's not around."

"I take it you want to talk about something, and you don't want him to hear you?"

"Yes…" Widow says, and pauses. He nearly calls her *ma'am* again. "There's something wrong about Snyder, and The Vidocq Society."

Silence, for a long beat, then Cameron says, "Widow, are you sure Snyder can't hear you?"

"Unless he's got my hotel room bugged, then I think I'm safe," Widow says, then he thinks for a second about how it was Snyder's idea to stop here, and he's the one who got the rooms. But he shakes it off. It's a stupid, paranoid thought.

"Okay, so tell me more."

Widow tells her about The Vidocq Society, particularly Judge Mautner and the six members of the elite group within the society. He tells her about how they kicked him out of the room at the end, like they were having some kind of secret vote. He tells her about the Fenian Boys, the mugging, how Snyder never pulled his badge or weapon, and how the Fenian Boys took Harper's bearer bonds. He explains Snyder's strange behavior, and his adverse reaction and shock at Widow's foot fetish theory.

Cameron listens, and asks, "What's strange about Snyder's reaction?"

"It's not that he didn't want to hear it. It's more like he didn't want to believe it, like he didn't want Peter Stamos not to be guilty. And then there're the bearer bonds. When I recovered the document bag, they were gone. The Fenian Boys passed them up the chain. At least, that's what they said."

"Hold up. What do you mean, recovered the document bag?"

Widow pauses a beat. He's nearly let the cat out of the bag now. So, he says, "Well, Agent Cameron, I couldn't let them steal Harper's money like that. So I tracked them down, and…I went on a recovery mission."

"A recovery mission?"

"Yes, I investigated them and discovered how to find them. Then I reconned, discovered their location, and infiltrated."

"Widow, before you tell me too many details, it sounds like you've broken some laws. So I'm going to just ask you tell me what I need to know from here on out."

"Okay, I infiltrated the enemy. I interrogated the enemy. And they told me they gave away Harper's bearer bonds to some scary dude," Widow says.

"A scary dude?"

"That's how they put it. And they indicated that when you go up their chain of command, you'll find powerful people, like…"

Cameron interrupts, and says, "Politicians? That's not surprising."

"I was going to say judges."

"Judges?"

"Yes, like a guy called Judge Mautner, whom I met. I believe that the Fenian Boys were trying to tell me that."

"You think Snyder and this Mautner are doing something more than just trying to find Mia's killer?"

"I do."

Cameron pauses a long beat.

Widow asks, "Agent Cameron?"

"I'm going to trust you, Widow. And you better not let me down. If you're playing me, I'll burn your career so badly it'll never recover. Got it?"

Widow's eyes widen. He says, "I got it."

"I looked into Snyder. He's got a less than stellar track record with the FBI. He's crossed the line in the past. At least, they suspect he has. In fact, from what I could find, they were going to kick him out, only he's so close to retirement, they're letting him hang on until then. But next year, he'll be out on his butt, living off his pension."

Widow stays quiet.

Cameron says, "Your instincts are right to suspect him. I know nothing about The Vidocq Society or Mautner, but I'll check them out."

"What about Stamos?"

"I've not found him yet, but I've got people working on it. It's after hours right now. Hopefully I'll have news on him tomorrow."

"What about Nabors?"

"The Corps gave me three addresses for him. They're all within driving distance of Bar Harbor. Two are in Maine, and one's outside of Portsmouth, New Hampshire. I'm going to visit them tomorrow."

"You're going to visit them?"

Cameron says, "That's right. I'm at the airport right now. I'll be in Portland tomorrow. I'll call Snyder's phone as soon as I've apprehended Nabors."

"That's if Nabors is guilty."

"We never knew about Mia Harper. This evidence about the missing shoes from both Mia Harper's and Elena Torres's case, plus Nabors's connection to both victims, is more than enough to arrest and question him," Cameron says, and pauses. "Widow, this is because of you. So, no matter how this other stuff with Snyder and Mautner turns out, you should know I'm grateful to you. You may have helped us bring justice to these families."

Widow smiles, and says, "Thanks. Maybe I'll see you in Maine. You know, if our paths cross."

"If things go right, then I suspect not. But keep me informed about those other guys. And anything else you see with Snyder and Mautner," Cameron says, and clicks off the phone.

Widow hangs his end up, sticks his dirty plates and all out into the Blackstone Inn's hall, on the tray. He leaves it there for the staff to pick up, and returns to his room. He showers, and calls Harper before going to bed.

Widow avoids talking with Harper about Snyder or Mautner. He keeps his suspicions of Nabors to himself.

CHAPTER 29

Widow wakes early in the morning, hungry, like the cheeseburger he ate the night before never existed. So, he goes to call room service for breakfast, but his hotel phone rings. He answers it.

It's Snyder. He says, "Morning, Widow. Get dressed and meet me downstairs. They got a café with a breakfast bar. We'll grab breakfast and hit the road after."

"Okay. Getting ready now."

Snyder says nothing else. He just hangs up.

Widow gets out of bed, stretches out his limbs. Standing on his tippytoes, he touches the ceiling with the tips of his fingers. He rubs his face, which is growing stubble already. He checks it in the mirror. It's okay for now, but by the end of the day it'll breach uniform code unless he grooms it. He's not going to be back at Annapolis, not today. So he could leave the stubble, but he doesn't.

Widow fishes a shaving kit out of his rucksack and goes to work at the bathroom sink. Afterwards, he washes his face, cleans the stubble mess from the sink, and returns the kit to his rucksack. Next, he brushes his teeth, dresses in his street clothes, repacks his rucksack, and leaves the room, leaving the hotel room keycard on a nightstand, on top of directions indicating this is the process for what the hotel advertises as *easy checkout*.

The breakfast bar isn't much in size and scale. But what it lacks in that department, it makes up for in quality. The choices are good, and the food's better than Widow expects. He really likes their hot, fresh coffee. His only complaint is they don't offer to-go cups for it.

During breakfast, Snyder mentions he called his contact in the Bar Harbor Police, and they're all set to view the evidence today, as soon as they get there.

Widow asks, "What about Bernabe and Idris?"

"It's too early to call Bernabe. I'll try later to set an interview with them."

"Sounds like we have a plan. How's your feet?" Widow asks.

"What?"

"Last night, you said you had arthritis in your feet?"

"Oh, yeah. They're better now," Snyder says, and eats the last forkful of eggs off his plate, and nods at Widow. *He's not a morning person*, Widow thinks.

Ten minutes later, they're back on the road, driving north on I-290, heading to I-495. Before that, there's a moment when Snyder's tempted to ditch Widow and drive east on Route 9, to face Judge Mautner at his Boston courthouse and convince him to pause their arrangement to find and kill Stamos. Of course, he doesn't. And it haunts him the entire drive up to Bar Harbor. He doesn't know that for Peter Stamos, the deal's done.

CHAPTER 30

Five hours north on the interstate, Snyder and Widow arrive in Bar Harbor, where it's like stepping into a scenic holiday postcard from a forgotten time. The hordes of summer tourists are long gone, leaving behind a picturesque town, a treasure shadowed between the eastern white pines and the icy cold Atlantic. The air's misty and snowy. Saltwater scents the air. It's only hinted at when they first drive across Bar Harbor's town border, but it grows stronger as they near the ocean.

Bar Harbor winter streets are the opposite of the summer streets. In the summer, the streets bustle with activity, but now they're nearly deserted. Old nineteenth-century store-fronts that rule the town huddle under thick blankets of white snow. Christmas decorations add color to the bleak scene, but they don't erase it. Local store windows, frosted over from the cold, glint under a weak winter sun. Townspeople seem to hold their collective breath, like they're waiting for the thaw. But they'll wait for a long time.

The harbor leads to the Atlantic Ocean. It's hard to believe that months ago it teemed with sailboats and expensive yachts, but now lies dormant. The icy Atlantic water crashes against the shore, a dark, unforgiving shade of blue, not unlike Widow's Navy dress blues.

Local fishing boats dock at the harbor, but lie empty, swaying with the tides. The fishing nets remain folded and dry, as if they've never been used.

In the distance, Widow sees Cadillac Mountain soaring over Acadia National Park. Heavy snow dusts the mountain's peak. It stands tall, like a monstrous creature looming over the town, its intentions unknown. More pine trees line the mountain's slopes.

Bar Harbor hits Widow with a wintry stillness, a solitude of silence, like there are dark secrets embedded in town's shadows. But it's not a dead place. Life endures in the town, spirited and hearty, as evidenced by the house lights spilling out of windows, the smoke curling out of brick chimneys, and the holiday season cheer. Christmas banners, and lights, and wreaths, hang on front doors. The town's both gloomy and beautiful, all at the same time.

Their first stop is the Bar Harbor police station, which sits hunched on the edge of town. It's not much to look at. It's old and rundown in places, like a relic from a bygone era, which Widow guesses is the 1950s. The building's once-proud red brick façade is now weathered and worn, stained by the saltwater air, and scarred by long, harsh winters. Time has eroded the building's edges, leaving the bricks chipped and faded. The building has a blurred appearance, like a once-treasured photograph slowly fading.

The roof sags and paint peels off the window frames, curling away from the wood like it can no longer hold on. In a distant past, the front door stood strong, reflecting police authority, but now it hangs slightly askew on aging hinges. Widow wouldn't be surprised if it groans every time someone opens the thing.

The parking lot and sidewalks are cracked. Weeds sprout through the concrete. Empty flower beds covered in snow line the sides of the building.

As they pull into the lot, Widow says, "Wow. This looks neglected."

"It's really old. This station hasn't changed since the day I left to join the Bureau."

"When was that?"

Snyder pulls the Impala into a visitor space, slips the gear into park, leans on the steering wheel, and gazes out the windshield at the old police station. Old memories flood his mind and reflect on his face. He says, "I left at the end of eighty-seven. I just outgrew this place." Mia's murder was the catalyst for the devastation of the rest of his life. Even though working for the FBI sounds like an upgrade, a step up in career, for Snyder, it only looked good on paper. In reality, Mia's murder sent him into an alcohol and drug-induced spiral of obsession that destroyed his marriage, ruined his work life, and nearly drove him to suicide a few times. One day he woke up staring down the business end of his service weapon, ready to end it all, and that's when he quit drinking and quit drugs. He cleaned up, went to night school, and got his law degree, which led him to the FBI.

Sure, he's done some good in the years since joining the Bureau, but Mia's ghost lingers in the back of his mind. Several times a day, he swears he sees her rotting corpse staring at him in haunting silence. She stands just off the edge of his vision. And when he turns to look at her, she's gone.

Widow says, "Well, should we get to it?"

Snyder glances at where his wristwatch used to be. It's gone. He forgot the Fenian Boys took it. And Widow realizes he forgot to retrieve it for him. Snyder glances at the clock on the car's radio. It's six minutes till noon. He says, "Actually, they'll be at lunch for the next two hours. Let's grab some for ourselves, and we'll come back."

"The entire department will be at lunch?"

"Back when I worked here, there were only ten cops. Most of the dayshift would take their lunch at the same time, leaving a crew too small to be bothered with the likes of us," Snyder says, and glances around the parking lot. The number of cars in the lot is low, and not one person is in view. "I doubt the department's much bigger now. Let's grab lunch, and we'll come back after."

Widow says, "Okay, I'm not going to turn down a chance to eat, and get coffee."

The two men go to lunch. Widow calls Harper on Snyder's phone and checks in with her. She says nothing about his excursion to Bar Harbor, but something about her tone gives Widow the impression she's upset with him about it. It feels like she expects him to come back to her, and not go off on an investigation based on a wild theory about feet.

Widow asks her about it, and she denies being mad. So he lets it go. Perhaps it's not what he thinks? Perhaps it's more symptoms of her brain tumor?

He can't be sure, so he drops it.

After lunch, they've got more time to kill, so Snyder drives Widow by his old house on his old street. Besides a new paint job, the house looks the same, according to Snyder. At one point, Snyder parks the car and gets out. Widow follows, unsure what they're doing. He thinks Snyder's going to knock on the door, introduce himself as a previous owner, and ask to look around. But that's not what he does. Instead, he walks up to the driveway, kneels, and brushes snow off a small section, revealing his and his ex-wife's initials written in the concrete.

"Nancy and I did this back when we first paved a new driveway," he says.

"What year was that?"

Snyder faces away from Widow, and stares at the initials. They're old and faded. Tearfully, like just the letters drag him through the muddy memories of a life lost, he says, "It was 1979. That's the year we redid the driveway."

"I guess the new owners don't mind it, since it's still there."

"Yeah."

After another minute, Snyder stands, and says, "Okay, it's probably time. Let's go look at the evidence."

Widow nods, stays quiet, and follows Snyder back to the Impala, leaving Snyder's old memories in their shadow.

CHAPTER 31

Back at the Bar Harbor police station, a local cop gets out of his car, like he just parked as Snyder and Widow pulled into the lot. The cop wears a standard Bar Harbor police uniform, which is everything dark: dark blue shirt, black pants, black belt, and boots to match. His uniform's decorated with shoulder patches, the department's insignia, a gold badge, a nameplate, and the American flag. Everything's standard issue, including a gun safety-snapped into a holster on his hip.

The cop is older than Widow, but younger than Snyder. He's shorter than Widow, but only by a couple of inches. His hair is fair, but graying at the temples. He stares at the Impala as it drives in and parks. He stands still at the trunk of his police cruiser and watches, not quite suspicious, but beyond curious as to who are these two strangers.

Snyder parks the car but leaves the engine idling, like they're not staying long. Widow steps out of the car first. The cop stares at him like he's trying to register Widow's face. Widow notices the cop's gun hand lowers to his sidearm. It stops and rests on the butt of the holstered gun.

Snyder gets out, closes his door, and pulls his jacket in closer. He exhales, and turns to face the cop. He smiles, and says, "Terry, it's good to see you."

The cop stands up straight, as if Admiral Harrington just ordered him to, and looks at Snyder's face like he's seeing a ghost. He says, "Howie?"

Snyder steps around the nose of the Impala, and walks over to Terry. He says, "It's me."

Terry smiles heartily, and says, "Oh my God!" And he abandons his instincts to keep his hand near his gun, and throws his hands up. The two men step to each other and hug, patting each other's backs in the way that long-lost buddies do.

They banter for a long moment, and eventually acknowledge Widow's presence. Snyder introduces the men to each other. *Terry Gosford, meet Jack Widow*, and so on, that sort of thing.

After all is said and done, Gosford's hearty smile remains, and he says, "Come on into the station. We still make that good coffee."

This invitation perks Widow's ears up. But Snyder kills the dream right there, because he says, "We're not here to visit. Sadly, I'm reworking the case."

Gosford's hearty smile slowly recedes, and he asks, "What case?"

"The Harper case."

Gosford's smile completely vanishes, and his face gives away the horrible memories that flash through his mind. Which tells Widow this guy's very familiar with Mia's brutal rape and murder. He must've been here when it happened. Judging by his age, he would've been a young rookie back then. What a way to start a law enforcement career.

Gosford's voice cracks as he asks, "Now why would you want to go dig up that old nightmare? Haven't you put yourself through enough?"

Snyder's eyes flick down at the ground, like the question stings him. He looks back into Gosford's eyes, puts a friendly hand on his shoulder, and says, "We got new leads."

Gosford's eyes perk up, and he asks, "What leads?"

"Just something new. Something we failed to notice, or failed to follow up on, back in eighty-four."

Gosford looks intrigued. He asks, "What is it?"

"I'd like to review the evidence. And then I'll tell you. First, we gotta be sure we're right."

Widow already knows he's right. The shoes and socks are missing. They're not listed in an otherwise thorough evidence list in the police reports. But hearing Snyder say it this way to a co-investigator Widow supposes paints a new picture of Snyder's motives. He wants to see with his own eyes, that he, and others, missed evidence. It's evidence that might've caught their killer back then.

Gosford says, "Okay. I should call ahead for you. That evidence box has been in storage for years. The custodians will need time to fish it out."

"I already called ahead. I just need someone to take us up there."

Gosford looks at his watch, and says, "I can take you. I got to run inside and let them know first."

Snyder squeezes his old friend's arm, and says, "I'd love the escort."

Gosford nods, and runs inside to tell whomever he needs to about the arrangement. While he's gone, Widow says, "He seems friendly. He likes you a lot."

"He was the first officer on the scene. He saw Mia in the stairwell before I did."

Widow asks, "Really? It wasn't the college cops first?"

"Sure, it was them first, but Gosford was the first *real* cop. College cops don't deal with homicides."

True, Widow thinks.

Gosford finally rejoins them in the parking lot and offers them a ride in his cruiser. But Snyder says he and Widow will follow him because they need to go to the college after.

With that, the men get into their cars, and drive to the storage lockup.

CHAPTER 32

I t's early afternoon before Snyder and Widow get to see the box of evidence. They follow Gosford for nearly an hour, beyond the town limits, onto snowy country roads patrolled by the county sheriffs, and, finally, arrive at a complex that resembles a prison more than it does a state storage facility. But that's what it is.

They go through automated security gates and wind up parking in a lot ten times nicer than the Bar Harbor police station's.

Snyder could see the questions in Widow's eyes. He says, "County tax money is better than town tax money, because it's backed by the federal government, and divvied out by the state. The state pays for nice facilities like this using, in part, federal subsidies."

Widow nods, but clearly doesn't understand government red tape, and doesn't care to. They park, and follow Gosford into the building. There're various layers of security, also similar to a prison. Most of it is automated. There's one minimal security checkpoint with a guy in a tie and sweater vest. He's got a name badge hanging from a lanyard. It turns out he's a custodian. He takes Snyder, Gosford, and Widow through various corridors, and they end up in a room inside a chain-link fence, which makes Widow feel like he's entering a cage fight.

Two boxes are on a bench table in the center of the room. The custodian tells them this is all they have on Mia's case, and it's all of her belongings.

The custodian leaves them to it. And the three men sift through all the documents, evidence, and Mia's belongings. Widow's first to go over the item list. He confirms there're no shoes or socks listed. So, he goes through the actual items. Snyder pays attention throughout. But once Widow goes over it all a second time, Snyder talks with Gosford, catching up on sixteen years of how their lives have been.

After an hour of Widow studying everything, Gosford's radio blips, and he steps away to take the call. When he returns, he tells them he's got to go, some kind of police business back in town. He and Snyder hug again, and shake hands. Before he leaves, Gosford shakes Widow's hand and says goodbye.

Snyder and Widow go over some more of the case, things that Widow has questions about. The main thing he asks about is something Snyder didn't mention at the Vidocq Conference. He asks about a statement that Stamos made. In it, he claims he and Bernabe saw each other in passing, that before Bernabe claimed he entered the library, they saw each other from a distance.

Snyder says, "Yeah, Bernabe denied it. He said he never saw Peter, or Mia."

"Interesting," Widow says, and flips the pages of a report, and stops. He says, "So, Nabors is potentially our guy, and not Stamos, but it says he was in the police shack, near the radio. Bernabe is the one outside, on foot."

"Yeah, but there's no way to verify that Nabors was where he says he was. The campus is big, and snow-covered in December. It takes an hour to patrol it."

Widow flips the page again, reads, and says, "It says here Nabors spoke to Bernabe twice over the radio?"

"Sure, but he could've been lying about where he was."

"So, Nabors could've lied about being back in the police shack. Instead, he could've been in the fire stairs with Mia, raping and killing her."

Snyder's face flushes with anger and sadness all at the same time. He's both angry with himself, realizing an alternate storyline of Nabors killing Mia instead of Stamos being the killer, and he's sad just by realizing his own failures. Then there's one more element. Snyder doesn't know that Stamos is dead, not yet. But he knows he's the man who gave Stamos's name to Mautner. He's the one who pushed Mautner, and the Seven, to take action. He just prays he's not too late.

Widow asks, "Are you okay?"

"Oh, yeah. Just mad at myself."

"Don't be. You worked with what you had. It's a complete mess. Which is doubly ironic, because the janitor cleaned it up. If he hadn't cleaned and moved stuff around, you probably would've noticed the shoes."

Snyder says, "What's that?"

"It says here that a lot of Mia's belongings were found in the trash or in the library's lost and found. So, the janitor threw away a lot of stuff, and he turned other things in to lost and found. That's why his fingerprints are all over everything."

"Do think it could be him? And not Nabors?"

Widow says, "They could've been working together. I guess we'll find out. We're talking to Idris too, right?"

"Yes. When I called Bernabe, I told him we need to talk to them both."

Widow glances at a wall clock, and asks, "What time?"

"Idris is working the nightshift. Bernabe said to come after the college closes officially for winter break. Which's today."

"What time?"

"After six."

CHAPTER 33

After eighteen hundred hours, Snyder and Widow drive onto the empty Atlantic Shores College campus. In the middle of December the college lies dormant, like a group of stoic gothic buildings marooned in a sea of snow. Like winter birds flying south for warmer climates, the college students have all departed, leaving everything behind in an eerie silence. Only the howl of the wind and the whispers of the trees are left.

In the warm months, lush green ivy clings to the old brick buildings. Now, the ivy's turned brittle, like a network of frozen blood vessels, the life pumping within hibernates, waiting for the spring thaw. Dorm windows stare out blankly like unseeing eyes, overlooking the stillness that was once filled with the excitement and chaos of college life.

Majestic old giant trees are left skeletal after autumn's robbed them of their leaves. The trees cast angular, creepy shadows across snowy drifts. The student quad, once a bustling hub of intellectual conversations and laughter, is now only an empty, abandoned space. Dozens of benches line the quad. During the school year they're filled with students studying and hanging out. Now, blankets of snow pile high, nearly covering them completely.

The Atlantic Ocean crashes over the rocky outskirts of the campus. The air is cold and crisp, like frozen glass. Widow's surprised it doesn't constantly shatter. It's so cold that he fears he'll find ice under every gap in his clothing when he undresses to shower for the night. He fears he could find ice in his underwear, even. This is what his mom used to call *long john weather* when they camped in the wintry Tennessee mountains.

Widow looks out over the majestic campus in awe. He thinks that somewhere, hidden from view, are the secrets of Mia's murder, lying buried beneath the snow, as quiet and still as the college itself. But secrets, like everything else hiding below the snow's surface, don't stay buried forever. Everything thaws eventually. All secrets come to light. Something deep in Widow's gut tells him that long-buried secrets of the past will emerge tonight.

The guard hutch at the front of the campus is unmanned, but that's not surprising, as the campus is completely empty. Pathways are so snow-covered that the only reason they're visible is because of gaslights showing where they are. Like the rest of the town, the college's streets are snowplowed, so Snyder's able to drive them easily enough.

They drive on. Widow asks, "Are there any students left on campus?"

"Bernabe said they just closed today. I imagine today was the last of finals."

"So everybody high-tailed it out of here."

"Can you blame them?"

"Where did they all go?"

"A lot head south, but many went inland. Some even return home to the north."

"How can people survive winters like this?"

Snyder glances at Widow, smiles, and says, "Mainers are used to it. Besides, this ain't nothing. Stick around till January, if you really want to see something."

"It's that bad?"

"Ever heard the term *snowed in*?"

"That's a real thing?"

"You better believe it," Snyder says, and drives on, making a right, following the road, then veering to the left.

Widow looks up at the gothic buildings. Large windows stare down at him, like giant, lifeless eyes. It's so spooky, he thinks he nearly sees something move in every window he looks at. He reminds himself it's just a trick of the light—he hopes.

Snyder slows, and turns in to a parking lot. He pulls the Impala into a space under a streetlight, and parks it, leaving the engine running so they can get heat.

Widow looks around, and asks, "I bet this is like the night Mia was murdered?"

Snyder glances out the windshield, looks at Widow, and says, "It's eerily similar."

Widow nods, puts his hands to the heat blowing out of the vent, and asks, "Where's Bernabe?"

They both scan the area, and see no one. Snyder says, "He told me to park here and wait. I'll call him if he doesn't show up."

Just then, they hear the growl of an engine, and see big headlights coming toward them from around a corner. It's an SUV.

As it gets closer, they see police decals on the doors and the lightbar on the roof. The SUV drives up and parks near them. Both front doors open, and two men get out, leaving the engine idling. It's two men dressed in campus police uniforms.

Snyder looks at them, and says, "Okay. That's him." He gets out of the Impala, and Widow puts his gloves on, gets out, and follows. Snyder leaves his door open and the engine running.

They stop out in the snow, behind the taillights of the Impala but in the cones of the police SUV's headlights. The two campus cops are a few feet away. Both of them are armed. Both stare at Widow, hardly paying attention to Snyder.

The campus cop who'd been driving the SUV steps to Snyder, puts a hand out, and says, "Detective Snyder. You look older."

"Thanks, I appreciate it," Snyder says, and shakes hands with the cop. "It's FBI agent now."

"Oh, right. Sorry, Agent Snyder," the campus cop says. "And who's your friend? He looks too young to be FBI."

"This is Widow. He's liaisoning with me."

"Widow? That's it? Just one word? Like Prince?"

Snyder says, "It's his last name. He's military."

"I see," the campus cop says, and salutes Widow.

Widow stays quiet.

The campus cop stops shaking Snyder's hand, and asks, "What branch are you, Mr. Widow?"

Before Widow can answer, Snyder interrupts. He exaggerates, "He's with NCIS."

"Oh, I see. Why's the Navy interested in a nineteen-year-old murder?" the campus cop asks, and then he realizes. He says, "Nabors was a Marine. Is that the connection?"

"I can't comment on that. It's an ongoing investigation," Snyder says.

"I see, well, Mr. Widow, I'm Joel Bernabe," the campus cop says. He doesn't introduce the other cop. He glances at Snyder, and says, "I'm Captain now. Not FBI, but not too shabby."

"Not at all," Snyder says.

The men stare at each other in a long, awkward silence. Until finally, the other cop speaks. He asks, "Hey Joel, you need me to stick around?"

"Nah. Go on home. I got this," Bernabe says. "Leave the truck. Do one last round, on your way back to base."

The other cop stares daggers at Widow, like he offended the guy. Then the cop turns and pops his coat. He walks slowly away, but Bernabe stops him. He calls out, "Hey, Carl!"

Carl turns around.

Bernabe says, "Have a Merry Christmas! I'll see you at the New Year's Eve Party in a couple of weeks."

"Oh, Merry Christmas to you, Joel. See you then," Carl says, and walks away, into the snowy air. They watch him until he's gone from sight.

Bernabe looks at Widow, and says, "Don't worry about him. My guys all know about what happened nineteen years ago. They know, back then, I was grilled about it. Hard. So was Nabors, my partner. Carl's just protective of me."

Snyder says, "Can we meet with Idris now?"

"Sure," Bernabe says, and looks at his watch. "He'll be at the top floor of the library building, working his way down. This is his busiest night of the year, because he cleans that building from top to bottom before he leaves for winter break."

Widow asks, "Wouldn't the student dorms be the messiest?"

"Idris doesn't work the dorms. That's a couple of other guys. Idris only works these buildings here, "Bernabe says, and points at a cluster of tall buildings around the corner. "This way, gentlemen. Follow me," Bernabe says, and leads them down snowy paths toward the library.

Widow's glad he packed a beanie into his rucksack before he left Annapolis, because it's so cold out. He wishes he had a scarf. He walks on the outside of Snyder and Bernabe. He asks, "How long did you know Nabors?"

"We were friends for years. He grew up in my town. We were friends in school. He went off to the Marine Corps. And I didn't," Bernabe says.

"Are you still friends?" Widow asks.

"I've not seen him since 1985. He quit a few months after Mia's murder, and moved on. I think he blamed himself. He knew her. We both did. Such a sweet girl. What a terrible thing to happen to her. You know, truthfully, I should've left with him. But I stayed," Bernabe says, and grins at Widow.

They walk on in silence for a while, following a path barely visible to Widow and Snyder, but Bernabe knows it, probably could walk it blindfolded. Which makes sense because he's worked the campus for so many years.

Finally, Bernabe breaks the silence. He asks, "So, am I still a suspect, or something?"

"You weren't a suspect," Snyder says, not really answering the question, because he said *weren't*, not *aren't*.

Neither was Nabors, Widow thinks.

"That's good to know. Because it sure felt like we were, back then." Bernabe says.

"I gotta run all the bases. You know how it is?" Snyder says.

They turn a corner, and Bernabe stops. In front of them stands a massive gothic building with columns that Roman Emperors would be proud of.

Snyder says to Widow, "That's the library."

Widow asks, "That's where Mia died?"

"Yes. It's been updated now, but the updates are all in the computer equipment used inside," Bernabe says, and points up at a big boxy security camera over the front door. "Except for the security system. After Mia's murder, the school installed these. State-of-the-art, back in 1985. Now, it's ancient. That camera glitches all the time.

Snyder asks, "Are the students gone for holiday break?"

Bernabe says, "Affirmative. Most are gone. Finals ended today. There're still some stragglers. Not all kids have families to go home to. So they stick around until the last day the college allows them to."

"Where do they go?" Widow asks.

Bernabe shrugs, and says, "Beats me. Wherever they can, I guess."

They approach the library's massive concrete steps. It's like walking up to the New York Met. Bernabe asks, "So why're you guys really here after all these years? Did you get a break in Mia's case? Personally, I always thought that boyfriend did it."

Snyder says, "He probably did. My opinion on that's not changed. We're just revisiting everything. Sort of a refresher on the case."

They climb the steps. Widow notices shoe prints in the snow, going up the same steps. One set is probably Idris's, but there's a second set.

Widow's gaze traces the footprints back to the point of origin. They seem to vanish into the trees. He squints his eyes, trying to focus beyond the pines. He barely makes out a parking lot, with one streetlight high on a pole. In the pole's shadow he sees what could be a parked car.

Widow takes another look at the footprints, back to the steps, and to the front doors, which are locked. Then he notices the footprints lead off in a new direction. They go back down the steps, and to the right, and vanish around the building, like someone tried to get into the library, found it locked, and went around to try another entrance. Maybe it's one of Bernabe's cops checking the locks?

Widow stays quiet about it.

Bernabe unlocks the library doors with a key from a ring filled with keys. He pushes open two heavy doors. They creak on metal hinges. Overhead lights flicker on automatically, like motion sensor lights. The library's main floor has two-story-high ceilings. They enter a grand foyer with paintings on it like some kind of ancient Roman church ceiling. Up more stairs, there's a front desk, nestled away at the center of the main floor. Surrounding it are enormous rows of library aisles, with shelves and shelves of books. Study tables are situated among the massive stacks.

"This way," Bernabe says to Widow. Snyder already knows the way.

Widow follows the two men. They lead him to the center of the floor, and veer to the left, towards a pair of elevators.

Snyder asks, "Where's Idris?"

"He's here somewhere. I told him we were meeting him. Hey Anton!" Bernabe shouts. The call echoes throughout the stacks.

There's no answer. They walk through the lower level of the library. Snyder asks, "Why not radio him?"

"Oh yeah. Duh," Bernabe says. He radios Idris, but gets no answer. "This weather could be a thing. It happens all the time. Or he doesn't have his radio on. That also happens," Bernabe says, and smiles. He stows his radio away.

They walk through the lower level of the library. Bernabe glances at his watch, pushing the wrist of his jacket up to see it. He says, "He usually starts at the top floor."

"Even though it's under construction?" Widow says, and points at a small pink sign taped to the wall next to the elevators. Lights flicker behind him. The sign is handwritten, in very neat handwriting, like it's done by a librarian. The pink paper is just some kind of construction paper. The writing's in big black marker. The sign reads: *4th Floor Under Construction.*

Snyder goes up some steps and walks a few feet toward the elevator. Now, he squints his eyes, trying to read the sign. He asks, "You can see that from there?"

Widow stays quiet.

Bernabe smiles, and says, "Your boy's young. He's got those young eyes."

Widow remains quiet.

Bernabe says, "Yeah, it's being renovated, but part of it is functional. He likes to start up there."

Snyder shrugs. Widow looks around the library, the stacks of books, and the flickering lights. He points to a room in the back, with a sign above it that reads: *Student Computer & Study Labs: Quiet Please!*

Widow asks, "Is that where Mia was?"

Snyder looks where he's pointing, and stares, like he's trying to remember. The memory seems to be too far in the past for him to recall exactly. Bernabe looks, stops heading toward the elevator, and walks toward the study lab, instead. He says, "This's where she was studying with her boyfriend, when he left her. According to the boyfriend, I mean."

Snyder and Widow follow behind Bernabe. Fifty feet from the lab, Snyder points at a fire door to the left. He says, "That's the stairwell we found her body in. And that's where she was killed."

Widow nods, stops, and inspects both. Then, he says, "Can we look at them?"

"Sure," Bernabe says. Snyder doesn't object.

They go through the lab first. Widow looks at everything, like he's picturing it in his mind. Then, he points at the fire doors, and asks, "Can we look in there next?"

Snyder says, "Of course."

They go to the fire door and push it open. Inside, they see a large, empty concrete stairwell. Widow steps into it, and looks under the stairs. He asks, "Is that where she was found?"

Snyder says, "It's different, but I think so."

Bernabe says, "That's the spot. They just stopped storing things in here. Fire hazard."

Widow nods, and inspects the area, like he's imagining the rape and murder in his mind.

Suddenly, they hear a loud noise from above, like a door banging open. Bernabe looks up, his hand sweeping over his holstered gun, like he's stunned there's anyone else in the building.

Snyder sees his reaction, and asks, "You okay? You seem antsy."

Bernabe moves his hand away from his gun, and says, "Oh yeah. The sound just startled me. I wasn't expecting anyone else to be here."

Widow says, "Except for Idris?"

"Right. Of course."

Snyder says, "Maybe that's him?"

"Yeah, could be," Bernabe says, "Idris? Is that you?"

They listen, but there's no answer, and no more sounds. Whatever it was is gone now. Bernabe says, "Could've been the wind. Come on, let's take the elevator."

Widow says, "We can just walk up from here, right?"

"Look, kid, I've worked a long day. I want to get home to my family. So let's ride the elevator. It's better on my knees. I'm not as young as you are," Bernabe says.

Snyder says nothing. They follow Bernabe out of the stairwell. Before he passes through the door, Widow feels a draft, turns and sees the outside fire door is wedged open with a stone. He starts to mention it, but Bernabe and Snyder are both nearly to the elevator, so he ignores it, and joins them.

Bernabe escorts them onto the elevator. They get in and ride to the top in silence.

At the top floor, they step out. Construction plastic hangs all over the place, covering up demolished sections of old wall.

Some of the exterior walls have been sledgehammered, exposing the area to the frosty elements. A cold breeze blows and whips the plastic, slow, but consistent, like there's a giant outside the building, sleep-breathing heavily.

The construction floodlights illuminate the floor in a low, yellow light. Various lights glimmer and flicker, creating ominous dancing shadows. Other than the wind, and the low hum of construction lights, the floor's quiet.

They walk deeper in and start searching. The floor consists mostly of long hallways and empty offices. The lights continue to flicker, like on the set of a haunted house movie.

Bernabe walks ahead, through thick, dark shadows. He stops, and points at a work cart shoved to one wall. "There's his cart. So he's gotta be here somewhere," he says, and calls out, "Idris? Where are you?"

Bernabe moves faster, turns a corner, and leads them further into the darkness, into the shadows of the half-renovated floor. Snyder and Widow follow. Widow takes up the rear. He freezes, glances behind him, down the hall, past the elevators. He swears he sees someone standing in the shadows. But he continues to follow Snyder and Bernabe.

After they turn another corner, Bernabe leads them to an office suite with no door. There's a big empty hole where a new door will be installed.

Bernabe's the first through the door, and he stops. Snyder follows, with Widow right behind him. Inside the suite, icy wind gusts in through a missing section of exterior wall. It's where a new set of windows will be installed. More construction plastic's stapled onto the wall, above the large hole. It's stopped most of the snow from getting in, but not all of it. Wind whistles through holes in the plastic.

But none of that is what's got their attention. The three men freeze in place and stare up in horror. They've found Idris, and he's dead. The janitor's corpse hangs from the ceiling. There's a noose around his neck. It looks like he tied a noose, threw the rope over an exposed beam, and hung himself.

Only that's not what happened to him. Widow knows instantly, because Idris's hands are handcuffed behind his back. Seeing the handcuffs makes Widow glance at Bernabe's belt. He sees the leather pocket intended for handcuffs, and it's empty.

Snyder knows Idris didn't kill himself, but not because he sees Bernabe's handcuffs on the dead man's wrists. He knows Idris didn't commit suicide because of where Bernabe's gun is.

Bernabe points his gun at them and says, "I guess old Idris was beside himself with guilt. Once he heard you boys were coming, he didn't know what to do. He expressed his fear to me earlier," Bernabe says, and slowly circles Snyder and Widow, keeping his gun shoved in their faces.

The thing about Bernabe's gun, Widow notices, is that it's not his service weapon. His ASC-issued gun is still in his holster. The one in his gloved hand came from out of his jacket pocket. It's a snub-nosed revolver, like a backup weapon or a throwaway gun. Which worries Widow about what Bernabe plans to do to them.

Bernabe shoves the throwaway gun in Snyder's face, forcing Snyder to raise his hands over his head. Widow does the same.

Bernabe says, "You boys show up, and old Idris sees you. He can't stand the guilt anymore. But worse than that, he'll die before he goes to prison. And that's what he does. He hangs himself."

Bernabe reaches into Snyder's jacket, and takes Snyder's gun out. He stuffs it into his coat pocket, where his snub-nosed came from originally. Then he checks Widow for a gun. He's surprised when he doesn't find one. He steps back from Widow, and asks, "No firearm? What kind of cop are you?"

Widow grins, and says, "Who said I was a cop?"

"Who's this kid?" Bernabe asks Snyder.

Widow says, "I'm a midshipman."

"What's that?"

"I'm a student at the United States Naval Academy."

Bernabe looks confused, backs away, and starts laughing uncontrollably. He says, "Snyder, you brought your intern with you?"

Neither Snyder nor Widow answer that.

Snyder asks, "How're you going to explain us?"

Bernabe says, "Isn't that obvious? Old Idris shot you both, then hung himself."

Widow says, "Nobody's going to believe that."

"Oh, they'll believe it."

Bernabe stops chuckling, and starts shuffling and circling around them. He barks at Widow to move back, and stop in one spot. He glances back at Idris, and then barks at Snyder to move to a different location in the suite. He adjusts them, like he's positioning them where they'll be when Idris supposedly shot them, in the story he's fabricated to tell the police.

Frantically, Snyder talks, saying various things to Bernabe, like he's trying to stall, to buy more time. He acts more scared here than he did back in that alley with the Fenian Boys.

Bernabe ignores his babbling, steps from one side to the other, stops, and stares down the gun's barrel like he's aiming at Widow.

Desperately, Snyder tries to keep Bernabe talking. He asks, "You killed her? You raped and murdered Mia Harper?"

Bernabe stops aiming, lowers the gun, and stares at Snyder. Emotions seem to march across his face. He looks offended, like the very accusation insults him. His eyes tear up, like nineteen years' worth of feelings and regrets suddenly burst through him, and, unbelievably, remorsefully, the man cries. Angrily, he says, "Did I kill her!? Did I!? No! I didn't kill her! I didn't want her to die! I never wanted her to die!"

"Then why do this?" Widow asks, glancing at a hole in the wall nearby. It's big enough for him to ball up and roll through. If he doesn't get stuck on loose nails. He's thinking about making a move for it. He could get shot in the back. In fact, the odds are high that'll be the outcome. But Bernabe's going to shoot them both anyway. At least, running for the hole in the wall might give him a sliver of a chance of survival.

Tears stream down Bernabe's face, and he says, "I didn't want her dead. But I raped her. Okay? I did! He made me do it! We both did it! I didn't know he was going to kill her!" Bernabe goes quiet for a long beat. Then he says, "I know I should go down for it. I know. I've lived with the guilt all these years. But...but I got a family now. I can't let you ruin it. I'm sorry, Snyder."

A gust of wind blows through the hole in the exterior wall. They all glance at it. Widow glances at that hole in the interior wall. He wonders how much of the surrounding drywall is just drywall, no studs behind it. He could charge, and try to burst through it.

Bernabe turns back to them. He says, "I did see Stamos that night. In fact, there wasn't a plan in place. It wasn't premeditated. We formed it the moment, we knew they were in the library. I'd seen Mia around a bunch of times. She was nice to me. But it was Nabors who got me thinking about doing it to her. That night we were drunk and just talking. You know? We'd joked about it several times before. Not about Mia, about other coeds. But that night, she was the one who was all alone. I radioed Bret. He showed up, and...," Bernabe says, and pauses, "It got out of hand."

Bernabe aims the throwaway gun at Snyder. Widow interrupts him, and says, "You might as well tell us. If you're going to kill us, anyway. Don't you think Snyder deserves to know the whole story?"

Bernabe aims at Snyder, squeezes the trigger, but stops before the gun fires. He lowers it, wipes tears from his eyes, and says, "Yes. You're right, of course. We ambushed her. We waited till Peter left. Then I came in and distracted her. She always liked me better than Bret. While she was looking my way, Bret came up behind her. He grabbed her from behind. It was like a joke, you know. He dragged her into the stairwell. I came after. But once he ripped her clothes off. I knew I had to have some. Afterward, Bret got weird. I felt bad. Immediately. I didn't know what to do next. She kept sniveling and crying. Bret told me to go grab a cord from one of the lamps. So I did. I thought he was just going to tie her up, you know? But he strangled her right in front of me. And..." He pauses a beat, and says, "I let him. I didn't stop him. He convinced me we could just pretend it didn't happen. That Peter killed her. He was a punk kid anyway. But then, Bret got even weirder. He took her shoes and socks. He caressed her feet, like some sick pervert. I told him to leave her shoes and socks. But he said he needed them. He said they were his trophies."

Snyder and Widow both stare at Bernabe, disgust in their eyes.

Bernabe says, "Bret said he earned them. He killed her, and he took her socks and shoes. The next morning, we made Idris clean up. We told him we saw Peter arguing with her. We thought he would find her body, and call the police. We had a whole story concocted about seeing that punk, Peter, pushing her around. But Idris was dumber than we thought. He actually cleaned up the crime scene. He never found her. Then she was found on Monday by some kids. And you know the rest."

Snyder says, "Wow!"

"What? It wasn't me! I told you it was Bret! I told him not to take her shoes. But he insisted. He was a madman. He kept her shoes and socks, like a prize."

Widow asks, "Joel, where's Nabors now?"

Bernabe stares at Widow, like he's asking him to betray his friend. But Widow says, "Why not tell us? If you're going to kill us, then what's it matter?"

Bernabe shrugs, and says, "Sandbar."

Widow says, "Sandbar? Where's that?"

"Enough about Bret already!" Bernabe shouts, angrily. He's done with the questions. Widow sees it. Bernabe's already decided their deaths. There's no turning back now.

They're all quiet a long moment. Finally, Widow says, "This is going to look staged, Bernabe."

"Shut up!" Bernabe shouts, and he aims at Widow instead of Snyder. He aims, and squeezes the trigger. Widow stares him down, and doesn't blink. But Bernabe stops again, before the gun fires, because they all hear a noise.

Just then, the elevator doors ding open from down the hall.

Snyder shouts, "Help us!"

Bernabe pistol-whips him across the face with the throwaway gun. Snyder folds over. Bernabe calls out, "Hello? Who's there?"

No answer.

Bernabe points the gun at Widow, and asks, "Did you boys bring backup? You tell someone else to meet you here?"

Before Widow can respond, all the construction lights and floodlights flicker and shut off, like someone pulled the fuse out of the electrical box. For a moment, they're left in complete darkness. But the emergency lights click on, taking away the darkness but leaving lots of shadows.

Widow charges Bernabe. He crashes into him hard. The two of them go flying through a wall that is all drywall, and burst through it out to the hallway. Snyder's gun falls out of Bernabe's pocket and clatters to the floor. Widow scrambles up. Covered in dust, he dives for Snyder's gun. He grabs it, turns and aims at Bernabe. But Bernabe's quick. He's on his feet. Coughing dust particles out of his mouth, he scurries away, fast. Snyder tries to stand in front of him, to stop him. But Bernabe punches him across the chin, knocking Snyder out cold.

Once Snyder's on the ground, and out of his line of fire, Widow fires the gun. Bernabe dives into the darkness, and runs with all his might. The bullets miss, spraying through the other wall.

Widow scrambles to his feet and chases after Bernabe, but stops at the edge of the darkness, over Snyder. He looks down at Snyder, prods him gently with his boot. Snyder comes to, and stares up at him. His vision blurs, but he knows Widow's unmistakable silhouette.

Widow asks, "Are you okay?"

Snyder says, "Yes, I'm okay! Go after him! Be careful!"

Widow goes out into the hall, into the darkness. He holds Snyder's gun out in front of him, moving quickly but cautiously. He rounds a corner and sees Bernabe turn the distant corner, down the hall. He's headed toward the elevator or the fire stairs, Widow figures.

Wind howls, and the emergency lights flicker. Widow runs past more holes in the walls. The snow and wind gust against his face. He gets to the end of the hall, stops, and hugs the wall at the corner. He prepares, breathes, and jets out into the next hall.

Bernabe is at the other end. He fires in Widow's direction. Bullets spray randomly and hit the walls around Widow.

Widow crouches and returns fire. The bullets miss Bernabe, who turns and runs past the elevator, probably figuring it's too slow. Widow scrambles after him.

Bernabe blind-fires his weapon in Widow's direction, slowing but not stopping Widow. The bullets all miss. Widow returns fire, but the darkness swallows Bernabe, and Widow's sure he missed him. He pursues him farther down the hall. Then Bernabe makes it to the fire stairs. He bashes through the fire door and slams into the opposite wall. He scrambles down the stairs.

Widow's right on his heels. Bernabe leaps in long strides down three flights of stairs.

At the bottom, he's almost home free. He sees the final fire door, the one that leads outside, out into the cold, but out to freedom, to escape.

He's only feet from bashing through the door, until a man from the shadows steps out in front of him. The shadow man holds a sound-suppressed gun in his hand. He aims at Bernabe, and shoots him right between the eyes.

Bernabe's dead before he flops forward into the fire door. His dead weight shoves the door open. His body lies in the doorway. But unlike Stamos, Bernabe faces downward, like he's looking at the dirt and snow. He dies in the same fire stairwell where, nineteen years ago, he helped murder Mia Harper.

Widow's lost sight of Bernabe, but he knows he went through the fire door at the end of the hall. Hoping it's not a trap, Widow recklessly bursts through the door, and turns on a dime, nearly sliding into the wall. He scrambles to the railing, and peers over with Snyder's gun, aiming it down, in case he's got to shoot Bernabe.

And he sees Bernabe. The man is lying face down in the open doorway, between the fire door and the outside world. But Bernabe's not alone. There's a shadowy figure standing over him. Widow gets a brief glimpse of the man standing there, sees the guy take a picture of Bernabe's side profile. Then the stranger holds Bernabe's head up so he can get a shot of his face.

After the flash, the stranger drops Bernabe's head and looks up the stairwell, at Widow.

Widow shouts down to him, yells, "Hey! Stay right there!" But the stranger doesn't stay there. He runs out the open doorway, past Bernabe's body.

Widow can't shoot him. The range is too far. He scrambles down the stairs, taking several steps at a time. He gets to the bottom, leaps over Bernabe's body, and chases after the stranger. Blood has pooled from Bernabe's head out into the snow.

Widow runs after the stranger, but by the time he gets to the edge of the tree line, he sees brake lights and hears a car engine roar to life. The stranger peels out of the parking lot beyond the trees.

The scales of justice man smiles as he drives away.

CHAPTER 34

Snow falls gently from the night sky. Outside the library, blue police lights strobe, washing across the buildings and the snow. Three Bar Harbor police SUVs scatter across the closest parking lot. The police SUVs drove in so fast, their tires skidded across the snowy roads, making it appear, from an aerial view, that they were just making snow angels.

Bar Harbor cops walk the perimeter, circling the library. A few of them thread through the trees, following the scale of justice man's footprints. They find where he parked his car in the distant parking lot.

A cop's already taken Widow's statement. They walk him through the entire night, step by step. He doesn't lie to them about his involvement, Snyder, Harper, or The Vidocq Society, but he doesn't volunteer the information either.

The other ASC campus cop, the one Snyder and Widow met with Bernabe, returns to campus after the Bar Harbor police call him back. He stands thirty feet away from Widow, giving a statement to the local cops. Widow watches the guy. Blue lights splash across Widow's face as he leans up against Snyder's Impala. The window behind him is buzzed all the way down, and the heater blasts inside the car. Widow warms himself by covering most of the open window with his back, a clever life hack he hopes to remember.

The other ASC cop's face floods with confusion, learning the murderous facts about his longtime boss and friend, Joel Bernabe. The other thought that crosses his mind is he's been promoted, like how a commander in the field gets promoted to captain the moment someone shoots the captain in the head.

Snyder sits in the back of an ambulance, wrapped in a warm blanket, while a paramedic stitches a cut above his eyebrow.

Widow turns down being looked at by the paramedics. He's certain he's unscathed. He nearly borrows Snyder's phone to call Harper. However, he decides against it, because she's going through enough right now and doesn't need to worry about him getting shot at. Plus, he wants to help bring Nabors down before telling her about Bernabe. With all that, there's also the fact that Stamos is innocent. Seeing how Snyder's not taking that news well, Widow can only imagine how Harper will take it. For nineteen years, the two of them, and probably many others, believed Stamos killed Mia. Learning that she blamed an innocent man for nearly two decades and sent so-called evidence to The Vidocq Society to prove his guilt will eat away at her. Widow thinks that because he thinks he knows Harper better than anyone.

Most of the time in the past hour, when Widow glanced at Snyder, Snyder was calling someone repeatedly from his phone, frantically texting, or just blankly staring at his phone like he was desperately trying to get someone to respond to him. So far, it appears that whoever it is hasn't responded.

After Snyder's wound is stitched up, he speaks with the local cops for a long time. Finally, he shakes hands with the high-est-ranking one, and leaves the group, returning to Widow.

"What'd they say?" Widow asks.

"Nothing useful. Get in the car. We better get out of here while we can."

Widow, unsure of what that means exactly, climbs into the Impala's passenger seat. Snyder switches the wipers to the lowest setting so they can combat the slow snowfall, and they leave. Snyder takes them away from the college campus and onto Route 3, leaving Bar Harbor behind them.

Minutes later, Widow asks, "The cops don't want us to stick around?"

"I handled it already. We've got more pressing matters."

Widow asks, "Like what?"

Snyder says nothing. They drive on, getting off Route 3 and onto I-95. Snyder drives fast, just over the speed limit, and stays quiet.

Widow asks, "Who's the guy who killed Bernabe?"

Snyder glances at him, but doesn't answer.

Widow asks, "Where're we going?"

Snyder says, "We got to get to Nabors, before he does."

"Before who does?"

"That guy back there. He'll kill Nabors next."

"How do you know that? Who is he?"

Snyder doesn't answer.

Widow says, "We don't even know where Nabors is."

Just then, Snyder's phone rings. He takes his foot off the gas, and coasts to the right lane. He glances at Widow, like he's debating if Widow should hear his phone conversation or not.

Snyder looks at the phone's caller ID, and sighs. He answers it, and says, "Yeah? He's right here. Hang on." Snyder passes the phone to Widow.

He answers it, "Hello?"

"Widow, it's Cameron. Is this a good time?"

"Sure."

"Am I on speakerphone?"

"Nope."

"Listen, Peter Stamos changed his name to Sean Casey. He moved to Atlanta. He was an architect. He married and had several kids."

Widow asks, "What do you mean he *was*?"

"Someone shot him, yesterday morning. They rang his door-bell, he answered it, and they shot him dead."

"What about his family?"

"They weren't there. The killer waited for them to leave, and killed Stamos right after. It sounds like a contract hit to me."

Widow asks, "Any witnesses?"

"Yes. One. A neighbor saw a stranger outside Stamos's house. But it was raining. She can't identify him. But what sticks out to me is her description of him. She says he was average height, weight, and build, but she said there was something about him that was off."

"You mean like scary?"

"Yeah, it made me think of your mysterious scary dude. You mentioned the Fenian Boys told you about a man like that."

"Yeah," Widow says, and thinks about the stranger he saw kill Bernabe, take his picture, and run away.

"And there's more. I've been talking with an FBI agent who's working an investigation. I can't tell you the details, but I can tell you it involves your pal, Judge Mautner, and when I mentioned Snyder to her, she got real interested."

"What do they think's going on?"

"Widow, I can't comment on that. That's an FBI matter. But I'd guess that from the sounds of it, Snyder doesn't suspect a thing."

"No, I don't think he does."

Snyder glances at Widow, and then looks back at the road ahead. Widow tells Cameron about what happened in the library with Bernabe, and the stranger that killed him and got away.

Cameron says, "That sounds like a harrowing night. Are you okay?"

"Yes, we're good. We're trying to find Nabors now," Widow says, and thinks, *Although I don't have a clue where we're heading.* He asks, "Did you find him?"

"Not yet. But we still got to check a couple of previous known addresses for him."

Snyder glances at Widow, and gives him the signal to cut the conversation short. So, Widow says, "Cameron, I gotta go. I'll call you back when I can." He doesn't wait for her to say goodbye. He clicks off the call and hands the phone back to Snyder, who sticks it in the cup holder next to him.

"She say anything useful?" Snyder asks.

Widow stays quiet, glances at Snyder's gun bulge in his jacket. Then he stares back out at the lonely, dark highway ahead. There's silence between them for a long mile, leaving nothing but road noise and the slow whooshes of the wiper blades across the windshield.

Until Snyder breaks the silence. He asks, "Did she know what Sandbar was?"

"No," Widow says, pauses a beat, and asks, "Howie, where're we going?"

Snyder drives in the passing lane, accelerating the Impala to ten mph over the speed limit. He drives like they're in a rush, and like he knows where he's going. He drives on, heading south, back the way they came. He says, "We gotta get to Nabors."

"Why?"

"We have to get to him before he does."

"Before who does?" Widow asks, slides his right hand down to his side, and balls it up into a fist, for fear that he might have to use it. He glances at Snyder's gun bulge again.

Snyder ignores the question, and says nothing.

Widow asks, "Howie, who was that guy back there? Why did he kill Bernabe?"

Snyder doesn't answer that. Instead, anxiously, he says, "You heard Bernabe! Nabors is our killer! We got to find him!"

Widow breathes, and stays calm. He says, "Sure, but we don't know where he is."

Snyder says nothing. He doesn't react. He just stares at the road ahead, and drives.

Widow asks, "Do you know where he is?"

Snyder says nothing.

Widow asks, "Where's Sandbar?"

Nothing.

Widow says, "Howie, if you know where Sandbar is, we can call the local cops to pick Nabors up. We don't need to rush there. We can call Cameron back, and tell her to pick him up."

Snyder says, "No! We got to get to him first!"

"But why?"

Snyder pauses a beat. His eyes flick from left to right and back several times, like he's reading a teleprompter, searching for the right answer. But all that's in his vision is the dark, lonely highway. Finally, he says, "Because that shooter is after him next."

"But how do you know that?"

Snyder says nothing.

Widow asks, "Howie, did you have something to do with this?"

Silence. The wiper blades slide trickles of snow off the windshield.

Widow's right hand remains out of sight, and balled up in case he needs to use it. He asks, "Does Mautner have something to do with the man who killed Bernabe?"

No answer.

A tear wells up in the corner of Widow's eye, involuntarily and unwelcomed. He asks, "Does Harper know about this?"

No response. Snyder keeps his eyes on the road ahead, and nearly says something, but closes his mouth before he can utter a word.

Widow says, "Stamos is dead."

Snyder turns his head, and stares directly at Widow.

Widow says, "Cameron told me. Someone shot him yesterday at his front door."

"They know who did it?" Snyder asks, his voice choking up.

Widow shakes his head, and says, "A total stranger. Cameron thinks it was a contracted hitman. Do you know anything about it?"

Snyder pulls the car off to the side of the road. The tires dust up snow. Snyder brakes, and comes to a complete stop. Snow falls in the headlights. And the wiper blades slide across the windshield like a slow tormenting pendulum in the stillness.

Snyder turns to Widow, looks him in the eyes, and starts to speak, but he chokes up and says nothing. Abruptly, he unbuckles his seatbelt, opens his door and jumps out, leaving the door wide open behind him. He walks out in front of the Impala and stomps through the snow. The headlights wash over him in cones of light. Part of him is in shadow. He stands there a long moment, and stares up at the sky like he's trying to find the right words to say to Widow. Then he keels over halfway, putting his hands on his knees, and starts crying.

Widow glances at the keys in the ignition. He thinks about just taking off with the car and leaving Snyder behind. He could call Cameron from the nearest gas station payphone. But he doesn't leave. Although he probably should.

Widow gets out of the car, shuts his door, and follows Snyder down the snowy highway shoulder. Traffic is sparse, but just then an eighteen-wheeler flies down the interstate past them. Wet wind trails behind it, slapping Widow in the face. The eighteen-wheeler's taillights fade into the distance.

Widow stops several feet behind Snyder. He says, "That guy who killed Bernabe. He killed Stamos too, right?"

Snyder looks away.

Widow asks, "Did you have something to do with it?"

No answer.

Widow takes a deep breath, exhales, and asks the questions he really wants answered. He asks, "Did you have the Fenian Boys mug us? Steal Harper's money? Did you steal money from her to pay those guys at The Vidocq Society to hunt down and assassinate Peter Stamos?"

Suddenly, Snyder spins around to face Widow. One hand reaches into his jacket, and pulls out his gun. He points it straight at Widow's center mass.

Widow freezes, and slowly raises his hands up to surrender. He keeps his palms open, to appear non-threatening.

With tears in his eyes, Snyder says, "Yes! I paid for a hit on Peter! I wanted him to pay for Mia's murder! And I used Harper's money to do it!"

Widow takes a step closer to Snyder, and asks, "Does Harper know what the money was for?"

Snyder says, "Stop right there!"

Widow doesn't listen. He steps closer, and says, "Howie, you're not going to shoot me." He said it, but he wasn't actually sure about it.

Snyder fires a round in Widow's direction, but off to the left. The gun booms in the icy stillness. The bullet rockets through a cluster of trees off the interstate shoulder before it lodges in a far-off dead tree.

Widow freezes, and shouts, "Okay! Okay! I stopped!"

Snyder stares at Widow over the barrel, and says, "I saw what you did to that Fenian Boy who pointed a gun at you in that alley! Don't even think about getting in reaching distance of me! Or you get the next one!"

Widow looks into Snyder's eyes. He's still pretty sure Snyder won't shoot him. But not a hundred percent certain. So, he aborts his plan of trying to overpower Snyder for the gun.

Snyder says, "Yes. I helped order the hit on Stamos. What was I supposed to do? I thought he killed her. I thought he ran, and got away with it. Mia haunts me. I see her in my nightmares. I...I didn't know Peter was innocent. Now I have to stop this. I can't let the hitman kill Nabors too. He should rot in prison. I swore an oath. I have to right it. I'm sorry, Widow. I gotta stop the hit."

"Do you know where Nabors is? You know where Sandbar is?" Widow asks.

Snyder says nothing.

Widow says, "Howie, we can call the local police in Sandbar, and get them to pick him up. We can get Cameron to do it."

"No! You don't understand. These people will get him. They'll kill him no matter where he is. They'll kill me too. Probably you. All of us."

Widow says, "Howie, come with me. Turn yourself in. We can fight them. I can help you."

Snyder pauses, like he's thinking it over. But in the end, he keeps the gun trained on Widow, and circles around him. He keeps a wide gap between them so Widow can't rush him.

Widow follows Snyder with his eyes. Snyder returns to the Impala, gets in, slams his door, and activates the locks. He takes off in a cloud of snow.

Widow watches his taillights until they're gone from sight.

CHAPTER 35

Cold and relentless, the wind whips across Widow's face, numbing his ears and freezing his cheeks. Around him, night birds trill and warble through the trees. A half-moon shimmers high in the sky through a hole in the clouds. Widow walks for more than a mile, following Snyder, before he finds his rucksack. Snyder pulled over and dumped it and its contents on the side of the road. He must've searched through it for a phone, in case Widow was lying about not having one. Widow doesn't carry a phone. He doesn't like to carry phones, because carrying a phone is a great way to be found. And if Widow's outside somewhere, why would he want to be found? The whole point of going out is to be unavailable. At least that's how he sees it.

Ironically, at this moment, Widow wishes he owned a phone. They certainly have their upsides, like emergencies just like this one.

Harper's engagement ring is still in his pocket, which is good because it would've been hard to find it had Snyder dumped it out onto the snowy interstate shoulder. Widow had enough of a bad time trying to wrangle all the loose documents from Mia's case files. Snyder opened the document bag and dumped its contents out too.

Widow spends several minutes locating them and gathering them up. The one thing that really angers him about Snyder dumping his stuff out like this is his toothbrush. It's head down, with the bristles completely submerged in muddy snow. He sighs and leaves the toothbrush there.

Both his dress uniforms are balled up and laid out, and dirty from the elements. He gets everything, and stuffs it back into his rucksack.

With his rucksack slung over one shoulder, Widow walks with the traffic for six miles—if there were any traffic, that is. In ninety minutes, he's not made much progress to catch up to Snyder. He's going to need wheels to get anywhere. So far, in that ninety minutes, he's seen one more eighteen-wheeler, three cars, and one pickup. No one stops for him. He isn't sure if it's because of how he looks, or what. At one point, he thought perhaps he should put his dress blues or whites on. He could appeal to drivers' patriotism. Seeing a Navy man stranded on the side of the road in cold weather might entice someone to stop for him. But he didn't put them on, because one, they're grimy from being on the side of the road, two, he didn't want to get undressed in the cold, and three, in his mind he could hear his CO cursing him for the weathered state of his Navy dress uniform after being exposed to this weather. It almost felt like it would be desecrating the American flag. So, he didn't.

Widow takes a break, and glances behind him for oncoming cars. He sees a pair of headlights. The beams come on fast. They wash over the shoulder as the vehicle rounds a bend. Widow sees the tracks he's left behind him in the snow. Even though he's only walked about six miles, it looks like his tracks go on forever.

The driver switches to high beams, and slows, but doesn't cross over into the right lane. Widow stands on the shoulder and sticks a thumb out. He edges toward the no-man's-land boundary of the right lane and the shoulder. Hopeful, he waits.

The vehicle's another pickup, and it doesn't stop. At first, he's crushed by the rejection. But then the pickup's high beams wash over a sign ahead. It indicates there's an exit over the hill. And then the sign goes dark because the pickup's high beams are gone.

Rejuvenated, Widow picks up the pace, and hikes up the hill until he gets close enough to read the sign in the dark. It indicates there's an exit to the town of Newport, Maine, and it's just a mile away.

Widow continues to hump the rest of the hill until he's over it, and he sees the exit in the distance. Before the exit, a new sign rejuvenates his spirits because there's a picture of a gas station on it. As he jogs the rest of the mile he sees the gas station lights, high up on poles. He prays they have a payphone.

Widow runs down Exit 157 and enters Newport, Maine. He hauls it to a Chevron station. It's a trucker service station as well, but not a big one. Running down the exit, Widow sees three eighteen-wheelers parked in a lot at the back of the station. And that puts it at half capacity.

Widow makes it into the station's parking lot, and slows. He stops to catch his breath, removing the rucksack and setting it on the ground. He rests until his breathing returns to normal.

After a long minute, he picks his rucksack up and walks to the Chevron's front doors. He passes one of the cars that didn't stop for him. The driver and passengers sit inside the front cabin, under the dome light, eating gas station food. They shy away from his gaze—out of embarrassment, he supposes.

Widow enters the gas station and asks an attendant behind bulletproof glass about a phone. The guy says nothing, but points to the back of the store. Widow heads back there, towards a restroom sign. There's a line for the men's bathroom, with both women and men in it. An out-of-order sign dangles off the handle to the women's bathroom.

On the wall in the far corner, a single payphone hangs, unoccupied. Widow threads through the line, garnering sneers and rude looks from the people in the queue, like they suspect he's trying to cut.

At the payphone, Widow removes his gloves. He shivers as he reaches into his pocket. He fishes a quarter out and slips it into the coin slot. But the phone doesn't give him a dial tone. He looks at the price stickered on the phone. It's thirty-five cents, not a quarter. So he fishes out two nickels and drops them in, and is rewarded with a dial tone.

Widow dials Cameron's number from memory. As the phone rings, Widow holds his free hand out and stares at it. He's still shivering. The gas station heat isn't a thing of wonder. It blows, keeping the gas station's interior just around sixty degrees Fahrenheit. Still, it's light-years better than being out in the Maine winter for ninety-plus minutes.

A voice answers the call. It's Cameron.

Widow says, "Agent Cameron, it's Widow." Only when he says it, his teeth chatter, causing him to jitter the words.

"Widow? Where are you?"

"I'm in Newport, Maine."

"Where?"

"I'm off I-95. It's the 157 exit, at a gas station. You were right about Snyder. He pulled a gun on me, and ditched me."

"What? Are you okay?"

"Yeah, I'm good, but I need someone to pick me up. I know where Nabors might be. And we need to get to him, fast. And we need to get to Snyder too."

"Why? What's happening?"

Widow tells her about Bernabe, the Atlantic Shores College, Idris's hanging, and the mysterious hitman. He tells her about Snyder, and that he suspects Snyder's involvement in the assassination of Stamos and Bernabe. By the end of it, an automated voice interrupts the call and informs Widow he'll need more money to continue. He tells Cameron, gives her the number off the phone, and gets cut off right at the last digit.

Cameron calls him back, and starts with, "Tell me where Nabors is."

Widow pauses a beat, and says, "I'll tell you, but on one condition."

"Name it!"

"I want someone to pick me up and take me there, now."

"No way. We'll handle it."

"Not good enough."

"We're the NCIS. I'm a federal agent. You're just a midshipman in the Navy."

"I got you this far. I can't be on the sidelines. I've got stake in this. I need to see it through," Widow says, twists Harper's ring in his free hand, and stares at it.

"I don't know."

Boldly, or idiotically, Widow says, "If I don't go with you, then I don't give you the location. And this whole thing will get really ugly."

"Blackmail? You're trying to blackmail me? You know that's a felony?"

"Yes or no, Agent Cameron?"

"Okay, yes!"

Widow asks, "Do you know a place called Sandbar?"

"Sandbar?"

"Yeah, Bernabe mentioned it before he died. Find out what Sandbar is."

"Sandbar? I never heard of it? Where is it?"

"I don't know. But it's gotta be a place. That's where Bernabe said Nabors is."

Cameron says, "Okay. Does the gas station have large parking lot?"

Widow thinks about the truck lot in the back. He says, "It does. Pretty big, why?"

"Go outside and wait. I'll be there in thirty minutes," Cameron says, and clicks off the phone. Widow steps back and stares at the phone. The dial tone turns into a loud busy signal. And then the phone goes dead.

Widow hangs it up, and thinks, *Thirty minutes? How's Cameron going to pick me up in thirty minutes?*

Widow figures maybe she's going to have a cop or someone in uniform pick him up from the gas station. *But why did she ask about the size of the parking lot? Weird*, he thinks.

Since he's got time, Widow grabs two large gas station coffees. He pays, and drinks one there inside the gas station, while watching out the window and keeping an eye on the clock on the wall.

CHAPTER 36

After one-and-a-half coffees are down, Widow takes the last of his remaining coffee out into the parking lot with him. He holds it barehanded for added warmth, and waits for Cameron's emissary to pick him up. He watches the interstate, but sees no police or military vehicles. He only sees more weary travelers coming off the freeway to become customers of Chevron.

Widow waits, and sees no sign of a ride for him. Suspecting that Cameron duped him, he returns to the gas station, and sees it's been thirty-five minutes. Only five minutes over, but he's tired, cold, and angry. Maybe he's just hangry, so he goes inside and buys a protein bar. He eats it, and finishes his coffee before it turns cold. He throws the trash in a bin outside the gas station, puts his gloves on, and waits.

Suddenly, a *whop-whop-whop* sound comes from beyond the trees to the south, across the freeway. Widow walks to the consumer side of the gas pumps. Two customers pumping gas stop and stare in the direction of the noise. It grows louder and louder. The sound echoes over the trees and the freeway. Skeletal treetops blow from an incoming force of wind.

Widow sees what it is over the trees, but isn't certain what type it is until it crosses over into the northbound lane of I-95. He sees the running lights, and then he's sure what it is. Coming in his direction is a MH-60 Jayhawk helicopter. It's painted red and white.

The Jayhawk flies over the northbound lane, bending the top branches of the trees in the median, and then passes over the southbound lane. It's flying towards the gas station.

No way, Widow thinks. He doubts it's for him, at first, but the MH-60 Jayhawk is a Coast Guard rescue helicopter. It's the workhorse of the United States Coast Guard. The coast that the USCG would guard is eighty miles in the direction he came from. So what else would it be doing here, other than picking him up?

Cameron's an NCIS agent, which comes with perks, but he never imagined it included USCG helicopters.

The Jayhawk flies in over both interstate lanes, and hovers over the Chevron station. Widow runs out into the truck parking lot in the back of the station, realizing why Cameron asked about parking. She wanted an area big enough for a helicopter to land.

Thirty minutes ago, the truck parking lot had three eighteen-wheelers in it. But now, two of them are gone. So there's plenty of room for the Jayhawk to land.

Widow scrambles out to the middle of the truck lot, rucksack slamming into his back as he runs. He waves his arms frantically, as if the pilot didn't already see him. The Jayhawk hovers over Widow's head. The rotor wash whips his clothes and sprays snow in his face. A voice speaks over a loudspeaker attached to the Jayhawk's undercarriage. The pilot says, "Stand aside so we can land."

Widow realizes that in his excitement he accidentally ran to the middle of the lot, blocking them from landing safely. Widow nods, and sprints to one side, away from the helicopter.

Gas station customers come out of the Chevron, and watch in amazement as the Jayhawk descends to the parking lot. Widow realizes none of them have probably ever witnessed a helicopter land before. How many ordinary people have?

Widow's seen the Sikorsky SH-60 Seahawk several times at Annapolis. It's the US Navy's workhorse. The ones he's seen at Annapolis are used for training exercises. He's never actually ridden in one before.

Widow waits, and the Jayhawk lands on its wheels. The cargo cabin door slides open, and a figure emerges, waving at Widow to come to the door.

Widow grips his rucksack's strap and runs to the Jayhawk. He hops in the cargo door, and is led to a jump seat. He slips off his rucksack, and stows it near the seat. The cargo cabin door slides shut before Widow's even in the seat. Before he's even buckled in, the Jayhawk ascends.

Widow sees that the hand that ushered him into the Jayhawk belongs to a woman. She sits across from him, strapped into another jump seat. Her blond hair, pulled back tight, shines in the cabin's low light. The woman's green eyes beam, like million-dollar emeralds. She's wearing a bulletproof vest over a sweater, but underneath a suit jacket, and a scarf. She's seated, making it hard to judge exactly how tall she is. But Widow guesstimates she's around five-foot-one. She's probably ten or fifteen years older than him. It's hard to say for sure, because she glows with youth and energy, but a wise look about her overshadows it somehow.

Looking around the cabin, Widow sees that the woman isn't alone. There's the pilot, and three armed men. They're all in black tactical gear, like they're planning a night raid. There're badges patched on their jackets. Their agency's initials are displayed on the backs of their jackets. They're with the NCIS. One of them hands Widow a heavy headset, with a curly cord attached to the ceiling. Widow takes it, puts it on, and hears a faint crackle. He looks at the woman.

In a familiar voice, she says, "Welcome aboard, Widow."

Widow asks, "Agent Cameron?"

"In the flesh," she says, and looks him up and down. "You look like you've had quite a night."

Widow suspects if they were closer acquaintances, she'd have said, *You look like shit.*

Widow says, "It's been a long one."

Cameron smiles, and says, "It seems you've had a long week."

Widow asks, "Did you find out where Sandbar is?"

Cameron switches the channel on her headset, and barks orders at the pilot to head to their destination. Then she looks at Widow, and says, "It's not a place. It's a thing. *Sandbar* is the name of Nabors's boat. And yes, we found it. It's in place called Marchport, outside of Portsmouth, New Hampshire."

"Did you get some local police out to him?"

"I've contacted them. I told them the situation, but they're not going to be of any use to us."

"Why not?"

"Bad weather," she says. "They're dealing with severe cold, and lots of ice on the freeways. Most of their force is spread thin already. We're on our own for now."

Widow stares out the porthole, and sees the snow on the wind.

Cameron says, "At least, Snyder and this hitman will probably not get to him before we do."

Widow nods, and just stares out the porthole.

CHAPTER 37

Staring out the porthole, Widow sees they're traveling very fast, and the weather's getting worse. The further south they fly, the worse visibility gets. The pilot announces it over everyone's headsets a couple of times. He announces, "Reports don't look good for us. There's a lot ahead to worry about. We're facing adverse weather. I expect heavy snow and reduced visibility. You guys be prepared for potential turbulence and icy conditions."

Cameron responds, "Just keep monitoring the weather and stay sharp."

The pilot nods and responds in the affirmative. Then he mentions distance and his estimated time of arrival, but that part's not shared in Widow's headset. So he does the calculations in his head. From the Atlantic Shores College campus in Bar Harbor, it's less than a four-hour drive. Snyder has a head start, but the Jayhawk could probably travel at 180 knots, or about 207 miles per hour. Which means it should take nearly two hours to get to Marchport.

It turns out not to be *nearly* two hours to get there; it's exactly two hours. They arrive in Marchport. Cameron's communicating with her guys and the pilot over a different channel than the one she talks with Widow on. And the wind and the rotor noise is too loud to hear her outside of the channel.

The Jayhawk slows, and the pilot announces they've arrived. At least, Widow's sure that's what he said, because they've slowed. He leans forward and stares down from a porthole. Visibility is spotty. But he can make out the ocean, and sees the crashing waves below. In normal times, the waves probably don't crash like this, he figures. If they do, it was a stupid place to build a harbor.

The Jayhawk circles a huge, rundown boat harbor. It's jampacked with newer boats, which probably had no choice but to dock here because of this storm, and old rundown boats to match the rest of the harbor. The old boats are home in their boat slips. The newer ones are anchored in the spare, temporary slips. Some boats have dim lights shining out of cabins. But most look empty.

The old harbor may be huge, but Widow sees no ships, or even space for them. The harbor's largest vessels are fishing and shrimping schooners. There're a couple of small yachts. Desperate to dock somewhere, they ended up here. With people leaving their boats docked for the winter, the preferred harbors were too overcrowded to support them before the storm.

Icy waves crash at the entrance to the harbor. The ripples lift and sway the docked boats, making it hard for Widow to believe that anyone onboard is sleeping.

It's late at night, suggesting the boats with lights on have people staying in them. Perhaps some of them live there full time. Others may only be taking shelter for the night. But the temperature's so cold, it surprises Widow the passengers can stay warm enough.

Widow sees no one walking the docks or the piers, not yet. There're several boat launches. All are empty. There's an enormous parking lot with several snow-covered vehicles. The roads around the harbor look barely drivable.

Suddenly, but somewhat predictably, they hear pounding outside the helicopter. Widow glances out the porthole. Visibility has dropped below the Coast Guard's safety ratings for flying. The pilot squawks over all channels, says, "Hail storm!"

Widow sees it before the pilot announces it. Huge chunks of ice slam into the rotors and the sides of the helicopter.

The pilot says, "We need to land, or get out of here!"

Cameron says, "Find a landing spot!"

The Jayhawk circles the harbor again. The pilot can't land in the water. And the piers aren't large enough. Plus, there's no telling if they can hold the helicopter's weight. A MH-60 Jayhawk, decked out with all the Coast Guard's rescue equipment, weighs more than 14,500 pounds. And that doesn't account for a load of six people. It's too heavy to risk landing on rickety-looking piers constructed from wood.

There're potential areas on land, but none look safe enough to clear the rotor blades. They might make it down, but helicopters have to take off again. Their best bet is the parking lot or the road.

As they circle the huge lot, looking for a safe landing space, Widow sees Snyder's Impala. It's parked in the lot. He tells Cameron. She acknowledges it, but reminds him they've got to find a safe spot to land first.

Widow searches for Snyder. He sees no one.

The pilot says, "There's a spot right there." And Cameron looks out her porthole. She approves it. The pilot takes the helicopter down for a landing. The hail's let up slightly, maybe because they're over land now. But the wind's still blowing around a lot of snow. The Jayhawk gets close to the ground, but then violent gusts of wind blind the pilot by covering the windshield with snow. The pilot calls back, "I don't think I can land."

Cameron unbuckles her seatbelt, turns around, faces the cockpit, and stares out the windshield. She assesses the situation and agrees with the pilot. She turns back to her guys, and says, "Okay! We're going to do a hover jump! Get ready!"

The three night raiders get out of their seatbelts and seats, and check their weapons. They're all carrying sidearms and submachine guns. After they're all ready, the leader informs Cameron. He says, "We're good to go!"

Cameron says, "Take them alive!"

Widow unbuckles his seatbelt, and stands, like he's going out behind them.

Cameron puts a hand up. She says, "Whoa! You're not going anywhere!"

"But you said I could be a part of it."

"No, I said we'd pick you up, and bring you along. That's more than I should've done. If something happens to you, I'll be in all sorts of trouble. It could even ruin the investigation. No, you're staying here with me. Let my guys do their jobs."

Widow slow-nods, and calls out, "Do they know what Snyder and Nabors look like?"

The leader says, "We got this, kid!"

Widow glances out the cargo cabin door's porthole behind them. Light hail and snow stream in the wind past them. He says, "Don't shoot Snyder! He's FBI! He's misguided, but still one of us!"

The leader grins at him, says nothing, slides open the cargo cabin door, and one by one, the night raiders jump out of the hovering helicopter, landing on the snow below. The last one signals to Cameron they're all safe and ready to search. She closes the door and orders the pilot to take them back up. He warns that the hail can get bad again at any moment. She acknowledges the risk, but tells him to circle the harbor anyway.

CHAPTER 38

The weather's bad, but the scales of justice man doesn't charge by bad weather. He doesn't charge by the danger. He charges by risk and legal exposure. For the first time, he's got to raise his rate above what Mautner thinks he's paying him, because the risk and legal exposure just went up.

With a ski mask covering his face, protecting him from the elements, the scales of justice man watches from the snowy shadows as a USCG helicopter flies in over the Marchport harbor and circles the area. At first, he's confused about why a rescue helicopter circles the place. But once they hover over the ground and three armed SWAT-looking cops hop out, he knows he's got more risk than he bargained for.

Still, he's never missed a mark. He's never backed away from a target, not once he's accepted the contract. He doesn't plan to start now. Nabors, Snyder, and that Widow kid all have to go. Mautner's orders.

He's got no idea where the kid is. But he knows Snyder's here because he followed the guy. And the Impala in the parking lot confirms it.

The helicopter takes off after the three cops leap out of it. They must be feds, he figures. Although, he's never heard of the FBI using the USCG as transport before. Still, in this weather, it makes sense.

The scales of justice man threads between buildings, staying low, staying behind trees. He's lost sight of Snyder, but that's okay. That old FBI has-been isn't leaving the harbor—not alive, anyway. The scales of justice man's already shot all four of the Impala's tires out. The only way Snyder's getting away is on that helicopter. So the scales of justice man has got to take care of it first.

If he had a rocket launcher, he'd shoot the bird out of the sky. However, with the bad weather, he may not have to. He figures the three SWAT cops are his only genuine concern. The pilot's not going to hunt him down. And if there's anyone else onboard, they're no threat, or they would've gotten out too.

He's armed with his suppressed pistol. It would be nice to have more firepower. But he'll make do. He's good at making do.

The scales of justice man glances up at the helicopter. It circles around the harbor like it's searching for Snyder too.

The scales of justice man isn't picky. He's not trying to play with his prey. He's going to use his biggest strength, the element of surprise.

The SWAT cops form up in a three-man pattern and head towards the harbor, and the boats. This confirms what the scales of justice man suspected that Nabors owns one of these boats. But he'll deal with that scum after the others.

The scales of justice man waits until they're all bottlenecked on the first pier, the entrance to the harbor. He already walked the same boards ten minutes ago. He knows the squeaky ones, and the safe ones. Of course, it doesn't matter that much. The hissing wind muffles most sounds anyway.

The scales of justice man moves in behind the three SWAT cops. They're looking ahead, scanning the boats and the piers in front of them. They're not even thinking about what's behind them.

He gets close enough to the one in the rear that he could leap forward and tackle him. But he doesn't.

The scales of justice man raises his gun, lining up his shots. In a violent flurry, he shoots the rearmost one in the back of the head, two shots. Blood mists out his face, with the two exiting bullets. The rearmost SWAT cop crumples forward. The second SWAT cop turns, but doesn't make a complete rotation. He never sees what's coming. The scales of justice man shoots him, three shots. Two bullets hit him just above the collarbone, bottom of his neck, inches above his bulletproof vest. The third bullet bursts through the guy's cheek, and exits out his ear. More red mist sprays into the air.

The leader makes a complete rotation. He sees that red mist, sees his partners crumpled on the pier. The wood squeaks under their bodies. He raises his submachine gun, aims, but doesn't pull the trigger.

The SWAT cop never gets to pull the trigger because the scales of justice man empties his gun's magazine into him. Bullets rip through the SWAT cop's neck and face, and he collapses into a pile of dead bones, tissue, and SWAT gear.

The scales of justice man ejects his magazine, but he doesn't let the magazine fall away, haphazardly, like in the movies. He pockets it in his jacket, and reloads the gun with a new magazine. He checks the SWAT cops to make sure they're dead.

On the last one, he finds an earpiece with a curly wire attached to a radio, like the Secret Service uses. He takes it out and puts the earpiece into his ear, and listens.

After a long minute, he hears a woman's voice. He figures she must be in the helicopter circling the harbor. He glances up, and sees it not too far from his position, but going the wrong way. He thinks for a moment. Then, he glances over at the dead SWAT cops, and their submachine guns. He grins.

CHAPTER 39

"Guys, are you there?" Cameron calls desperately over her radio. She was just speaking with the night raider leader, and now she hears nothing but static. She stops talking, stands up, and goes from porthole to porthole, trying to catch a glimpse of her guys.

"I don't understand. Where the hell are they?" Cameron asks.

Widow stays quiet.

The pilot calls out to her over all channels, not caring what Widow hears, and says, "It could be the weather. Maybe they're not getting a signal."

They circle around over the water, staying high enough to get a good aerial view, but low enough to make out what's what, and who's who.

Cameron says, "Maybe. Get back around to the parking lot. Maybe we'll see them in passing."

The pilot nods, and takes them back around over the vast complex of boats and piers, to the parking lot. Widow gets up and stares out the opposite porthole from Cameron's position.

He reads the boats, searching for the *Sandbar*. The hail starts up again, pounding the helicopter. It's not bad enough to worry about. Not yet.

In the blink of an eye, Widow spots movement. It's down on one of the piers, between boats. He sees a flashlight beam and a bit of a jacket. He leans against the glass. He sees the man holding the flashlight. But it's a quick glimpse. The flashlight goes dark, and the man vanishes from sight. Widow only saw the man for a moment, but he thinks it's Snyder. It looked like him.

He says nothing about it.

The helicopter flies around, and passes over the harbor's parking lot entrance. Cameron stares out a porthole in terror. She barks orders at the pilot.

"Hold on!" she says. "Take us down." Cameron moves into the cockpit, and points at a pier. She says, "Right there."

The pilot yaws the Jayhawk and descends to less than a hundred feet from the ground. Then the helicopter hovers. Widow joins them in the opening to the cockpit.

"Oh, no!" Cameron says.

Below the helicopter, on a pier, they see the night raiders—or rather, the pile of dead bodies that used to be them.

The pilot says, "They're all dead. How?"

Cameron says, "We just dropped them off. How's this possible?"

The pilot says, "A group of professionals must've ambushed them."

Cameron doesn't cry, but she tears up, like it's the first time she's lost cops under her command.

Widow can't see them that well, so he moves to the porthole in the cargo cabin door and peers down at them. He says, "It's him."

Cameron asks, "Who?"

"The hitman. The guy from Bar Harbor. Probably the guy who killed Peter Stamos," Widow says. He leans away and peers down in several directions, like he's searching for the hitman. But he sees no one.

The pilot asks, "You mean one guy did this?"

Cameron says, "Not possible."

Widow looks at her, and says, "It's possible."

The pilot lowers the helicopter, like he wants a better view.

Suddenly, Widow charges the cockpit, like he's going to leap into the other pilot seat. He stops in the opening, and shouts, "No! Don't take us lower!"

But it's too late. A dark figure appears from out of the cabin of an empty boat, steps up onto a second-level cockpit, and shoots at the helicopter. He's using a dead night raider's submachine gun. He's set it to full auto.

Widow grabs Cameron, and dives to the floor with her. He shields her body with his. Bullets spray through the thin parts of the helicopter's undercarriage. Bullets fly through windshield. Navigational and piloting equipment explodes and sparks. The pilot fights to keep them airborne. He pulls the throttle back, bringing the helicopter's nose up.

Widow and Cameron roll around and bounce violently off various parts of the back of the helicopter. They bounce around like they're in a pinball machine.

The pilot fights with the damaged controls, trying to escape the bullet fire. But the bullets keep coming.

The scales of justice man unloads an entire magazine at the helicopter. He ejects the empty one, and reloads. Then he shoots the other magazine, aiming for the Jayhawk's vital mechanical organs. Sparks fly off the helicopter's under-carriage.

The Jayhawk flies out to sea.

Moments later, Widow stands and checks Cameron. He asks, "Are you hit?"

"No. I'm fine. Check the pilot."

The helicopter is flying, but it's flying crooked. Various alerts beep from the cockpit. And several onboard machines and measuring instruments spark, but nothing's on fire. At least, nothing's on fire inside the craft. The outside may be a different story. Luckily, the hail and snow will most likely put out any fires on the body. The rotors still spin, they're mostly upright, and still in the air. That's the important thing.

Widow makes it to the cockpit and checks the pilot. Cold gusts of wind slap his face. The windshield's partially gone, and what's left is covered in bullet holes.

Widow grabs the pilot's shoulder and asks, "Are you okay?"

The pilot says, "Yeah. I'm okay."

But Widow feels something wet on his hand, from the pilot's shoulder. He lifts his hand, and inspects it. There's blood on his glove. He says, "You've been shot."

The pilot says, "I think it's only my arm." But blood trickles out of his mouth.

Widow unbuckles the guy, and checks the rest of his body aggressively. He finds one bullet's gone through the pilot's arm, and another's grazed his leg. But there's nothing serious enough to be fatal. The trickle of blood from his mouth is just where he bumped his head in the struggle to stay upright through all the gunfire.

Widow tells him all of this, and says, "You're going to be fine. But what about the bird?"

The pilot says, "I doubt she'll make it far. But I can land us somewhere. Maybe back at that parking lot."

Widow looks out the windshield and sees the crashing waves. Then he sees a boat at the end of one pier, with a light on. A man steps out of the boat to check what all the commotion is. He stretches his arms, like he's been awakened from a deep sleep. Widow's not sure whether the guy heard the gunshots or not. With all this hail and wind, he might have, or he might not have. But he heard the helicopter overhead. He looks right up at them.

The thing Widow notices about this boat is the name. It's the *Sandbar*.

The pilot coughs violently. And the helicopter yaws, forcing Widow back a step. He looks at the pilot again. There's more blood trickling out of his mouth.

Widow says, "Okay. Take us back to the parking lot. Stay over the water until we're south, away from the guy with the submachine gun. But first, go low, over the waves." Widow pauses, and searches for a spot. He points to a clear spot with no boats. He says, "There. Get as low as you can."

The pilot asks, "What for?"

"Just do it."

The pilot nods.

Widow returns to Cameron. He says, "I'm all you got now."

The pilot flies the helicopter to where Widow pointed, just off several meters from a pier, and a boat in a slip. He calls back to Widow, and says, "Okay, we're there. Not sure how long I can stay in this position."

Widow goes to the cargo cabin door, slides it open, and stares at Cameron. She says, "Wait! Take my gun!"

Widow puts a hand up, and says, "Keep it! Call the cops when you land. Tell them to send all they got."

Before Cameron can protest, Widow falls backward from the helicopter. He falls dozens of feet and crashes into the surf below.

Cameron darts to the open door, and stares down, looking for him. But all she sees is the rippling water he splashed through, and the crashing whitecaps.

CHAPTER 40

In the water, Widow regrets jumping from the helicopter so recklessly. But he feared that if he didn't take the leap, Cameron would talk him out of it. Or he might chicken out. And he has to find Snyder, and stop the hitman.

The ocean's freezing. It hits him like a ton of frozen bricks. His veins bulge in his arms like the blood inside is going to freeze over.

Widow surfaces to see Cameron's worried face staring down at him before the pilot spins the helicopter's nose south. The helicopter flies away, tracing the coastline to avoid the hitman shooting at it.

Widow swims to the nearest boat, which sways up and down with the waves. The swim is hard, the hardest swim he's done yet. He's a pretty good swimmer and has always liked the water. But he's going to need a lot of training to become any kind of Special Forces swimmer. If he was auditioning for the Navy's swim team, they'd laugh him out of the water.

Sluggishly, Widow swims to the boat. He regrets leaving his bomber jacket on. Harper will be angry that he's ruined it.

Besides that, it's also weighing him down. It turns out leather jackets soak up water.

He makes it to the boat, reaches up, grabs the gunwale, and hauls himself up onto the deck. He drops onto it, and rests. He shivers from the icy water, but just concentrates on breathing.

After a long minute, he's calm, but still shivers. He scrambles to his feet, realizing that the boat may not be empty. The last thing he wants is for a boat owner to shoot him for trespassing. But the boat's unoccupied.

Widow searches it as quickly as possible, looking for anything he can use. He's mostly hoping for warm clothes that would fit him, or a weapon. He finds neither.

There's no time to waste, so he sucks up the chill, and stumbles onto the pier. He stays low and follows the pier back to the next branch. He looks to the north, and sees the *Sandbar*. The man onboard is gone. He thinks it was Nabors, but he isn't sure that's who he saw.

Widow shivers and trembles with each step. He's trying to be quiet, in case he stumbles upon the hitman. So far, if the hitman had been within twenty feet of him, he would've heard Widow's teeth chattering.

Widow makes it to the end of the pier and comes to a large fork. There's a good-sized area with a covered bulletin wall. He walks over to it and gets under the roof. It helps to keep the hail and snowy wind off him for a moment.

Various announcements about the fishing season, job offers, and boats for sale cover the bulletin wall. There're a couple of photocopied ads for prostitutes. There're pictures of girls on them. One headline reads: *To get your boat rocking call Jocelyn!* There're several more examples like that.

But there's also a section of bulletin wall that's labeled: *Missing Persons.* There're several posters of missing women. Widow looks at the faces. Every one of them looks young. They all share a similar story. *A young girl is last seen in blah blah. Call so and so, if you've seen her.* A couple of them offer big cash rewards.

The locations of each girl's disappearance all seem to be within a hundred miles of Marchport. The timeframe also seems pretty recent. Several of them are in the last year. Many of the photos have faded so badly, he can't even make out a face. The elements would destroy them completely if the glass didn't protect them.

Widow presses on, leaving the bulletin wall and the missing girls behind. He sneaks along the pier, unaware of where Snyder and the hitman are. But he knows where Nabors is, so that's where he's going.

He snakes along the piers. Boards creak under his steps. Other boards creak around him, making him paranoid that the hitman's creeping up behind him. Every time he spins around to check, there's no one there. Only shadows surround him.

Widow stops at another fork in the piers, looks left, toward the hitman's last known location and the three dead night raiders. Widow sees no one coming. He looks right. It's the direction of the *Sandbar*. He goes down its pier. Carefully, he walks along the pier, passing swaying boats, and shadows.

Widow makes it to the *Sandbar*. He reads the name on the boat's stern. The boat is a forty-five-footer, which is pretty nice, but it's an old boat. The lettering on the name, along with the rest of the boat, has seen better days.

Lights are on below deck. Widow hears coughing, and low rock music playing, something with screaming, and undiscernible lyrics. The light is red, like the red alert on a nuclear submarine. Which is weird—or evil, he thinks.

Widow steps onto the boat. He creeps to the stairs that lead below deck, when a step creaks loudly, like the boards of the pier, only much more audible under the boat's cover. He freezes.

Crap, he thinks, and waits for a sign that Nabors heard him. Instead, he hears something horrifying. It's the sound of whimpering. It sounds female. And it's piercing, the way a terrified child sounds.

The music comes back on, and the whimpering's drowned out.

Widow gets to the bottom of the stairs. He steps into the low red light. The cabin of the boat starts with a decent kitchen, then a sitting area, and a nook with benches that could double as beds.

The music plays over loudspeakers throughout the cabin.

Widow sees him. Bret Nabors lies on one of the benches. His arm stretches over his face, covering his eyes. He snores lightly. There's a near-empty bottle of vodka on the tabletop next to him.

Widow starts to approach him, but freezes because he hears a noise behind him. He turns around, quietly, and looks. Behind the stairs, going toward the boat's stern, there's a short hallway. Two doors are back there. Both are closed. But Widow hears whimpering coming from behind one of them. It sounds like crying, like a girl crying. It might even be a child.

Widow can't help himself. He's got to know. So he leaves Nabors, and sidles down the hall, boards creaking under his bulk. The boat rocks and sways. He gets to the first door. The whimpering's so low, he can't tell where it's coming from, not directly.

Slowly, he slides the first door open. It's a small bedroom. The bed's empty, but there's a closet. The door's closed. Widow peeks back toward Nabors. The man sleeps, like he's slept through worse storms at sea. Plus, he's probably blackout drunk, Widow figures.

Widow enters the bedroom. The bedroom is so small, his tall stature feels like it's crushed in, like a sardine in a can. He grabs the closet door handle, and slides it open. He stares in horror at the contents.

Girls' shoes fill the closet. Socks are rolled up and stuffed inside each pair. Countless pairs of women's shoes are stacked from floor to ceiling, in a kind of methodical chaos. Some shoes aren't even big enough to belong to a woman. Many of them are small enough to only fit teenagers. Some are smaller than that.

And they smell. They smell like old, unwashed shoes and socks. There's dried blood on many of them.

Widow steps back, and backs out of the bedroom. He glances back at Nabors. The maniac is still asleep.

Widow goes to the other door and slides it open. There's a girl inside. She's on the floor of the shower. Nabors had handcuffed her hands around a nozzle. Blood dries around her wrists, where she's tried to pull herself free, without success.

The girl might be eighteen. She might even be younger. Widow can't tell. Her hair's matted. Dark mascara runs down her face from crying. She's completely naked, except for a pair of sneakers and socks on her feet.

She looks up at Widow, and cringes. She scooches further into the shower stall, trying to escape him, like he's a monster worse than the one she knows.

Widow immediately recognizes her. He saw her face on one of those missing person posters, back at the bulletin wall.

Widow wants to cover her up with something, but all he sees is a used bath towel hanging off a hook. He can't imagine that she wants covered up with the towel used by the man who's abducted, held her captive, and probably raped her. So, he backs out of the bathroom. Finding the handcuff key is more important than covering her.

Widow doesn't know where it is, but he knows the man who does—*Nabors*, he thinks, and clenches his fists, both of them.

Widow realizes something's different. The music still plays. The low red lights are the same, but Nabors's snoring has stopped.

Widow spins around and looks down the hall. Nabors stands at the other end, beyond the stairs. He's holding a gun, and pointing it at Widow.

"Who the hell are you?" he slurs, drunkenly. But he doesn't wait for an answer. He just pulls the trigger.

CHAPTER 41

Widow dives back into the bathroom and grabs the naked girl, who's screaming and shouting. Widow hauls her up and over, out of the line of fire. He covers her with his body, pulling them all the way into the shower stall, away from the open doorway.

Nabors fires the gun empty. He may have been faking being asleep, but he's not faking being intoxicated. He shoots like a blind man, because the bullets hit everything but Widow and the girl.

The gun's a revolver. Nabors pops open the cylinder and empties the casings out. They clatter to the floor, sounding like falling change.

Widow releases the girl and scrambles out of the bathroom. He gets into the hallway. The distance from him to Nabors isn't far. The cabin feels small, especially the cramped hallway. It boxes Widow in tighter than he's comfortable with.

Widow charges Nabors. The stairs are the biggest obstacle. They slow him down.

Nabors reloads the revolver, but only with one round, because he knows a giant stranger is barreling down on him. He loads the gun, snaps the cylinder shut, and aims at Widow.

Widow gets mere inches from Nabors, and slaps the gun away. The revolver fires, and the bullet rockets past Widow. It slams into the bathroom, shattering wall tile right next to the girl's head. She screams in horror.

Widow grabs Nabors by the throat, lifts him off his feet, and slams him into the ceiling. Old ceiling tiles crumble and dust down on the two men.

Nabors is drunk, but he's not a weak, small man, not physically, anyway. He smashes Widow across the head with the revolver. Widow drops him, and Nabors tumbles to the floor.

Widow's dazed and spins around into the kitchen. Blood trickles from a cut over one of his eyes. He makes a colossal mistake. He checks the wound. With one hand, he touches it, and feels the blood.

Meanwhile, Nabors snaps open the gun's cylinder again. This time one casing falls out of the gun.

Nabors reloads the revolver and snaps the gun shut.

Where's he getting all these bullets? Widow thinks. *Nabors must've been sleeping with his pockets filled with bullets.*

However, that's not the worrying issue. The worrying issue is how fast he reloads the weapon, and he's drunk. If the guy had been sober, Widow would already be dead. He has no doubt.

Widow grabs a dirty cast iron frying pan off the kitchen stove, and scrambles towards Nabors. Widow's no Navy SEAL, or an expert in combat, not yet, but he knows handguns are close-quarter combat weapons. However, they work best when there's some distance between the shooter and the target. The distance for a handgun to be extremely deadly isn't much. It can be a few feet to kill a target easily enough. However, close the gap from feet to inches, and it's much harder to maneuver a firearm.

Nabors aims the gun at Widow, but he's so drunk, he's not sure which Widow's the right one because he's seeing double. So, he shoots both of them. But he starts with the one on the left. That one turns out not to be Widow. His first bullet slams into a refrigerator, pierces the exterior plastic, and pops a hole in a carton of milk inside the fridge.

The second bullet almost hits the right Widow, but before he shoots, the right Widow hits him across the face with his own filthy frying pan. Nabors pulls the gun's trigger, but the bullet veers off into the stairs and goes through the hull of the boat.

Nabors doesn't know any of that because the force of the cast-iron pan nearly breaks his jaw clean off his face. He spits out half his teeth and topples over. He drops the gun and pukes on the floor. More teeth spill out of his bloody half-mouth.

He looks up at Widow and tries to speak, but all that comes out of his half-mouth is even more teeth. Blood oozes out of the guy's mouth, like a blood faucet.

Widow tosses the pan and scoops up the gun. It's still got three in the cylinder and one in the chamber. He pockets it and grabs Nabors by the arm, and hauls him to his feet like a crash test dummy.

Widow checks Nabors's pockets, finds the handcuff key, and takes it. He turns to go free the girl, but quickly learns that's a mistake. He hears an audible click from behind him.

He spins around to see that Nabors has a folding knife. Which makes him wish he'd kept the folding knife from Frankie, the Fenian Boy from the day crew.

Nabors slashes at Widow, forcing him to release Nabors from his grip. Widow hops back into the kitchen, avoiding another knife slash. But now, the crammed space is he's biggest problem. Widow's a big man, the crammed space limits his mobility. The kitchen counter stops him from dodging another slash.

Nabors cuts Widow across the forearm, and Widow drops the handcuff key. His bomber jacket slices open, and he gets cut on the arm, bad. He feels the pain. It's immense. He grabs his arm. Blood seeps out the open leather and through his fingers.

Nabors goes in for another swipe, but Widow aims the gun at him. He shoots once, but Nabors dodges left and swipes at him again. This time the blade misses Widow, but it hits the revolver, which goes flying off into a corner.

Nabors winces and grins a bloody, evil smile at Widow. It's all half-mouth, and no teeth.

Nabors comes in at Widow with the blade again.

Suddenly, a gunshot rings out in the boat's cabin, from behind Widow. A bullet fires through the bow. A familiar voice says, "Freeze! Drop the knife, asshole!"

Nabors pauses, and stares at two figures standing on two sets of stairs. Only it's just one of each, and not two.

"Who the hell're you now?" Nabors slurs again drunkenly, but also inhumanly from his bloody half-mouth.

Widow looks back at the stairs. And Snyder steps off the bottom step and enters the cabin. He walks right up to Nabors, shoves the gun in his face, and says, "I'm not going to say it twice. Drop the knife, asshole, or die!"

Nabors releases the knife. It drops to the tile. He raises his hands in surrender.

Snyder keeps his eyes on Nabors, he asks, "Widow, you okay?"

Widow catches his breath, and says, "He cut me pretty bad, but I'll live. There's a girl, end of the hall, handcuffed. I had Nabors's handcuff key, but I dropped it."

Snyder glances back down the hall. He sees the girl's shoes and bare legs. Nabors steps to him, like he's going to attack, but Snyder pistol whips him right in the broken, bloody jaw. Nabors would scream, if he could scream. But his jaw's too far gone to scream. So he just snivels.

Snyder says, "Take the key out of my pocket. It'll open those cuffs."

Widow reaches for Snyder's outside jacket pocket, but Snyder says, "Left one."

Widow finds the handcuff key, takes it, and walks down the hall. He takes his bomber jacket off, unlocks the girl, and covers her with his coat. He offers to carry her, but she's still afraid of him. So, he backs away, giving her space. She slips her arms through his jacket and zips it up. Widow's bomber jacket is huge on her. It looks like she's wearing an oversized leather kaftan.

She walks herself out to the front.

"I'm an FBI agent," Snyder says to her, without taking his eyes off Nabors. "Go topside, and wait for me on the dock.

Terrified, the girl says nothing. She scrambles up the stairs and out of sight.

Widow returns the handcuff key to Snyder's pocket, and takes out the handcuffs. He offers them to Snyder. But Snyder doesn't take them. Instead, he says, "Widow, why don't you go up there and wait with her?"

Widow lowers the handcuffs, and asks, "Why?"

"Go join her."

"What're you going to do?"

"This maniac killed Mia, and others. He's gotta pay."

Widow says, "Howie, don't do this. He should face justice."

Snyder says nothing.

Widow says, "Howie, this isn't justice. He should face a judge and a jury of his peers."

"Why? Because he deserves his day in court?" Snyder says, "You're young and idealistic. Trust me, this is for the best. He doesn't deserve to live."

"It's not for him," Widow says, and points up the stairs, where the girl ran. "It's for her, and Mia, all the others, and their families. They deserve see him stand trial. They deserve to be there the day the judge sentences him. They deserve to say their piece. It's not for him. It's for them."

Snyder says nothing.

Widow says, "This isn't justice. This is murder. He's an unarmed prisoner. If you shoot him now, it's just cold-blooded murder. You gotta take him in."

"I can't," Snyder says, pauses a long beat. He tears up, and says, "Peter's dead because of him."

Widow says, "Howie?"

"Peter's dead because of me," Snyder says, and glances at Widow. "I killed him. I ordered the hit on him. I thought he killed Mia. For all those years, I thought it was him. But it was this animal!"

Widow stays quiet.

Snyder looks at Nabors, who now seems to understand the gravity of his situation, like he's only just now recognizing Snyder's face after all this time. Nabors begs for his life, only he speaks garble.

Snyder barks at him, "SHUT UP!" Snyder shoves the gun back in Nabors's face. He squeezes the trigger, nearly all the way to kill point, but stops.

Widow puts his bloody hand on Snyder's shoulder. He says, "If you kill him, it's murder. You'll be no better than Mautner and the others."

Snyder looks at Widow, but there's no surprise on his face that Widow's figured it out.

"You're better than them. You're better than that," Widow says, pauses, and adds, "Mia would think so."

Snyder aims at Nabors, closes his eyes, takes a deep breath, and slow-opens them again. He steps back, stares at Nabors, and says, "Bret Nabors, you're under arrest for the murder and rape of Mia Harper. And for abduction and false imprisonment of that girl we just freed."

Snyder orders him to turn around and assume the arresting position. Snyder holsters his gun, cuffs Nabors, and recites the Miranda rights to him. He notices Nabors's gun on the floor, and tells Widow to grab it. Widow does, and pockets it.

They climb the stairs and exit the boat. They take him off the boat and onto the pier. Widow steps out last, behind Nabors, only they're not alone on the pier.

Ten feet in front of them, the scales of justice man stands on the pier with the girl from the *missing* posters.

CHAPTER 42

The scales of justice man takes the suppressor off his gun. No need for stealth anymore. He aims the gun, but not at Widow, Snyder, or Nabors. He aims it at the head of the girl wearing Widow's bomber jacket. She stands in front of him, terrified. He's holding her in place with one hand around the back of her neck. He's behind her as if she's a human shield, only she's a human shield who's been living a nightmare that won't stop getting worse. The poor girl's figuratively gone from the frying pan into the fire. And she's got no idea what's going on.

Snyder and Widow stay where they are. Nabors looks at the scales of justice man in total confusion. He slurs, "Hey man! You here for some fun too? Let me go, and you can keep her."

The scales of justice man says, "Slowly, take out your guns and toss them."

Snyder goes for his gun. The scales of justice man tightens his grip around the girl's neck. She squeals in pain. He points his gun at Snyder, and says, "Slowly!"

Snyder nods, and unholsters his gun. He tosses it toward the scales of justice man, and raises his hands above his head. The scales of justice man smiles, and points his gun at Widow. He says, "Now, you."

Widow says, "I'm unarmed."

The scales of justice man glares at him, mistrustfully.

Nabors squawks, "He lyin', man! My gun's in his pocket!"

The scales of justice man aims at Widow. So, Widow reluctantly pulls the revolver out of his pocket.

The scales of justice man says, "Toss it."

Widow tosses the revolver into the water, to his right.

Nabors rattles his handcuffs, and says, "Okay, man. Now free me!"

The scales of justice man stares at Nabors, blankly.

"I'm on your side!" Nabors barks.

Widow says, "Let the girl go! She's not part of this!"

The scales of justice man stares at Widow, and steps back. He releases his grip on the girl. She doesn't wait for any second thoughts. She spins around him like a basketball player on the court and runs away quickly, down the pier, and never looks back.

Widow doesn't thank the scales of justice man. He just gives him a slight nod.

Nabors slurs, "Ah, man! You let her go!"

The scales of justice man steps close to Nabors, who says, "Get the key from that one!" Nabors gestures his head towards Snyder. But the scales of justice man doesn't move. He raises his gun and aims it at Nabors. He presses the muzzle to Nabors's forehead. Nabors stares up at the muzzle, cross-eyed.

Snyder says, "Wait! It's different now! He's not a target! No more targets! I call the whole thing off! You guys can keep the money! Keep whatever they paid you!"

The scales of justice man says nothing. He steps back, moving the muzzle back a few inches from Nabors's head, and squeezes the trigger. The gunshot booms across the water, the pier, and the boats.

The bullet rips through Nabors's head. Blood and brains spray out the back, creating that red mist Widow's getting used to seeing. Nabors falls back, lifeless. His torso hangs half off the pier, over the water.

Widow freezes, and stares in horror, realizing they're next. He glances to the right at the water, where the revolver went. *How deep's the water under there?* he wonders.

The scales of justice man turns to Snyder, who says, "You didn't have to do that. I told you it's over. Call Mautner! Get him on the phone!"

The scales of justice man smiles at Snyder, and shoots him. It's a quick double tap, a quick *pop-pop* to the chest.

Widow doesn't wait for his turn to die. He wants to go for the revolver underwater. The problem is that the angled position of the scales of justice man and his gun speed leave Widow with no opportunity to dive right. So, he dives to the left, back onto Nabors's boat. He rolls onto the deck and scrambles around the port side, taking cover along the helm and the walls.

The scales of justice man fires after him. Three rounds. They all barely miss.

Slowly, the scales of justice man steps onto the stern of the boat. He takes his time, because he's not worried about some kid. He calls out to Widow, saying, "Sorry, kid. I can't let you live." He walks slowly, turning corners with caution. He aims around the curves of the old, beat-up boat. Each time he turns a corner, the gun goes first, ready to fire, ready to kill.

He listens, carefully, but doesn't hear Widow. The boat sways. Waves crash against the harbor's outer walls in the distance. But there're no sounds from Widow.

The scales of justice man says, "It's nothing personal, kid. I get paid to do a job, and you're the last item on my checklist. You're the last thing to be crossed off."

The scales of justice man walks toward the bow of the boat. There's nowhere left for Widow to go. The scales of justice man leaps around the last stretch of cover and sees Widow dive off the bow pulpit and into the water.

The scales of justice man rushes to the bow, and fires into the dark water below, blindly. He stares, trying to see the kid. He hopes to see blood rise to the surface.

Finally, he does. Blood rises to the water's surface, merging with the white ripples Widow left behind.

Still, it's not much blood. The scales of justice man wants to be sure, but he's not jumping into the freezing ocean. He's not much of a swimmer—terrible, in fact. It's his weakness.

But if Widow's still alive, he'll have to surface, eventually. So, the scales of justice man waits.

CHAPTER 43

Widow's killed no one before. But tonight, he might just have to.

After he dives into the water, Widow swims deep, holding his breath like he's never done before. The hitman is right on his heels. The guy fires several rounds into the water. But Widow's already pulled himself too close to the boat to be seen. He grabs the anchor dangling out of its hole. It's pulled up, but not all the way. Nabors wasn't the most by-the-book type, and Widow's grateful for it.

After the hitman stops shooting, Widow leans back out and lets the blood from his arm trickle up in the water. Against his better judgment, he surfaces behind the boat and takes a quiet breath. Then he dives and traces along the boat's hull until he reaches the starboard quarter. He quietly surfaces, grabs the motor and hauls himself back up onto the boat. This makes a bunch of noise.

The hitman hears it, and scrambles toward the stern. Widow's got no time to go diving for the revolver. There's a better option anyway.

Widow scrambles to the pier, runs, and dives over Snyder's dead body. Snyder's eyes are still open, staring up at him.

Widow grabs Snyder's gun and spins around.

The hitman leaps over the motor and onto the pier. He scrambles around a pole and stops, facing Widow, who's soaking wet, shivering, and standing there, aiming Snyder's gun at the hitman.

The hitman holds his gun down by his side. He walks to Widow, slowly.

Widow shouts, "Drop it!"

The hitman pauses a beat, and asks, "Have you ever shot someone before?"

"I'll shoot you!"

The hitman doesn't believe him. He steps closer, holds his gun out, pointed at the ground. His finger's on the trigger.

"Don't make me!" Widow says.

The hitman asks, "Have you ever killed someone before?"

"Stop right there!"

"Son, you're shaking," the hitman says, grins, and slow-raises his weapon.

Widow shouts, "No! Don't!"

The hitman brings his weapon up quickly, ready to fire. But Widow shoots him first. He doesn't blink. He doesn't flinch. He squeezes the trigger, once, twice. It's a double tap, straight into the hitman's chest.

Widow fires a third time. The bullet rips through the hitman's forehead. That red mist explodes around the hitman's head.

The hitman collapses backwards into the water—dead. His body floats. Blood pools all around him. His dead eyes stare up into the snowy night's blackness.

CHAPTER 44

On Friday, Bostonians all over the city go back to work from their lunch breaks. Gray skies hover over the city. Everyone wears warm clothes. Cops walk the streets, decked out in their winter gear. People walk the sidewalks cautiously, trying not to slip on icy concrete.

The US District Court of Massachusetts stands majestically on the corner of Northern Avenue and Courthouse Way. The building stands out from the surrounding ones as an architectural marvel of masonry.

Judge Mautner dismisses court for the day. The case he's presiding over isn't done, far from it, but he let the court go early for the weekend, before the lunchbreak. He plans to have lunch in his chambers. He's got a lot on his mind today. The biggest thing is that he's not heard from the scales of justice man at all. Which probably isn't a reason to panic. Not yet. But it is highly unusual.

The thing is, the scales of justice man usually checks in after a job's done. And the job should be finished by now. He's never disappointed Mautner before.

Mautner steps down from the bench as members of the court exit the courtroom, and picks up today's folded newspaper, that he's not yet read. He nods goodbye to the bailiff, and exits through a huge oak door behind the bench. He steps through short hallway, removes his black robes, and enters his chambers. He hangs his robes over a coat rack.

Mautner's office is at the north side of the building. It's a corner office with enormous windows. The office overlooks Fan Pier Park and the Boston Channel. In the distance, gigantic ships pass each other. Some are on their way out to the Atlantic, and others are coming into the Boston Harbor.

The office is bright and spacious. Tons of books line shelves across the walls.

Mautner reads his newspaper and never looks up. He walks straight into his huge office, past a fireplace, over to his desk. Knowing she can hear him through the office door, he calls out to his secretary as he walks, asking her to get him some coffee.

Mautner threads around his desk and dumps himself down in the seat. He continues reading his newspaper and completely misses the man sitting in a visitor's chair.

The man stands up. He's tall and towers over Mautner. The man steps closer to Mautner and tosses a metal object onto the desktop. It clangs and bounces on the thick oak, until it stops, facing up at Mautner.

Startled, Mautner nearly jumps out of his chair. He doesn't look at the object. First, he looks up at the giant man.

Towering over him, wearing a neat and clean set of Navy dress whites, with the only thing out of place being one arm stitched and bandaged, and hanging in a sling from around his neck, Widow stares down at Mautner. He says, "I took that off a man who tried to kill me last night."

Wide-eyed, Mautner glances down at the metal object. It's a scales of justice pin. The gold shines under the bright office bulbs above.

Mautner looks up at Widow, and says, "Widow? What're you doing here? How did you get in?" Mautner looks at his door, and considers calling out for his secretary.

Widow pounds the desktop with a fist from his uninjured arm. He shouts, "Pay attention! No one's coming to help you!"

Mautner trembles, stares up at Widow, and asks, "What's this about?"

Widow says, "Snyder's dead."

Mautner squirms in his chair. He asks, "What? How?"

"Your guy killed him."

"What're you talking about?"

"The hitman you sent murdered him right in front of me. And he nearly killed me, but I was faster."

Mautner glances at the door. He could shout. He could scream out for help. But then he thinks about how he called out for coffee, and his secretary never answered. She usually responds right away, but this time she didn't.

Widow says, "She's not there, Mautner. No one can hear us. It's just you and me."

"What do you mean?"

"Why did you send this guy to kill Snyder? To kill me?" Widow asks.

"I never did such a thing!"

"Yes, you did!" Widow says, and points at the scales of justice pin. "He told me before I killed him."

"You...killed him?"

"Yes!" Widow says, and pounds his heavy fist on the desk again. He pounds so hard; it rattles the scales of justice pin.

Mautner says nothing, not with his lips, anyway. But his eyes tell a different story. Widow killed the hitman. *What'll this kid do to me?* Mautner wonders.

"You took an oath. To uphold the law, to serve justice. But you bent it! You broke it!" Widow says, pushing Mautner. "What kind of judge are you? What kind of man are you? You took money from desperate victims. And hired a hitman to murder people."

Mautner rages from the accusation. He says, "Justice? Tell me, Widow, what the hell do you know of justice? I've sat on the bench for thirty years. I've been the DOJ's tool! What've you done? You're just a kid! Sometimes the system misses the mark! So what?!"

"So what? You offer a better kind of justice? It's not for us to decide. We can't just take the law into our own hands."

"Can't we? Our system fails, all the time, every day! I see it! So many victims walk through that courtroom, begging me for help, begging for justice. And yet killers get off because of technicalities. What kind of justice is that? You tell me!"

Widow stays quiet, and just listens.

Mautner says, "What should I do? Should I just stand by and watch miscarriages of justice replay, over and over? I've seen murderers walk free, and victims left with nothing. If the law won't do what's needed, then who will?"

"You're not talking about justice! You're talking about revenge!"

Mautner rubs his forehead. His skin turns red. Anger creeps in at the thought that anyone dares question him, especially some kid. He says, "What's wrong with that? Revenge is the next best thing. At least, it's honest. Revenge doesn't hide behind fancy legal words and our system's false promises.

"But what do you know? You're young, Widow. You still believe the world works the way they told you it does, the way they promised us it would. But it doesn't. The good guys don't always win. And good, helpless people continue to get robbed, raped, and murdered."

"Cynicism blinds you, Judge! Bitterness corrupts you! And your corruption has ruined lives! You think because monsters walk through your court, that means you can become one?" Widow says, and backs away a step. He stares into Mautner's eyes, and is stunned, like he's seeing the monster lurking back there for the first time. "You tell yourself that you're doing good, but you're just playing God. You're no better than the monsters in orange prison suits."

"I'm necessary. You think I like this? That I take pleasure in breaking the oath that I swore? I do it because I must, because someone needs to make the hard choices. And if it's not me, then who?"

"Who the hell gave you that right, Judge? You sit there, in your robe, inside your big fancy chambers, going to your expensive clubs, and pretending to be a man of the people. But you're just a wolf in sheep's clothing."

"Someone's got to make the necessary calls!" Mautner shouts, and stands angrily. "You want to talk about morals, about law and justice? I've seen humanity's filth, and I've had to wash it from my hands. You...you still have the luxury of your morals! You see the world in black and white, in right and wrong! But there's no black and white! There's no right and wrong! There's only gray!"

"Our system's flawed? Sure. But it's blind, and it works if we stay honest. And that's worth fighting for."

Mautner stares at Widow. His eyes rage with angry fires. His cheeks flush red. He says, "I took out the trash. I ordered those scum dead. I heard the victims of the most heinous crimes you can imagine, far worse than Mia Harper! I've heard the families of so many victims! They cried at my feet! They begged me to take action! And that's what I did! It was my orders that got them the retribution that they sought! MINE!"

Widow asks, "And how many of the men you killed were innocent?"

Mautner says nothing.

Widow says, "What about Peter Stamos?"

"What about him?"

"He was innocent. He had nothing to do with Mia Harper's murder."

Mautner pauses a long beat. He breathes heatedly, and says, "Eggshells. Stamos is just broken eggshells. So what? Life moves on!"

"How many others were innocent, Judge? How many people have you murdered who were innocent?"

Mautner says nothing.

"You chose the wrong path, Your Honor. Justice takes work, but it also takes faith. And you've lost yours. Justice takes not losing yourself to the darkness. But darkness has consumed you," Widow says, and backs away from Mautner's desk.

Mautner asks, "Are you here to kill me?"

Widow smirks, turns, and walks out of Mautner's opulent office.

"You'll learn, Widow. In time, you'll see. You'll become just like me!" Mautner shouts, and reaches into a drawer. He pulls out a shiny silver gun, and points it at Widow.

Widow stops at Mautner's office door. He opens it, steps into the doorway, and turns to face Mautner. He stares past the gun, into the judge's eyes. He sees a crushed, dark soul. Widow says, "You're wrong, Mautner. I'm nothing like you."

Before Mautner can pull the trigger, several armed FBI agents storm in, pushing Widow out of the doorway.

They aim guns at Mautner, and shout at him: *Drop the gun! Get on the ground!*

Widow watches from behind the armed agents. Mautner, terrified, gazes at them, puts the gun to his head, and pulls the trigger.

CHAPTER 45

It clicks empty because Widow unloaded it when he came in. He thought Mautner might feel the weight of the gun and realize it was empty. But he never thought the man's ego would overshadow his judgment. But apparently, it's done that for years.

The FBI agents enter Mautner's chambers and swarm him. They jerk the gun out of his hand and slam him facedown onto his desk, where he's spent years making decisions about the fates of others.

FBI agents throw handcuffs on Mautner, arresting him so he can face his own fate. An FBI agent named Carla Sabin, dressed in street clothes, walks in past Widow. She does the honors of explaining Mautner the charges he faces and reading his Miranda rights to him.

Widow steps away, and waits at the end of the hall. They haul Mautner away in shame. He passes Widow in the hallway but doesn't make eye contact. He holds his head down, also avoiding eye contact with his staff and the colleagues who worked with him on that floor for years.

At the stairs, Sabin reaches her hand out to Widow, but not to shake. He unbuttons part of his dress uniform shirt and removes a tiny black microphone the FBI had taped to his undershirt. He gives it to her, along with a small recorder. It's the wire Widow agreed to wear before they sent him in.

It seemed like a tremendous gamble to bet it all on Widow's suggestion they wire him up, but he knew Mautner's ego, and the surprise of seeing Widow alive, would get the better of the man. A man who plays God will have a God complex. And Widow knew it.

Sabin says, "Nice work! I've been after these guys for years."

"I couldn't have done it if the FBI hadn't been nice enough to get my uniformed dry cleaned so quickly. I doubt Mautner would've taken me seriously without it."

"The uniform does add a nice touch to it. It's too bad about Snyder, though," Sabin says, and they follow Mautner and several armed agents.

Widow asks, "Does he have family?"

"He's got a son. We'll reach out to him. Don't worry about that. Snyder's part in this is going to mended to reflect the good he did. His family has nothing to feel dishonored about."

Widow nods, and asks, "And the girl from Nabors's boat?"

"We've returned her to her family. She's going to have a long road to go before she stops having nightmares, I'm sure. But she's alive, thanks to you."

Widow says nothing.

Sabin asks, "What time's your graduation?"

"It's tonight. I should get back."

"We'll take you to the airport."

"I don't have plane tickets."

Sabin smiles, and says, "Don't worry about that. We've arranged a ride for you."

An hour later, Widow gets out of a car and steps onto the tarmac of the private jet terminal at Boston Logan International Airport. Sabin thanks him again, and watches him board a government jet, already fueled and cleared for takeoff.

Widow gets on, and suddenly thinks about his rucksack and the bomber jacket that Harper gave him for his birthday. To his surprise, both are on the plane already. When he steps on, he's greeted by NCIS agent Rachel Cameron. She hugs him, grateful for him. They embrace like old friends, not knowing that they'll become closer than friends someday. She brought his rucksack and bomber jacket with her.

"Ready for a first-class ride?" she jokes.

"I've never flown on a private jet before."

"Working for the government's got some perks," she says.

They take seats next to each other. Their private jet flies into Baltimore/Washington International Thurgood Marshall Airport, arriving an hour and five minutes after they took off from Boston. The sun sets to the west, turning the short winter Friday into night in a matter of minutes. Widow's graduation ceremony is soon.

Cameron walks Widow through the terminal and rents a black Cadillac, on the Navy's dime. She drives Widow to the place he wants to go first, the hospital. She waits outside in the parking lot with the car running, as Widow requests.

Nervously, Widow walks into the hospital, carrying his rucksack. He goes to Harper's room, but it's empty. Even the woman who had her second endarterectomy is gone.

He turns around, goes to the nurses' station. They remember him. A nurse informs him that Harper has been discharged.

Widow returns to the parking lot and gets back in the Cadillac. Cameron takes him to his next destination: Harper's apartment.

Widow starts to take his rucksack, but gut instinct tells him he won't need it. So he leaves it with Cameron, and takes Harper's document bag. He asks Cameron to wait for him. That he'll be back. She agrees.

He climbs the steps, enters the building using the extra key Harp gave him. He rides the elevator to her floor, and gets out. His stomach feels twisted in knots. His heart beats cold and distant, like he's got to do something he doesn't want to do. He walks the longest walk of his life to her front door.

Widow sticks his key in the door, but stops. Shaking, he takes the key out and pockets it, next to the engagement ring. He slow-knocks on the door.

Harper unlocks it and opens it. She sees him, and her eyes get huge. She leaps on him, hugging him tightly. They embrace for a long, long moment, like lovers who thought they'd never see each other again.

She takes his hand and leads him into the apartment. She says, "I worried about you. When I didn't hear from you for so long. I worried."

Widow stays quiet.

Harper looks him up and down, and says, "You're so handsome in your uniform."

Widow says, "They let you out?"

"Yeah, I discharged today. They said I was okay to go home. Of course, I've got more appointments and...," she pauses, and goes to him. She takes his free hand in both of hers. She stares up at him, smiling, like she's gotten the best news of her life. She says, "I've decided to fight it! I'm going to start chemo again!"

Widow stares at her, expressionless. But, on the inside, he breaks like a house of glass.

"You're speechless! I knew you would be!" she says, and kisses him. Then she backs away, and glances at a clock on the wall. She says, "Good heavens! Your graduation's in, like an hour. At least, you're already dressed for it. Let me get my little black dress on. You know? The one you like so much? I don't care how cold it is, I'm wearing it!"

Widow stays quiet.

Harper nearly skips away in blissful happiness. She vanishes down the hall to her bedroom, and starts changing her clothes. Widow drags himself over to her kitchen, dreading what comes next. He sets her document bag onto a stool, and leaves it there.

In the corner of his eye, he spots an opened package and a digital camera sitting out on the kitchen bar. Widow inspects the package. There's no address on it, but it was sealed like something delivered by mail. On the box, Widow sees a familiar symbol. The package is stamped with the scales of justice in gold.

Hesitantly, Widow peers inside the package, but it's empty. He glances at the hallway door, and hears Harper singing to herself, which she often does when she's in an exceptional mood.

Widow picks up the digital camera and goes through the pictures in the viewing window. But the camera only has one picture to view.

Widow stares at it in horror, but not disbelief. He already knew it, the truth. He knew it in his bones, in his blood, in his fears. He doesn't stare in disbelief or surprise. He stares at the picture with a feeling of betrayal. It's a deep betrayal. It's not just a betrayal of his trust. It's a betrayal of everything he stands for.

Right there in the photo is Peter Stamos. He's dead, shot to death. There's a bullet hole in the center of his forehead, identical to the one in Bernabe's forehead. And there's a hand in the picture. The hand holds Stamos's head up, posing it for the photo. It's the hitman's hand.

Widow's shoulders drop in utter disappointment. But he knew he would find this. Of course he would.

Jaime Harper, the first woman he ever loved, the woman he wanted to spend the rest of his life with, sent him with a bag full of money to pay for a hit on an innocent man. He had inadvertently killed Peter Stamos, like he pulled the trigger himself.

Widow takes the camera and walks down Harper's hallway to her bedroom. He enters. She's smiling hugely, singing, and staring into her bathroom mirror. She's scantily clad in a robe, doing her hair and makeup. He stands there for a long second, lurking like a killer in the shadows. He's unsure what to say or do.

Finally, Harper sees him, and says, "Widow, you sneaking up on me now?"

Widow stays quiet.

She says, "I'm doing everything as fast as I can. I'll be done in a flash. I'm so excited to see you walk the stage tonight!"

Widow steps out of the shadows, and stares at her in the mirror. She stops singing, and asks, "Widow? What is it?"

Widow steps into the light, and puts the camera on the bathroom counter in front of her. Peter Stamos's death picture faces her. She stares down at it without remorse.

Widow steps back to the edge of the shadows. Harper stares at the image. Her smile recedes.

She whispers, "Widow?"

"You sent me to pay a hired gun to kill him?" Widow asks, tears streaming down his face.

Harper whispers, "He killed my sister."

Widow drops his head, avoiding eye contact with her. He says, "You used me."

She releases her hair, and puts down the items in her hand. She spins around to face him, and leans on the bathroom counter. She stares up at him, and says, "Widow, he killed my sister. He raped and murdered Mia, my big sister, my hero."

Widow raises his head, and shakes it. He says, "Snyder's dead."

"What? How?"

"I nearly died too."

Harper steps close to him, puts her hand on his chest, and looks up into his eyes. She asks, "How?"

Widow gently pushes her away, but holds her by the wrists, stares down into her eyes, and says, "Peter didn't kill Mia."

Harper pulls away from him. She steps back into the bathroom light. Confusion floods her face. She says, "What're you talking about? He murdered my sister!"

Widow shakes his head, and stares at her.

Tears fill her eyes. She says, "YES! HE DID!"

"No! He didn't! Peter was innocent. And now he's dead."

Harper struggles to believe, struggles to breath, struggles to hear what he's saying to her.

Widow says, "Peter, Snyder, Idris, and three federal agents are all dead because of you. Because you sent me to The Vidocq Society with blood money. Peter's wife and kids will never see him again. All of their families will never see them again. They're dead! You killed him! And I helped you do it!"

"NO! THAT CAN'T BE TRUE!" Harper shouts, and cries uncontrollably. "It can't be true!"

Widow looks at her one last time, turns around, and leaves her there.

He takes off the bomber jacket she gave him for his birthday, and drapes it over the bar, next to her opened package, her proof of death from the Shadow Club. He leaves his keys to her place inside the bomber jacket's pocket.

Widow walks out of the apartment, and out of Harper's life forever.

CHAPTER 46

Widow barely makes his graduation ceremony. But Cameron gets him in and vouches for his unapproved leave by flashing her badge around. She speaks to Widow's CO and to Harrington on Widow's behalf, and covers for him. Of course, she doesn't tell them what he's done. *It's official NCIS business*, she tells them.

At the end of the ceremony, Widow looks for Harper in the crowd, thinking she might show up. Wishing, in a way, that she would show up. But she doesn't.

He never sees Harper again, except in his dreams. He sees no reason to turn her in to Sabin, or to the FBI. What for? Living with the guilt in the short time she has left is more punishment than Widow could ever imagine. And he didn't want her to hurt any more than she already is.

Cameron stays for his graduation ceremony. She talks with him as everyone else hugs their families and celebrates with the ones they love about their accomplishments. Widow's grateful she does, because he'd be all alone otherwise.

Cameron doesn't ask about him being alone on such an occasion. She just says, "You're a good man, Widow."

Widow replies, "Thank you."

"Well, glad I could be here for you. You're going to be alright," she says, and turns to walk away, to leave him to his future. But she stops, and turns back to Widow. She asks, "Widow?"

Widow nods and looks down at her.

"You got orders yet?" she asks.

"I got leave time, then I ship out somewhere."

"I hope you're going somewhere exotic?"

Widow nods, and says, "It's definitely far away."

Cameron puts a hand up, and says, "Don't tell me where. I'll find you. When the time's right. I'll be watching." And with that, she vanishes into the crowd of white uniforms, and family members loving on their sons and daughters.

Widow watches Cameron until she's gone from sight. Then he leaves the auditorium and the crowds of sailors, past his company. He goes back to his dorm, and stops at the community phone. It's unoccupied. Most of the midshipmen have gone home for the holidays, or are out celebrating with all the other graduates.

Widow picks up the phone, and dials. Nervously, he waits.

A voice says, "Killian Crossing Sheriff's Office."

Widow says, "Can I speak to the chief?"

"Hold one."

A familiar voice comes over the line. She says, "This is Deveraux."

Widow hears his mother's voice, and nearly speaks. But shame fills him, and he hangs up, not knowing what to say.

* * *

SEVERAL WEEKS LATER, a huge Navy ship rocks and sways in a storm off the coast of Taiwan, in the South China Sea, at night. A sailor stands alone on the deck, near the railing. He's off duty at the moment. He stares out over the water, into the storm ahead. No one's around. He drinks a hot black coffee from the mess. He looks like he's deep in thought.

Widow takes Harper's engagement ring out of his pocket, and stares at it.

Time to let go, he thinks. He heaves the ring over the side, into the darkness, into the choppy waves below.

A SPECIAL OFFER

THE GHOST LINE
PREORDER BOOK 20

A family in need, terrorized by a local backwoods criminal group, and a drifter who won't stand for it. (Actual cover to be revealed in 2024)

A WORD FROM SCOTT

Thank you for reading THE SHADOW CLUB. You got this far —I'm guessing that you enjoyed Widow.

The story continues…

The next book in the series is THE GHOST LINE, coming in 2024!

To find out more, sign up for the Scott Blade Book Club and get notified of upcoming new releases. See next page.

THE SCOTT BLADE
BOOK CLUB

Building a relationship with my readers is the very best thing about writing. I occasionally send newsletters with details on new releases, special offers, and other bits of news relating to the Jack Widow Series.

If you are new to the series, you can join the Scott Blade Book Club and get the starter kit.

Sign up for exclusive free stories, special offers, access to bonus content, info on the latest releases, and coming-soon Jack Widow novels. Sign up at ScottBlade.com.

THE NOMADVELIST

NOMAD + NOVELIST = NOMADVELIST

Scott Blade is a Nomadvelist, a drifter and author of the breakout Jack Widow series. Scott travels the world, hitchhiking, drinking coffee, and writing.

Jack Widow has sold over a million copies.

Visit @: ScottBlade.com

Contact @: scott@scottblade.com

Follow @:

Facebook.com/ScottBladeAuthor

Bookbub.com/profile/scott-blade

Amazon.com/Scott-Blade/e/B00AU7ZRS8

BOOKS BY SCOTT BLADE

The Jack Widow Series

Gone Forever

Winter Territory

A Reason to Kill

Without Measure

Once Quiet

Name Not Given

The Midnight Caller

Fire Watch

The Last Rainmaker

The Devil's Stop

Black Daylight

The Standoff

Foreign and Domestic

Patriot Lies

The Double Man

Nothing Left

The Protector

Kill Promise

The Shadow Club

The Ghost Line

Jack Widow Shorts

Night Swim

Made in the USA
Las Vegas, NV
15 January 2024

84415921R00215